Secrets

Satisfy your desire for more.

Kiss Me at Midnight by Kate St. James

TV co-hosts Callie Hutchins and Marc Shaw fake an on-air romance to top November sweeps. Callie thinks Marc is a womanizer who should help her snag her dream job... on the other side of the country. As the month progresses, she realizes Marc isn't the handsome playboy he portrays on their show—he's funny, kind, and too sexy for words, damn it.

Mind Games by Kathleen Scott

Damien Storm is a Varti—a psychic who can communicate telepathically to one special person. He's tried in vain to get his Vartek partner, Jade, to acknowledge their link, but fear has made her keep him at a distance. He will do anything to know the sweetness of her body and mind in closer proximity, but first he must save her from the forces who wish to see all Varti destroyed.

Seducing Serena by Jennifer Lynne

Serena Hewitt has given up on love. Her experience has taught her there's no such thing as 'Mister Right', but when she interviews for a potential partner she's not prepared for her overpowering sexual attraction to Nicholas Wade, a fun-loving bachelor with bad-boy good looks and a determination to prove her wrong. But Nick's hiding a secret that might just do the opposite. Can two people afraid of love risk exposing their hearts one last time?

Pirate's Possession by Juliet Burns

When Lady Gertrude Fitzpatrick tries to bargain with a fierce pirate for escape across the water, she unwittingly becomes the possession of Merciless MacGowan, a fierce privateer on the run from Cromwell's army. Ewan MacGowan has been betrayed and mistakenly exacts revenge on this proud noblewoman. He may have stolen the lady's innocence, but buried beneath her plain exterior lies a hidden treasure he never thought to find: the true woman of his heart.

Kate St. James

Kathleen Scott

Jennifer Lynne

Juliet Burns

Volume 28

Secrets

Satisfy your desire for more.

SECRETS Volume 28
This is an original publication of Red Sage Publishing and each individual story herein has never before appeared in print. These stories are a collection of fiction and any similarity to actual persons or events is purely coincidental.

Red Sage Publishing, Inc.
P.O. Box 4844
Seminole, FL 33775
727-391-3847
www.redsagepub.com

SECRETS Volume 28
A Red Sage Publishing book
All Rights Reserved/December 2009
Copyright © 2009 by Red Sage Publishing, Inc.

ISBN: 1-60310-008-3 / ISBN 13: 978-1-60310-008-3

Book typesetting by:
Quill & Mouse Studios, Inc.
www.quillandmouse.com

Contents

Kiss Me at Midnight

by Kate St. James

To My Reader:

Don't you love a feisty heroine who isn't afraid to go head-to-head with a sexy-as-sin hero? How about when she discovers there's more to him than meets the eye... and lips, and hot, roaming hands? In *Kiss Me at Midnight*, late-night TV personality Callie Hutchins knows what she wants—the best ratings in the business—and she's willing to do just about anything to get them. Even if that means putting up with a month of arrogant co-host Marc Shaw's sizzling, rigged-for-the-audience kisses. Even if it means pursuing their attraction off-camera... for the betterment of their careers, of course. But is she ever surprised when she falls in love.

Callie and Marc are two of my favorite characters, and I had a wonderful time writing their story. Please join them on their sensual adventures as they find their way into each other's hearts.

My thanks to Rebecca Martinez for answering my multitude of questions about TV production. All errors and fictional liberties are mine.

This story is dedicated to my parents, James and Ines, who taught me the fine art of banter.

The Los Angeles Post
Monday, September 18th Edition

Hollywood Gab
by Celia Fiennes, Gossip Columnist

Did You See That?

Hollywood bad girl Jada Reilly stopped hearts across the nation last night when she publicly dumped fab-u-licious L.A. talk show host Marc Shaw with a faux wardrobe malfunction during the live broadcast of the Best of Film & Television Awards.

After accepting a BOFTA for her role as sexy nurse Amy Divine on the campy primetime hit, *Psycho Suburbanites*, Jada shocked viewers by tearing off her satin Donna Karan vest to reveal "Marc Shaw Is A Pig!" scrawled on a skin-tight tank top artfully painted to look like the two "girls" which first shot Jada to fame as a lingerie supermodel. The stunt prompted a commercial break that interrupted Jada mid-rant while BOFTA producer Sid Walters scrambled to ensure the actress hadn't violated FCC regulations.

Score a win for Jada in the skyrocketing publicity department, but what's to become of Marc Shaw? The chiseled face of Channel 16's late-night offering, *L.A. Tonight*, enjoyed minor celebrity while dating the outrageous Ms. Reilly. Their pairing focused attention on Marc's "He Vs. She" segment with lively co-host Callie Hutchins, who often rebuked Marc for his womanizing ways.

Oh, clever Callie, what will you rake our spurned Marc over the coals about now?

Chapter 1

Late October

"It doesn't matter how you try to justify your attitudes, Marc." Callie Hutchins glared at her handsome nemesis beneath the eyeball-searing bright TV studio lights. "I'm a woman, and I'm telling you today's women still like to be romanced."

Marc Shaw flaunted his aggravatingly perfect smile at camera one. "And I say chicks today appreciate a guy who knows how to cut to the chase. It's a busy world, too much to do... too many women to do it with." He winked, eliciting low chuckles from the men in the small studio audience. "Why waste her time with flowers and chocolates when a king-sized mattress awaits?"

The jerk's knee bumped Callie's thigh beneath the tiny desk they shared for the "He Vs. She" segment of *L.A. Tonight*. Despite the warm tingles scooting to body parts north, Callie refused to budge. Marc always prodded her when he realized he was losing one of the battle-of-the-sexes spots they taped three out of the five weeknights *L.A. Tonight* aired. He did it to throw her off-balance, and it drove her insane.

"Oh, please." She rolled her eyes at camera two for the benefit of their female viewers. "What chase? In your world, relationships fast-track from 'How ya doin'?' to 'Let's get it on.' Honestly, you're nothing more than an overblown Joey Tribbiani." Mindful of plugging their guests whenever possible, she mentioned a character from the syndicated *Friends* TV show immortalized by the actor they'd interviewed last night.

Marc's gray eyes twinkled. "Ouch." He grinned into camera one, then followed the floor director's hand signals to camera three, which spanned them both. "How about it, L.A.? Is Callie right about relationships today, or am I? Light up the callboards, zap us some emails, and we'll give you the verdict Monday. Until then, have a great time in L.A. tonight and stay safe this weekend. So long from Marc Shaw."

"And Callie Hutchins." Callie smiled stiffly for camera three until the floor director counted down the seconds and the red light blinked off.

"We're clear!" the burly man announced.

Callie blew out a breath and detached the microphone clip from her blouse. "Marc, what the hell was that?" she mumbled through tight lips so the exiting audience wouldn't notice. Normally, she interacted with viewers following a taping, but tonight embarrassment kept her seated. "I've seen you off your game once or twice since Jada kicked your ass to the curb, but tonight was bad."

He lifted a hand. "I know plenty of women who appreciate the efficiency of my approach."

"I'm sure you do." But she'd never be one of them. Marc Shaw was conceited, arrogant, and too sexy for his own good. *And* hers. She might dream about him whenever exhaustion left her incapable of banishing the erotic images of his hands and mouth all over her body, but she'd die before letting him know how strongly he affected her. Until the actress Jada Reilly publicly humiliated Marc six weeks ago, his love-'em-and-leave-'em reputation had assumed epic proportions within local television circles. While the breakup had sucked some of the wind from his sails, his ego certainly didn't need any help from Callie.

"So what's the problem?" he asked. "'He Vs. She' doesn't work if we agree with each other."

"You're kidding, right?" Callie pushed back her chair and removed the mic transmitter hooked to her skirt. Standing, she wrapped the wire around the miniature black box. "Your argument rehashed one of our July shows. It's like you weren't even watching the teleprompter."

"Uh…" Easy humor relaxed his face as he stood and removed his own mic. With his sun-streaked dark blond hair and devil-boy smile, he resembled a thirty-ish version of Brad Pitt.

"Ugh, don't tell me," she half-whispered. "You weren't watching the tele-prompter, were you?"

He shrugged and pocketed his transmitter in his navy sports jacket. "The segment relies on spontaneity and ad-libbing—"

"But usually we try to follow our hazy outline!"

"Tut-tut, Hutchins. I thought we decided not to critique one another on-stage."

Callie counted to three. "Marc. Not that I don't love creaming you on 'He Vs. She,' but if you don't take the segment seriously, ratings will continue to tank." She turned toward their dressing rooms, but couldn't out-pace his long strides. His black dress shoes scuffed the concrete floor.

"If Angela isn't happy with our work tonight, she'll tell us at the post-production meeting," he said, referring to their producer, who supervised the taping from the upstairs booth while communicating with assistants and the floor director through headsets. "She can always replace the segment with a back-up. That's the beauty of taping at eight and airing after the eleven o'clock news."

"A pre-taped segment with canned laughter? No thanks." Callie shot him a glance. "And maybe you don't care if tonight's segment stinks, but I do." She sounded like a shrew, but the success of the show meant everything to her. "The network will never notice me at this rate." She entered her shoebox-sized dressing room.

"Still dreaming of New York, huh?"

Callie waited for him to cross the hall. Instead, he leaned against her doorjamb, crowding her, his spicy aftershave oozing sex appeal. Not many men radiated do-me vibes in stage makeup, but Marc Shaw managed it, damn him.

"Yes," she bit out. Her national-morning-show aspirations were no secret at

KCLA. "I might have ridden your coattails our first year co-hosting *L.A. Tonight*, but I have more experience to offer the network now."

"You've never ridden my coattails, Callie. Granted, I've been with KCLA longer, but you're the hardest worker I know. You're disciplined and creative—a rare breed. Plus, you're only slightly irritating." Grinning, he brushed the tip of her nose with a finger. Her nerve-endings sparkled to life. "For the record, I care. More than you know."

His gaze held hers for a mystifying moment, and tremors of attraction rippled low in her belly.

Move. She needed to escape Marc Shaw's undeniable magnetism. Now.

She strode toward the lit mirror, gaze darting to her reflection. "Crap!" Pulse racing, she whirled on Marc. "Why didn't you tell me there's a knot of hair sticking up at the back of my head?"

His grin broadened. "Thought it was part of the 'do."

"You know it's not!" She wore her hair in a simple, shoulder-length style every night. "Marc, I looked like a fool on-camera!" She squashed the sticky blond lump, but it returned with a bounce.

"Maybe if you didn't use so much hairspray, it wouldn't have stayed in that position." He shut the door and watched her idly.

Callie plunked her transmitter on the counter. "I don't use too much hairspray—Zeta does." Damn the third-trimester pregnancy that sent their hair and makeup artist waddling to the restroom every twenty seconds lately. Zeta had sprayed Callie's fine, flyaway hair during the break preceding the battle-of-the-sexes segment, so at least she hadn't suffered this hair indignity long.

Still, she asked Marc, "When did it happen?"

"After I articulated one of my more salient points near the end of 'He Vs. She,' and you scratched your head."

He'd had no salient points. "I did not scratch my head."

"Yeah, you did."

She checked the mirror again. "Well, not alerting me to the problem was juvenile."

He laughed. "Callie, I tried to tell you. Why do you think I kept bumping your leg?"

To turn me on. "To annoy me." She frowned at their reflections. She hated the animalistic lust that kept her fine-tuned to this Lothario.

"Believe what you will, Hutchins, but I was not put on this earth simply to annoy you."

He moved behind her, forcing her against the counter. Of course, his jacket and tie didn't have one thread out of place.

He reached around her waist, his reflection growing thoughtful. Her nipples tightened.

"Wh-what are you doing?" she asked as her panties warmed.

"Fixing the knot before we meet Angela."

He gently tugged the clump with a hair pick. Callie struggled not to shiver in ecstasy as his well-honed body pressed against her. That she considered him the finest specimen of male pulchritude this side of the Sierra Nevadas served as a great source of mortification in the middle of her lonely nights. She couldn't have him realizing she actually enjoyed their nearness. He'd never let her live it down.

Suddenly, she detected rigid evidence that he enjoyed their proximity, too. At his six-one to her five-five, his pelvis settled just above her butt. His cock moved.

Callie stiffened. Marc's favorite pet followed suit.

"Nearly done," he murmured, plucking the knot.

Again with the movement!

Callie pushed off the counter, shoving him backward.

"Oof." He groaned—in pain, not pleasure. Served him right.

"Marc Shaw, you're disgusting." She jabbed his chest. "You got an erection untangling my hair."

"Ow." He rubbed the impressive bulge in his pants. "Sorry. It's not like I'm in control of the thing. It's a compliment."

"A compliment, my ass." Any woman in a pinch, that was Marc.

His devil-boy grin returned. "You're right. It's a compliment to your ass."

Callie snatched her purse off the chair. "We need to meet Angela."

"Sure, but later we could go to my place and… compliment each other?"

"In my nightmares."

More like her fantasies.

And there her pathetic cravings for Marc Shaw would remain.

Three days later, Marc dug his hands into his trouser pockets and paced Ed Lumley's office. "Callie won't be happy about this," he cautioned the KCLA program director.

"Callie won't be happy? I'm not happy," the middle-aged man blustered. "Friday night's broadcast was a train wreck."

"I know." Angela had pointed out several areas where Marc's performance had floundered. Callie had shone, firmly trouncing him on "He Vs. She," as she had during most of October. Marc hadn't sabotaged the segment on purpose—he couldn't help himself. Callie's fantastic legs and feisty blue eyes distracted him. "What does Iris think?"

The tall, wiry man scowled at Marc's mention of the station manager, their boss. "She's a walking category five hurricane—what did you expect? 'He Vs. She' was her concept. If it fails, in Iris's mind she fails. If she fails, I get canned. You might be ready to ditch your career and raise rugrats in Wyoming, Shaw, but I'm too old to start over in this cut-throat industry someplace else."

"Who said anything about Wyoming?"

"Wyoming, Arkansas, Timbuktu. What's the difference? Your mind's on extended vacation, Shaw. You haven't been yourself since Jada dumped you, and it's affecting the show." A knock tapped at the door. "Yeah!" Ed bellowed.

Callie entered, a tiny frown bunching her eyebrows. "Angela said there's a meeting, Ed. Is something wrong?"

Her gaze swung to Marc, and, like every time he first saw her at the two p.m.

start to their workdays, heat swarmed his chest and his pulse kicked. Her light pink suit hugged her breasts and hips, her blond hair and flawless skin as yet unspoiled by the overly made-up eyes and lips the studio lights required.

Ed grabbed a sheaf of papers off his desk. "This is wrong."

Callie bit her lip. "Emails about Friday's show?"

"And phone calls. Lord knows you did your best, Callie, and Angela smoothed out the worst of the bloops, but the viewers recognized recycled material. You two—" he pointed the scrunched papers at Callie, then Marc "—once had something amazing happening. The audience couldn't wait to tune in and watch the fireworks. Now our formerly top-rated segment is heading for the dumpster."

Callie winced. "I'm sorry, Ed. I'll try to do better tonight."

"*We'll* try," Marc amended. He'd botched the segment, not Callie, but they stood as a team.

"Take a tip from Yoda, kiddies. There is no frickin' *try*."

"We *will* do better then," Marc said.

"Damn straight you will." Ed chucked the papers onto his desk. "November sweeps starts in three days. I need some brainstorming from you two, and I need it fast. We gotta take this segment hotter than when you were dating Jada Reilly. Goddammit, Shaw, couldn't you have kept our little ratings machine happy another couple of months?"

Callie smirked. "Yes, Marc, what's your problem?"

She would know if she'd ever allow him a chance to explain. "I only dated Jada eight weeks—"

"But, oh, what weeks they were." She snickered.

Ed sat on the couch, nodding. "That relationship did more for 'He Vs. She' than anything before or since. You always screw up with your women, Shaw, but the poor twits usually stick around. Callie blasts you for acting like a dick, eventually you break the twit-of-the-moment's heart, and ratings soar. It was an unbeatable formula."

"My love life—a buffet for public consumption. I'm surprised any woman wants to date me."

Callie's smile could have sliced an ice cube. "So am I."

"Then Jada came along, and *kapow*." Ed punched his palm. "Instant celebrity appeal—our demographic went nuts. We need to generate that same kind of excitement for sweeps."

Marc scrubbed a hand over his face. "I'm not dating another actress for ratings. The viewers will see right through it."

"Don't date an actress, then," Ed conceded. "I see your point."

"Thank you."

"But give me something. Anything." Their boss's head turned. "Callie?"

"Don't look at me!"

Marc crossed his arms. "He said he wants us to brainstorm."

"I didn't create this mess."

Okay, but she was the reason he kept screwing up. "Maybe we should date." Marc chuckled to disguise how much the idea intrigued him.

Callie snorted. "Yeah."

Ed sprang off the couch. "Shaw, you're a natural! A romance between our co-hosts!"

"Give me a break." Callie rolled her eyes.

Ed clapped and pointed, as hyper as Jeff Goldblum on ten vats of espresso. "It's time to dig in the sandbox, kidlets, or not play at all. Marc's concept is fresh and reality-driven."

Callie stared at him. "You can't seriously mean a real romance between me and Marc?"

"No, of course not."

"Christ, Hutchins, I'm not that bad." Marc unfolded his arms.

Ed's fingers flexed. "You gotta admit, though, the idea has possibilities. Can we work with it? Callie, could you?"

"No. No. No and no and no."

Marc ignored her. "We'd need enough reality that the fans would buy into it. We could start small, build momentum. Begin with cute looks and comments on-camera. Lead to staged kisses, maybe leak a story to the tabloids...." *Kissing Callie. Yeah, I like it.*

Ed shadow-boxed an invisible opponent. "Iris would pee her pants!"

Callie jammed her hands on her hips. "Well, I hate it. I won't do it."

Marc turned to her. "I, I, I. Ever heard of teamwork, Hutchins? If all you can do is criticize, you might as well leave."

Chapter 2

"Yeah, you'd like that, wouldn't you?" No way would she inch one toenail out of Ed Lumley's office. This was her career. She wouldn't let Marc play tiddlywinks with it.

"She can't leave," Ed said. "We need her agreement."

Marc's gray eyes challenged her. "Then stop bitching and help us brainstorm. Have any bright ideas?"

Callie's jaw stiffened. "No." That was the problem. From a ratings viewpoint, Marc's publicity-stunt brainwave screamed pure brilliance. Anything less she suggested now might paint her as difficult to work with. She wanted Ed thinking she'd do anything necessary to put *L.A. Tonight* back on top, not come across as a whiny diva willing to risk the show. "I'm concerned about the believability quotient. Isn't there a fraternization policy that would prevent us from carrying this out?"

"Good point." Ed finger-jabbed the air.

"Pam and Rex from *Gourmet Cook-Fest* got married last year," Marc said.

Ed whirled to face him. "Equally good!"

"Weren't Pam and Rex considered an exception? They'd worked together ten years."

Ed looked at her. "Right."

"If corporate can make an exception for them…" Marc shrugged.

"Shaw has something there—the precedent has been set." Ed wagged a finger. "You know, corporate might frown on another trampling of the fraternization policy so soon, but at least they'd be paying attention to you two." He stepped toward Callie. "I would never allow a ratings stunt to hurt your career. Instead, consider how hot ratings could help you." He patted her shoulder. "I understand you're not responsible for this mess, but it's not like you have to sleep with the guy."

"Although that could be arranged," Marc murmured, rocking back on his heels.

Ed glared at him. "Can it, Shaw."

Callie paced the office. "But—but Ed, I can't force myself to feel an attraction that doesn't exist." Except it did. Even now, with Marc behaving like an ass, her panties sizzled just from being in the same room with him.

"You don't have to feel it. You just gotta fake it."

Easy for Ed to say—he didn't realize the source of her turmoil. "How many shows are we talking about?" Agh, don't ask that!

Ed smiled. "Just November."

"All of November?"

"Sweeps ends the 29th this year. So, until then?"

"Sounds fun," Marc said as Callie's stomach churned.

"It would be." Ed rubbed his palms like a kid anticipating trick-or-treating tomorrow night. "Callie, you want network attention? A staged romance with Marc ought to get it. In fact, if you come on-board and do everything in your power to increase the numbers and satisfy Iris, I'll start pressuring her to push you to New York. How does that sound?"

"What about me?" Marc asked.

"You could give a shit about New York."

"True."

"However, you make this thing with Callie look real, and you'll get approval of her replacement when she leaves."

"A female replacement?"

"Definitely."

Callie's throat tightened at the thought of Marc sharing their set with a new co-host. The unfortunate girl wouldn't survive his ego.

"*If* I leave, Ed. There's no guarantee a fake romance will work—for ratings or the network." Damn it, was she actually considering this ridiculous idea? For the ratings. God, she wanted those ratings.

"Oh, it'll work." Ed's eyes gleamed. "We have a photo shoot scheduled for Wednesday. Let's make the most of it. Once the audience accepts the romance, we'll plaster posters of you all over buses and billboards. Replace our usual we-hate-each-other ads with shots of you warming to Marc, then progress to you in his arms. The public will eat it up."

In Marc's arms? Her stomach fluttered. *Help.*

The desk phone rang. Gesturing for silence, Ed answered. After mumbling a few words, he disconnected. "Iris needs me, but I want to do more brainstorming. You two wait here."

The office door closed. Callie narrowed her eyes at Marc. "You just had to go and piss off Jada, didn't you?"

"Stuff it, Hutchins." He retrieved Ed's tension ball from the credenza. "We couldn't date forever."

"No, you'd need an attention span for that to happen."

"She broke up with me."

"That's not the story you fed me last time."

He flipped the silver ball from hand to hand. "Well, you didn't want to hear the truth, so why not stick with the P.R.?"

"Jada Reilly's a smart woman—that's why she dumped you. If she could swing some publicity by taking your trashing public, good for her."

The ball stopped bouncing. Marc gripped the shiny orb in one hand, a sexy smile playing on his mouth. "I won't argue with you there." He moved closer. "But don't you want to know what really happened?" he half-whispered.

Her nerves jumped. "Why? It has nothing to do with me."

"Ah, but you're wrong." Winking, he tossed her the ball. She caught it, and he stepped beside her. "You're too chicken to hear the truth, aren't you?" he asked softly.

"I'm not afraid of anything."

He grinned. "Yeah?" His large hand covering hers, he pressed her fingers into the warm tension ball until it compressed and expanded in her palm. Leaning closer, he murmured slowly, "Cluck, cluck."

His breath near her ear raised stimulating goose bumps on her neck. His musky cologne tantalized her senses.

"Step away, Shaw."

"Cluck." His deep voice soft and erotic, he squeezed her fingers around the ball again, and visions of them having sex filled her mind. Her nipples peaked.

Damn it, how'd he do that?

He released her hand. The ball plopped onto the carpet as he stepped back. His lashes were thick, dark blond, his gray eyes self-assured and mellow.

"Think we'll need to kiss for the photo shoot?" he asked.

Callie swallowed. "No."

"Well, I think we will—for the ratings. And I know I'll like it."

"You'd like it with a blow-up doll." She tried to sound caustic, but her voice trembled, and he laughed.

"We could find a hotel and satisfy your curiosity."

"God, Marc, you're so full of yourself."

He smoothed his tie. "Prove you're not afraid to get close to me, Callie. We won't make it through the session if you are."

"I am close to you. Right now." And she wouldn't back away. He couldn't intimidate her with his over-confident sex appeal.

He shrugged. "So, kiss me."

Her skin tingled. "Excuse me?"

"Better we try in private today than act self-conscious with the photographer Wednesday."

He made too much sense. She ran her hands down her skirt. "One kiss. Shaw, I swear, if you try anything…."

"Like I'd want to feel you up in Ed's office."

"You know what I mean. No hard-ons."

"I'll think of Joan Rivers." A small smile tipped his mouth as his head lowered. His lips hovered above hers, and he paused.

Callie's heart pounded. What was his problem? "Hurry up."

"I'm anticipating," he whispered.

"Well, I'm having second thoughts."

"Like hell." He kissed her. His hand swept around her neck, fingers grazing her skin as their lips touched. Sparks flickered behind her shut eyes. *Pop-pop-pop.*

His lips moved far too gently, triggering an indescribable longing inside her. She parted her mouth, inviting him in.

Oh, he tasted sublime. Hot and needy and brimming with wanting.

Exactly how she felt.

His mouth broke away, and a puff of sensual breath warmed her face.

Callie whimpered. *Not yet.*

"I'm no chicken," she whispered, wrapping her arms around him and tugging him back where he belonged.

To her mouth.

A chuckle rose in his throat, and her stiff nipples poked her suit jacket. She'd kiss the arrogance right out of him.

The office door opened. Whipping away, she wiped her lips. "Hi, Ed."

The tall man's eyes bugged. "What's going on?"

"Preparation." Marc snatched up the tension ball and returned it to the credenza. "For the photo shoot."

Callie fiddled with her blouse collar. "Um, yeah."

"Yes!" Ed victory-pumped the air. "I knew I could count on you two. So, how was it? Can you do this?"

"It was incredi—"

"It was passable," Callie interrupted.

"Good, we can work with passable. Now, kiss him again. I'll give you pointers. We need to get this right."

"Oh, Lauren, it was hell." Callie didn't think she'd ever dislodge her head from her hands. She and her friend, Lauren Flannigan, an account executive for KCLA, shared a booth in a diner across the street from the station in an old area of Hollywood. Callie's lunch break fell at the end of Lauren's work day, and this afternoon Callie needed to vent something fierce.

"Doesn't sound like hell to me." Ironic humor resonated in Lauren's throaty voice. Callie rested one arm on the Formica table and stared at her.

"Right. I had to stand there and kiss Marc Shaw half a dozen times while Ed Lumley 'directed' us." Mindful of the other patrons crowding the diner, she maintained a quiet tone. "If that's not your definition of hell, what is?"

Lauren laughed. "Okay, I can see how Ed's presence might unnerve a girl."

"He looks like a frog with those Don Knotts eyes. Picture Don Knotts watching you trade spit with someone you can barely tolerate."

Lauren pushed her chestnut brown hair over one shoulder. "Yeah, like I buy that kissing Marc Shaw is anything but a fantasy come to life."

Callie lifted her head. "You've kissed Marc?" No, no, no. She did not feel green.

Lauren smiled. "I wish. No. But I can imagine."

"You can have him." The guy might be gorgeous, but his conceit knew no bounds. Every time Ed had approved another kiss, Marc had zapped her a mysterious wink. She'd felt like he was keeping score: Shaw 6, Hutchins 1. The only kiss she counted successful on her part occurred before Ed returned to his office. Nerves had assailed her after that, heating her cheeks and making her fidget like a thirteen-year-old girl.

"You're wrong." Lauren sipped her soft drink.

"About what?"

"I tried to catch Marc's attention after he and Jada Reilly split. He wasn't interested."

All men were interested in Lauren. "His ego was probably still in recovery mode," Callie said, relief flooding her. Or was it nausea?

"Whatever. I'm eyeing the new guy in engineering now."

The waitress arrived with their Caesar salads. Callie picked up her fork. She wanted to send Marc a clear message during tonight's taping—no more unnecessary kissing.

"You must admit, though, Marc is hot." Lauren ground pepper onto her salad.

"He's a dickhead."

"A hot dickhead. And no doubt he has a hot dick."

"Okay, stop." Callie laughed. "I'm never finding that out."

Her friend's head tilted. "Maybe you should."

"Lauren Flannigan, bite your tongue."

"Maybe Marc will bite yours. You know, just a sexy nibble, a sultry little suck."

Callie's lap heated. "Lauren, he's an idiot. I can't."

Her friend smiled. "Idiots are perfect for just this sort of thing. Callie, I'm telling you, if you don't have sex more than once every eight years, you'll turn back into a virgin."

"I had sex last year."

"Which proves my point. All you do is work. These next few weeks with Marc could be fun. I say take him for every bit of sex-godness he can dish out."

Callie stabbed garlicky romaine. "And when November ends?"

"You'll worry about what to do then. You'll have to 'break up' for the cameras, so you'll do it in real life, too. It's perfect."

Callie chewed her salad. In this town, everyone knew "perfect" translated into "too good to be true."

Chapter 3

"I hope we're getting paid overtime for this."

Marc glanced up from a magazine in the reception area of the photography studio to see Callie standing in front of his chair, wearing a pristine white suit and spiked dominatrix heels that perfectly accentuated her long legs.

"Wow. You look great." Forcing his mouth shut before drool escaped, he tossed his reading material onto a side table.

She brushed invisible lint off her skirt. "Thanks. So do you."

"This old thing?" He grinned and flicked his tie. The rich red color duplicated the shade of the snug top peeking out from Callie's jacket. "Angela chose it."

"She must want us to match."

"Maybe she wants the new ads to send a subliminal message to viewers. Red represents love, after all."

Callie's lips pursed in a manner that reminded him of sex. "Shaw, I'm impressed."

"I can feign intelligence when necessary." Of course, with her, everything reminded him of sex.

"No, you're right about the subliminal messages," she said, indicating his monkey suit. "You're dressed in black, symbolizing the bad guy. I'm wearing white, so naturally I'm the good girl."

"Or you're a sacrificial virgin." He grinned.

She eyed him. "Now I really hope I get overtime."

He chuckled. "You know we won't. Starting an hour early hardly constitutes employee abuse."

She plunked onto a chair. "Yeah? Well, just because I agreed to this sideshow doesn't mean I have to like it."

No, admitting she enjoyed working with him in any way would decimate the hostile air she struggled so hard to maintain. However, after their passionate kiss in Ed's office two days ago, she could bitch until the next century and not convince Marc she didn't feel the same attraction that had boiled in his veins for months.

She rubbed the tiny purse on her lap. "Where's Angela?"

"Upstairs talking to the photographer about the confidentiality agreement."

"I guess we're not the only ones who need to worry about keeping this charade under wraps."

"I'm not worried."

Her blue gaze lifted. "You wouldn't be. You never seem to stress about anything,

Marc. Why is that?"

Because he was a slack-ass? No doubt, that was what she thought.

He shifted his leg to adjust his trousers at one knee. "Because I have no incentive to stress out over my job, Callie. I'm tired of this damn town. I'm tired of the traffic, the smog, the sunshine. I'm tired of collagen lips and plastic boobs, and I'm tired of working in TV."

She gripped her chair arm. "You want off *L.A. Tonight*?"

"Not exactly." How to explain his restlessness of the last year? "I'm happy to stay with the show. But I'd be just as happy to get kicked off. I need a change. I don't know how or what yet, but I do know it's not what I already have."

"So, grab some goals. Make a life list."

"A life list?" He laughed. "Not my style."

She rolled her eyes.

"Don't worry, Hutchins. I know our show is the ticket to your dreams. I won't screw up."

"Marc, your lack of focus is what got us here."

"True. I dug the damn hole. But together we'll climb out. I promise." He clasped her hand, but she tugged it free.

"Don't get the wrong idea, Shaw. I want the dating concept to succeed because of what improved ratings can do for my career. No other reason."

"I'm not a moron. I know that."

Her gaze skipped away. "I think the show could survive without you, if that's what you want," she said quietly. "I just can't have you leaving soon."

He snorted. "Of course not. You need me. For now."

She nodded.

"But we're in trouble if you can't even hold my hand, Callie."

Her gaze met his again, determination shining in her eyes. "I've already proven I can perform when it counts. How about you?"

"I can perform anytime, anywhere, baby. Just let me know."

She shook her head. "You're impossible."

"But charming."

A tiny smile curved her mouth, and he grinned, pleasure flooding him. She wasn't as immune to their chemistry as she wished.

Angela's clunky shoes echoed on the hardwood stairs leading to the studio proper. Her round face poked over the railing. "Marc, Callie? We're ready for you."

Callie shot off her chair as if he'd lit a bomb beneath it. Marc followed her up the stairs behind Angela. Callie's perfect ass swayed with each step—a mesmerizing view.

"Eyes up, Shaw," she muttered without turning.

"Make me," he whispered.

Her pace faltered. The movement of her hips tight and awkward, she raced up the remaining steps, and he laughed. He loved to goad her.

A woman in her late fifties with long silver hair and animated green eyes greeted them. "Good afternoon, Marc. It's been awhile."

"Hi, Kay." He shook her hand, and she turned to Callie.

"Ms. Hutchins, I haven't had the pleasure. My associate worked with you and Marc last time. However, I've seen the show, and I'm a fan." They shook hands. "Kay Wharton."

"Please, call me Callie. And thank you about the show. I'm sure, with your help, we'll increase the numbers again."

"You bet." Kay directed Marc and Callie to the center of the large room crowded with lights, reflectors, and assorted backgrounds. "We'll start with your usual back-to-back stance, against a white setting this time. Marc, instead of crossing your arms, I want you to slide your hands into your pants pockets, elbows out a bit, jacket casually creased. Perfect. Now give me a self-assured look."

Feeling like a mannequin, he complied. Kay placed her hands on his shoulders and adjusted his position toward the large, wide-format camera used for billboard ads. "Tilt your head a smidge. This way. Great."

Kay took Callie's purse and passed it to Angela. "Snuggle your back close to Marc's," Kay instructed. "Arms crossed, but twist your waist slightly. Good. Now glance around coyly at him. Lift your left hand off your elbow, as if caught off-guard by your feelings."

"That won't be a stretch," Callie mumbled, and Kay's husky laughter filled the studio.

"Hah, hah, Hutchins," Marc murmured as Callie's spine twitched against his. The scent of peaches lifted from her hair, fogging his brain and stirring excitement in his cock.

"Nice shampoo," he whispered once Kay had retreated to the camera. "Or is that a soap you use all over?"

"You'll never know," she whispered back.

"Don't tempt me. I love a challenge."

She clammed up. But rosy color infused her cheeks, signaling her arousal.

Kay dusted her hands on her men's-style trousers and focused the camera on the tripod. Angela stood beside her, hands propped on jeans-clad hips and Callie's purse sticking out from her grasp like a little white flag of surrender.

"Let's have fun with this," Angela said. "Hate each other on your time—and in private. For the next twenty-one days, in public and while taping, you're falling in love."

Callie's shoulders squirmed against him. "Why only twenty-one days? Sweeps lasts all of November."

Angela fluffed her short dark hair with one hand. "On day twenty-one, trouble brews in paradise. On day twenty-eight, Marc breaks your heart."

"But I want to leave him!"

Marc scratched his eyebrow.

"Positions, please," Kay ordered.

Angela set Callie's purse on a stool near the camera. "Our fans—what few we have left of them—prefer Marc as the villain. The latest focus group report clearly states that the breakup with Jada Reilly castrated his image."

Marc coughed. "Let's not use that word in my presence."

"Sorry, dude. Callie, strange as it seems, our women viewers feel that when Marc instigates his breakups, they might then have a chance with him. Become his next victim, so to speak. Which they'd gladly do. Considering that, when Jada left him, you'd think he would have captured public sympathy—the 'poor baby' factor. And he might have, if he'd listened to my advice and played the situation properly." Angela arrowed him a stern look.

"My bad," Marc murmured, amused at the irony of the female fans' response. If only they knew that he had dumped Jada.

But they didn't know. No one did.

Including Callie.

"However, the focus group findings reveal that when Marc gets dumped, he looks weak. Our female viewers don't approve," Angela finished.

Marc shrugged. "Women. You want to be dominant *and* submissive. I'll never figure any of you out."

"Which will work in the show's favor after your 'romance' with Callie puts us back on track," Angela said.

"Unbelievable," Callie muttered, breath feathering his shoulder.

Kay smiled. "All right, let's do this. Callie, lift your hand a bit, remember. That's it. Marc, how about a wolf-grin? Great!" The camera flashed several frames.

"Let's see some movement," Kay directed. "Marc, give her a sexy, come-to-me crook of your finger." The flash popped. "Fantastic! Callie, now turn and tug his tie—I love it!"

Talking them through a series of poses, Kay snapped enough frames to fill a photo album. Leaving the camera, she strode behind them, pulled down a dark shade, and adjusted a red spotlight to cast a vibrant glow.

She returned to the camera.

"Ah, the red looks lovely." She reached for the remote shutter control. "Okay, Marc, take her in your arms."

He whispered to Callie, "Told you we'd have to."

She stepped into his embrace, spine rigid as a ruler.

"Relax," he whispered. "I'm not packing wood." His cock hardened. "Oops. Spoken too soon." He now flew at half-mast.

A blush spattered her cheeks, and he grinned. "Sorry. Guess it needs training."

"Or a sharp knife," she mumbled, but the softness of her voice betrayed her. Desire arced between them, vibrant and electric.

"Keep your hips pressed against me," he murmured. "To conceal the evidence." Like the intimate contact would help. However, he didn't want to embarrass Kay or Angela.

On the other hand, shocking Callie gave him a carnal thrill he'd yet to experience with another woman. The more she tried to resist their attraction, the more he wanted to pursue it, regardless that she was the most irritable female he'd ever met.

He was a sick puppy.

Shaking her head in apparent frustration, she moved closer.

"Smile like you mean it," Kay said.

"Which one of us?" Marc asked without tearing his gaze from Callie's insanely arousing indignant expression. The blush on her cheeks reminded him of cotton candy. He wanted to lick them. Wanted to lick her.

All over.

"Both." Kay's commanding voice hauled his attention back to the task of taming—not encouraging—his erection. "We can't have aggravation radiating from you, Callie. Try an understated, dreamy smile. If it helps, pretend he's your celebrity crush of the moment. And, Marc, she's not your lunch, she's your sweetheart. You adore her. You want to protect her."

He wanted to devour her.

However, keeping his goal of deflation in mind, he visualized the words of every syrupy greeting card he'd received from female fans over the years. Callie's features assumed a blissful expression.

"Excellent." Kay shot several frames. "Let's try the same pose, but kiss her. Romantically, mind you. No slobber."

"With pleasure," Marc murmured in a velvety tone meant only for Callie.

He pressed his mouth to hers, a feather-light sweep for the camera. Her lips moved cautiously, almost shy, considering they'd kissed several times already in Ed's office. Marc's chest tightened.

"Wonderful!" Kay cheered as the camera zoomed and whirred.

Angela's zestful response followed, "I'm convinced!"

Marc lifted his head. "You get all you need?" He intended the question for Kay, but couldn't tear his gaze away from the surprise parting Callie's succulent mouth.

"Um, yes," she answered instead of Kay, and he smiled.

"Too bad. Because I haven't."

Aside from the necessity of being civil to Marc on-camera, Callie spent the next two days avoiding the guy and trying not to think about Lauren's suggestion that she go after him for real.

Never in her life had she pursued a man just to satisfy a temporary itch. Although, she had to admit, the idea intrigued her. Clearly, Marc suffered from erectile function—he couldn't stop getting it up!

Maybe if she sapped him of a few thousand gallons of testosterone, he'd recover. And her nightly sex dreams would cease. Then their relationship could revert to her keeping him off-balance, rather than the other way around.

She compensated for her descent into lust-inspired madness by upping her grouch quotient whenever dodging him proved impossible. Friday night, after the post-production meeting, she managed to slip into her dressing room and remove her makeup without him following and hounding her to confess her celebrity crush. If Marc learned that thoughts of him and only him had filled her mind during their amazingly tender kiss at the photo shoot, his big head would swell just as rapidly as his marginally smaller one.

That was all she needed, Marc Shaw more impressed with himself.

After checking the hallway and finding no evidence of the sexy annoyance, she headed for the deserted, streetlight-brightened parking lot. The warm night breeze fluttered her cream-colored pantsuit as her shoes tapped asphalt. She spied Marc lounging against her white coupe.

Now what? Fighting her attraction to him was exhausting. Couldn't he cut her a break?

Nearing him, she pulled her keys out of her purse. "Excuse me."

He stayed put. "You didn't come to the makeup room."

"Zeta's pregnancy tires her out. I thought she'd like to leave early tonight, so I removed my makeup myself."

He nodded. "Want to get a drink?"

"Why? Our publicity stunt date is next week."

"Yep. And I'd rather you didn't bite off my head during it."

"I won't, Marc. I'm a professional."

"A professional pain in the ass." He grinned. "Come on, Callie, what can it hurt? Just one drink. I'm not asking to sleep with you."

A sensual thrill zinged her. "I wasn't aware you asked any of your conquests." No, they probably begged him.

"What do you think I do? Force them?" He pushed off the car. "Fuck, Hutchins, you're cute, smart, quick as a whip. I've heard rumors you can act human when you want to. Yet you're always busting my balls. Who made you hate men?"

"*What?*"

"Who taught you men are the enemy? Or *is* it just me?"

"What an ego! I don't jump at a drink, so automatically you think a bad experience with some asshole turned me evil."

"Yeah, I do. Because I have a hunch I'm not the only man in this town to show a little interest and get his nuts crushed in return."

Callie's heart lurched. Marc was interested in her?

She clenched her purse. "I hate to break it to you, but sporting a boner whenever you're within two feet of a woman isn't interest, Marc. It's insulting."

He laughed. "Well, you have me there. I've never heard that one."

She jammed her key into the car lock with trembling fingers. *Damn it.* "Haven't you learned anything from 'He Vs. She'? Treating women like sex objects went out with burned bras."

He planted a hand on the car hood. "I'm not trying to get into your pants without an invitation, Callie. I'm thinking of the show, that's it."

Stemming the swift bite of tears, Callie stared into the driver's window. Marc had her pegged. She did always look for the worst in men.

No wonder she couldn't hold the attention of guys she liked. Apparently, she launched "don't touch" vibes to the entire gender.

She glanced at him. "I'm sorry for the conquest comment. It was out of line."

"Yes. It was. But if you want to try slipping into your human skin tonight and agree to that drink, I'll forgive you."

A troubled look shadowed his gaze, and her throat pinched.

Had she hurt his feelings? Why should she care?

Because they needed to survive November sweeps. She needed the show to triumph. And continuing her personal smear campaign against Marc Shaw wouldn't help.

But playing nice this early in the game might.

Chapter 4

Following a forty-minute drive stuffed with clumsy silences, Callie found herself in Santa Monica outside an Old English pub that didn't suit Marc at all.

"Why here?" she asked as he held open the door.

"You'll see."

She entered The Sly Fox ahead of him, and the friendly atmosphere engulfed her. Occupied tables flanked her right, and a dark walnut bar with a mirrored backdrop bordered an area that opened into a pool room. Callie glimpsed the pool tables and dartboards. Secluded booths lined the walls.

Marc placed his hand on her back, the light pressure undemanding against her jacket-styled top. Still, her skin trembled and her tummy tumbled.

"Head for the bar." His low, deep voice resonated beneath the soft, classic rock music. "There's someone I want you to meet."

"How often do you come here?"

"A couple times a week. The people who frequent this place don't hassle celebrities."

A smile tugging her lips, she glanced back. "Minor celebrities."

"You wouldn't believe some of the shit I went through with Jada. The Sly Fox became my haven."

"You turned into a lush?"

A grin crinkled his eyes. "Not quite."

They reached the bar and squeezed in beside a vacant stool. Marc waved over the bartender, a sturdy-looking fellow of about sixty with blue eyes and white hair.

"Hey, Marc." The bartender set down his cloth and smiled. "You finally brought her in."

Callie shook his hand. "Hello. I'm Callie Hutchins. Pleased to meet you." She smiled.

The man chuckled. "I know who you are. I watch you and my nephew here on TV every weeknight without fail."

Callie blinked. "Your nephew?" However, now that Marc's uncle mentioned the connection, she noted a resemblance around the older man's friendly eyes.

"Callie, this is my uncle, Bob Firman," Marc said.

Bob explained, "Marc's mother was my sister."

"Oh." Bob had said "was." Was Marc's mother dead? Cheeks heating, Callie realized how little she knew about his life outside of KCLA.

"Do you own The Sly Fox?" she asked Bob.

"Marc and I own it together."

Marc nodded. "Bob's father—my grandfather—owned it for twenty years, although Bob's managed it the last ten. My father died when I was young, so when Granddad passed away last winter, Bob and I inherited the place together."

Both of Marc's parents were gone? For a strange nano-second, Callie's heart squeezed as images of a lonely, gray-eyed boy brimmed her mind.

Bob's smile broadened. "I do all the work while Marc rakes in half the profits."

"Hey, it's thirty-seventy, and I'm on the short end," Marc razzed him. "The split is fair."

"Sure is." Bob leaned on the bar. "My father wanted a fifty-fifty split, but Marc insisted I take another twenty regardless that I don't have my own kids to leave the place to."

"It's good business." Marc clapped his uncle's shoulder. "With a thirty share, I don't feel guilty not pulling my load, and I know that when you kick the bucket, I'll get it all."

"You sure about that? Maybe I'll leave my seventy to Rosie on the corner."

"Which corner? The one in your dreams?"

"Could be. Or maybe the one in yours."

Callie shifted on her pumps as she watched the camaraderie between Marc and his uncle. Had Marc asked her here to make her feel foolish for thinking him one-dimensional? Or because he honestly wanted to open up and improve their relationship?

With abrupt clarity, she realized she needed to give him the benefit of the doubt. No matter his motivation, she'd treat tonight as an important step forward for the show.

Bob straightened. "What'll you have?"

"Two drafts," Marc answered. "On the house. And don't bitch."

Bob laughed and stepped away to draw the beers. After passing them the glasses, he retrieved his bar cloth. "Can't stand around and entertain you all night, you know. I have other customers, and my partner's a slave-driver."

"So, leave," Marc teased. "Who's stopping you?"

Bob winked at Callie—now he definitely reminded her of his nephew. "This cute little thing."

"I promise she'll say goodnight before we go. Won't you, Callie?"

"Sure." She liked Bob. His sharp wit kept Marc in line.

Bob greeted another customer. Callie glanced at Marc, her stomach chasing butterflies. "What now?" she asked.

"We sit and drink."

He maneuvered them through the crowd. Heads turned, and Callie noticed a few glances of recognition, but no one bothered them.

She sat at a small table and sipped her frosty glass of beer. Marc parked in the second chair and grabbed a handful of peanuts from a bowl. As he popped two into his mouth and chewed, she caught herself staring at his sensual lips.

Heat burned between her legs, and she lowered her gaze. He wore the same white shirt and deep lavender tie from tonight's broadcast, but had traded his blazer for a charcoal jacket that emphasized his gray eyes.

Damn it, staring again. And he knew it. Humor filled his gaze as he flashed a bone-melting grin.

Callie's pulse raced. "I didn't even know you had a grandfather, much less that he died," she blurted. *Crap! How crass.*

"There's a lot you don't know about me, Callie." He tossed another peanut into his mouth. "I think we should change that. Let's try to be friends."

"Do I have a choice?" she mumbled so the other customers wouldn't overhear. His husky chuckle rolled over her, doing crazy things to her suddenly perky nipples. "But I'm antsy tonight. I can't just sit here." She scraped back her chair. "A table's free. Let's play pool."

Marc's eyebrows lifted. "You want to shoot pool?"

"Well, I figure you don't want me near a dartboard. For some reason, I see a huge bull's eye painted in the middle of your forehead." She grinned.

"Pool it is." He stood and retrieved their beer glasses. "Do you like snooker?"

She feigned confusion. "I know eight ball."

"Okay. Not my favorite, though. How about nine ball?"

Callie Betty-Boop blinked.

"I'll teach you," he said. "It'll be fun.'"

I'll cream you. It'll be awesome. Her competitive nature rejoicing, she trailed him to the bar.

"We'll leave your purse behind the bar," Marc murmured, then asked his uncle, "Do you have the nine ball rack?"

Bob nodded, reaching beneath the bar and handing Callie a diamond-shaped rack in exchange for her purse. Marc removed his jacket and passed it to his uncle.

Callie stared at the rack. "Why isn't it a triangle?"

Marc's smile held an edge of superiority she often encountered on "He Vs. She." "Nine ball uses its own rack. The regulars know to ask for it."

Callie just smiled.

She allowed him to lead them through the crowd again. He set their beers on the side rail of an empty pool table.

She pretended to listen as he instructed how to choose a cue in typical Me-Big-Strong-Tarzan-You-Adoring-Jane fashion. Scattered murmurs of recognition rose from the booths.

Callie glanced at a middle-aged couple, who grinned and waved. After watching her and Marc argue on "He Vs. She," the pair probably wondered when she'd pull out her six-shooters.

They'd see.

Marc explained the rules while assembling the balls in the rack.

"Does whoever sink the black ball win?" Callie asked, securing her trap. Really, could she help it if a colossal male ego lurked beneath his cute "let's be friends" veneer?

"Nope." He chalked his stick. "In this game, the eight's just a regular ball. You want to sink the nine last."

"Weird."

He laughed. "It's not. Ladies' choice. Want to break?"

She nodded. "That's the best part."

"Okay." He placed the cue ball on the table. "Generally, if you don't sink a ball or send four balls to the rails on the break, we'd call your shot foul and I'd get ball in hand."

"No need to be rude, Shaw."

He grinned. "However, seeing as this is your first nine ball game, if you don't sink a ball on the break, we won't count it as a foul."

"Gee, thanks." Callie levered her cue.

"You might want to chalk your stick first."

"Oh. Right." She lobbed him a "sucka" smile and reached for the tiny cube of blue chalk.

Marc admired Callie's ability to make the best of their situation. He'd ambushed her outside KCLA with his nut-crushing comments, yet instead of telling him to fuck off, she'd pushed aside her antagonism and accepted his invitation for drinks.

For the good of *L.A. Tonight.* He wouldn't fool himself that she'd have come to The Sly Fox otherwise.

However, now that she had, he wouldn't let her leave until she realized he was more than an over-sexed asshole who sprouted an erection whenever he neared any warm female body.

His erections were woman-specific.

And, lately, they only occurred around Callie.

Like now.

He peeled his gaze off the snug pants hugging her ass as she positioned herself at the pool table.

She glanced over her shoulder. "You said to hit down the nine ball last. Does it matter which ball I sink first?"

He shook his head. "The idea is for the white cue ball to strike the yellow one ball first. If the one sinks, great. However, if the one ball then hits six, sinking it instead, equally good. After the one ball drops, the same format follows for striking the two ball first."

Forehead puckering, Callie plunked her cue stick on the parquet floor stretching beneath the pool tables. "What if I accidentally sink the nine?"

"That's a foul. I'd re-spot it and get ball in hand—my turn—with the cue ball again."

Her lips twitched. "You're really obsessed with this ball in hand thing, aren't you?"

He chuckled. "Start us off, Callie."

She nodded, murmuring, "Thank God the one ball is at the top of the diamond."

Her sunshiny hair drifted over her shoulders as she lifted her stick and bit her lower lip.

She paused, inhaled, struck the white cue ball. The colored balls flew, three hitting the rails but none sinking. "Damn it."

Marc patted her shoulder. The brief contact seared his palm. "Actually, that's a great break shot." The one ball now hid behind the purple four. Beginner's luck for Callie. "It's my turn, but I still need the white cue ball to strike the yellow one ball first."

Callie leaned on her stick. "How're you gonna do that?

Marc grinned. "Smart ass."

Two men playing at the next table ogled her. Marc resisted the urge to thunder on over there and knock them senseless—Callie would have his hide. He doubted they eyed her only because of her local celebrity, but because she exuded sexiness, elegance, and feisty attitude all at once.

She had no idea how beautiful she was, how strong the temptation to tame her.

"I'll try coming at her from behind," he murmured.

Mischievous humor sparkled in her eyes. "Oh, first you're obsessed with balls, now with 'coming at her from behind.' Honestly, Marc, is everything about sex with you?"

He laughed. "You'd think so, to hear you talk. But, no, sorry to disappoint you."

"I'm not disappointed."

"Sure, you are." He lined up a shot. The white ball whizzed down the table and banked to strike the one, but didn't sink it. *Shit.*

"That's rough, Shaw." Callie drank her beer. "Do I still need to hit that crafty yellow ball first?"

"Yep." Thanks to his crappy shot, the damn thing stood in direct line to a corner pocket. "I'd advise—"

"Uh-uh. No tips." She smiled sweetly. "Unless I ask."

As she set up her shot, her stick wobbled. "Nerves," she murmured before refocusing her attention on the table.

Her ass wiggled. *Snap-crack-plunk!* "Yes!"

Marc yanked up his gaze. "You sank it?"

"Yep." She sounded as gleeful as a little girl out to impress her favorite teacher.

Too bad they weren't playing bedroom games.

Nibbling her lip, she sauntered around the table. He'd follow, but her swaying ass would just sidetrack him again. So he watched as she examined the layout.

She twirled her stick. Reaching the foot of the table, she leaned down, created a perfect arch on the felt with her fingers, and stretched her stick onto the back of her hand like a pro. Her shrewd gaze calculated shot lines and angles as the stick slid back and forth, back and forth.

Her movements were slow and seductive, designed to keep his mind off the game and firmly rooted in his pants.

He swallowed a chuckle. The little hustler. He'd been had.

He gripped his stick and prepared to enjoy the show.

As Callie drew back her cue again, her head turned and she grinned. She took her shot. The white ball bounced over the six to sink the two.

She stepped away from the table and blew chalk off her stick like a gunslinger.

Marc mock-growled, "'I know eight ball,' my foot."

"It's true." Grin blossoming into a beautiful smile, she surveyed the table. "I've played eight ball and snooker, but never nine ball before." *Whack.* The three dropped into a corner pocket. She strolled past him. "I haven't played in years—"

"Braggart."

"—but I guess it's like riding a bicycle."

"Or other things."

Her eyebrows lifted.

"Like sex," he added. "We might suffer dry spells, but we never forget."

Her gaze lowered, but she calmly chalked her cue. "You can't fluster me, Shaw."

"Well, that's one of us." She stood so close, her perfume floated up from the hint of cleavage her jacket-top displayed. Spicy. Enthralling. All Callie. "Your play."

In every way.

"I'll sink four now." She grinned. "I've been saving it."

"So we're doing them in order?"

"'Doing' them? Shaw, grow up. We're hitting and pocketing the balls in order, if that's what you mean. No more pansy-assed doesn't-matter-which-ball-goes-in crap."

"You're a wily one, Hutchins."

"You should have known better than to patronize me, Marc."

She sunk the four and five in rapid order, and he groaned. "I'll have to get you drunk to level the playing field, won't I?"

Chapter 5

"Where did you work before KCLA?" Callie asked Marc over juicy mushroom burgers in a shadowy corner booth. Despite his declaration to get her sloshed, he'd fallen for her argument that his fragile male ego couldn't survive a drunk-female thrashing, and they'd enjoyed four sober games of nine ball before agreeing to a tournament tie.

In fact, once he'd learned each of their grandfathers had taught them pool, he'd played hard, which suited Callie. She liked a man who didn't shy away from her competitive nature.

The next logical conclusion surprised her. Because it meant she liked Marc—more than as a handy body in her dreams.

"You mean you haven't snooped in my employee files like a worthy little adversary?" he asked before licking burger sauce off his thumb. "I know everything there is to know about you."

Callie laughed. "Except for my skill with a pool cue."

"Okay, so your files don't reveal all your secrets."

Wasn't that the truth? She bit into her burger. A tiny mushroom popped out, landing on her chin.

Marc's gaze honed in on her fingers as she slid the morsel into her mouth. She didn't bother suppressing the sensual thrill vibrating through her. She'd experienced the same arousing sensation every time he'd brushed past her at the pool table, and had quickly discovered its addictive qualities.

Several times while they'd played, she'd fantasized about chasing away his uncle and the customers before having her wicked way with Marc on the felt. She'd sit on a side rail and open her legs, inviting him between her thighs. He'd caress her outside her pants, feel her heat, then go wild and strip her bare. To his touch, his hands, his mouth and stiff cock….

Her clit buzzed, panties moistening. She squirmed on the booth seat. "Maybe if you tell me your secrets, I'll let you in on some of mine." She took another bite of her burger and washed it down with a slug of beer.

Marc smothered a French fry in ketchup. "Communications major. I did features at small stations around the state. I didn't set out to work in TV, though. I was lucky and fell into it."

"Connections?"

His dark blond eyebrows wiggled. "My very own Mrs. Robinson. She believed I had talent and helped me along."

"You slept your way into your first job?" Callie expected annoyance to wash over her. Instead, faint jealousy toward his Mrs. Robinson stabbed her.

Oh-oh.

"That's how it might look, but I really cared for her, Callie. Unfortunately, it turned out she loved her husband's money more than she wanted me."

"So she used you." *Bitch.*

He shook his head. "I knew what I was getting into. She taught me an important lesson about how complicated emotions can become. Tag them with a marriage license, and they grow even more complex—third parties don't belong. I'll never take up with a married woman again." He grinned. "Unless she's my wife."

Callie swallowed. "I can't imagine you married."

"I can." He ate more French fries. Nearby, pool balls clacked, and a victorious player cheered. An old Rolling Stones song thrummed from the loudspeakers spaced throughout the large room. "How about you?"

"Um, sure, I'd like to get married someday. I'm focusing on my career for now, though."

He chuckled. "I meant your background."

"Oh." Her face warmed. "I attended UCLA for a B.A. in film and television. I loved drama in high school, so at first I pursued a liberal arts degree, intending to enter the theater. Then I realized I needed more than a stage presence. I wanted to connect with people, talk with them, influence their lives." Babble, babble.

"Which explains wanting to work in national morning TV."

She nodded. "I love hosting *L.A. Tonight*, but morning shows are more personal and homey."

"Kelly Ripa, watch out. Callie Hutchin's after your job."

She laughed. "A network show is a nice dream, and I'll work my hardest to make it happen." She lifted her burger. The rich sauce tantalized her nostrils, and damn it if Marc's nearness didn't seduce every last one of her senses.

Oh, boy, if she didn't watch herself, she'd have him flat on his back by midnight.

"I have no doubt that you will make it happen, Callie." He smiled. Not teasing or flirtatious for once, but warm, honest, genuine.

An affectionate, caring smile any woman would love to wake up to every morning for the rest of her life.

No wonder their female viewers forgave him his asinine opinions on relationships. He probably held them spellbound with the charismatic power of his smile.

Now, for the first time, she wondered, had he formulated his viewpoints for the camera? Was there more to Marc Shaw than she'd allowed herself to believe?

"Thank you." She set her unfinished burger on her plate. She was stuffed.

"Where were you born?" he asked.

She toyed with her napkin. "Nebraska."

"I don't hear a Midwestern accent."

"I've worked hard to lose it."

"Here I've always pegged you for a city girl."

"Spoken like a true city boy who doesn't believe there's intelligent life outside L.A."

"You're wrong. My parents farmed outside Fresno until my father died."

Callie fingered a cool drop of condensation on her beer glass. "If you don't mind me asking, Marc, what happened?"

"Tractor accident. I'll spare you the details. It's gory."

She shuddered. "But your mother's family is from L.A.?"

Nodding, he reached for another French fry. "She always felt close to Dad's sisters, so after his accident she moved us to Berkeley to be near them. Eventually, she and two aunts opened a chain of designer baby clothes stores and made a mint. Babeez—they're all over the state now."

Callie nodded. "Impressive." The stores were hugely successful.

"One of my cousins wants to expand to Manhattan."

"That's a great idea! I can easily imagine the Sarah Jessica Parkers of the world shopping at a place like that." She pushed aside her plate. "Marc, I don't mean to pry, but is your mother still alive? Your uncle, um, spoke of her in the past tense."

"Good catch. She died of a massive brain aneurysm my senior year in high school. She went upstairs to rest, and a little while later I heard her scream. By the time I reached her, she was gone."

"Oh, no." Callie's heart clenched. "What did you do?"

"Went crazy, swore a lot, held her, cried, called the ambulance." His deep voice turned gruff.

Callie placed a hand on her chest. "I'm sorry I mentioned it."

"Don't be." He half-smiled. "I don't talk about my mother much. When people hear both your parents died under tragic circumstances, they tend to pity you."

"I don't pity you."

"You shouldn't. My aunts took great care of me. So did my Mrs. Robinson." He winked. "When I moved here, I had Bob and my grandfather. I have a wonderful family, Callie."

His returned his attention to his meal. Their waitress appeared and whisked away Callie's plate. She sipped her beer, considering how much of her own family history to reveal. Marc had shared so much of his life, she wouldn't feel right not reciprocating.

Finally, she murmured, "The grandfather who taught me to play pool—you could say he raised me. My mother and I lived with him after my father left."

Marc's gaze lifted. "Your father left you?" Sharpness entered his tone.

"My father and stepfather both deserted my mother and me. Mom tried her best, but her self-confidence nose-dived after my stepfather left, and we moved in with my grandfather for good. It really bothered her that she couldn't make herself into someone men wanted, so she stopped trying."

Marc grunted. "Sounds like she wasn't the problem. She just chose assholes."

"Self-esteem is a delicate issue for a lot of women, Marc. My father and stepfather both treated my mom like crap, but she shouldered the blame." Callie drew in a breath. "After my stepfather left, Mom went through the motions of raising me, and she didn't do a horrible job. But it was my grandfather who taught me never to let any man undermine my self-worth."

"Any man?" Marc's eyebrows arched. "Not anyone?"

"Excuse me?"

"Nothing." He shrugged. "Now I know."

Callie shook her head. "What?"

"Why you hold such strong opinions about jerk-offs.'"

She chuckled. "Like I should hold good opinions about them?"

"I didn't say that. But not all men are assholes, Callie."

A variation on his remarks back at KCLA. "You have a point," she conceded.

"I do?" Surprise widened his gray eyes, and she laughed.

"Yes. But I'd rather we didn't analyze my deficiencies when things are going so well."

His gaze softened. He reached across the table and grasped her hand. "Callie, I don't want to tick you off."

She grinned. "Then stop talking."

"But you need to understand—I'm not the bad guy."

The heat of his touch seeped into her… comforting, provoking, exhilarating. "That's not what your press says," she teased to counter her rapidly beating heart.

Chuckling, he pulled his hand away and wiped his mouth with a napkin. *No, no*, Callie's body clamored. *Touch me again.*

"You know better than to believe the tabloids," he murmured.

Yes, she did. She also knew better than to suggest they extend their evening beyond the emotionally safe confines of his uncle's bar. However, right now, nothing short of a Richter 8 earthquake could stop her.

She drew in a breath. "Marc, if it's okay with you, I think I'd like to continue this conversation someplace else."

***

"Who's this?" Marc bent and scratched the ears of the huge orange cat hulking in the entrance of Callie's apartment. The beast stretched and purred.

"Hector." Smiling, she hung his jacket in a closet. "Don't worry, he won't bother us."

The cat snaked between her ankles before slinking to the kitchen. She slung her purse onto the back of an armchair in the small living room decorated in pale shades that reminded him of peaches and raspberries—and eating them off her flat stomach.

"Would you like a drink?" she asked.

"Is that why you invited me up?" He pushed his hands into his trouser pockets.

"If you want to leave—"

"I didn't say that."

She ran her hands down her slacks. "I want to show you something."

Her panties? "What?"

She laughed. "You look like I'm sending you to the executioner."

If so, he masked his need for her well. They'd broken through a lot of barriers tonight, and he didn't want to say or do anything to screw up the fragile trust building between them. But his entire body ached for her. If she decided to pursue their attraction, could he resist her?

Hell, could a mouse survive Hector?

"What—" his throat constricted "—do you want to show me?"

"Something that might help explain my bitchiness since we met."

"You mean besides my fucked-up relationship with Jada?"

"And your other women? Yes." Callie's lips pressed together, and uncertainty shaded her blue eyes. She gestured to the armchair. "Please. Sit down."

He squinted. "Why?"

"Just do it, Marc."

"Yes, ma'am." Smiling, he sank onto the chair and planted his feet apart on the off-white carpet. His hands rested on his thighs, and the purse strap on the chair lodged against one shoulder blade.

She moved to stand in front of him, and his heart racketed in his chest. He should have accepted that damn drink, because the vulnerability on her pretty face parched his mouth and trapped his breath in his lungs.

He nodded, forcing out, "All right, I'm sitting."

She bit her bottom lip, a blush sweeping her cheeks. Without releasing his gaze, she reached down shaky hands and tugged off her high-heeled sandals one at a time. Marc kept his hands glued to his thighs as she slipped her fingers beneath the hip-grazing hem of her jacket-top and unzipped her pants.

"Holy fuck." Blood rushed to his cock. "Callie, what are you doing?"

Her mouth curved in a half-smile. "You'll see."

She released the zipper. Sucking in a breath, she pushed her thumbs into the waistband of her pants and inched both her slacks and her skin-toned panties down. Over her slim hips, past her knees. Her head lowered as she bent to complete the job, her blond hair dangling above the carpet. Marc gulped, gripping his thighs as she eased her slacks and panties to the floor, then stepped out of both garments and nudged them aside with a bare foot.

Naked below the waist, she straightened. Her jacket crested the top of her sparse blond pubic hair. Her pink pussy lips looked plump and juicy—just perfect for feasting on.

God, he hoped she wasn't a tease, because now that he'd seen her like this, he had to have her.

"Look," she murmured, half-turning her firm ass toward him.

"I'm looking." Her pussy entranced him. *Touch yourself*, he commanded silently, unwilling to shatter the haze of sensuality enshrouding them by speaking the words and possibly scaring her off. *Slide your fingers inside that hot little box and drive me insane.*

Her soft chuckle reached his ears. "Not my front, Marc. My rear."

"Huh?" The erotic humming in his brain nearly drowned out her voice.

"My butt," she said louder, turning her ass more fully into his line of vision and pushing it toward him. "Look."

Her pussy peeked out between her legs, the swollen seam of her outer lips encasing her dainty inner labia. Cock hard as granite in his pants, he moved forward on the chair. The subtle scent of her desire urged him closer.

"Can I touch?" he whispered hoarsely.

"Not yet." She sounded breathless. "Just look. The left cheek. To the side."

Not yet. As in hopefully sometime fucking soon.

As he gazed at her ass, a tiny, swirly design came into focus on the top swell of her left cheek. "A tattoo," he croaked out when all he wanted to do was plunge his fingers inside her and stroke her until she dripped. "Is it symbolic?"

"It's a name," she whispered. "In script."

She expected him to read at a time like this? "Callie, I have to touch you."

After a moment's hesitation, she nodded.

Leaning in, he palmed her left cheek. Her warm skin puckered, and her breath hissed from her mouth. As he traced the tattoo with a finger, recognition smacked him between the eyes.

"Mark?" With a fucking K. He blinked. "You spelled it wrong."

She laughed. "It's not your name, silly."

"You have some other Mark's name tattooed on your ass?"

"Well, if that's how you're going to react." She stepped away from his touch.

"Shit! Sorry!"

She turned. "I haven't had sex in over a year, Marc. Now you know why. Nobody knows about this tattoo. Just you and the first Mark."

Her pussy hovered inches from his face. He forced up his gaze. "Your girlfriends don't know?"

Expression unreadable, she shook her head.

"Hector?"

She smiled. "He can't read."

She unbuttoned her jacket and let it fall open, revealing a filmy bra that matched her discarded panties. Without removing either piece of clothing, she took another step closer, spread her legs, and straddled him. Her bare knees knocked the edges of the armchair, and the heat of her naked pussy burned his zipper, branding his erection. His cock twitched and throbbed beneath his restrictive trousers.

"Who the hell is Mark with a K?" He slipped his hands beneath her jacket and caressed her bare spine. Her nipples stiffened against the translucent bra.

She licked her lips. "Promise you won't tell anyone?"

"Why would I?" He wanted his name on her, not some asshole's with a K.

Her gaze dropped, and she whispered, "Mark Rafael."

"The baseball player?"

Nodding, she clasped his tie and loosened the knot. Marc held her naked hips, her jacket hem brushing his hands. "Callie, everybody knows he's a womanizing son of a bitch."

"I didn't." She untied the knot. "I met him two years ago, when I first moved here. I fell hard for him, Marc."

He hated hearing this. But he let her talk.

"I thought he felt the same about me." Her gaze remained riveted to the task of whisking his tie out from under his shirt collar. "He asked me to have it done." She curled both ends of the tie around her hands.

"To tattoo his name on your ass, like you're his possession?"

"*Were.*"

"Did he reciprocate?" Now that would be sexy—if it were him and Callie.

She shook her head. "Not his style."

"Yet he expected you to—"

Pink washed her face. "Remember that self-esteem I mentioned? I wasn't only speaking about my mother, Marc. I was talking about me."

"But your grandfather—"

"Taught me to stand up for myself." She blinked rapidly. "Yes, but I slipped. Mark with a K wormed into my psyche more than he ever lived in my heart. He had this mesmerizing effect on me that I'm not proud of. In the end, it meant nothing. When I found him with another woman, I realized I meant less than nothing to him. After that, it was like I grew an extra layer of skin. I vowed I'd always have the upper hand with any other men in my life."

"Make so mistake, woman, you have the upper hand with Marc with a C." He rolled his hips beneath her.

"You sure about that?" She smiled.

"Definitely." He cupped her ass. His rigid cock bumped her pussy through the thin fabric of his trousers. Her hot moistness seeped into the cloth, dizzying him. "There must have been someone since him." She'd said she hadn't had sex in a year, not two.

"One guy. Last year. I wouldn't let him see me naked with the lights on."

"Because of your tattoo?"

"Yes." She snapped his tie between her hands.

Yet she'd shared her secret with him. Was that a good thing?

"Why not get it removed?"

"I thought keeping it would help remind me not to let another man go to my head that way again."

He caressed her smooth, silky thighs. "And now?"

A seductive smile flirted on her mouth. "I think it's time I learned not to take relationships so seriously." She whipped the tie over his head like a lasso. Tightening the silk against the back of his neck, she coaxed his mouth to hers. "And you're just the man to help me."

Chapter 6

Callie's body was on fire. Her arousal dampened Marc's pants whenever she pressed against him, her swollen clit buzzing from the rough brushing of fabric against her bare skin. His tongue swept into her mouth, twining and twisting with hers. She steeled her grip on his tie, wrapping the slippery silk around her fists and holding his mouth captive. His groan of approval encouraging her, she swayed forward. Her breasts met his large hands, and he teased her stiff nipples through her nylon bra. The tantalizing sensations shot to her clit.

She allowed the tie to slacken, but didn't let go. Marc pinched her nipples, and she squirmed against him, releasing his mouth and whispering, "We do this my way."

His warm breath fanned her face as he nodded.

She slipped the tie out from behind his neck and draped it on the chair arm. Although he'd moved forward on the seat, her inner thighs ached from being spread so wide. His hand slipped to her mound, thumb searching for her clit. He made contact, and she moaned.

"What did I just say?" she murmured.

He swore. "Sorry."

"Well, maybe just for a second."

"Thank God."

His thumb found her clit again, and she smiled. She loved Marc like this—so hot for her that he'd do whatever she asked.

Closing her eyes, she savored the sensations of his fingertips dancing on her fattening clitoris. His index finger glided inside her slick opening while his thumb continued the light pressure on her clit. Desire swamped her, but if she gave him free rein with her body, she'd climax all too soon.

Whimpering, she backed off his legs and knelt on the plush carpet. He groaned, reaching for her, but she murmured, "Unbutton your shirt."

He unlatched the first button. Callie yanked off his shoes and socks, then grappled for his belt.

Their breathing grew faster as Marc ripped through his buttons and she unzipped him. His snug boxer-briefs molded a monster erection. Still sitting on the chair, he lifted his hips. Callie's pulse raced. She dragged his pants down his legs and chucked them aside. He stood and whipped off his shirt and boxer-briefs. Callie remained kneeling, mouth watering as his erection and tight sac bobbed above her head at the apex of his muscular thighs.

He tugged her to standing, and his head lowered as if he meant to kiss her. Ducking away, she pushed him backward. He toppled onto the chair, laughing. His spine hit her purse strap.

"Can we move this thing?" He lifted the strap with a thumb.

"Poor baby. Does it bother you?"

"It digs into my back."

"Aw." Stepping to the side, she knocked the purse to the carpet.

He reached for the handbag. "Want it on the coffee table?"

She shook her head. "Leave it. For the condoms. Unless you have some?"

His eyebrows raised. "No."

"I do. In my purse." Lauren had stocked her up following their conversation at the diner last week. Callie had protested, but now her friend's insistence was very welcome indeed.

She needed this time with Marc. If only to prove to herself that she could handle the one-night stands he favored when he wasn't dating some gorgeous sex goddess like Jada Reilly.

However, not only did she need this night with him, damn it. She wanted it. Wanted him. With no regrets and no looking backward.

Tonight was for her.

He leaned back in the chair, erection jutting from the dark blond curls between his legs. "Take off your bra, Callie."

"I thought we were doing this my way."

"I'm assuming you'll mount me at some point. If I can't feel your naked tits in my hands, I think I'll die."

Her nipples tightened at the raw need in his voice, and she smiled. "We can't have that."

She shucked off her jacket top, then unclasped her bra and tossed both pieces onto the clothes pile. Straddling Marc again, she leaned forward. With his cock trapped between their abdomens, warming her skin, he lifted one breast to his mouth and sucked the rigid nipple. Callie wove her fingers in his hair, holding him close to her rapidly pounding heart as he licked and tugged. Her clit pulsed, and her pussy ached to have him inside her. However, as soon as her breast popped out of his mouth, she slid back onto the carpet, grabbing the tie off the chair. He groaned.

"Want me to tie you up?" she whispered.

"Whatever you need, babe."

"Goodie." She quickly looped the cool silk around the base of his cock.

"Shit!" His erection bucked against the thick ribbon she'd created, and she grinned.

"Surprised?"

"Yeah. But don't stop, Callie. It feels fantastic."

She had no intention of stopping. She wrapped another swathe of wide silk around the base of his cock. His erection swelled, a drop of pre-come glistening on the plum-shaped head. The deep lavender tie partially covering the ivory skin of his shaft looked incredibly erotic. Desire swirling in her clit, her pussy, throughout her entire body, Callie massaged the silk up and down his hard length. His fingers dug into the chair arms, and he pumped his hips, head thrown back on the aqua armchair, chest rising and falling with his rapid breathing, his nipples tight discs amid the light furring of dark blond chest hair.

Urgency built within her. She tugged the tie, angling his cock forward. A lust-ful moan rushed from him. He sat up straighter, his erection bouncing against her open mouth.

With another tug on the tie, she sucked him down her throat.

"God, Callie."

His voice sounded hoarse. Tingles spun through her stiff nipples, her breasts grazing the coarse hair of his thighs as she sucked him. His hands cupped her jaw, coaxing her to increase her tempo. Her hair swung forward and back again. He tangled the strands in his fingers, swirling them around his cock in rhythm with the up-and-down and back-and-forth movements of the tie. His musky pre-come salted her tongue. She felt his sac tighten and draw up, his abdomen tensing.

"Callie, you have to stop," he ground out.

Sensual power surged within her. *Don't stop. Stop.* Couldn't he make up his mind?

She sucked, licked, and nibbled, hearing his breathing grow increasingly labored and feeling his thighs stiffen as he struggled for restraint. Finally, his breathing progressed to moans indicating he was about to come, and she pulled away.

Gazing up, she licked pre-come off her lips. "You have a beautiful cock, Marc."

"Sweet Jesus." He dragged a hand through his hair. "Thank you. But if you don't climb up here and let me pleasure you, I can't promise I can keep holding out." He reached for her.

Smiling, evading his touch, she loosened the tie around the base of his erection so that only one loop of silk remained. She tugged the tie back and forth, and he groaned. "Callie, I'm warning you."

"Maybe this is what I want."

"Screw that. I want to fuck you. Either you climb on top of me, or I'll take you on the floor."

Her pussy throbbed. "And stain my ivory carpet?" She rocked her hips. "Shaw, you should know better." She'd never been so wet.

He chuckled. "Get up here, Hutchins."

Leaving the tie looped once around his erection, she retrieved a condom from her purse. Marc rolled it on while she kissed and caressed his inner thighs. He reached for her again, and this time she went, spreading her legs and grasping his cock, guiding it to her entrance.

As she slid down onto him, her puffy pussy lips connected with the cool silk of the tie wrapped around his shaft. He held her hips, and she rode up and down, up and down, her juices soaking the tie with every slide. Marc's hands flew up to mold her breasts, thumbs flicking her nipples. Her breath caught, and a mini-climax swept her. Biting her lip and closing her eyes, she rode out the sensations with a slower tempo, then kissed him.

"Did you like that?" he asked.

She nodded, pulse going crazy. "I want more," she murmured. More of their amazing sex. A strong, pulsing orgasm.

More of Marc.

He cupped her face in his hands as she continued to ride him against the tie. His hips pumped. Caressing the hollow at the base of one ear, he kissed her. Tenderly. Then adding tongue. Deeper. Faster.

Hotter.

"Callie, you're beautiful," he whispered. "So wild and free. Incredible. Amazing. Wow."

Yes, wow. Definitely wow. Their connection was fierce and strong, electric. Elemental. Pure ecstasy. Heaven.

Like nothing she'd ever experienced.

He took her mouth again, one hand slipping between their moving bodies to rub her engorged clit. Her second climax rushed upon her. He rubbed, and her clit stiffened, the walls of her pussy clamping his cock as her legs and arms tingled and burned. Her clit exploded, and a full-body orgasm claimed her.

"Marc!" She cried out again and again, continuing to ride him through the swarming sensations, saturating the tie with her passion.

He pumped up hard, growling. His hips stiffened, eyes squeezing tight as they kissed. Their bodies burned and melted together.

And he came.

Marc slipped out of Callie's bed in the wee hours of Saturday morning, making room for the green-eyed tomcat glaring at him from the open bedroom door. The damn beast had sat there throughout their last lovemaking session. Deviant feline. While Callie, her beautiful eyes glazed with heat and her body drugged on passion, hadn't noticed, Marc damn sure had. Luckily, Callie's enthusiasm for their sexual gymnastics had overshadowed the cat's presence, and Marc had enjoyed another mind-blowing orgasm. That made three tonight—for him. Five for her.

Was the woman trying to kill him with sex?

He chuckled. He wouldn't put it past her.

A smile tugging his mouth, he caressed her hair as she slept on her side facing him, the pale pink sheets draped low on her spine, revealing her swirly tattoo. Mouth swollen from their kisses. Hair a mess.

She looked beautiful.

However, no doubt the first rays of morning would bring her a bucketful of regrets. Callie Hutchins didn't go from tolerating a "jerk" one minute to wanting a relationship with him the next. Wanting anything beyond what they'd shared tonight. Fantastic sex.

Too bad. Because he'd love to experience more. A real relationship with a woman who truly cared for him.

Could that woman ever be Callie?

He released a heavy sigh. Leaving her, he strode into the living room and got dressed. His tie sat crumpled on the carpet. As he picked it up, the musky scent of her juices floated to his nostrils. His chest tightened and his cock thickened, but he wouldn't wake her for another round. Come Monday, their ratings-engineered romance would hit the ground running. Callie didn't need him pressuring her about taking their relationship seriously when she had November sweeps on the brain.

He retrieved his jacket from the closet and stuffed the tie in a pocket. When he returned to the bedroom, Callie still slept like a rock. Hector now lay curled beside her pillow where Marc's head had rested.

"Take care of her, buddy," he whispered.

The beast slit an accusing eye. Callie didn't budge.

Marc found a notepad and felt-tipped pen on the feminine desk occupying a corner of her bedroom. *Callie*, he wrote. *Last night was incredible. However you want to play this, I'll follow your lead. See you Monday. Marc.*

He placed the note on her nightstand. Gazed at her sleeping form.

Grinning, he scrawled a note of another kind.

Then he left.

Brrringg!

Callie yanked herself up through fuzzy layers of sleep and reached for the ringing phone. "'Lo?" The numbers on her bedside clock read 10:20 a.m. Late for nine-to-fivers, but ten precious minutes pre-clanging-alarm for her Monday mornings.

"What the hell did you and Marc do together Friday night?" Lauren's voice pelted her ear. "Emails are glutting the station."

Callie rubbed her eyes. "They are?" She crawled out of bed with the cordless in hand. Hector rolled off her legs onto the foot of the bed, meowing. "We went to his uncle's bar in Santa Monica. But the crowd there is mainly middle-aged men—not the demographic for *L.A. Tonight.*" Although, Bob had mentioned watching the show. Had he tuned in Friday night's broadcast after she and Marc left?

Oh, God. Friday night. When they'd screwed like monkeys on speed and she'd woken to find him gone, a note on her nightstand and a big felt-pen C concealing the K of the tattoo on her butt.

She smiled, nipples tightening beneath her sleep shirt in the morning air. Despite that she'd showered twice since Marc Shaw had branded her with black ink, she'd taken great care not to scrub off the C.

"Well, these emails aren't from middle-aged men," Lauren said. "They're from women, wanting to know what's going on."

Callie padded into the bathroom, catching sight of herself in the mirror. Mangled sleep shirt, hair askew, eyes drawn. She'd passed her weekend conjuring ways to avoid Marc outside of the week's tapings. As much as she appreciated Friday night's multiple orgasms, she hadn't counted on their appearance at The Sly Fox throwing their fake romance into premature high gear.

"Nothing's going on," she lied. Just the most amazing sex of her life with a man who might give her more if she asked him.

Dared she ask him?

Lauren said, "That's not what I'm reading." Papers rustled over the phone. "I'm quoting, 'My husband says the looks Callie gave Marc were like she was inviting him to do a lap dance.'"

"They were not!" Callie grabbed a washcloth and tossed it into the sink. Crap, had they been?

"'The way that woman holds a pool cue should be outlawed,'" Lauren continued. "Okay, that was from someone named Max." She giggled. "Here's another. 'She can fondle my stick any day.'"

Callie blasted hot water onto the washcloth. "That's crude."

"Don't kill the messenger." More paper-rustling. "Back to the women. Quote. 'What's with the hand-holding? I thought those two hated each other.'"

"Now, that's ridiculous. We did not hold hands." Unless the email-writer counted the all-too-brief seconds when Marc's hand covered hers on the booth table. "I can't believe people watched us that closely. I thought we were safe there."

Lauren laughed. "Being seen together outside the station is the idea. Callie, you've jumpstarted sweeps. You're a genius."

"I am?" Steam rose from the soaked washcloth. Callie dammed the flow of water in the sink and squeezed the excess from the cloth with one hand, scorching her fingertips.

"Yes, you definitely are. One hundred percent, certifiable, the Hollywood Einstein of Fake Love."

She was certifiable, all right. Just not how Lauren thought.

Forget the potential for more Marc-induced orgasms, she needed to get this publicity free-for-all back under her control. Fast.

"Ed! You're crushing me." Marc untangled himself from the program director's bear hug. If his boss were any happier, he'd be nursing broken bones. "What's this about?"

Ed's hearty laugh boomed in the office. "We're on a roll! And you started it. Fantastic idea to date Callie Friday night."

"What are you talking about?" How did Ed know? Their appearance at his uncle's bar must have caused a stir with the patrons. Or had Callie told one of her friends at the station that they'd made love?

"The first billboards are going up this week," Ed blazed on, clueless to Marc's confusion. "Your timing couldn't have been more perfect."

"Well, we didn't plan it." Not the date, nor the spectacular sex.

"Spontaneity." Ed snapped his fingers. "Perfect."

Marc thought so, too.

"Luckily, both the photographer and my contact at the ad agency owe me favors," Ed said. "Or we'd never get the billboards done fast enough for how this thing is progressing."

A knock rapped at the door, and Callie breezed in, wearing another of her two-piece skirt suits. A light sky blue this time, like her beautiful eyes.

Uncertainty settled on her features when she saw him. Her gaze lowered to his tie, and he grinned. She blushed, glancing away.

"Congratulations!" Ed planted a sloppy kiss on her cheek.

"Let's not get ahead of ourselves." She swept a strand of her hair behind one ear. "It's just a few emails."

Ed chortled. "Try a few hundred."

Her eyebrows lifted. "That many?"

"Wait a minute." Marc turned to her. "You already know?"

"Lauren woke me with the news. It's good for the show, huh?" Her gaze wouldn't quite meet his.

"Damn right it's good," Ed said. "Now we need to keep the ball rolling. I've sent for Angela and also Tony from Promotions to help brainstorm tonight's call-in."

"Since when do we do call-ins?" Callie asked.

"Since your fans want to know a million times more than they wish the smog would melt away why you and Marc were holding hands Friday night… and if you'll do it again." Ed studied her. "What's wrong, Callie? You look sick."

"I'm not." Color dusted her face. "But what about our scheduled guests? What about 'He Vs. She'?"

"The guests stay. The spew-fest goes on vacation."

"For good?"

"For tonight. We'll take the rest as it comes." Ed clapped. "Spontaneity. You two started it. Together, we'll build on it." His head swung to Marc. "You with us, Shaw?"

"Definitely." They just needed to convince Callie. He walked over and squeezed her hand. "I'm with you. Always.'"

And damn it if he didn't mean it. He wanted her in his bed, sure. However, during their year as co-hosts, she'd also wriggled her way into his heart.

Without trying to. Without realizing she had.

Hell, she was why he'd left Jada Reilly, only one of the sexiest women on the planet. However, even in Jada's Victoria's-Secret perfection, she couldn't compete with Callie.

Her cheeks blazed, gaze dropping to his tie again. The same one he'd worn Friday night.

He really shouldn't torment her like this.

Chuckling, he lowered his head. "One-hour dry-cleaning," he whispered, squeezing her hand again. "I had to. It belongs to Wardrobe. They need it back."

"Oh, shit," she whispered, then licked her lips. "Th-thank you."

Ed's head poked between them. "You two are good! It's like you really feel something for each other."

"Yes," Marc said without releasing Callie's gaze. "It is."

Chapter 7

Callie's stomach fluttered and jumped as if hyperactive butterflies bowled with glass marbles inside her. Rarely had she felt so nervous, which was ridiculous. She and Marc had taped in front of larger studio audiences before, particularly during the heyday of his relationship with Jada Reilly.

However, usually the blinding stage lights obscured the audience's expressions. Not tonight. After they'd interviewed their guests, the house lights had brightened for Marc's humorous recap of a pre-taped on-the-street question and their upcoming call-in, which the station had promoted throughout the day.

Anticipation grew on the viewers' faces, several of whom glanced back and forth between Marc and Callie, despite that he stood center stage while she occupied the interview set, commenting when he directed a remark her way.

Finally, the recap ended, and they broke for commercial. Marc ambled across to join her.

"Relax," he said beneath his breath, sinking into a contemporary ochre armchair while the audience warmer-upper launched into a series of jokes and cheerful canned music played. "We've taken questions from the audience before. Adding phone calls isn't a stretch."

"We haven't been grilled about us before," Callie murmured. Ridiculous though the idea seemed, she felt like everyone in the studio knew she and Marc had slept together.

Not good.

Very bad.

Before he could reply, a production assistant arrived and passed them tiny earpieces for the call-in. Callie inserted the bud in her ear while Zeta touched up her makeup. The pregnant woman moved on to Marc, and the junior hairdresser stepped in.

"Check that spot in back," Callie said. "But don't over-spray." Angela wanted no repeat hair disasters.

"Yes, ma'am," Tommy murmured, and Callie winced at her bossy tone.

"Thank you." She shut her eyes as the mist of spray fell.

Zeta and Tommy departed. The P.A. set fresh mugs of decaf on the small table between Callie's eggplant-colored loveseat and Marc's armchair. Once the P.A. left, Marc reached around and patted her knee. Quivery sensations danced on her thigh.

"Hey, this entire show is about us," he said, picking up their conversation in soothing tones. "No matter who I'm dating, on set it's always about how I respond to you and how you respond to me. The audience knows that, Cal. They love it."

His voice softened when he shortened her name, and her butterflies ebbed.

Offering a wobbly smile, she half-whispered, "But you're used to being the center of media attention. You're our star, Marc. I just bounce off you."

"No, you don't. You hold your own."

"Well, it feels like I bounce off you."

"That's nerves talking." He kept speaking in hushed tones. "If you're serious about New York, you need to get comfortable with stardom. Unless you don't want New York, Cal?"

Her stomach cramped. "You know I do."

"Then now's the time to step up. Keep your eyes on your goal. Never waver."

"Quiet on the set!" the floor director called in preparation for returning from commercial.

Callie cast Marc a glance. "Okay," she whispered, then smiled. "Thank you."

"You're welcome," he mouthed. Caring shone from his eyes and face, expanding and drawing her in until she all saw was him. Marc. There. For her. Encouraging and supportive.

Then he grinned, and their ever-present attraction slammed her in the chest, spiking up her pulse and stealing her breath.

Heart pounding, she grinned back like a lamebrain.

"Coming out in ten… nine…!"

The floor director's loud voice broke her trance. Jerking her gaze from Marc's, she studied the cameras.

"Seven… six…." The floor director fell silent, continuing the countdown with his fingers. He pointed to Callie and then camera two. The red light indicating taping blinked.

"Welcome back, L.A.!" Callie said in the vivacious tone she reserved for the show. "Tonight, instead of 'He Vs. She,' which you all know I'd win, anyway, we're opening the floor and the phone lines to your questions."

A laugh rose from the audience. Re-energized by their response, she smiled. "Emails have flooded the station since I whipped Marc in our nine ball tournament Friday night, so if anyone needs pool tips, I'm your girl."

The robotic camera controlled from the production booth wheeled across the set to catch Marc's feigned expression of affront. "Callie, it was a tie. You did not whip me."

Did he have to say tie?

"But I'd bet she'd like to whip you!" a female audience member shouted.

Callie forced a laugh, and Marc's gaze swung toward the woman's voice. "I heard that! For the record, I'm not into S and M." His head tilted. "Well, maybe fuzzy handcuffs and silk scarves."

The blood drained from Callie's face. However, again the audience laughed. A woman of about thirty approached the microphone at the bottom of the bleachers. She glanced at a P.A., and the P.A. prompted Callie through her earpiece.

"Yes, we have a question from the floor?" Callie asked.

The woman wrung her hands. "Uh, hi, I'm Susan. Um, Callie, on Friday night's 'He Vs. She,' you and Marc debated, uh, about if whether a guy wears boxers or briefs—"

"Or boxer-briefs," Marc broke in, and Callie's panties heated.

Susan giggled. "Um, you discussed what a man's choice of underwear says about him, you know, as a guy."

"One of our more ridiculous topics," Callie quipped.

Marc scoffed, "I stand by what I said. Just because a man doesn't want to strut around Thanksgiving Day wearing boxers decorated with cartoon turkeys beneath his clothes doesn't mean he's insecure with his masculinity."

"I agree," Susan said. "My point is, usually Callie argues you into the ground. But on Friday, she, um, had this look like she was thinking of you in the boxers."

Callie made a comical show of examining her fingernail polish. During Friday's taping, she had fantasized about Marc in underwear, or preferably nothing at all. She hadn't realized she'd been so obvious.

Of course, now she knew he wore boxer-briefs. And filled them out quite nicely, too.

After the audience's chuckles abated, Susan added, "Then my sister's husband said that at the bar in Santa Monica Callie acted like a teenager with a crush. Callie, I'm confused. Don't you hate Marc and everything he stands for?"

Callie studied her nails a moment longer, eliciting more audience laughter. Looking at Susan, she did her best imitation of a snooty Diane Chambers from the old TV hit, *Cheers*. "Marc and I are colleagues. Of course I don't hate him. Before Friday night, I just wasn't aware that I tolerate him as well as I do." Now there was an understatement.

Marc lifted a finger. "What she's trying to say is she thinks I'm sexy as sin and she's tired of fighting it."

Callie shrugged impishly, and the audience roared.

She and Marc answered more questions before Angela's voice traveled over the earpieces, informing them that she'd coached their callers to pretend they watched the show live—as if they were on the air now instead of taping for broadcast after the eleven o'clock news.

Angela directed Marc to take the first call, and he faced camera one. "I believe we have our first ever on-air *L.A. Tonight* phone call. This is history in the making, people! Go ahead, Les from Sherman Oaks. What would you like to know?"

A gruff voice emerged onto the set. "I been listening to the questions, and my wife and me think this whole set-up is goofy." Embarrassment shaded the man's tone, as if his wife had nagged him to call. "She says she won't, uh, be happy until you kiss her. Then we'll know for sure."

Marc stared into the camera, deadpanning, "Your wife wants me to kiss her?"

Boisterous laughter erupted from the bleachers.

"Er, Callie." Les coughed. "She wants you to kiss Callie right now."

The audience cheered. Callie raised her hands. "Uh, Les, isn't that a little Jerry Springer?"

"It gets worse. The wife wants Marc to kiss you, um, every show around midnight."

Callie arched her eyebrows. A likely story. Apparently, Angela had coached poor Les from Sherman Oaks well. The kissing concept screamed Ed, and the caller had the time frame down pat.

Marc chuckled. "I think the wife has something there, Les!"

"So you'll do it?" Les asked.

"Do it! Do it!" the audience chanted to the enthusiastic gestures of the warmer-upper.

Callie gulped. They seriously expected Marc to kiss her now?

She glanced at him. A sexy gleam lighting his gaze, he planted a hand on his chair arm. He was getting up.

Oh, no, you don't.

Shooting off her seat, she channeled Diane. "Please. If anyone's kissing anybody around here, it's me."

Marching two strides to Marc, she grabbed the forest green tie he'd changed into for the broadcast. She yanked him upright.

"What are you doing?" he whispered, gaze widening.

"Ensuring I get to New York," she murmured. She planted a big, juicy, wet one on him while the audience went orgasmic.

The Los Angeles Post
Thursday, November 16th Edition

Hollywood Gab
by Celia Fiennes, Gossip Columnist

Is it Real or for Ratings?

TV insiders are abuzz with the latest developments at KCLA. Seems *L.A. Tonight* co-hosts Callie Hutchins and Marc Shaw can't keep their hands—or lips—off each other. Since Callie's impromptu kiss on Marc's smacker ten days ago, each broadcast at midnight the growing studio audience chants "Kiss her, kiss her!" until Marc does… or Callie beats him to the punch. A far cry from when these two couldn't stand each other.

Was that only a few short weeks ago?

What's up? Definitely the ratings (and probably parts of Marc, but this is a family publication). *L.A. Tonight* hasn't enjoyed this level of popularity since Callie's summertime "He Vs. She" lashings over Marc's poor treatment of actress Jada Reilly. Which prompts this clever reporter to ask: is the love-fest between Callie and Marc a stunt for November sweeps? Or have these former adversaries fallen for each other for real?

Either way, they're a hoot to watch. But if December arrives and the love-fest vamooses, the viewers I've spoken with won't be happy. In this age of reality TV, we're accustomed to "showmances" that wither away once the cameras stop rolling. But that doesn't mean we like it. We're rooting for true love!

So, Callie and Marc, are you willing to sacrifice long-term benefits for temporary ratings? The fun and games might you put on the TV map, but who wins in the end? And who loses? The network, the audience, or... might I ask... you?

Marc tossed the newspaper onto the makeup counter as Zeta dabbed thick pancake gunk onto his forehead.

"Good press?" she asked his expression in the lit mirrors.

He smiled stiffly. "It's great." And about all he was getting lately.

She chuckled. "Don't worry, I won't tell Callie."

"Tell her what?"

Zeta's raven eyebrows rose. "That the love-fest is real. For you, anyway."

He grunted. "Don't make me laugh." Aside from their staged kisses, where Callie drove him crazy with her scent and her silky skin and enthusiasm, her withdrawal since they'd made love announced loud and clear that she only wanted to focus on the show.

Or discuss how to act on their fake dates.

Or rehash the success of the billboard and bus ads.

Or remind him how their skyrocketing ratings would help her achieve her New York dream.

Any topics or touches remotely personal had her sputtering like a steaming tea kettle about to blast off its lid. While Marc had always chased ratings himself, this charade he now played with Callie hit home why he'd grown so tired of the game.

Whose idea had it been to say he'd follow her lead, anyway? To advise her to keep her eyes on her goal and never waver? The woman had "never wavering" down pat. Meanwhile, his need for her had spiraled out of control.

And then—okay, he missed the vulnerable Callie he'd caught glimpses of at The Sly Fox two weeks ago. He wanted that Callie back—but only if she made it clear she wanted him on the same terms.

Otherwise, when she finally went to New York, he'd find a gaping hole in his life.

Zeta stepped between his director's chair and the mirrors, her pregnant belly bursting her striped top. "Come on, Marc, I've known you for years, and I'm one of the few people who figured out what really happened with Jada." She lifted one shoulder. "Maybe it's time you told Callie. You're getting along well with her, right?"

"Just hunky-dory."

"Only hunky-dory?" Zeta nudged him. "I've seen how she looks at you. It's more than that."

"I bet you have a bridge to sell me, too." He shook his head. "I've tried telling Callie the truth about Jada a dozen times in the past. She never listened."

"Maybe she had her reasons. Then." Zeta smeared makeup on his chin. "Maybe she'll listen now."

Marc frowned. Zeta had a point. How could he expect Callie to let down her guard when Jada Reilly still stood between them?

The unmistakable tapping of Callie's high heels on the concrete floor signaled her arrival. Zeta mimed zippering her lips shut and returned her attention to Marc's makeup.

Callie floated in. "Hi, Zeta."

"Hi."

All sunshine and smiles in a light yellow skirt and white top, Callie sat in the director's chair beside his. She crossed her legs, and her top shoe dangled off her foot.

"What's on for tonight, Shaw?" she asked with the building confidence evident since the night of their first on-set kiss. "Do we smooch before or after the last interview?"

The woman thrived on torturing him. "It's your call."

Smiling, she leaned over his chair and rubbed a bit of makeup on his jaw. His skin burned.

She said to Zeta, "You missed a spot."

The makeup artist blinked. "I did?"

Yeah, on purpose, the pregnant matchmaker. And his libido didn't appreciate it.

Callie pouted at him. "You're grouchy tonight."

Only because he wanted those rosebud lips on his again—for real.

"No, I'm not," he lied.

She laughed and sat back in her chair. "Did you hear the good news?" she asked his reflection. "Ed spoke to Iris. Thanks to our wonderful performances lately, she's more than happy to promote me to the network executives."

Marc grunted. Trust Iris. Callie's concerns about the fraternization policy had come to naught. As soon as Iris realized the massive upside, she'd jumped all over the idea.

In the mirror, Zeta's lips pursed. "But if she loses you to New York, what happens to our ratings?"

"Oh, Marc will be kissing the new girl in no time."

No, he wouldn't.

"Iris would have grabbed the chance to prove she can groom talent with national potential," he explained to Zeta. "Callie's success is Iris's success, pay boost included."

"Sounds like I signed up for the wrong gig," Zeta replied. "Callie, if you don't mind waiting, I need to hit the can."

"Go ahead."

Zeta set down Marc's makeup kit and left the room.

Callie's crossed leg bounced. "Ed wants us to go to Nine Tails nightclub after tonight's taping. Take our pairing as public as possible, maybe catch the paparazzi's eye."

"Yeah, I read his email. He gets off way too much on our publicity dates."

"Well, you're getting something from them, too, Marc. We both are."

Okay, that did it. He had to know.

He gazed at her. Waited a beat. "But are you getting what you really want, Callie? Because I'm sure as hell not."

Her lips parted. "What do you want?"

"Isn't that clear by now? You."

Chapter 8

Callie scanned the crowded nightclub for Marc, who'd gone to the bar for drinks. In the makeup room before tonight's taping, when he'd said he wanted her, her breath had stopped in her throat and her heart had skittered wildly. She'd been about to ask if he'd meant for another night of great sex—or something more. However, then Tommy had arrived to do Marc's hair, and a minute later Zeta had returned. Between the show and Callie's trip home to shower and change before driving to meet Marc a discreet distance from Nine Tails, they hadn't shared another moment alone.

Or maybe she was just too scared to.

After all, Marc Shaw had broken dozens of female hearts. Why should things turn out any differently for her?

She had to watch herself, because, aside from the physical benefits of making love with him throughout that one amazing night, the last two weeks of overexposure to his intelligence, sincerity, and sense of humor had put her in danger of developing genuine feelings for the man.

And that way lay trouble.

The last thing she wanted was to land in New York pining for a guy several time zones away.

Conscious of her short white dress inching up her thighs in her chair, she folded her hands over her crossed legs. A dark-haired man who'd watched her on and off since their arrival approached the miniscule glass table.

"Your friend coming back?" the man shouted above the blaring dance music. She nodded.

"Because, if he's not, I'd love to be his replacement." The guy leered.

Heat swarmed her face.

"Back off, buddy," Marc suddenly announced behind her. Shouldering the guy away, he set their drinks on the table.

"Hey! Is that any way to treat a fan?" the stranger complained.

"It is if you're hassling my woman."

A smile coaxed Callie's lips. His woman?

The man snorted. "You weren't this possessive with Jada."

Marc peered at him. "Do I know you?"

The guy snickered and disappeared into the crowd.

Marc sat in the second chair. "Asshole."

"Did you recognize him?"

"I'm not sure." He lifted his glass. "He probably lusts after celebrities, but I didn't like how he was looking at you."

Her tummy fluttered. "Well, he said he was a fan, so that was a nice touch, Marc, calling me your woman."

He plunked down the glass without drinking. "Let's dance."

He stood and pulled her out of the chair. Squeaking, she adjusted the hem of her dress as he blazed a trail to the dance floor.

The seductive beat of the deafening music thumped above and between the dancers' bodies. Marc smiled at her and began moving, keeping her close with clasped hands, then releasing her to dance on her own. Gorgeous women gyrated all around him, but his intense gaze locked on her, telegraphing, *You're mine.*

Callie's nipples tightened beneath her wispy halter dress. Marc looked at her as if he wanted to eat her up. And—no big surprise—she didn't want him to stop.

She'd missed his touch these last two weeks. His talented hands, his stiff cock, his rock-hard body.

The music pulsed into her bones. She swayed with her hands in her hair, dancing within touching distance of him before spinning off.

She continued the flirtatious dance steps, facing away from him and sensing him intimately shadowing her movements.

Her butt bumped his thigh, and he muttered, "Danger zone, Callie."

He twirled her around, pulling her close, his knee between her legs and his erection rubbing her mound.

Her practical thoughts while waiting for him at the table vanished. The music possessed her, Marc's hands and gaze caressed her. A girl could only handle so much forced togetherness, and she'd reached her limit—future heartbreak be damned.

She pressed her mouth to his ear. "Is it real or for ratings?" she whispered, echoing the gossip column headline.

"It's real, all right," he murmured, hands cupping her ass. "But this isn't how I want you, Cal, in public with everyone watching."

Didn't sound so bad to her. She slipped a hand between their bodies and rubbed his erection through his pants. "Oh, no? And just how do you want me?'"

"Alone," he growled, embracing her as the music slowed.

His hands slipped beneath her hair, cradling her face, and when he gazed into her eyes, she almost bought that he believed what they shared was real.

Her throat squeezed. "Marc."

He brushed her bottom lip with his thumb. "Shh."

Lowering his head, he kissed her in a gently seductive manner. His tongue dipped into her mouth, enticing hot desire and somersaulting sensations from deep inside her.

Callie looped her arms around his neck and returned his kiss with more yearning and passion than she'd ever offered any other man.

He moaned. "Ah, Cal, sweet Cal," he whispered against her mouth. "I can't take it anymore. Let's get out of here."

"Where are we going?"

Marc glanced at Callie in the passenger seat of his black sports car. "Anywhere you want. Hopefully, somewhere private."

Her fingertips danced on her thigh. "Okay."

He restrained a chuckle. She'd left all her daring in the nightclub. Since they'd left Nine Tails and chosen his ride for their getaway, she'd acted as timid as a production intern her first day on the job.

"Your place?" he asked as they sped down the busy street.

A pause elapsed, and her gaze sought his. "I'd like that."

He smiled. "Me, too."

The high-beams of the idiot behind them glared in the rear view mirror. Lifting one hand off the wheel, Marc tipped the mirror for night viewing. The small pickup darted into the alongside lane, a telephoto lens snaking out the window. *Snapsnapsnap!*

The camera flashed several times, and Callie's head swung away. "Marc!"

"Fucking paparazzi." The pickup zoomed off, horn honking. Marc glanced at her. "Sorry about that."

She swept her hair off her face. "Ed should be happy, but I didn't expect paparazzi tonight. They've never followed me before."

"They have me, when I was with Jada."

"Did it happen a lot?"

He nodded.

"Well, I guess it comes with the territory, but I don't like it."

"Get used to it." He downshifted for a red light. "You know, I think I pegged the dark-haired jerk with the camera."

She looked at him. "The man from the club?"

"Yep. Don't ask me why I didn't recognize him there." The sight of Callie in her sexy white dress had obliterated most of his brain cells. "He's a weasel, and if the cocksucker driving is his usual compadre, I don't want them knowing where you live."

"They could find that information in the phone book."

"Then let them. I won't do their leg work." He checked the rear-view. "Looks like they're coming around again. Must be a slow night."

Callie turned in her seat to peer out the tiny back window. The position plumped her breasts, deepening her cleavage. "Ed will have an orgasm."

Marc chuckled. "Want to have some fun?"

She licked her lips. "I don't want a dangerous situation developing here, Marc."

"Hey, I'm not Lindsay Lohan. I hate to burst your bubble, sweetheart, but neither are you. They'll lose interest fast enough. Let's tease them a little."

"A daredevil, hmm? Okay, I'll put my life in your hands."

"You're safe with me, Cal. Uncle Bob used to drag race."

"I take it you believe that's comforting. And I suppose he taught you?"

"Yep on both counts." The light turned green. Marc gunned the car through the intersection. The little truck followed. Marc downshifted and turned a corner.

"We'll lead them to my place. They already know it. It'll bore them."

Callie laughed, blue eyes shining brightly in the hazy dashboard light. "Is it weird that I'm having a good time?"

He grinned. "Probably."

Several minutes later, they reached a congested area. He adjusted his speed and checked the mirror. "They've backed off."

Callie glanced over her shoulder. "We've lost them?"

"Nope. They just want us to think so."

He eased onto a side street and allowed the creeps time to catch up. They trailed several vehicles behind, doubtless thinking they were sneaky.

Six turns later, Marc parked on the road in front of his modest bungalow built in the 1960s. "Here we are."

Callie gazed out the window. "Wow, a whole house."

Marc switched off the ignition, knowing she intended the remark as a compliment. L.A. real estate was insane. "That's nothing. Wait until you're celebrating your fiftieth Emmy from your New York penthouse overlooking Central Park."

She glanced at him. "You give me too much credit."

"I think you'll blow them away."

"I'm not in New York yet."

"No. However, someday soon, you will be." And, if he had any say in the matter, he'd love to follow, cheer her on.

Leaning over the hand brake, he kissed her thoroughly. As usual, his cock jumped, but this time a deep, satisfying warmth filled his chest, accompanying the brainless physical reaction.

He deepened the kiss, relishing her sultry moans. When they parted, her face glowed.

"That was for Ed," he murmured. At her quizzical look, he added, "The paparazzi is up half a block. See the small navy truck parked in front of the white van?"

She stared out the windshield, nodded.

"I bet they snapped us kissing."

"You kissed me for Ed?"

"Uh huh." And to help achieve the ratings that would get her where she wanted. "Now this one is for me," he half-whispered, retrieving a folded newspaper from the joke-of-a-back-seat and holding it in front of their faces.

He kissed her again, soft and slow, savoring her sweetness. Callie, full of spirit and spark, then at other times shy and unsure. But always challenging him. Always inspiring him.

How he loved her.

His heart thudded. He loved her.

"Marc?" she whispered when they came up for air, hand coaxing his to lower the newspaper. "I'm tired of hiding how I feel about you. Let's go inside."

Chapter 9

As Marc shut the living room blinds, Callie wondered about her judgment. She knew without a doubt that she wanted to make love with him again. However, despite his assertion at the nightclub that their explosive attraction was real, without November sweeps spurring them on, would they have grown this close?

He inserted CDs into the stereo unit, then approached her with a sensual look on his face.

"Where were we?" His hands settled on her waist, and desire shimmered through her body, dampening her satin thong with her juices and scattering her thoughts.

She lifted her face to his. "Right here."

The smoky jazz washed over them as his mouth devoured hers. Need pulsed in her, low and heavy. Her nipples pointed.

Breaking the kiss, she whispered, "Bedroom."

He glanced back wistfully at his couch, and she said, "They could still be out there."

Fire gleamed in his eyes. "You don't like being watched?"

"Maybe later, if you're good. However, since you closed the blinds, I figured…"

He chuckled. "You figured right."

He scooped her into his arms, and she giggled. "I feel like Scarlett O'Hara."

"Too bad I don't have a staircase."

They resumed kissing while he carried her down a dark hall and toed open a door. The same music playing in the living room drifted from concealed speakers above the big bed.

Callie tried to banish thoughts of Marc sharing this space with Jada Reilly. She wanted to pretend she was the only woman in the world he'd ever wanted, or would want again.

As if reading her mind, he whispered, "I want you to know I never brought Jada here." He lowered her to the mattress and switched on the lamp. A soft glow from the low-wattage bulb illuminated the dark taupe bedspread. "It didn't feel right."

"Why not?" Callie smoothed her dress and propped up on one arm, tucking her legs behind her.

"Because of you." Marc sat on the bed in the V of space created by her half-reclining position. His hips grazed her thighs, the brief touch starting an erotic throbbing in her clit. His hand covered hers on the bedspread. "I might have been with her, Cal, but I wanted you."

Her heart skipped a beat. Several times since his televised breakup with Jada, Marc had tried explaining the relationship, but Callie had either ignored him or brushed him off.

No longer.

"There's more to the story." He caressed her hand, and delicious sensations sprinted up her arm.

"I want to hear it," she half-whispered.

A sexy smile crooked his mouth. "I fell hard for you, Cal. I've never felt such a strong attraction for a woman. Unfortunately, outside of work, you wouldn't give me the time of day—which I understand, considering my reputation."

"It's a beauty, all right." Callie grinned, and he chuckled. Then his expression sobered.

"I'm not proud to admit this, but Jada and I realized early on that we were basically friends using each other for sex."

Callie swallowed. Like she and Marc were now?

"She was tired of her actor boy-toys, and I thought I had zero chance with you, so it seemed like there was no downside," he continued.

"But there was a downside?"

"Definitely." His gaze locked on hers, his voice low and husky. "Because I didn't care about her the way I cared—and still care—about you."

A lumped formed in her throat. "Marc."

"Jada didn't ditch me at the BOFTAs, Cal. I wanted to end things, and she got pissed, saying I'd benefited from her celebrity in a way she couldn't hope to achieve with me. So I agreed to the BOFTA circus to help her save face and create a buzz."

Callie's heart pounded. "No publicity is bad publicity?"

He nodded. "I figured I owed her. No woman likes learning her guy has the hots for someone else."

Callie traced a lazy number eight on the gray denim covering his thigh. "Poor Jada."

"It doesn't upset you that I used a woman for sex?"

"No. After my experience with Mark Rafael, it probably should, but your bad-boy image is one of the many things that drew me to you, as non-P.C. as that sounds."

"Oh, yeah? What else drew you to me?"

Callie grinned. "Your incredible body." She rose to her knees, reached for the hem of his V-necked shirt, and tugged it off. Golden hair dusted his chest and spiraled around his dusky nipples.

She placed her hands on his six-pack abdomen and rubbed his lower ribs with her thumbs. "You might not believe this, Marc, but I've wanted you from the moment Iris hired me and you and I collided in the hallway outside the KCLA restrooms."

"I remember. When you saw who I was, you looked horrified. I didn't get a chance to introduce myself before you took off."

"I already knew who you were. I had a crush on you from watching the show. Of course, what woman didn't—or doesn't?"

"Those women don't know me, Cal. They just think they do."

Like her. Then.

"I understand that now. But, back then, I didn't want you to get so much as an inkling that I was as star-struck as everyone else. So I convinced myself you were a user like Rafael, and I treated you accordingly." She whispered, "Sorry."

He cupped her face. "Are you still star-struck, Callie?"

"No. I know the real you now. That's who I want."

He smiled. "Good."

Their mouths fused, and they tumbled onto the bed, his hands stroking her shoulders and spine the cut of her dress revealed.

She fumbled with his belt, and his fingers skipped down to unbuckle it. He whisked the thick leather through the loops of his jeans and tossed the belt to the carpet. Their footwear followed.

Callie sat up slightly. He released her neck strap, and the bodice of her dress skidded over her sensitized nipples to drape at her waist.

Groaning, he caressed her breasts, then dipped his head to tug a stiff nipple into his mouth. She gasped as aching desire overwhelmed her. His thumb flicked her other nipple, speeding arousal to her pussy.

While his mouth and thumb lavished her breasts, he let her drop onto the bed then pushed his free hand beneath her dress secured at her waist by a tiny back zipper.

His deft fingers discovered her thong now saturated with hot pussy juices, and he groaned, lips slipping off her nipple. His kisses roved from the underside of her breast to her shoulder and neck, blazing sensation everywhere before his mouth captured hers for another kiss.

Clit throbbing, Callie popped the button of his jeans and inched down his zipper.

His fingers prodded beneath her thong, one easily sliding inside her and pushing deep.

His thumb found the swollen hood of her clit, rubbing it in swirling motions, and her inner muscles gripped his thrusting finger.

"Oooh." Her head sagged onto a pillow.

"You like that?" he whispered.

"Like is too tame a word." Hot tingles radiated from her clit to her pussy. "Marc. Now."

She shoved his jeans down his hips, uncovering his boxer-briefs. The soft cotton molded his cock, thick and hard beneath her palm. She squeezed him outside the fabric, and his erection swelled further.

Impatient to feel his rigid shaft inside her, she grappled for the waistband of his boxers and freed the head.

"Not yet." His finger glided out of her pussy to trail beneath the satin T curving her ass.

She caught her bottom lip between her teeth, eager to learn his intentions.

He bundled her dress at her waist, then grasped the T of her thong and tugged, tightening the panties' front over her thumping clit.

Repeating the motion faster and faster, he blew short, hot breaths on her satin-covered mound.

"Aaah." The pleasurable friction built until her hands fell off his jeans. His fingers found her nipple again and rolled it while he continued tugging her panties and heating her clit through the satin.

Suddenly, the erotic sensations careened into a knot of intense pleasure, and she came.

He tugged aside the satin and sucked, demanding every ounce of satisfaction from her body as her legs squeezed his hand and the waves consumed her. When she thought she would pass out if he didn't stop, he ceased nibbling her clit and rested his head on her tummy.

She clapped her hands over her chest to still her racing heart. Glancing down at his dark blond head below her belly button, she murmured, "Marc, that was amazing."

He smiled at her. "Have I worn you out?"

Warmth flooded her. Stroking his hair, she smiled back. "For the time being, yes. But that doesn't mean I can't do you." Playfully, she smacked his ass. "Get out of those jeans." They trapped his erection half-beneath the boxer-briefs.

"Gladly. But first your dress." He got to his knees, urging her up. His gaze lingered on her breasts before dropping to the pooled fabric at her waist. "Is there a trick to this thing? I don't want to ruin it."

Laughing, she reached behind herself. "A hidden zipper."

"Had to make it difficult for me, huh?"

"Well, I figured I was too easy last time."

"I don't know about that." He slapped her ass, dislodging her fingers from the zipper. "Stripping halfway and then showing me your tattoo while forcing me to sit in that chair and keep my hands to myself for even a few seconds was very hard."

Like he was now. She smiled. "Thanks for the C."

"My cock?"

She laughed. "The felt-pen C on my butt. I found it the next morning."

"You didn't say anything. I wondered if it came off in the shower before you saw it."

"Oh, I saw it. And I like it. Every time it washes off, I draw it back on."

He chuckled. "We'll have to see about getting it permanently changed."

"Only if you get Callie tattooed on your ass."

"Entirely possible."

She knew he was only teasing about getting his-and-her tattoos, but she loved how free they were with each other, not afraid to talk about past lovers when they were about to have sex. If anything, their candid discussion made her feel closer to him. As if she could share her most intimate thoughts, fears, and dreams, and trust that he wouldn't judge her.

Marc embraced her, sweeping a hand around to locate the zipper of her dress. Following a quick tug, he pulled the garment off over her head, tousling her hair.

He climbed off the bed. As he shed his clothes, renewed desire kindled in Callie, and she whisked off her thong, murmuring, "Sit on the bed."

When he complied, she knelt on the mattress and drew his cock into her mouth.

He groaned. "Callie."

She gazed up. "Tut-tut. Give a girl what she wants."

His head lolled back. Callie licked and sucked while the dim light of the bedside lamp played over his naked body.

A guttural sound tore from him, and his hips pumped. He fondled her back and ass, his breathing shallow as his fingers dipped into her pussy from behind and mimicked the movements of her mouth.

She squirmed from the pleasurable sensations, and he groaned again. "Cal, if you don't stop, I'll explode."

She smiled against the velvety skin of his cock. "Not a problem." She loved the effect she had on him.

"It is for me." Grasping her arms, he pulled her on top of him and collapsed on the bed. Their gazes linked. For several quiet moments, he caressed her face and hair, his expression so serious it scared her.

"What are you thinking?" she whispered, heart hammering.

"How right this feels."

"I know. It's kind of freaky."

He chuckled. "Condoms are in the nightstand."

"Your wish is my command." Reaching over, she opened the drawer and withdrew a packet from the unopened box, then moved down his body to roll the protection onto his engorged cock with her mouth.

When she finished, he flipped them over so she lay beneath him. He turned off the lamp, blanketing them in darkness, and relief swept her. She'd loved having the light on during their foreplay, but the dark would help hide her increasingly conflicting emotions.

Because Marc felt more than right to her. He felt special. *They* felt special. Which was ridiculous. Sure, they got along like sugar and water, but tonight was about exploring their physical attraction—nothing more.

And she'd prove it.

She slid her hand between their bodies and gripped his iron-hard cock, smoothing her thumb over the soft latex condom before lowering her fingers to cup his balls. He groaned as she squeezed and fondled, lightly dragging her fingernails over the sensitive skin behind the base of his sac. His body stiffened.

"Cal."

"I could make you come right now," she whispered in his ear.

"You wouldn't dare."

"Care to test me?" She massaged his nuts again, and his cock bucked.

He moaned. "You're relentless. But this time we're doing things my way." He grabbed her fingers and released her grip on his sac, swooping her arm out from between them and pinning it above her head on the sheets. A second later, her other hand joined the first, and he grinned down wickedly at her. "I'm coming inside you."

Hot sensations pooled within her as he gripped both wrists in one hand and lifted her ass with the other. The thick head of his erection nudged her wet pussy, his mouth claiming hers, tongues tangling.

He drew back, then plunged, sinking into her again and again. He pinned her wrists with both his hands now—when had that happened? Her head swam.

His mouth left hers to claim a breast, teasing her aching nipple until the spiraling heat consumed her anew and she neared her second climax.

"Marc, I want to touch you," she murmured, straining against the bonds of his strong hands while he sucked her nipple.

He glanced up, smiling, and the unchecked emotion shining in his gray eyes seduced her in a way the wildest sex tricks couldn't match.

Seduced her body and soul.

What a fool she'd been, thinking making love with Marc again wouldn't mean anything to her.

It meant everything.

It meant she'd given him her heart.

He let go of her wrists, snuggling her deep within his arms while he continued to pump. She swept her hands over his back and ass, holding her to him and lifting her knees so he thrust deeper.

"Callie." His jaw tightened against her neck, and her pussy pulsed, signaling the onslaught of a mega-orgasm.

"I'm there with you," she whispered as the first crest broke over her.

He adjusted the angle of his hips. Her pussy clenched in rapturous spasms, and she screamed as her climax swept her.

"God, Callie." He kissed her, and, with one last thrust, they rode out the strong waves of his release together.

⁂

"Any chance they're still out there?" the beautiful woman in Marc's arms asked, parting the slats of his living room blinds while he hugged her from behind.

"I doubt it. They have spoiled heiresses and immature actors to chase around. They don't need us." He kissed her neck above the collar of his shirt she'd donned for their post-lovemaking foray into his kitchen for a snack. The hem skimmed her thighs, exposing her legs, and the warmth of her bare ass through the wrinkled fabric half-stiffened his penis beneath his boxers.

He kissed her again, and her head wriggled as if the contact tickled her skin. "They needed us earlier," she murmured.

"And we gave them what they wanted. They should leave us alone now."

She grew silent. Then, "What about us?"

"I never want to leave you alone." He squeezed her.

Remaining within his embrace, she turned. The curve of her breasts peeked out from the skewed front of the unbuttoned shirt. Thanks to the faint light spilling from the hall and kitchen, he could make out the outline of her nipples.

Desire spiking, he swept up a hand to brush them.

"I'm not talking about sex," she whispered. Her eyes closed, and she moaned as he continued to tease her nipples. "Well, maybe I am. But not completely."

A smile tweaked his lips. "Hmm?"

Her eyes opened. Doubt filled her gaze. "I know we've done this before, but I can't help feeling that tonight… you, me, us… it's been building for months, Marc. What do we do about it now that we've given each other what we wanted?"

He dragged in a breath. He knew he loved her, but was she ready to hear it?

"You're thinking too much." He kissed the tip of her nose. "Let's enjoy what we have."

She smiled. "And worry about it tomorrow?"

"We'll worry about it when what we share doesn't work anymore." Preferably never.

He caressed her breast, and she shivered, longing glazing her eyes and her rosy mouth parting.

His cock hardened to full mast, nudging her thigh, and her smile stretched into a sexy grin.

"It's working now," she whispered, kissing him. "Marc." Husky appeal softened her voice. "I want to make love."

His balls tightened. "Here?"

She nodded.

Her tongue delved into his mouth, tasting of the oranges they'd feasted on. She shoved his underwear down his hips.

Their lips briefly broke contact as he helped release his cock and kicked off the boxers.

Mouths joined, he slid his hands around her back beneath the shirt and maneuvered them to the wall cornering the living room window. Levering her against the wall, he lifted one of her legs and hooked it around his hips.

Her moist cleft wet his erection.

Sensing her stretching on tiptoe to accommodate their height difference, he boosted her up. Her legs wrapped around him, the intimate pressure intensifying his arousal.

He pushed aside the shirt fabric and palmed her breast; her nipple beaded in his hand. When he skated his hand between her legs and played with her clit, she rested her head on his shoulder, her breath releasing in soft gasps and her hair brushing his naked shoulders.

Her passion soaked his fingers. Marc lifted his hand to his mouth, sniffed her essence and licked it off, then probed her slick folds and massaged her swollen clit.

Her hips wiggled against him. As if struggling with the effort to speak, she whispered hoarsely, "P-protection."

He grunted. "In the bedroom."

Her head drew back, and she smiled. "Shirt pocket."

"Nice work, Hutchins."

Callie unhooked her legs, and he lowered her to standing. Grinning, she retrieved the condom and ripped open the packet. Marc chuckled as she tossed the trash aside.

However, when she grasped his erection, stroked a few times, then rolled on the condom while gazing into his eyes, his heart lurched and the need to tell her how he felt about her surged within him so strongly that only kissing her deeply while visualizing his stiff cock filling her hot pussy tamed it.

"Up," she murmured, moving closer.

He hoisted her onto his hips. Her legs encircling him, she lifted her body away slightly and whispered, "In."

Supporting her against the wall, he gripped his erection and swiped the head over her wet slit.

"In," she repeated.

Groaning, he thrust to the hilt. Her slick heat gripped him tight, and she gasped. "Ohhh. Marc, pump. Pump now."

Sweeping his hands beneath her ass, he drove into her.

"Yes." She kissed him. "Yessss."

Her mouth captured his, her cries spurring his passion. Her heat squeezed and pulsed, milking him. He pumped again, and his orgasm grabbed him, spilling into her, making her his.

Chapter 10

On Monday, Marc found Callie in the KCLA break room. She sat at a table with her back to the door, turning magazine pages and nursing a mug of coffee.

A sales guy and a young woman he recognized from Human Resources chatted near the sink. The guy drained his mug and rinsed it. The pair continued talking as they exited the room, leaving Marc alone with Callie.

He crept to her chair and whispered, "Hi."

"Shit!" Coffee sloshed onto the table, and she laughed. "You're lucky I didn't get burned."

"Sorry." He knelt beside her. "I'd have kissed it better."

"I'm sure you would have." The sexy light softening her gaze revealed that, burn aside, she'd have enjoyed every moment.

Remaining crouched, he brushed her arm. "Why'd you disappear this morning?"

"I needed to feed Hector and change my clothes." She sopped the spilled coffee with a paper napkin. "When I leave out huge bowls of chow and water, he thinks I'm abandoning him and claws the furniture. Besides, as much as I love lounging around in your shirts, you couldn't expect me to come to work today wearing one of them, could you?"

Marc chuckled. "I'd have taken you home first."

"I didn't want to wake you, so I hiked over a couple of streets and caught a cab." With a glance to the open door, she half-whispered, "You know, Marc, when we got my car Friday, we agreed that our appearance at Nine Tails was for the tabloids and everything else that happened this weekend was for us. No one at the station needs to know."

He nodded. "And arriving at work together this afternoon might have told them. Fair enough."

"Thanks for understanding." She rubbed his hand.

Marc plastered on a smile to offset the uneasy sensations invading his gut. Regardless of their agreement, he yearned to shout to the world how much he loved her, now and eons beyond their damn ratings prank.

Their making love again Thursday night had set the tone for a fantastic weekend. Early Friday, they'd retrieved her car from Nine Tails so it wouldn't get vandalized or impounded. However, following Friday's taping, she'd parked at her apartment and driven with him to his place for a late dinner and more great sex.

She hadn't mentioned leaving again, so neither had he. Aside from popping out for muffins, lattes, and condoms, they'd spent the weekend in bed—and on his couch, in the shower, on the kitchen table.

Erotic memories filled his mind, stirring desire low in his body. He caught her gaze. "This weekend was incredible."

Her lips trembled. "I know."

Love flashed through him, swift and intense. Over the last two days, when not making love, they'd laughed and talked for hours. Following coffee and Sunday crosswords, he'd regaled her with stories of the year he'd lived with his cousins following his mother's death. In return, she'd divulged her wish to rekindle her relationship with her own mother and recounted cute tales of life as a teenager on her grandfather's farm.

"I enjoyed our talks." He stroked her arm. "I can't wait to be alone with you again."

Her gaze dipped. "Same here."

"I want to kiss you so badly, it's killing me. A slow, deep kiss, like the ones we shared last night."

A pixie smile curved her lips. "I don't think this is the right place. Knowing Ed, he'll rush in soon with the tabloids."

Marc groaned. "Just so you realize I'm suffering."

"I'll make it up to you," she whispered.

"Deal." His knees ached from crouching. He got up and sat in a chair. "Speaking of the tabloids, have you seen them?"

She shook her head. "But I heard we're in them. You know Lauren Flannigan, right?"

"The account executive. A little."

"She's a friend of mine. Lucky thing I went home this morning, because she called me there with the news. I didn't have time to hear specifics, but I didn't buy copies myself—"

"Because no doubt Ed bought a million. Same here."

Just then, a tall man clutching a stack of newspapers sailed in and shut the door.

"Speak of the devil." Marc murmured.

Callie twisted in her chair. "Hi, Ed."

"Hi? Fan-fricasseed-hallelujah!" Ed slipped between their chairs and slapped the tabloids onto the table. "You two are brilliant, you're amazing, you're freakin' lifesavers!"

"C'mon, Ed, tell us how you really feel." Marc grinned.

"I feel like Superman in a world devoid of Kryptonite, kidlets!" Ed flipped open the top publication and indicated a shot of Callie wearing one of Marc's shirts while fetching the Sunday paper from the stoop. Photos of them baiting the paparazzi Thursday night topped the shirt-skimming-thighs shot, and the zoom-in of them kissing in his car sat beneath a blazing headline.

Ed poked the Callie-with-newspaper picture. "It says this one's from Sunday. Were you and Marc really together all weekend, Callie?"

A blush splotched her face. "Uh." She glanced at Marc, and he shook his head at Ed.

"You know how these rags are," he said. "That picture was taken Friday morning, not Sunday."

"Callie stayed the night after your publicity date?" Glee saturated Ed's voice.

Marc nodded. "In my guest room. We wanted to make the scenario appear believable." The lie came easily—because it was for her.

"So you took it up a notch, and it worked! The phone lines and emails are going crazy." Ed jabbed the photo of Callie in Marc's shirt again. "You must have had a restless sleep, Callie. Your hair's all mangled."

"Um, I teased it with a comb."

"Huh. It actually looks like you had mind-blowing sex."

"That was the idea." She emitted a nervous chuckle.

"Well, I appreciate it, and so does Iris. She damn near kissed me when she saw the pictures." Ed clapped. "Now to maintain our momentum. On tonight's show, pretend you haven't seen these. But exaggerate the sexual tension you have going on. We want the audience to believe it hasn't faded."

"Sexual tension?" Marc laughed. "Ed, what have you been reading?"

"My wife's romance novels. Don't smirk, Shaw—they're good."

Callie laughed, and Ed chortled, adding, "Your breakup happens in nine days, kiddies. But first we need some conflict to keep the audience guessing. The ratings will shoot through the roof."

The next two days whipped by in a flurry of viewer and media speculation about Callie and Marc. Callie barely had time to field interview requests and confer with suddenly interested agents, much less seize more alone time with him. With Thanksgiving approaching and one week remaining in sweeps, out of necessity their energies revolved around taping advance broadcasts and staging Nielson-motivated public appearances.

Wednesday night, following back-to-back tapings, they arrived at a trendy West Hollywood restaurant to play out Ed and Angela's "trouble brews in paradise" brainwave.

As scripted, Callie fawned over Marc, scooting her chair next to his so their legs rubbed beneath the table and clasping his hand whenever he set down his knife or wineglass.

Sexy leg action aside, which she loved, acting the clingy girlfriend in public fell so far outside her range of experience that she felt like an air-headed idiot. Even when she was at her most pathetic with Mark Rafael, she'd kept her fawning private.

However, if Ed and Angela believed "clingy Callie" would help them trump sweeps, then "clingy Callie" they'd get.

In the middle of their meal, she scratched her cheek—her and Marc's signal to proceed to the "trouble."

As planned, Marc shook his head. "I'm not sure I like what you're saying, Callie," he said in a raised voice.

She pouted and toyed with the shirtsleeve peeking out from his blazer. "What do you mean?"

"The sooner you accept who I am, the happier we'll be."

Several curious gazes turned toward them. Callie bit back a grin. Ed's cheesy writing had produced the desired effect.

"I'm just asking you to be faithful over Thanksgiving," she griped. "Is that too much to ask?"

Marc rolled his eyes. "I knew this wouldn't work." He pushed back his chair and stood.

She forced alarm into her gaze. "Marc, please sit down."

"You can come with me now and take what I have to offer, or stay here and eat alone."

She glared at him. "You're an asshole." Standing, she grabbed her glass of Shiraz and tossed the contents at him. The red wine bloomed on his shirt and splattered his jacket.

Genuine shock pelted his features—she'd ad-libbed. "Shit!"

Three couples nearby snickered, and a woman in Callie's peripheral vision cheered.

Emboldened, Callie gripped Marc's glass, but he stole it away, grumbling, "I think one is enough, don't you?"

"It's not near enough," she hissed, snatching her purse and wrap and striding for the door.

She stormed out of the restaurant as cameras flashed from the sidewalk. With several A-list celebrities dining inside, the likelihood that the paparazzi would follow her and Marc tonight sat squarely below zero.

The vultures wanted their main courses—she and her guy were mere appetizers.

Very soon, she'd have him all to herself. Her body buzzed.

Adjusting her wrap around her shoulders, she pushed through the paparazzi and hurried down the sidewalk.

The cool breeze blew her hair around her face, obscuring her vision as she pulled her cell out of her purse and punched in a fake number.

Marc raced behind her and grasped her arm. "Wine-throwing wasn't in the script," he whispered.

"The crowd loved it," she whispered back. "'Clingy Callie,' indeed." Then, in a loud voice, she said, "All right, I'll pay for your damn dry-cleaning!" Jamming her ringing cell phone to her ear, she murmured, "Return to the script."

"Huh?" the man answering the phone asked.

Marc grabbed the cell, mumbling into it, "Wrong number."

Back in character, he scowled and slapped shut the phone. "Who the fuck was that?"

"A taxi, you ignorant caveman. You want me gone, I'm gone."

He swore again. "I brought you here, I'll take you home."

"Whatever." She flicked a hand.

They continued sniping at each other like a couple on the brink of divorce. Several yards down the sidewalk, Marc looked over his shoulder. "They bought it." He passed her the cell.

"Good." Giggling, she took his hand and ducked into the parking garage. "To the car, Shaw—go, go, go!"

"Yes, Jane Bond!"

Minutes later, laughing and breathless, they clambered into his low black sports car. He leaned over the stick shift and kissed her. The intoxicating tastes of grilled steak, wine, and sexy man played on her tongue.

"You were great back there, Cal."

"So were you! Sorry about the wine. I couldn't resist."

"You can lick it off me." He pushed the key into the ignition. "Your place?"

She stopped his hand on the steering wheel. "I can't wait."

"Miss Bond, what are you suggesting?"

"A celebration." The car huddled in a dark corner of the parking garage. Besides, this was L.A. She could strangle Marc in his car and no one would notice.

"Unbuckle your belt," she said, throwing her purse and wrap into the puny backseat.

He laughed. "Callie, this is a tiny car."

"Go with the moment, Shaw. Slide back the damn seat and pull down your pants. I'm climbing on-board."

"Fuck." Excitement resounded in his voice, and she grinned.

"That's the idea."

He scrambled for his belt, tugged down his pants and boxers. The seat scooted back, gaining them another few inches.

Lifting her dress, she kicked off her shoes and crawled over the gear shift. Her head bumped the car roof, and her big toe knocked the GPS screen.

Marc's breath skidded out of him. "You're not wearing panties."

"Nope."

He probed her slick folds. "God, you're wet."

"Ahh… mmm… yes."

His cock poked her slit, and she sank down, gasping as he filled her deep with no latex barrier between them.

Finally. She sighed.

"Callie." Marc swore softly. "We forgot a condom."

"I'm on the pill," she whispered. "For my cycle."

"Are you sure you want to—?"

Her heart squeezed. "Yes. I've never done skin-on-skin before."

"And you chose me? I'm honored." His voice sounded thick and husky.

Closing her eyes, Callie slid her slick inner muscles up and down his cock. The bulging tip kissed her womb, and she moaned. "Oh, Marc, you feel incredible."

"You feel like heaven."

He held her hips, supporting her while she dug her knees into the soft leather of the car seat and rode him.

A million emotions showered her as she sank fully onto him. Love, radiant happiness, desire. In that moment, she knew them all.

Chapter 11

"Explain again why you're having fried chicken with me and Hector instead of sharing a romantic Thanksgiving with Marc?"

Callie licked chicken grease off her fingers before dropping a morsel to her cat meowing beneath the dinette chair. "Lauren, are you deaf? Marc's uncle throws a huge turkey party at the bar, and Marc always attends. If I went with him, the fight we staged at the restaurant last night would go to waste."

"Why not continue the pretend squabbling at the bar?"

"Because I'm 'out of town' until Saturday." Callie mimed quotation marks. "Besides, even if I were 'here,' I wouldn't want to stretch the fight to the Fox. Bob thinks what's happening between me and Marc is real. He's a sweetheart. I don't want to upset him."

"Doesn't he know about last night? And I thought he watched the show."

"Hearing Marc and I are having problems and witnessing them in action are two different things." Callie picked at her coleslaw. "I wouldn't feel right faking arguments in front of him. Marc cares about him a lot."

"You care about Marc, too, don't you?"

"Yes, I do. Are you happy?"

Lauren laughed. "Actually, yes. When I suggested you have hot sex with the guy, I never imagined you'd fall in love. It would look great on you, by the way, if you'd just accept it."

Callie blinked. "How do you know I'm in love?"

"Ah ha! You admit it!"

She shook her head. "I said I care for him."

"A euphemism for, 'I love the man, but I'm too much of a wuss to admit it.'"

Callie put down her fork. "Lauren, what if how I feel about Marc is a byproduct of the situation? Actors think they fall in love all the time, but when film production ends, the 'love' dies, too."

"Byproduct, schmyproduct. You're not an idiot, Callie. And, unlike you thought a few weeks ago, neither is Marc. You know this is real. That's why it scares you. I don't blame you, either. I'd be freaking out all over the place if it were me."

"That's supportive."

"I try. And I'll bet the last chicken breast in the bucket that Marc loves you, too." Lauren swiped the breast.

"Hey, I was saving that!"

"Finders keepers, losers creep me out." Lauren bit into the breast. "Mmm. Can we have fried chicken at the wedding?" Hector meowed at her feet, and she zapped him a stern look. "Scram."

"I can't begin to express how much I don't want to do this," Marc murmured to Callie while they waited backstage for the audience warmer-upper to introduce them. Clipboard-wielding production assistants scurried on and off set, and Angela, heading to the upstairs booth, gave an enthusiastic thumbs-up.

"You mean the breakup?" Callie whispered, returning their producer's smile. "We have to, Marc, for ratings. All our appearances lately point toward you dumping me, and sweeps ends tonight."

Bending his head to her ear, he whispered, "Screw sweeps. Let's not do it, Cal. Let's tell L.A. we're really an item."

Her baby-blues widened. "You're serious?"

"After the last few weeks, do you doubt it?"

"N-no. But—I don't know, Marc. Ed would kill us."

He brushed her shoulder as if sweeping off a strand of hair. The gesture provided an excuse to touch her without raising the crew's suspicions. "From what I've read, if we do split, the show could lose as many viewers as it's gained."

A smile curved her lips. "And where did you read this, hmm? A gossip rag?"

A P.A. hurried past them, and Callie's smile faltered.

"Ed and Angela don't believe the breakup will cost us viewers," she murmured. "As long as the set-up remains secret, we're safe. So are the ratings."

"Cal, how I feel about you has nothing to do with ratings."

"Same here. But…." Worry filled her gaze.

Marc frowned. "What's wrong?"

She rubbed her hands on her skirt, glancing away.

His stomach knotted. "Callie?"

A P.A. scooted in from the set. "Callie, Marc, you're about to go on. Callie's first tonight."

They attached their mics while the P.A. listened through her headset. The warmer-upper's voice rang out, and the P.A. shooed them forward, saying, "Tape's rolling. Callie, go."

Callie darted an anxious glance Marc's way before strolling onto the stage. Ever the professional, she waved to the audience, a big smile brightening her features and her jitters non-apparent.

Marc pasted on his game face and strode out after her.

What was eating her? Did she doubt his sincerity? He'd yet to tell her he loved her. He'd wanted to wait, keep the declaration separate from the zoo their lives had become.

Time for a different approach.

And, if he played it right, not only would he get the girl, but Ed and Angela would have their precious ratings, too.

Nerves pelted Callie throughout her and Marc's interview of a bubbly sitcom star's breakthrough film role. She needed to talk to him. But when? Appointments had separated them until they'd met backstage minutes before taping, and Ed was hosting an end-of-sweeps party following their post-production meeting with Angela.

If the breakup proceeded smoothly, the meeting wouldn't last long. Maybe Callie could snatch a few moments alone with Marc before they joined Ed.

She sucked in a breath. She hoped so. Because she didn't want him hearing her news from anyone else.

The interview ended, and they broke for commercial. The sitcom star flirted with Marc while Zeta and Tommy checked Callie's hair and makeup.

When the star finally flounced off, the floor director counted down to Callie's gag segment with an eccentric Venice Beach woman who claimed she read fortunes in handfuls of crushed taco chips.

A lot of laughter and another commercial break later, Callie sat at the tiny desk with Marc for "He Vs. She." During the first two segments, they'd buttered up their guests while acting barely tolerant of one another. Now, Marc scowled as if her very proximity irked him.

Hand subtly covering his mic, he murmured, "Remember when you said you wanted to spearhead the breakup?"

Trying to appear disgruntled, she jerked her head in an impolite nod.

"Now's your chance," he whispered.

"Excuse me?" Fake-coughing, she pressed a hand to her blouse to muffle her mic. "What do you mean?" she mumbled.

"You can dump me, Cal. I won't do it."

She looked at him. He wanted to alter Angela's plans now?

"Marc," she whispered.

"I'm not doing it, Callie. You can ad-lib, can't you? Of course, you can. I have the wine-stained shirt to prove it." His mouth twitched in a barely there smile. "After the grief I gave you in public this past week, despite what Angela's focus groups say, believe me, the audience wants you to kick me out on my ass."

"Maybe, but—"

"Coming out in ten… nine…!" the floor director called.

Callie lifted her hand from her mic. The stage lights blazed, and the studio audience clapped while the "He Vs. She" *Jaws*-like theme music played.

The P.A. listened through her headset, communicating with their producer. The floor director indicated camera two.

"Welcome back, L.A.!" Callie scanned the teleprompter. Until she decided how to adapt the scripted dialogue preceding their "spontaneous" breakup, she'd follow the original plan. "Tonight, for 'He Vs. She,' I have a challenge for Marc. Fortunately, for the men in our audience, this challenge includes visuals."

On cue, Marc shifted in his chair. "What visuals?"

"Hot chicks," Callie snapped with the tone of a teacher aggravated with a misbehaving pupil. "Curvy young women."

The audience laughed when she slid off her chair, grabbed a telescopic laser pointer off the desk, and extended it.

A screen emerged from the stage floor. Callie swept the pointer toward a slide of an elderly comedienne comically covering her half-naked body. The red laser danced over the comedienne's shocked expression, and Callie feigned surprise. "Whoops!"

The audience guffawed.

A parade of slides featuring gorgeous models, some of whom had dated Marc, flashed one by one onto the screen. Callie "quizzed" him on names, birthdates, where he'd met a woman, how long a relationship had lasted.

However, as per the script, he "only" recalled bra size, quirky erogenous zones, and, in the case of one model, how much money she owed him.

If they adhered to Angela's outline, any moment now, he'd "break" from the scripted skit to portray growing irritation with Callie's critical appraisal of his dating patterns. He'd storm offset, interrupting the show. Angela would race from the booth, hauling a portable camera operator backstage to resume taping while she "convinced" Marc to return to the set.

Once back, he'd impulsively dump Callie. Promos advertising the breakup would run until the 11:30 broadcast—and ratings would explode.

True to his pronouncement, Marc didn't follow through with the plan. Instead of appearing ticked off, he looked and sounded increasingly repentant.

Angela materialized from the booth to stand near the floor director. She must have decided to trust Marc's ad-libbing, because tape kept rolling.

Cleary, if Callie were to assume control of the breakup, she needed to do so now.

She ignored the script on the teleprompter. "As we can see, Marc's serial womanizing has resulted in a lot of broken hearts."

Angela gestured to the P.A., who held up a placard. The audience, following the sign's directions, booed.

Callie narrowed her gaze at the audience. "Isn't it time he suffered some payback?" This time, the viewers cheered.

She faced the screen. "Luckily, I have a great role model."

For a nerve-wracking moment, the screen remained static. Then the slide of Jada Reilly flashed on, and Callie, catching a glimpse of Angela nodding, released a breath. Her producer had given her the go-ahead to play out the breakup as she saw fit.

"Uh, Teach?" Behind the desk, Marc raised a hand.

Callie swung toward him. "*What?*"

"I think I know where this is leading." He looked at camera one. "Callie's had enough of my B.S. Isn't that right, Cal?"

Callie tensed. What was he doing? Was she instigating the breakup or not?

"You may not speak," she scolded, refusing to acknowledge the cameras for fear the viewers would smell a set-up.

Marc stepped out from behind the desk, and the studio fell quiet.

"Oh, I'm speaking, all right." He came toward her. "In fact, I want everyone here to know that you're the first woman in my life to inspire me to speak from the heart."

Callie's pulse raced, and a weird humming noise filled her ears.

Gaze locked on hers, Marc tugged the laser pointer from her grasp. After collapsing the instrument, he tucked it into her skirt pocket. Her body tingled at the brief contact. He clasped her hands.

"Don't dump me, Callie. And please don't ever leave me." His voice softened, husky, sexy, sincere. "I love you."

Gasps and excited cries flew from the audience. Callie's feet glued to the stage. "What?" she squeaked.

"I love you. If you'll have me, I want to marry you. Will you marry me, Callie?"

Her mind went blank.

"What do you say, L.A?" Marc asked the audience. "Should she put an end to my miserable bachelor existence and say yes?"

The entire house stood and cheered, and Callie's heart pinched. "I—I can't!" She ran off the set.

🙟🙜🙞

"Angela, I said no cameras!" Yanking off his mic, Marc aimed a hand against the mini-crew hounding him backstage.

"But, Marc, this is great stuff!" The producer scurried beside him. "We'll feed it to the screen onstage. It'll almost feel like we're going live!"

He blocked the dressing room door. "No cameras. If I have to break every damn one of them to make my point, I will."

"Okay, okay. Don't go psycho on me." Angela studied him. "You honestly love her?"

He nodded.

She grinned. "Then go get her, hotshot."

"I have every intention."

Angela led the camera guys back down the corridor. The hallway clear, Marc rapped on the door. "Callie?"

No response. Several harrowing seconds passed. Then her voice transmitted through the thin wood, "Are you alone?"

"Yes. I promise."

"Then come in. It's unlocked."

He entered to find her hugging her waist, and he swore. "Aw, Cal, I'm an idiot. I'm sorry."

She blinked. "What the hell happened out there?"

"A marriage proposal. A shitty one, obviously. I guess you can tell I'm inexperienced in these matters."

"A real proposal?" She shook her head. "You're telling me that stunt had nothing to do with boosting ratings?"

"No, it partly did. Only because I know how badly you want to get to New

York. Tonight was my lousy attempt to help. But just because I screwed up doesn't mean I love you any less."

"Marc!" Her eyes widened. "The first time you say you love me, it's in front of ninety strangers! You asked me to marry you onstage!"

He cast a sheepish and hopefully charming smile. "It worked for Johnny Cash in *Walk the Line.*"

"I'm no June Carter."

"God, I hope not. The sound of that harp thing she played in the movie hurt my ears."

One corner of Callie's mouth twitched. "It was an autoharp."

"I don't care if it was a freaking brass band." He grasped her gently by the upper arms and searched her face for a hint—just a drop of hope—that she'd understand.

Her gaze softened, and his spirits lifted. "Maybe I chose the wrong way to show you how much I care, but I meant every word. I love you, Callie. I'm tired of pretending I don't." He patted the blazer sleeve concealing his right upper arm. "Know what's under here?"

She shook her head. "What?"

"Until it heals, a thick piece of gauze covering my new tattoo: Callie Forever."

"Oh, Marc." Tears brightened her eyes as her fingers grazed the sleeve. "But how can you trust that what you're feeling is real? How do you know it's not an illusion created by the situation?"

He laughed. "Because I have half a brain, and I always follow my instincts. What I feel is no illusion. Is it for you?"

"No," she answered without hesitation. "I love you, too. I have for weeks. But—"

"No 'buts,' Cal. I love you, and you love me. We're halfway home." He pulled her into his arms and kissed her. A soft, slow kiss brimming with tenderness and passion.

All too quickly, she broke away. "But, I have to tell you, I have an audition in New York next week. I found out a few hours ago."

"Callie, that's great!"

"No, it's not! If by some miracle I get the job, where will that leave us?"

"In New York?"

She shook her head. "I can't ask you to leave your home, the bar, and your uncle to follow me."

He clasped her hand. "You don't have to ask me, sweetheart. I'm offering. In the first place, Bob would kill me if I sacrificed the best thing that's ever happened to me to keep his sorry ass company. Second, don't you remember when I said I didn't know what I wanted from life, but it definitely wasn't what I have here?"

She nodded.

"Well, I want you. If being with you means leaving L.A., I'll go in a second. No more TV jobs for me, though. It was fun while it lasted, but my heart's never truly been in it. I think finally leaving this place would be a great chance to expand my involvement in Babeez."

She smiled. "Your aunts' stores?"

"My stores, too, Cal. I inherited my mother's share. After helping Bob with the bar over the last year—and, yes, I earn my thirty percent, I don't care what the old bastard says—I've discovered I love business. So what am I waiting for?"

She smiled. "And if I don't get the job?"

"We'll cross that bridge when someone builds it. You and me, for the rest of our lives. What do you say, Cal?"

"Do I have to fix my tattoo?"

"As quickly as possible."

She grinned. "Then I say get down on one knee, Shaw."

"Still bossing me around?" He hauled her into his arms. "I'll do you one better."

"Oh, you will? Where? On the flimsy counter?"

"If that's what it takes."

"I think it might."

"Not just this moment, though."

Her lips bowed in a sexy pout, and desire leapt within him.

"Don't distract me, woman." He nodded to the wall clock. "What time is it?"

"Eight-thirty?"

"Now think what time it would be if we were broadcasting."

She laughed. "Midnight."

"So, kiss me, Callie."

She did. Passionately and thoroughly. Filling him with more love, desire, and happiness than he'd ever thought possible.

"Marry me, marry me, marry me, Hutchins," he murmured against her mouth.

"Yes, yes, for a million midnights and then some, yes."

"Mmm, let me lock the door, my future Emmy winner, and I'll meet you at the counter."

The Los Angeles Post
Monday, May 7th Edition

Hollywood Gab
by Celia Fiennes, Gossip Columnist

True Love Triumphs!

A little lovebird tells me that former L.A. Tonight co-hosts Callie Hutchins and Marc Shaw got hitched Saturday afternoon at a simple ceremony in the bride's hometown of Whitten, Nebraska. Fans of Channel 16's late-night talk show will recall November's ratings frenzy when Callie and Marc's on-and-offstage romance rejuvenated interest in local KCLA. The station hasn't looked back since.

Several family members and close friends witnessed the romantic nuptials in a small country church. The bride wore a classic Vera Wang sheathe with her mother's pearls, and the groom cut a sexy figure in a dark charcoal Armani tux.

Following a honeymoon in the Bahamas, Marc and Callie will divide their time between their upstate New York retreat and Manhattan, where Callie takes over from retiring Sheri-Ann Webber to team with TV morning show veteran Garrett Lord.

And, get this, word has it Marc has hung up his microphone for good to assist in the expansion of the ultrachic Babeez boutiques. Apparently, he's one-third owner of the chain. Who knew?

Callie and Marc, we'll miss you! True love is rare, and skeptics of this "made-for-TV" pairing numbered in the thousands when the couple confessed their romance began as a ratings stunt. However, time reveals all, and fans say they foresee blue skies for "L.A.'s Sweethearts."

I gotta admit, this jaded reporter agrees.

About the Author:

Kate St. James lives in the Pacific Northwest with her husband and two sons. When she's not trying to whip her disobedient muse into submission, you can find her chasing her dog in the hills above an azure lake, ignoring the smoke alarms blaring from the kitchen, or endlessly renovating her house. This is Kate's third story with Red Sage Secrets. Kate loves to hear from readers, so feel free to drop her a line at kate@katestjames.com, *or visit her on the web at* www.katestjames.com *where you can subscribe to her newsletter and learn about her back list and upcoming releases.*

Mind Games

by Kathleen Scott

To My Reader:

After finishing my novella, *Fatal Error*, I knew I wanted to revisit the future and see what happened to Soran and Jesse. Imagine my surprise when the sequel happened thirty years later and involved their grown son, Damien, and his lover, Jade. I hope you enjoy discovering their love story as much as I did.

Chapter 1

Damien Storm sat in the recliner with his head tilted back and hands relaxed on the arm rests. His eyes were closed against the intrusion of outside stimuli. Earpieces drown out the noise from the busy street below his apartment window. He could not fail to connect his mind to Jade's. Her life—their lives—depended upon his success.

He hoped this time she wouldn't draw away from him in fear. He had to do something to convince her that the voice she heard in her head was that of a Vartek partner and not the manifestation of schizophrenia.

"Jade?" The thought moved out along the mental pathways that connected a Vartek pairing. *"Jade, I know you're there."*

He wound his thoughts around hers, trying to bracket them into a protective cocoon. Jade's mind brushed lightly against his, gentle as a cobweb floating on a breeze then withdrew and tried to rush from the safety of his hold.

"Jade, please don't run away. We need to talk."

A shiver shimmered along the psychic bond. He was losing her, she was preparing to flee and set up her natural mind shields. At least Damien assumed they were natural, he didn't believe for even a moment that Jade had ever learned to control her mind. No, it felt too disorganized in there to have been the recipient of any formal training.

He laughed at that. Any 'formal' training for a Varti was usually received in a dark cellar lined with lead in order to outwit the government agents who searched for Vartek pairs for mandatory imprisonment or institutionalization. Luckily, his parents had known people to teach him everything he knew. Everything he planned to pass on to Jade if she would ever let him stay inside her sweet mind.

"Ah, babe I've missed you so much." The admission felt as if it had been ripped from his soul. *"You've shut me out for two weeks."*

"Leave me alone. You aren't real," came the shaky answer.

Damien gouged the armrests with curled fingers. Shock jarred him into losing the grip he had on her. She had never answered him before. Never acknowledged his existence when he spoke to her, though he quite often bared his soul to her.

He focused his concentration. *"I* am *real."*

"What's wrong with me? What have I done?"

"You've done nothing wrong. There's nothing wrong with you or me."

He swore he could hear a sob. *"Then why are you hounding me?"*

"Because I want to protect you."

There was a beat of silence then nothing. She had pulled away and closed him out again.

"Damn it all." He pulled the earpieces from his ears and threw them across the room. So close. The bitch of the matter was he couldn't pinpoint her exact location without having her cooperation. So far he'd only been able to contact her while her unconscious mind had control of her thoughts, or while doing right brain activities.

He knew she wrote poetry. He'd been able to glimpse the lines she composed before her delicate hands ever committed them to paper. The thought made him smile. Yes, paper. The woman was still enough of a romantic to use that long out-dated form of communication.

She had to have some major source of income to be able to afford ink and paper to scribble her ideas on. None of his acquaintances had been able to afford the stuff and his family was considered upper middle class.

He rose from the chair and went to look out the window. With the spotty images he'd gotten from her he'd been able to track her as far as Glendown, Virginia, but not the exact address.

The town was small enough that most people didn't take their gliders above street level. It had been one of the things that struck him as odd and rather charming when he'd first wondered into town following the psychic signals Jade had unwittingly threw his way—before she had stopped letting him in.

For all accounts Glendown looked like a throwback to a bygone era. The buildings up and down the main street sported edifices reminiscent of the early 1930's, though the materials used were modern. Flowering trees filled the air with fragrance, and bathed the area in color. The scene looked like something out of a story.

"Where are you, baby?" he said to the wide-open streets. But the streets didn't answer him.

Chapter 2

Jade closed the journal and sat back in her seat. Her hands shook so badly she could barely twist the pen to retract the tip. For two weeks, she hadn't pulled out her poetry because every time she did she ended up with that strange voice inside her head.

Today he'd said he was real. How far over the edge had she gone exactly? Often she wondered if she should just let the voice take over and then she wouldn't have to walk around terrified of someone finding out her nasty little secret. And in her house that would be a very bad thing.

A bitter laugh escaped and broke the silence of the room. Boards creaked over her head and a light shown at the top of the basement stairs.

"Are you all right down there?"

Chills swam down her spine. "Yes, father."

"I thought I heard laughter. Is there someone down there with you?"

Only my multiple personality. "No, father. I just wrote something I found amusing."

The top stair creaked as he started down.

She swallowed the panic that choked her whenever the voice surfaced from that deep broken side of her mind. If her family ever discovered her mental illness they would send her away to the State Hospital at the outskirts of town. Not that being away from their overbearing control would be a loss, but it was still better to live in the hell you knew than to go to one unknown. But even as she watched her father's shadow grow as he neared, the words *go, run* punctured her mind and threatened to explode from her mouth.

She took a deep calming breath and tried to center her thoughts. Control was of the utmost importance.

"Jade?" Her father stepped into the light and regarded her with a wary expression. "Put your book away. It will be time to eat soon."

Like she could even think of food when her entire life felt like it was about to blow up in her face. "Can I eat down here tonight? There's a poem I want to finish…"

He held up his hand for silence. "You don't need to be told again of the rules of this house, do you?"

She stood and ran her shaking hands down her dress, more to calm herself than to smooth any wrinkles. It wouldn't do to let her family know how much she feared them. How much she feared their good will would end if they knew how sick she was. There was nothing for it. She would have to listen to the voice and leave. Afraid or not, she'd spent too long worrying that they would turn her out. If the decision was hers and she left on her own, escaping the prison of her life, they would no longer have dominion over her.

"I'll be right up."

He nodded, but narrowed his eyes as if not believing a word from her mouth.

After he left, she closed her eyes and took a deep breath and tried desperately to feel her way to the voice inside her head. *"Are you there?"*

A strange feeling rippled across her consciousness, sending out waves like a pebble dropped on a pond. *"I'm here."*

"I want proof you aren't just a figment. That I'm not listening to my mind fracturing into shards." Just the thought made her breath hitch. Tears splashed down her face. She really couldn't take it if the voice who offered salvation was nothing more than psychosis. Or worse, a Vartek partner.

"Listen, my name is Damien, and I'm a flesh and blood man. Meet me at the café at the corner of Maplethorpe and Rose. I'll be waiting there for you."

Her heart pounded. She knew the café but had never been inside. Her parents wouldn't have allowed it. They barely let her out of doors to begin with and then only with an armed escort of her father's personal guard. God in heaven this was no way for an adult to be treated. *"When? I may not be able to sneak away for hours."*

"That's fine. I'll wait forever if I have to."

Of course he would. He was only a voice, regardless of what he'd have her believe. Mental illness could do that to a person.

The basement door opened again. "Jade."

"I have to go," she said to the voice. *"I'll be there when I can."*

Dinner seemed to move in slow motion. She pushed the food around on her plate, having lost her appetite when she agreed to sneak out of the house. How was she ever going to pull that one off? The promise spread out before her like her own personal Rubicon. Once she crossed there would be no going back.

"Are you not hungry, honey?" Her mother considered her with a deep frown creasing her elegant brow. "Cook went through a lot of trouble to make your favorites."

Cook needn't have bothered.

"No, not really. I have an assignment do and I can't think of a topic."

Her father looked up from his plate and down the long expanse of table at her. "You should have been doing that rather than wasting your time with your poetry."

She looked down at her chest to be sure the knife wound to her heart wasn't real. It wasn't. But it bled like it was. He'd never understood her, much less her creative side.

Jade put her napkin on the table. "May I be excused?"

"Oh, Jade. Your father didn't mean that the way it sounded."

Farroll Tanner's face told a different story. He did mean it.

Jade shrugged. "It's all right. Not everyone can appreciate poetry. I understand that. You have to have a soul for that."

He cleared his throat. It was the only warning she'd get. Eyes so much like her own glared at her.

Her mother took the clue and rang for the servant. When he appeared at her elbow she said, "Jade will have this saved for later, please. She is unwell."

"Very good, ma'am."

She left the table before her father could impose any more threats on her, or inflict punishment for her rudeness. How awful to live in a house where she wasn't even tolerated by the people who gave her life. They should have practiced birth control more carefully if they didn't want children. No, that was unfair to her mother. Glenda Tanner loved her daughter, though she had never once stood up to her husband to prove it.

As she hurried through the house, Jade looked at the grandfather clock in the hallway and kept walking on towards the library. Doors in that room led out to the gardens, from the gardens she could leave the premises without being discovered. Security cameras kept a watchful eye on the Tanner estate at all times, but a quick redirect command and she wouldn't have to worry about the ones watching the back gate.

Quickly she made a detour to the security room. Both guards, Reis and Dale, watched a soccer match on television rather than the monitors. Good, they wouldn't notice the view shift on the cameras until much later.

A few commands into the house's mainframe network and she could escape. It was an action she'd practiced before, back when Quenton still lived. It was how they would manage to sneak away and be alone. Her breath hitched at the thought of him and she pressed on.

An hour later and she entered the café. People sat at tables, or on couches, and sipped coffees while they talked in low tones. Soft background music filtered through the room from hidden speakers, and delicious smells of fresh baked cookies and breads filled her nose.

In the back of the café a man sat with his head in his hand. A small LCD screen lay on the table in front of him. As he read he flipped his wrist up to look at his watch, then darted a look her way. And froze.

Air refused to move through her lungs. She tried to exhale, but couldn't. She tried to inhale and couldn't. Nothing seemed to work for the length of two heartbeats then everything seemed to move in real time again.

He stood and ran a hand through his already disheveled hair. "Jade?"

Oh God, it's true. He really is flesh and blood, or have I completely come unglued.

Chapter 3

Damien watched as Jade's fair skin grew even paler. He had to get her out of the coffee house before she passed out. However, there was always the chance she wouldn't follow him.

His gaze caressed the column of a very slender throat and moved on down to her chest. Her breathing had become erratic.

Large green eyes were caught somewhere between fear and sadness. "Come on, we need to talk, but not here." He said the words out loud, rather than in her mind, hoping that would calm her somewhat.

She started to back up as he came near and put his hand out for her to take.

"I have an apartment upstairs; we can talk there."

"Oh God, you are real." For some reason that seemed to upset her even more.

"Here, let me buy you something to drink, and we can sit here and talk."

She shook her head and clutched her hands together in the folds of her dress. Christ, was she ever nervous. How was he going to get her to trust him if she wouldn't even talk to him?

"Please? You came all the way here to meet me. Don't run away without even talking to me." At her slight nod of acceptance, Damien went to the counter and asked for a small coffee. He didn't know what she preferred so decided to get it black and she could put in it what she wanted.

When a sleek silver glider crawled near the curb and stopped outside the café, Jade looked at the door, looked at the ladies' room, and hauled a shapely ass.

Two men entered the café. One had on what looked like an old-fashioned chauffeur's uniform; the other dressed in an expensively tailored suit. They scanned the patrons and when they didn't see who they were looking for they took up positions on either side of the bathrooms to wait.

Damien stood with the warm cup in his hand trying to decide what to do. They didn't look government, they looked like concerned family. Or rather concerned father and employee. But the father looked damn familiar. He knew that face, but it was out of context.

Unfortunately, he didn't have time to figure out where he knew the guy from. He had to work on the more immediate problem of getting Jade out of the café and away from them. They looked as dangerous as government officials. And to a Varti that was as good as dead.

In order to get Jade out he had to get them away from the bathrooms and out of the café first. He set the cup on a table and sauntered over to the two men. "You two looking for someone?"

The suit looked at him and dismissed him as unimportant and beneath him. If the guy only knew he owed everything he was to Damien's parents, he'd be down on his knees thanking God. If not for Jesse and Soran Storm, the government would still be run by a maniacal computer and free will would be nothing but a myth.

Uniform came towards Damien, hands up, as if to push him away.

"Hey, if you don't want to know where that pretty little number in the yellow dress went, then fuck you."

Suit's head snapped around and finally considered Damien as more than a spot on the tiled floor. "Where is she?" If the man's lips were any tighter he'd have farted the words.

"Ran out the backdoor when she saw you two coming. Can't say I blame her. Not the most friendly fellows I've ever encountered…" Damien exhaled as the men split up. One went out the front the other continued on to the back where he pushed open the door, tripping the alarm.

The manager poked her head out of her office and looked at the open back door.

"That guy just tried to rob you!" He shook a finger toward in the direction suit fled.

She hurried out the door with her personal com-unit in hand and talked into what must have been a straight line to dispatch for the local police. Sirens began to sound in the distance.

While chaos prevailed in the café, Damien snuck into the ladies room to find Jade hiding by standing on top of a toilet seat behind a closed door. It wasn't an original way to hide, but at least she hadn't tried to climb out the window.

He held out his hand to her again. "Come on, we've only got a few minutes to clear the area. Cops will be all over this place real soon."

"What did you do?" She gave him her hand and let him help her down off the toilet seat.

Her hand felt cool and a little damp in his. Just the fact he was finally touching her made him smile. He'd begun to doubt he'd ever get so close to her. "Let's just say your father will have a lot of explaining to do with the local authorities."

"Not him. He is the local authorities."

Cold seared him through. "Then we better move."

After a quick scan to make sure the coast was clear, he pulled her out the back door and across the parking lot on the opposite side of the building from the entrance. Trees obstructed the view of his glider so he didn't worry they would be seen getting in, only if she would get in. He hit the remote unlock and starter and hurried to the driver's seat.

Jade stopped mid-stride. "Where are you taking me?"

Damien waited until she got into the glider before he answered. It proved her anxiousness to be away from Glendown that she even moved into the vehicle without yet knowing their destination.

"To meet my parents." He grabbed the manual door handle and pulled, engaging the duel control that closed both at the same time. "Strap in. We've a long ride ahead and I have a feeling the first part is going to be bad."

Chapter 4

Jade had lost count of the passing miles as they left her small town of Glendown, for the heavier populated sections of the country. They'd hurried by the Beltway and downtown D.C. then took an exit and headed northwest. It was hard to tell where one town ended and the next began. The only discernable images were the hulking outlines of buildings as the highways twisted and turned through the cities.

She'd never been away from Glendown before. The only traveling she'd ever done was on the computer, accessing files of distant lands and cultures, trying to escape the hell of her own existence. For some reason the vast expanse of concrete and glass, and the traffic zooming by at high speeds looked less intimidating on the screen, but it had never felt as exhilarating.

They stayed to the major arteries and only then advanced to middle tier roadways that hung precariously over the cities. Damien explained they would be better hidden that way. With decks of moving gliders above and below them it would be hard to find one dark glider among many.

Jade begged to differ, the damn thing stood out as if it had neon signs plastered to it. Damien's glider was only one on the most basic level. It was probably thirty years old or more. The thing shuddered and rumbled as it moved, and something in the back seat smelled a little less than fresh. Jade doubted the glider would make a decent junker for parts. But she shouldn't complain. She was free.

Damien offered no more information on his parents or where in the vast network of urban sprawl known as the U.S. they lived. Nor had he mentioned if they would stop at any point to answer the call of nature. She crossed her legs and hoped it would be soon.

She turned and studied his profile in the dim light coming in from the highway lights as they passed by. He was probably the most handsome man she'd ever seen. Not in the conventional sense, but in an intangible way. And she doubted few women had refused attention from him. His dark wavy hair didn't seem to understand the concept of a comb or brush, but he did run his fingers through it quite often.

She sighed louder than she wished to and felt her face grow hot as he turned.

"I know you're tired, babe, but we need to put as much distance between us and the good people of Glendown as possible."

"I know." She didn't take her gaze off him. "I just don't know why, other than my father disliking his commands being ignored."

"No man in power likes having his commands disregarded. I'll tell you what I know, but you have to wait until we stop. Can you hold on that long?" His gaze darted to the console computer that displayed a grid of surrounding traffic. He frowned. "Look behind us. Do you see a glider that looks familiar to you?"

Jade turned in her seat and looked out the back glass. There were other gliders on the road, but she wasn't sure if she recognized them or not. "It's too dark to tell. They all look alike to me."

"Damn." He pulled the toggle to the right and they sped down the off ramp and into the city proper, whatever city it happened to be. She'd stopped watching signs about the time they passed Pittsburgh. A few blocks down they roared up the onramp and onto the southwest spur of the highway.

"What's wrong?"

"I'm pretty sure we're being followed." The worried expression on his face did nothing to calm her growing fears.

This time when she turned around she studied the other gliders and personal transports for any sign of one staying close on their trail.

Then she spotted it.

Three gliders back and off to their left. It came up onto the highway from the same ramp. The glider had that same silver sheen as her father's, and looked just as purposeful and cold as the man who owned it.

"Could you go a little faster?" She turned back around and faced forward.

Damien tapped a few commands into the dashboard computer to display another screen. The display belched and sputtered. He hit it a few times for motivation. "See something?"

"My father, I think." The thought alone sent an unpleasant rumble through her gut. What would he do when he caught her?

"Damn! I was afraid you'd say that." He jerked the toggle to the right and flew off the highway and down into the middle of the city proper once again.

A quick glance over her shoulder and the unpleasant rumble turned into full-blown fear. "They're right behind us."

"Strap yourself in good and tight, babe. I'm gonna try and shake them loose."

From the condition of the glider, Jade wasn't so sure he could manage to shake anything loose. Her father's glider was top of the line and mint, it would catch them sooner or later, but the thought of going back held very little appeal.

She strapped herself in and held the door handle as Damien pulled back on the toggle and punched the accelerator. Jesus, the glider was old enough to still have an accelerator. The protesting vehicle jerked and shimmied then, after a loud belch and backfire, they rocketed up to the next level.

Jade closed her eyes. She had left her family and placed her life in the hands of a maniac.

A deep chuckle made her open her eyes and stare at him. He took his concentration from the roadway to glance at her. "I'm not a maniac, just determined."

"I know you're used to listening in on my private thoughts, but stop it. It's rude."

He only smiled wider. "I can't help it when you're broadcasting like that."

"I didn't realize I was." She gave a quick glance to the computer screen and noticed a glider cutting through traffic right on their tail. "They're gaining on us."

"I know. Hang on, you're about to get a crash course in offensive driving." He jammed the accelerator to the floor and the glider bolted forward again.

"Don't say crash."

Suddenly Damien began to weave in and out, up and down, between other gliders, taking them on a carnival ride sans safety measures. He turned them sideways to sneak between two transport trucks.

Jade hugged the door panel and prayed to every god and saint she'd ever learned a name for. She'd just begun the rosary when the glider leveled out again, only to lose altitude. They hit the pavement hard. The safety harness bit into her skin with the impact. Blood seeped from the wound and ran down the front of her dress.

"Jade?" Damien took one hand from the toggle and caressed her face.

"I'm all right. What happened?"

"A little evasive maneuvering." He flicked her hair from her shoulder. "You're not all right, you're bleeding."

"It's nothing."

He clenched his jaw and concentrated on the road. "I'm sorry." He made for the next exit ramp, which turned out to have several exits that separated off each other about a hundred feet down. He slipped in between a new glider carrier and a dump truck. When it looked as if they would take one direction, he pulled the toggle a hard left and they took the exit for downtown.

Desperately lost, Jade looked around as buildings rose up on either side of them. The metropolitan behemoths blocked out the night sky and made it impossible to sense direction from ground level. One had to know their way around, or trust the navigational package on their personal transport. Jade didn't trust anything about Damien's glider, let alone the nav system.

Without warning they shot up onto the second tier level again. "Damn, your father's driver is good."

A pit of despair knotted her stomach. Quenton had been good, too. So good he'd died for it. She closed her eyes against the painful memory and tried to blot it out. Or block it before Damien discovered it.

"Hold on, babe. We'll have to go down the back allies and bad sections of town to shake him."

They turned down a one-way street, where minimal traffic moved at the late hour. "Shit. I hoped there'd be more people out and about tonight." He accelerated to full tilt just as the silver glider moved onto the road.

A red light at the next intersection showed that street crowded with traffic, and Jade braced herself for the force of a hard stop. It didn't happen. Instead, Damien lowered their altitude by half the distance of a tier and plunged onto the street, sandwiched snuggly between the first and second tier gliders.

"Oh, God!" At best they'd get stopped and ticketed for the illegal move, at the worst they'd be caught by her father.

A break in the conveyances had him lifting higher. "We have to find a place to hide for a while. Clare can't keep this pace up for much longer."

Clare? He'd named his glider Clare. Jade glanced to Clare's instrument panel just as a red light began to blink. So he could read the glider as well as her mind? "Where are we going to go?"

"I know a place, but I don't want to take you there until we shake your father and his evil sidekick."

A billboard overhead caught Jade's attention. It flashed a brilliant image of Little Ray's Used Gliders. "There!" She pointed to the sign. "Find that lot and pull in."

"Good girl," he said and slowed down a bit.

Panic rose inside her. "Why are we slowing down?"

Instead of answering, she got the image of her father's glider sliding in under them, then Damien pulling off a side road.

"Oh?" She blocked her doubts that it would work. If Damien was as determined as he said, her father had made it his life's work to bring determined self-thinkers to heel.

No sooner had the word left her mouth than Damien executed the maneuver, and Clare shuddered in protest. The poor vehicle wouldn't make it to their final destination, of that Jade had no doubt. As it stood, Clare seemed to be on her last good thruster.

Jade watched as her father's glider slid under them and lifted up into a break between traffic and up into the second then third tiers then bolted away.

"We lost them."

"Not quite, he's probably just trying to find a way to get turned around and come back for us." They pulled down a side street and cut across down under cover of office buildings and industrial parks.

Chapter 5

Damien finally pulled onto the glider lot and killed the engine and thrusters. Hopefully their pursuers wouldn't lift to the second story levels and see the dust settle from the landing. He hadn't told Jade they were spotted again. He'd watched her worry her lip with her teeth and squirm in her seat ever since he'd mentioned they were being followed.

"We'll wait here for a bit and then grab another ride." He bent forward to look out and up at the sky.

Jade bent forward as well and looked up with him. His glance slid from studying the nearby rooftops to the curve of her arched throat. He could see the pounding of her pulse beneath her delicate skin. Fear dripped from her in a steady bead, like some ancient Chinese torture. Angry red welts marred her skin, and blood spotted the neck of her dress.

Impotent rage closed his fist. How dare her own father hunt her like a dog for a simple act of disobedience. And Damien was positive it had been her sudden streak of defiance that had Jade's father so outraged. Five seconds in the man's presence and Damien knew her father to be a total control freak.

Lights scanned the lot above street level.

"Get down on the floor!" Damien leaned over the seat and pushed her down onto the floorboards. He covered her body, hoping the back of his black shirt would make them harder to spot.

Heat from her body radiated through his clothing. Sweet feminine scents filled his head and brought his mind and body to attention. Soft curves fit his, as he curled his arms around her, part in protection, part in desire.

A slight tremor passed through her body. "Shhh, Jade. I promise it'll be all right."

She turned her head and his lips brushed against her cheek. "You don't know my father."

"And you do, but you still left." Resistance low, he pressed a slow kiss to her face. "When we leave here, I'm taking you to a safe house. I know some people here. They'll hide us until it's clear."

They waited in silence for fifteen more minutes before Damien decided the way would be clear for them to move. "Get out."

"What?" Frightened eyes stared into his as she straightened in the seat.

"We're taking a different glider. I'm already getting warning lights all over the board. She won't make it to the third level garage where we need to park. Besides, it'll be harder for them to spot us straight off if we change vehicles."

She nodded and started to open the door.

Damon grabbed her before she could get out. "Please, don't think I would leave you on your own. I won't do that."

Silence said more than she ever could. He would just have to show her he meant to take care of her. Damn, his father never told him being a hero was so hard. But Jade was worth everything. His freedom, his sanity, even his life.

"When we get out, stay low. We'll be seen on the security cams, but any traffic from the street will have a hard time spotting us."

Jade nodded then exited the vehicle. Damien did the same and duck-walked around to the passenger side and took her hand. "Stay with me, babe."

Her hand squeezed his in answer.

It took him less than a minute to jack the glider closest to them. It was a fairly new model and had dark tint on all the windows. Damien smiled. It would be harder for Jade's father to track them in this vehicle.

When he was sure Jade was buckled in and safe, he went back to Clare and started to transfer what meager belongings he had chucked into the glider while waiting for her to join him at the café.

With a quick prayer he lifted the glider to only the street level and rolled them off the lot. A fist of guilt hit him square in the stomach as he looked back and saw Clare sitting on the lot abandoned like a used toy. She'd served his family well over the years. Back when his parents had saved the country from the maniacal mainframe computer, NATNET, his father had rescued Clare from the destruction of a parking garage and brought her back to his mother as a surprise.

"We can come back for her," Jade offered, reading his mood correctly.

"No, we can't. I'll ask Sam or Major to come back for her later." She didn't ask about the names, and he was thankful for that. She'd meet them soon enough and then she'd understand everything.

No lights were on in the third floor apartment, but what did Damien expect. He glanced at his watch. It was almost time for morning rush to begin. He and Jade had spent the better part of the night hauling ass and trying to evade capture. Exhausted and sick over her injury, he rang the doorbell.

It took a few minutes, but finally vibrations from inside the apartment announced that someone was at least awake enough to answer the door. A panel flashed to life beside the door. No video feed opened, only audio.

"Who is it?" Came a sleep-roughed voice.

"Damien and Jade. I need…" he didn't have a chance to get the rest of the words out before the door opened and a huge bear of a man hauled them into the apartment and relocked the door.

"Jesus Christ, Damien. What have you done?" Major ran a hand through gray hair and shook his head in disbelief.

"Did I hear you say Damien?" A low female voice came from the hallway.

Damien stepped around Major and held his arms out for Sam. "You did." His petite waif-like sister came to him and threw herself against his chest. "We've been so worried. Mom and dad are going crazy wondering what happened to you tonight."

"They know part of it then?"

Sam's dark gaze slid from his to look at Jade. "Just that you've kidnapped the only child of a very prominent member of the government."

Damien let out a long, slow breath. Well, she'd said her father was the local authorities.

"It's all over the vids," Major added and handed Damien a communication disk. "Call your mother now before you do anything else."

Damien took the disk. "I'd rather get Jade cleaned up and to bed before she drops. We took a nasty fall during the chase."

"I'll help her." Sam moved from Damien and held her hand out to Jade. "Sam Storm, Damien's sister."

Jade held her hand out and took it. "Jade Tanner."

Damien closed his eyes as a sick feeling moved through him. Of all the women to have as a Vartek partner she would be the daughter of the Director for the Eradication of Psychics.

Chapter 6

Sam helped Jade to cleanse her wounds and gave her a t-shirt and a pair of baggy drawstring pants to wear. The material felt soft and well broken in. Jade had never been allowed to wear pants, only dresses in the most expensive cuts and designs.

When she showed her to a bedroom, Damien was already ensconced in the bed, his arms folded behind his head, his gaze on the door.

He sat up when she came in. Sam bid them both good night and closed the door, sealing Jade in with a man whose entire attitude toward her had undergone a drastic metamorphosis when she introduced herself to his sister.

She stood there not knowing quite what to do with her hands, let alone where to sit.

"Come here, Jade." Damien lifted a hand from behind his head and held it out to her.

Instead of doing as she was told, she stood her ground. "Look, I know my father isn't a very nice man, but please don't hate me because of what he's done…"

"I'd never do that. I'll admit it was a shock realizing who your father is, but I'd never blame you, or hate you for something he's done. You're as much his victim as anyone."

Like Quenton.

Jade blew out the breath she'd been unaware of holding. She moved toward the bed and Damien scooted over to give her room. Weariness made her limbs heavy, but the uncertainties of her future made her head swim in possibilities. The foam mattress pressed down under her weight, cushioning her fatigued body in comfort.

"Did you talk to your mother?" Jade turned toward him and folded a pillow under her head.

"Yeah." Impossibly blue eyes studied her face, then moved to glance at the bandage on her neck and shoulder. "I'm sorry you got hurt."

"I know, but like I said it's nothing. I've been hurt worse." However, she wasn't going to tell him the worst of her scars would never show.

Silence descended on them. Jade had almost fallen asleep when he asked, "How much do you know about Varteks?"

"Enough to realize now that the voice I heard inside my head wasn't a mental breakdown and was my Vartek partner." She shrugged. "Though in all honesty, I'm finding little comfort in the knowledge."

His eyes went soft and caring. Compassion moved along the tenuous thread of their psychic connection. "Growing up with your father, I'd believe it."

For now, she'd skip telling him that it was worse than he could ever imagine. But when the time came, would Farroll Tanner be able to order the execution of his own daughter like he had so many others who had not agreed to conform to the standards and practices of the government? Or would he use her like a Guinea pig in some horrible lab experiment performed courtesy of her father's medical henchman, Dr. Onslow Ruskin.

She shuddered at the mere memory of the doctor. How many times had he come to the house for dinner and sat across from her, staring at her like he wanted to eat her instead of the meal.

Jade tried to push those thoughts from her mind and concentrate on the moment.

"You should have forgotten about me, Damien."

"And if you know anything about Varti males, you know that's impossible." Even as he said that she could feel how close he came to reaching for her. His want echoed through their link and nestled in her nerve endings.

Male Varti DNA was programmed to seek its mate and reproduce. Jade still found it odd that a byproduct of pollution and over-industrialization had created mutant genes that made psychic awareness and telepathy provable and more widespread than in the past. Thus began the government's need to contain and control a segment of the population that could very easily tip the scales of power. Some rumors said that Varti could communicate telepathically with other than their partners, but Jade had no knowledge to the validity of that statement. So, far she'd only picked up Damien's voice.

"So what do we do now?" She tried to steer the conversation away from the eventuality of their relationship. And deep down, Jade knew she would give in to his desire. Even now her own blood screamed to have him inside her.

His eyes dilated, but he shook his head and moved back from her a bit. An attempt to take temptation out of his way, no doubt. "Mom said it's too dangerous for us to come there. The authorities have already been to the house and questioned them."

"What about Sam? Isn't she in danger, too?"

"Eventually, but she usually uses my mom's maiden name hyphenated with Major's surname. It may take a while for the authorities to track her." He rubbed a hand down his face, scrubbing at the stubble that had grown in as they fled her father. "When we leave here, we'll go to a training facility in the Black Hills. You need to learn how to control your ability and I can only teach you so much."

She nodded.

He opened his arms for her. "Let me hold you while we sleep."

"Should we risk it?"

"Oh yeah, I think we should."

Hesitantly, Jade slid her hands around his waist and let him rest her head against his chest. She felt him kiss the top of her head. Such a small, tender action she hadn't been given in such a long time. It brought tears to her eyes.

He pulled her slightly closer so the stiff rise of his erection was cradled in the hollow between her legs. A slight moan left his throat. "I'm sorry."

Why would he be sorry over something he had no control over? She lifted her mouth and kissed the base of his throat. She settled back again and tried to concentrate on the softness of the bed and the fact she was free for the first time in her life.

The steady beat of Damien's heart and the brush of his hand up and down her back lulled her into a deep sleep.

Jade woke alone in the bed. She felt the sheets and discovered they were still warm. Damien hadn't left her too long before. The day had shifted into evening again, if the lack of light that came around the window treatments was any indication.

Deciding she'd better find her hosts and partner, she stood and opened the door. Hushed voices carried down the hall in a soft whisper of sound. A slight tremor of emotion filled her gut, just below her heart and made it hard for her to draw breath.

"You need to take her home, Damien. She's in danger being with you."

"She's in danger at home. Especially now. Do you honestly think her father's going to let her live when he discovers she's a Varti?" Damien stood by the kitchen counter, his body tense and ready for a fight.

Sam Storm stood on the other side of the room from him, stirring a pot that heated on the stove. "I don't think her father will have her killed. He'll probably just lock her up somewhere."

"That's still unacceptable." He looked at his sister, his eyes pleading with her to understand. "How would you feel if someone told you, you couldn't be with Major?"

She said nothing, but continued to stir the pot.

Jade walked into the room, uncomfortable with them talking about her and her future. She'd had enough of people deciding what her life would be or become. Now she was away from her father, she had no intentions of going back.

"I appreciate you taking us in, Sam, but I won't be bundled up and carted off to my father like an errant child." She crossed the room and stood close to Damien. She could feel his heat through the borrowed cotton pants she wore.

He shifted closer to her, his arm came around her waist. His hand spread wide across her rib cage and his thumb moved to caress the underside of her right breast.

Instantly, desire shot through her body, bringing her nipples to aching attention and pooling wetness between her thighs. Jade locked her jaws together so the moan would stay in her throat. But Damien knew it was there. She could tell by the way his body went rigid beside her.

He let his hand drop and shifted to put a little distance between them. "I need to get Jade some formal training. Mom suggested we go to the Black Hills and hide at the facility with Evangeline for a while."

Sam's gaze fell on her brother then turned to Jade. "Take my glider. I'll have Major return the one you took from the lot and try and get Clare back."

Damien shook his head. "Tell him not to risk it. The authorities will be all over you as soon as they discover you're connected in some way to the glider used to abduct Jade Tanner. They probably already have Clare impounded."

Jade's heart caught at the thought. He'd seemed really attached to that glider, and now he'd lost it in order to save her. She slid her hand into his and squeezed. The simple contact soothed as much as it ignited her again. "I'm sorry, Damien."

He shook his head, then slid his hand around her neck and pulled her close enough to put his lips against her forehead. His erection brushed against her stomach. "Don't worry about it, babe. I would much rather have you with me than Clare." The sincerity of his words shimmered on the pathways that linked their minds. He turned to Sam then. "We'll clear out of here in a few minutes."

The sheen of tears stood in Sam's dark eyes as she looked at her brother. "At least have some dinner before you go."

He shook his head. "We've imposed on you enough."

"Don't be silly. You're my brother. I love you. I'm glad you came to me for help." She started to pull containers out of the cabinets and place them on the counter. "At least take something to eat on the road. It's a long way to the Black Hills."

After a moment, Damien nodded. In this, at least, she was glad he took the decision making out of her hands.

The buzzer sounded on the front door, disrupting their goodbyes. Sam shot a worried look over her shoulder and hit the intercom but left the video off. "Yes?"

"Police. Open up."

Chapter 7

Damien took Jade by the hand and headed for the back of the apartment. There had to be a fire escape or a balcony somewhere they could climb out on.

"Where are you going?" Sam used a stage whisper.

"Trying to find another way out of this place. I'm not about to let them have Jade." And he knew as sure as the world was round that they had come for Jade. Him, they would execute immediately for taking her, but she would be taken back to her father to live only God knew what horrors.

"The back of our closet has a door into the adjacent unit. You'll come out on the other side of the parking garage, but they probably have it covered already." Sam shooed them down the hall with a frantic hand gesture. The door buzzer continued to sound. Insistent. Frantic.

"Come on." He didn't wait to call another hasty farewell to his sister. There wasn't time.

The closet was a large, double-door affair on sliding tracks with strip lighting. Damien pushed one side open and skid the clothes down the track. Damn it, Sam hadn't given them a clue as to how the door opened. There had to be a mechanism of some sort, but time was running out for them. They didn't have time to figure it out for themselves.

He started to move a box out of the way and there on the bottom of the wall, near the floorboard was an electrical outlet complete with red reset button.

Loud voices carried down the hallway as the police spread out to search the apartment.

With everything to lose, Damien pressed the button in hopes it was just a cleverly disguised door release. A click and a hiss sounded and the back wall of the closet popped.

"Hurry. Through here." He pushed Jade through the opening then resettled the clothes and the outer door as best he could before following her through into the next apartment.

No one was home, but the place definitely had occupants. No telling when they'd be home. At this time of evening it could very well be soon.

"We'll go to the garage stairs and up two flights. They'll expect us to work our way down to street level." Damien put his hand in the small of Jade's back. Anxiety zapped him like an electrical charge. He didn't have time to stop and comfort her, but he would make sure and do so later. At length.

Her silence worried him, but she hadn't stopped moving or refusing to do as he instructed, so he figured they were all right. If she started to drag her feet or argue they'd not get away from the police in time.

Before they could make it to the exit, the lock on the front door disengaged with a sharp click. Their luck seemed to go from bad to worse. The owner just came home. Damien pulled Jade up short and backed her into a dark alcove. Hands gripped his shirt, trembling through the fabric. He opened his mind and sent her a soothing thought. The grip turned into a soft caress.

Footsteps came closer, and Damien pressed backward from the small nimbus of light that spilled from the kitchen area. He held his breath, even while light puffs of air bathed him between the shoulder blades compliments of Jade. Instant desire swarmed through him like bees, stinging deeply beneath the skin.

Every breath she took drove her hard little nipples into his back. His hands fisted at his sides and his jaws clenched in the effort to keep from moaning.

A comm unit chirped.

"Hello." A male voice came just beyond the wall. He was really close.

The one-sided conversation continued, but moved away down the hall, Damien suspected the occupant headed to the bedrooms. At least that would give him and Jade time to escape.

He took her hand and pulled her along, staying close to the walls in case there were squeaky floors. Most wear occurred on the heaviest traveled parts of the boards, in other words, the middles. Plus, they were less likely to throw shadows down the hallway if they stayed to the sides.

The door made a creaky sound as Damien opened it. He stuck his head out and looked around. "Stay low." With that he pushed Jade out of the door.

This particular apartment opened up to the garage proper. The plan to walk up two flights was thwarted when the door to the stairwell opened and cops flooded into the deck, fanning out in search of the fugitives.

"Hurry, babe. Find a glider and stay there." He spoke into her mind, afraid to say anything out loud in case their voices echoed through the garage.

"What are you going to do?"

"We're going to steal another glider. We haven't got a choice."

She stopped in front of a very non-descript black glider with dark tinted windows.

"Good choice." It took him less than ten seconds to break in and jack the glider. He opened the passenger door for her.

The vehicle was luxury all around. The console was filled with an array of screens that showed various angles outside the vehicle. The cockpit had more bells and whistles than a band.

The owner would no doubt miss this pride and joy, but good insurance should cover the loss. Unlike Clare, this ride still had pneumatic closures on the doors. They lowered with a quietness that was truly a godsend. Now, if they could only leave the garage as quietly.

Damien and Jade buckled their harnesses. The liftoff was smooth and silent. But Damien only allowed the fine glider to rise a foot off the ground. Much more and they'd be caught. He pushed the toggle forward and they started forward.

"Halt!"

"Shit!" No sense in waiting to be caught. Damien pulled the toggle up and they rose quicker than he thought possible. Higher, too. They hit the garage roof and bounced off.

"Are you all right?" He turned to Jade who remained in a wince. The controls were much more sensitive than Clare's. It would take him a bit to get used to them. That's what happened with higher end, newer models. They could practically navigate themselves. All a driver had to do was get in and set a course.

Shots rang out, ricocheting off the glider's body in loud percussion.

"Get down, Jade! Don't get up until I say it's safe."

The harness opened with a loud click. She slid from the seat and hunkered down on the floorboards.

Had the police lost their minds? How did they even know they were firing on Damien and Jade? They could be some well-off businessperson on his or her way to work, or the opera, or whatever. They had only yelled the command to halt once. What if the person inside the vehicle had the music playing loud, or listened to messages on the communications system?

He shook his head at a system run amuck. Hadn't his parents risked their lives to fight such a thing?

He gunned the power and they shot out of the parking deck, leaving the angry police behind. They would follow. Even now they were probably searching for the stolen glider—though the owner had yet to realize it was even gone.

Damien glanced down at Jade. She'd curled herself into a ball, knees to chest with her arms holding her legs. She rocked back and forth.

For the second time that day he sent a soothing touch of his mind to her. She looked up at him and her eyes softened.

"I'm going to get us out of this, I promise."

"I believe you."

He let out a long breath. It was too early to tell if he deserved her confidence. "The next twenty-four to forty-eight hours might be a little rough. We have to get all the way to the Black Hills without being caught, which means a less than direct route."

"Would you think I'm weak if I told you I'm scared?"

A small bubble of laughter escaped him. "Baby, I'd think you were crazy if you weren't."

"Are you scared?"

"Terrified." It was the truth. He'd been scared to death since he'd realized his Vartek partner was somewhere out in the world waiting for him. Being with her now only intensified his fear. It was no longer about just his safety, but also Jade's. And damn it, it made all the difference in the world.

Chapter 8

Jade remained huddled on the floorboard. One hand gripped the dash, the other the seat. Both had white knuckles as Damien buzzed the glider in and out of heavy evening traffic. From her hiding place, she couldn't see much of what was going on. Occasionally she could see the lit undercarriage of a glider or transport as it passed overhead and shone through the sunroof. But that was it. The view and jarring of the glider as Damien moved expertly through evening rush hour traffic made her dizzy.

The onboard computer flashed, giving updates on other traffic in the area. Emergency vehicles such as police appeared as bright red dots on the screen. And they were coming up fast and hot on their tails.

Jade turned just enough to access the computer. It was too easy to find them with the global tracking device onboard. Most newer model gliders had them, and the most expensive ones had a computer interface that could disable them. At least that's what Quenton had told her. He'd turned off her father's GTD whenever they'd sneak away. Until that one awful night.

She swallowed down the memory.

Taking in a long shuddery breath, Jade tried to block the thoughts from her mind. She didn't want to be accused of broadcasting again, especially about something so private. Instead she centered her concentration on scrolling through the onboard computer's programs.

"Welcome to Astro Systems Advanced Driving Technology." The computer had a nice deep voice. Male. And since the computer spoke, it was probably on a voice activated control. However, most systems had overrides that could be utilized by technicians at the dealerships. She knew this from Quenton as well. He'd been the one to take her parents' personal transports into the shop for work.

"What are you doing?" Damien looked down at her, his brows pulled together in a frown.

"Trying to disengage the GTD. We're pretty much toast with it still active."

He shot her a hot smile that went straight to her groin, dampening the crotch of her panties. "Is it too early to tell you I love you?"

Her heart did a funny little cartwheel in her chest. "Save it until you mean it."

"Do you really wish to disengage the global tracking device?" The computer asked.

"Is there a button for 'hell yes'?" Damien turned the toggle to a hard left and

Jade had to brace herself. "How much longer until that kicks in? They're closing in on us fast."

"Give me a minute."

"I don't think we have a minute."

She pressed the confirm button and an unanticipated screen popped up. "It wants an access code."

"Don't tell me that." They rolled to the right, sending Jade against the passenger door. "Are you all right?"

She shifted her weight, and rubbed her head where she'd bumped it. She gave the screen another look. As she'd fallen away she'd hit the screen. The one now showing had color selections. Yes! Astrotint. It wouldn't solve the GTD problem, but it would definitely buy them some time.

Jade looked up through the sunroof, but couldn't make out anything. She rose up to sit on her seat. With the tinted windows she shouldn't be seen and it appeared the cops had quit shooting at them—at least temporarily.

Just ahead of them, two transport trucks hugged the two bottom tier lanes. Remembering their harrowing ride the night before, Jade couldn't believe the words that came out of her mouth. "Can you squeeze us between those trucks?"

"Do you have any doubt?" His eyes twinkled in the oncoming lights at the mere thought of doing more fancy driving. She didn't have to feel his thoughts moving through his mind in order to know that, she could see it on his face.

She leaned back and fastened her harness as Damien turned the glider up on its side and slid in between the two large transport vehicles. She held onto the straps and closed her eyes. "Tell me when we're through."

A sudden acceleration pushed her back against the seat. Then the vehicle jerked and righted.

"We're through."

Jade unfastened the harness again and leaned forward. Altering the car's appearance would help them marginally on a visual search, and might buy them time until she could figure out how to bypass the access code requirement. She had to at least try. So far she'd been nothing but a liability to Damien. Time to put her meager computer skills to work. Face it, if she could reprogram her father's security system, she could definitely figure out how to reprogram a glider.

He'd put his life on the line to save her. More than once. She owed him something.

In the back of her mind she wondered if she deserved it. Being a Varti wasn't anything she'd aspired to be, not like writing her poetry, it just happened through some accident of pollution. And yet, the most amazing man in the world had come into her life to try and bring her kicking and screaming into her own.

Scanning the Astrotint color selections she chose red for the interior and moonshine white for the exterior.

"Engaging Astrotint color change." The computer whirled and a warm feeling moved through Jade's bottom as the chameleon dyes changed the seat under her from black to red.

"Astrotint? This car's got the total package." Damien lifted his hand off the toggle and opened and closed it a few times. The heat must have shot through the navigation system as well.

"My mother has the same model glider. She changes the tint according to what she's wearing that day." Jade had always thought the option frivolous and a terrible waste of money and resources, but her mother loved it and if it bought them time, Jade would learn to love it, too.

Now, to tackle the GTD again.

There had to be a manual override for the access code. Quenton told her that every front door had to have a back one. That was just the way human nature worked. Everyone needed an escape plan. Programs were no different.

"What are you doing now?" Damien accelerated and took them down an off ramp into the south-bound lane of the highway.

"Never mind what I'm doing, where are you taking us?"

"Around the outskirts of the city. They won't expect us to go back the way we came. We'll pick up the highway west when we reach the turnoff."

It sounded like a dangerous plan, but it would work if she could get the damn tracker disabled.

She took stock of their position and the red dots on the screen as they swerved in and out between other vehicles. "Can you find us a pocket to hide in? Preferably one around an off ramp."

"Yes, ma'am." He lifted them to the third tier and over the tops of a caravan of heavy construction equipment. They came down right in the middle of the pack and hovered at second tier.

The quarters were tight, but at least they were surrounded by a wall of other transports. Jade set to work on the GTD. The first thing she did was turn off the voice interface. She didn't need the distraction of the computer telling her what she could very well read on the screen.

It took a few minutes but she finally found the override menu. It wasn't just for the GTD but for all the glider's functions. She touched the tracking control and switched it off. The dot on the nav screen that indicated their glider now had a black X over it.

"I think I did it." She leaned back in her seat.

A sensuous mental caress moved through her mind. Her nipples tightened painfully in response. Damien definitely knew how to make his appreciation felt.

It had been so long since anyone had appreciated her in such a manner. Men in particular. Her father never let her get close enough to one after Quenton to give them a chance.

The thought left a deep achy feeling under her breast bone.

Damien spared her a glance. "Something wrong?"

"No." She shook her head and looked out the window. "Disengaging the GTD only stops the flow of some signals, but the ones that are still emitted should get lost in the other transmission traffic."

A slow smile played at the corner of his mouth. "How did you learn that?"

Words choked up into her throat. All she managed to say was, "A friend."

Chapter 9

The sadness in her voice moved through their psychic bond. The person she referred to was more than a friend, and he didn't have to be her Vartek partner to guess that one. "When we stop for a minute, I'll take the chip out."

Jade only nodded and stared out the window.

He wanted to get her to open up to him, to share something of herself. So far all he knew he'd gleaned from those stolen snippets he'd gotten before she closed him out. But he could only imagine what her life was like living under the thumb of Farroll Tanner.

He took the next off ramp down and in through the city. Heat moved through his hand and rear as they passed under the viaduct in a smooth white color and came out as a safety-orange monstrosity.

"Good thing it's dark out."

She looked over at him and smiled. Looking at that slight curl to her lip was like putting his heart in a vice. He really couldn't wait to get her some place safe, where they could stop and take a deep breath and not have to worry about looking over their shoulders for her father and the cops. There wasn't a spot on her body he didn't want to take his time and explore. But if she were as private with her physical self as she was with her mind, he'd have a real long wait. Holding her while they slept had been good, but it hadn't been enough. It had been like sexual torture for him.

For months he'd dreamed of Jade, of how it would be when they finally met, so far his dreams hadn't been anything like his reality. Mostly because in his dreams they weren't trying to outrun the vary agency responsible for imprisoning and executing their kind.

He glanced at the nav screen. Only two lone dots followed them now. The rest of the police vehicles had split off from the pack to follow other off ramps and tertiary roads. The numbers were looking much better, but they weren't out of the frying pan yet.

The next off ramp took them into the downtown area again.

Jade turned and looked around as if just waking out of a trance. "I thought you said we were going to skirt the city?"

"I think it's safe to stop and change the registration and pull out the chip now. We'll just pull down an alley and find a glider to switch plates with."

Jade raised a brow at him. "Just like that?"

"All in the name of survival, babe."

She laid her hand on his arm as he took a left through the restaurant district. Her stomach let out a loud growl. "Can we stop for something to eat?"

They really needed to. When the police arrived at Sam's, he hadn't waited around to grab the food she'd put in bags for them. His first concern had been getting Jade to safety.

"Yeah. Once we get away from here. We'll stop in the next metroplex and grab something."

He found a glider parked on a side street and set their stolen one down beside it. It took Damien only a few minutes to change plates with the vehicle parked at the curb. He climbed back in and pulled the harness over him. "Change the color again. I don't want to risk being seen exiting the alley in case someone's watching from one of the storefronts."

She tapped the screen a few times. The glider turned a light sea blue.

"Much better than the orange." He smiled and lifted them off to second tier. "Now for some grub."

Full night had fallen hours before. Well fed, Jade slept in the seat beside him. After a quick bite on the run, she'd drifted off looking out the window at the passing miles. She hadn't spoken much to him either while or after they ate and the silence between them stretched as far as the distance before them. He could only imagine what was going on in her mind. Though he could pry, he wouldn't. Her secrets would be all the sweeter if she revealed them herself.

That didn't stop him from worrying about her opinion. He'd taken her from her home and put her on the run, chased by the police and made her afraid to show her face in the daylight.

Next time they stopped they'd have to find a way to disguise their looks. But how? He turned his gaze to her and drank her in.

She was even more beautiful than he'd imagined. Her long blonde hair looked like spun gold in the moonlight. Her profile was sheer perfection. Lips soft in repose begged to be kissed.

Damien leaned over and moved his hand down her cheek. Damn, was she ever soft. He let his mind wonder how she would feel all over. How it would feel to move inside her, her body tightening around him before she lost control and fell headlong into orgasm.

He shifted in the seat. His pants fit uncomfortably now. Sex between Vartek partners was rumored to be the most intense coupling imaginable, and Damien had waited so long to find out.

Jade stirred in her sleep. A sigh escaped past her parted lips. A glance down her body showed pert nipples pressed against the thin fabric of her borrowed shirt.

God, she'd picked up on his arousal in her sleep and had started to get aroused as well. He needed to reel in his emotions so he couldn't be blamed for coercing her into an act she would regret.

Her back arched off the seat as a throaty moan rose from her. Slim thighs parted. In a moment she'd have them both coming. He was damn near to bursting the seams of his pants.

Damien pulled the glider over and hovered on the shoulder. He powered down and set the glider on the ground then turned to her.

"Jade, wake up." Electricity shot through his hand when he touched her shoulder.

Green eyes glowed hot under heavy lids. A smile lifted the corner of her mouth. She reached out a hand for him and caressed his cheek.

Regret that they hadn't time to explore their feelings rocketed through him. He moved her hand away from his face, but instead of letting her go, he pulled her closer. Their lips met and hunger exploded in an arc of psychic awareness.

Her past moved through his mind in a kaleidoscope of sight and sound, as if it had happened to him. Loneliness enveloped him. How could such an amazing and beautiful woman be so lonely? Without friend or a family member to give her the love she so deserved. A face flashed through his mind, one smiling expression among many stern ones. It hadn't been just any face, but that of a lover.

Coldness surfaced at the thought Jade could have had another man in her life.

Then just as he began to feel the very essence of her memories, the mental door slammed shut on him and she broke away. Her hand covered her mouth and the sound of her heavy breathing filled the close confines.

Damien's breathing wasn't all that steady either. Every time he drew air in he could smell her, taste her on his tongue. Unconsciously he licked his lips, finding her there. A painful erection made it difficult for him to move back into his seat, let alone buckle the harness back over him.

Jade stared at him with accusing eyes. "You had no right."

"No right to what? Kiss you?"

She folded her arms under her breasts, lifting them in a tempting display she in no way meant. Her nipples were still hard and undermined her anger. Especially since his attention kept straying to them.

"No. To go through my memories like that. I could feel you sifting through them."

"What did I tell you yesterday about broadcasting? When we touch, it just amplifies what you're thinking. We need to get you some training, then you won't feel like you're being mentally raped." He turned away from her and started the glider. It was less torturous than staring at her amazingly pert breasts.

She rested a gentle hand on his arm. "Damien, please. I don't feel that way. There are just some things that I would like to keep private."

He took her hand and lifted it to his mouth, placing a gentle kiss on her fingertips. "That's all you have to say. I understand." But Damien knew what Jade didn't, as they became closer and their Vartek bond strengthened there was nothing she'd be able to keep from him, nor would she want to.

Through the front window he could see rays of light burning low in the eastern sky. Morning and sunrise would be upon them soon. Like a couple of vampires, it was time to find a place to hide for the day and get some sleep.

They rode in silence until he found a hotel off the beaten path and paid the desk clerk with untraceable credits. He never let Jade out of the glider, but told her to stay where the hotel staff or guests wouldn't see her.

When he got back to the glider he strapped in and put the guest register in the front windshield for the free parking. He turned and handed Jade a room key. "We're in 1212."

She took the small red disk from him and looked at it. He doubted she'd ever been to a cheap hotel like this, but too damn bad. Being an outlaw didn't include many luxuries.

Damien chewed the inside of his jaw in thought. Damn, it wasn't her fault he'd fucked up back there. He'd wanted to kiss her like that since he'd damn well laid eyes on her. And she'd given it right back until her memories had started leaking out. Could he help it if she didn't know how to keep her thoughts to herself? He'd already apologized, what more did she want from him?

The garage was as tall as the hotel with each floor having its own designated parking area. He took the up ramp and parked in the spot close to the catwalk that would take them to the hotel proper.

He hit the up button for the passenger door. "Go ahead to the room. I have some things I need to get before I come in."

She frowned at him and turned the key disk over in her long fingers. *"I'm sorry, Damien."*

The words spoke directly into his mind came with a gentle stroke. God, she was driving him mad and she didn't even realize it. He put up his hand to stop her apology. "Don't… don't be."

She placed a hand over her heart. A suspicious sheen filled her eyes and made them shine under the soft glow of the garage lights. If she cried, he wouldn't be going anywhere, and what he needed to get would see their next day go much smoother than today ever did.

"Go on. You'll feel much better after a shower and a nap."

She nodded and turned her back on him and walked into the hotel, shining her disk in front of the security doors. Damien waited until she was out of sight before he pulled away from the door.

Back on the street he pulled over again and looked through the onboard computer for a communication center. When he found it he placed a call he'd promised hours ago. They probably weren't even awake at this hour, but…

"Damien?"

His mother's anxious face showed on the screen. He could see his father moving around behind her. "Mom. I just wanted you and dad to know we're all right."

His father came into view. "You take care of that girl, and don't let her out of your sight. Tanner and Ruskin are both on the hunt for her."

What did the damn Doctor of Horrors want with Jade other than to lock her up in his so-called 'treatment facility'?

No, while they were on the road he'd be careful with Jade. But the guilt of leaving her in the hotel alone must have shone on his face, because his father let out a deep growl. "Where did you stash her? No, never mind. Don't say a thing. I don't know if this line is secure."

"She's safe. I'll call you again when we arrive."

"We love you, Damien," his mother said, tears standing in her eyes.

"I know. I love you both, too." He cut the transmission before the lump in his throat could choke him. They were his heroes and his role models. Everything he knew about being a man he'd learned from his father. His mother was the gentlest woman he'd ever met, but she had a steely core that made her one tough lady when the need arose. He saw the same quiet resolve in Jade.

He let out a slow breath and started the glider again. There were things he needed to do before he went back to the hotel.

Chapter 10

Jade moved around the room. It was quiet and comfortable. Small, but cozy. The bed was soft and pliable. She didn't care about that—she only wanted Damien back. As the minutes stretched out into an hour or more, she began to wonder if he'd thought better of the problems he'd gotten into by asking her to come with him? Would he just leave her here? Where would she go? What would she do with herself? One thing she'd never do would be to go home.

She sat on the bed and drew her legs up to her chin. Her hair, damp from her shower, hung down her back and made her shirt stick to her skin. The air conditioner cooled her, making her shiver.

If Damien never came back, she wouldn't give him up to the authorities. She'd swear she got away on her own and had no outside help. He'd given her freedom, and she would never forget him for that. It was a gift she could never repay.

The door hissed, causing her to jump. It opened and Damien came in carrying several large bags.

She rose and hurried to help him as he lugged them across the room. "You should have taken me with you if you intended to buy all these things."

"No. It would have been more dangerous. Besides I wanted to give you a chance to rest." He set the bags down on the bed and then reached for her. "Come here, woman."

She did and was enveloped in his arms. Warm breath stirred the hair around her face where it had begun to dry.

"I wasn't going to leave you. I just wanted to keep you out of danger."

The words came low and intimate into her mind. She loved it when he spoke like that to her. Considering how only a mere forty-eight hours ago the very idea of hearing his voice in her head filled her with fear, it was a major improvement.

"Did I broadcast that to you from so far away?"

"How do you think I found you? I could hear you if you were on the moon, babe."

Jade looked up into his face. Her lips parted as he dipped his head to take her mouth. This is what she needed. What she wanted from him. To feel the desire spiraling up from the very core of his being and out to touch the psychic cord that connected them, until it became part of her.

His tongue was warm and soft as it filled her mouth, stroking against hers. He tasted faintly of mint. She smiled.

"What?" He backed away and looked down into her face.

"You taste good."

He let out a moan. "So, do you."

He backed her up to the bed and when she fell back, he followed her down. Their legs tangled together. His hand slipped under her shirt and stopped just short of touching her breast. Jade looked down at her body. Her nipples stood out as if they wanted attention.

Damien's gaze locked on them and he smiled. "You've got the most sensitive breasts I've ever seen." His voice held a note of awe in it.

Slowly, his hand snaked up, moving the shirt up higher until he'd exposed her. "So beautiful," he breathed against them.

"So small." She started to cover them up. A man as sexy as Damien had to have had women with better endowments than she'd been blessed with.

"Perfect." He leaned over her and took one aching tip into his mouth.

Automatically her back arched off the bed. It had been so long since she'd made love. So long since she felt a man's tongue on her body. So long since such delicious sensations fissured through her.

Suddenly she had on too many clothes. She wanted to be naked and under Damien, his long hard cock deep inside her, giving her the release she needed so desperately.

His tongue worked her nipple until she thought she'd come from that alone. He laughed slightly and moved to the other one. "We don't want that yet, do we?"

She planted her hands in his lush dark hair. "Was I thinking out loud again?"

"Yes, but I don't mind it when I'm making love to you."

"It just feels so good."

"I know, babe. I know." Earnest blue eyes studied her for a moment. The look on his face solemn. "I promise you before we fall asleep you'll know what it feels like to have me inside you."

"I don't think I can wait."

"Maybe I can take the edge off a bit." He loosened the tie on her pants and pulled them down her legs. She hadn't put her underpants back on after her shower. "Lift your knees."

There wasn't enough air in the room. Jade tried to do as he said while she concentrated on breathing.

"Open your legs, babe."

Oh God, he would see her. All of her. And she was dripping wet.

Quenton and she had always made love in the dark, inside the car. Or he'd sneak into her room at the estate, but they'd never had a chance to see each other—just feel.

Damien laid a hand on her knee and gently wedged it between her thighs. "Please. You don't have to be shy with me. I want you so much…"

As if to test the truth of his words, she opened her mind to him. Heat, sharp and exotic, filled her veins. Desire rode him hard and he held nothing of it back from her. His mind grabbed onto hers and held firm. His pupils dilated. "*That's it, babe. Open your mind to me.*"

His hand skimmed lower and Jade let her thighs open for him. Gently, his thumb slid from her clit to her anus. An audible moan rose from his throat. "I have to taste you."

The breath in her lungs hitched. No. She wanted to stop him, pull him away, but excitement from him poured into her. Desperation tinged his thoughts, and made her unable to resist.

Then his mouth was there. His tongue taking the opposite path of his thumb. Nothing had ever felt as exquisite as his soft tongue lashing her clit and stroking her cunt. Her lips parted and she swore she could taste her heady woman's musk on her own lips. She licked them wondering if they'd be wet.

"You taste like sex should. So good and pure and mind-blowing."

Jade held his head and moved her hips back and forth as he worked. *"If you keep on that spot I'm going to come."*

"Hold onto it, babe. If you come now, so will I. I can feel how close you are."

What was she supposed to do? She wanted to come so much. He would have to have remarkable control, because she didn't.

He moved away from her suddenly and unfastened his pants. He pushed them down his legs then entered her in almost one fluid movement.

"Jade. Jade."

Mental sobs tore through her as she clamped down on him. He was big, and long and hard as velvet over steel. No man should feel so damn good inside a woman. Like he belonged there and no where else.

He moved his hips a few times. A slow torturous grind so deep inside her she was forged to him.

It was too much sensation. The act of making love with her Vartek partner gave new meaning to the saying, "Go fuck yourself." Not only could she feel him inside her, but how being inside her felt to him. The unbearable tight wetness of her cunt was incredible. How could he stand to feel so much along the length of his shaft?

She came on a cry that ripped straight from her heart. Hot pulses from Damien filled her. He bent down and rested his forehead to hers.

"I promise it will last longer next time."

"How can it. You touch me and I want you so much..." Her thought cut off as he bent over and kissed her, long and hard. The taste that filled her mouth was the same one she had on her tongue when he had been licking her pussy.

Jade ended the kiss and pulled back to look at him. "Do you like the way I taste?"

"I wanted that to last longer, too. But you're so damn hot. Christ, Jade." He shook his head and shifted his weight away from her, but remained inside. "You had me thinking of making love to you since the moment I touched your mind. Earlier today you had me so close, I almost came in my pants and that was just watching you get turned on in your sleep. It doesn't take much for me where you're concerned."

Heat rose to her cheeks and she tried to cover her face. The shirt remained rolled up under her chin, her breasts still exposed. She pulled the tail up to hide her face.

Damien laughed and rolled off her. "Don't be embarrassed. We'll get better at controlling our minds and bodies the more we're together."

Jade frowned and looked away. Damien took advantage of her turned head and nuzzled her neck. "What's the matter now?"

"I didn't disappoint you, did I? I don't have much experience."

He placed a finger under her chin and moved her face so she didn't have a choice but to look at him. "Neither do I."

She blinked a few times, unsure if she just heard what she thought she did. "I find that hard to believe."

He gave a sexy laugh. "Is that a compliment of my prowess or my good looks and charm?"

Jade found her own smile. "Well, the performance was too short to judge prowess on, so we'll say it's your good looks and charm."

"Oh, she knows how to hurt a guy." He rolled off her and lay on his back looking up at the ceiling. Their legs remained twisted together. Jade ran her foot up and down his calf. "The next time will last so long you won't be able to walk back to the glider."

She giggled and rolled so she could snuggle against his chest. His arms came around her and he put his face in her hair. "I love hearing you laugh, babe."

It had been so long since she'd laughed she didn't even realize she had. The thought sobered her.

Before the moment could weigh too heavy on her thoughts and Damien discovered how much it disturbed her, she sat up. "What's in the bags?"

He studied her for a long silent moment then sat up with her. He began pulling stuff out of the bags and placing it in piles. "Clothes for both of us. Shoes. We can't have you going around barefoot all the time." He gave her one of those slow sly smiles that turned up just the corner of his mouth. "Though I have to say, you have very sexy feet."

She smiled at him. "What else?"

"You've got a great ass."

There was no way she could keep from laughing at that, even as her blush intensified. "No, I mean what else is in the bags?"

"Oh." He pretended to break his focus on assessing her various body parts and pulled out two small colorful tubes from the bag. "Hair dye. We need to change how we look."

Just that quickly reality crashed back down on her. For a moment she'd been able to forget the danger they were in.

She'd never changed her hair color before, but there was logic to his suggestion. "I like my hair color, but for the sake of safety I'll change. What color did you bring me?"

He handed her a tube. "You'll be a sexy redhead when we leave this hotel. I'll be the hot blond."

Next he pulled scissors out of the bag. "And you'll need to cut my hair some for me."

"I've never cut anyone's hair before. What if I mess it up?"

"Cut it short, and we'll dye it afterwards."

Jade shook her head. "I love your hair."

Heat shot through her body directly from him as they both remembered how she'd grabbed it to hold him to her body while he made love to her.

"We'll leave it long enough for you to hold onto."

This time she turned red all the way down to her breasts. She pulled the shirt back down to cover herself.

Damien leaned over and kissed her softly. "Does it make you feel better to know that I think you're so beautiful it hurts to look at you? You're hair looks just like spun gold in the moonlight and the thought of you changing it tears my guts out. But I would rather have you with me and a redhead than blonde and taken away from me."

Was there any way she could shield her heart from him? If there was she didn't know what it could be. No power on earth could stop the outpouring of love she felt coming from her Vartek partner. No wonder the government feared their kind so much. The lengths one partner would go to in order to make the other one happy could probably be extraordinary if the situation called for it. Being loved and accepted so unconditionally was unlike anything she'd ever experienced in her life.

When she could finally speak again, her voice was low and emotional. "What else did you get?"

"A couple more changes of clothes for us, some snacks for the road," he reached into the bag and pulled out a large flat LCD plate, "and this."

He handed it to her, and she almost cried. She waved her hand over the on button and pulled the stylus from the clip. The light blinked a few times and the screen came on.

"I can't afford paper, but these are great. You can store thousands of gigs on one. I wanted you to have something to write your poetry on if you wanted to."

Not even her parents would have given her such a meaningful gift and especially when resources were so low. Not that her parents were ever low on resources.

"Thank you." The words didn't seem enough. She leaned over and kissed him thoroughly, letting her lips and tongue express the words that wouldn't come.

She pushed him down onto the bed and straddled his hips. His cock rose up full and thick between them. "Let me make love to you this time."

"So, you like it?" His hands snuck up her back, caressing her ever so softly.

"It's the most thoughtful gift I've ever received."

His smile was breathtaking, but he sobered quickly, his hands more insistent on her back. "I'd do anything for you."

As she rose up and slid down, impaling herself on him, she closed her eyes and whispered, "I know."

"I won't ever leave you."

She rose up and came down on him again. "I know."

Once again she opened her mind to him. It was a bit overwhelming to be able to feel not only her own enjoyment, but Damien's as well. And not just by taking cues from his body—she actually knew how it felt to have her tight hot passage slide down the length of him. The sensations flooding his cock felt as if they happened to Jade. She wondered if he understood how good he felt so deep inside her, filling and stretching to accommodate his size.

"*Yes.*" His hands settled on her hips and moved her back and forth a little harder.

"*Can you feel how it is for me? To have you inside me?*"

"Yes" The word broke through his lips and his back arched off the bed.

No wonder the sex was so unbelievably good. He knew exactly where to touch her, where to move to hit that sweet hidden spot in her.

He spread her butt cheeks apart opening her wider for his thrusts. It wasn't enough. She wanted more. Had to have more.

Reading her mind, he slipped a finger down between her cheeks and began to massage the rim of her anus.

As she came down on him, she pressed back against his finger.

"*Is that what you want?*" His mind voice had taken on a velvet quality.

"*Yes.*"

Gathering some of her wetness, he rubbed her anus again then slipped a finger in.

"More," she begged.

"You're so incredible."

Jade continued to move over him. His finger went in and out of her in a counterpoint to his cock. Leisurely, she slid her hands down the front of her body, massaging her breasts and plucking her nipples as she made her way down to her pussy.

"Yeah, touch yourself, babe."

Oh, she had every intention of touching herself. Damien made her feel so sexy she wanted to explore with him every sensual thought she'd ever had.

Spreading her fingers, she ran them through the soft hair covering her mound and found the sweet throb of her clit. She brushed her finger against herself as she rode him.

"Let go, Jade."

As if his words were a command she had no ability to resist, her body began to convulse around him. When she looked into his face, his eyes were narrowed and his jaw was clenched.

"Don't fight it." She kept the words in the open. She had a feeling he had his shields up anyways. He was determined to have a longer lovemaking session this time. She could tell.

When the last of her orgasm passed, Damien gently nudged her over onto her side. He brought one of her legs over his hip, coming into her as they lay gazing at each other.

Sweat broke out on his skin as he pumped into her. The sexy quiver of his abdominal muscles as he moved made Jade's fingers itch to touch him. She didn't resist. Running her fingertips down his body, she smiled when he sucked in his belly at her touch. She slid her hand farther, wrapping her finger and thumb around the base of his cock and holding him tightly.

Fevered blue eyes gazed into hers. "Incredible," he whispered before he leaned forward and claimed her mouth.

The taste of his passion was unlike anything else. She had kissed men before—well, Quenton—and though there was passion involved, it hadn't tasted the same as what came from Damien. His had a unique flavor, and it wasn't just the fact she could taste her own desire filtered back to her. No, this was something more. Something elusive.

His tongue stroked along hers. Just a gentle brush, cherishing the moments they were together, acting as if they were two normal lovers spending the day making love. Not two outlaw Varti on a cross-country adventure to outrun her murderous father.

Damien broke the kiss and frowned at her. "No thinking about anything other than us right now."

She nodded. "Kiss me again."

He obliged, rolling her to her back as he enfolded her in his arms.

The movement of his hips was much slower than it had been. Almost teasing now. He drew all the way out of her then came in inch by torturous inch. When he lay balls deep inside her, he gave a slow rotation of his hips, grinding his cock against a hidden spot that made her toes curl.

At her moan, he pulled out and repeated the process.

This time she anticipated the feeling of him hitting that one indescribable place and bore down on him when he touched her there. A cry tore out of her throat. Exquisite pleasure rolled through her like a new tide coming in.

Once again he pulled out and moved slowly to that spot. Her back arched and tears seeped from her eyes. Bliss broke over her and an unexpected cry rose from her throat. The orgasm blinded her in its intensity and depth. Then the warm rush of Damien losing himself in her started her coming again.

Jade could do nothing but throw her arms over his shoulders and bury her face in his neck. Sobs tore from her body.

"Jade?"

Once she started, she couldn't seem to stop.

Damien cradled her face in his hands and pulled her away from him. He looked worried and a bit scared. "Did I hurt you?"

She gave him a watery smile and shook her head. Really, speech was too much at the moment. Opening her mind to him, she let him see her feelings. The experience of making love with him that time had been so intense it had started a chain reaction. Emotions she'd tried to suppress for years, living under the thumb of her father had risen to the surface and been released.

Damien closed his eyes and rested his forehead on hers, still holding her face. No words were exchanged. The only thing that moved between them was the emotions that snapped like live power lines.

Chapter 11

Jade woke sometime later. She could hear Damien rummaging around in the bathroom. He hummed some tune off-key. There was a sound like the swish of metal. Scissors?

Did he get it into his head to cut his own hair? What a disaster that would be.

Jade hurried off the bed and found her pants wadded at the foot. Her shirt she couldn't find so she walked into the bathroom with only her pants on.

Wavy locks of dark brown covered the floor like a fur carpet at Damien's feet.

"What are you doing? I thought you wanted me to cut your hair?" She tried to take the scissors from him, but he stepped back. His longer reach held the shears far from her.

"You seemed a little squeamish about it, so I thought I'd at least get it started."

She closed the toilet seat and pointed. "Sit down and I'll even it up. You look like you've gotten bad hair advice from a demented stylist."

Taking up a stance in front of him, she lifted the jagged pieces of hair and tried to see how to go about evening them up. Under the harsh bathroom lights she could see varying shades of color, each strand different from the next. There were golds, coppers, auburns and sables. Gorgeous. She leaned forward and kissed the top of his head.

"Are you going to cut my hair or stand there with your pretty breasts in my face, driving me crazy?"

Jade glanced down and noticed he'd gotten hard again. She gave him a smile and started snipping.

With her hands up, Damien began to massage her breasts, plucking at her nipples until they were hard as pebbles. He leaned forward and ran his tongue around the puckered areola, barely touching the hard tip with the velvety side.

"Can't you wait?" The question was more obligatory than protest. If he wanted his hair even he wouldn't be doing that, but she didn't want him to stop either. Delicious sparks of desire threaded through her body.

He shook his head, his tongue lashing her as he did.

"I'll end up having to shave your head because your hair will be unfixable."

"You don't get it do you?" He pulled away and looked up into her face.

"Get what? I'm trying to finish your hair and you're trying to distract me? I get that." She tugged his hair and snipped.

He wrapped his arms around her, bringing her even closer. "That I've waited for so long for you, and now we're together and we're lovers and I want to spend as much time making love to you as I can."

"Well, I promise after we finish our hair you can make love to me all you want. Remember, this was your idea."

After that he really tried to behave, and Jade appreciated it. She finished his hair and stood back to inspect her work. It wasn't bad, but it wasn't good either. It had a kind of grungic chic to it that fit Damien Storm. "Once it's blond and we have some gel on it, it won't be half bad." Now the next phase of their transformations began. They took turns applying the hair color to each other then rinsing it out. Too bad they didn't make hair with Astrotint. The procedure would have been a whole lot simpler.

Jade lifted the edge of the towel, afraid of what she'd see. A coppery strand fell before her face and made her eyes go wide. The new shade would be anything but inconspicuous. The new look would be louder than a siren, sure to draw attention wherever they went.

"Come on, don't be shy. I showed you mine."

Jade met his gaze in the mirror. He looked great as a blond. They had only taken a few strands here and there and added to the gold of his hair. It looked more like he'd spent weeks in the sun. The result gave his hair depth and texture. For something that had been a disaster in the making, his hair turned out looking very natural.

Damien unwrapped her hair and let out a low whistle. "Wow."

She frowned. "It's your fault."

"No, I didn't mean that as an insult. Just. Wow." He pulled the dryer from the wall and started to separate her hair into sections. A few times their gazes met in the mirror, but mostly he concentrated on his work. His fingers were busy running through the strands and making sure they were dry.

When he finished, Jade watched him as he stood back and admired his work. "You look amazing."

Unsure what that meant in relation to how she looked before, though he'd already said she was beautiful, she had to admit the red against her skin made the green of her eyes stand out more.

Damien pulled her hair to the side, baring her neck. He pressed warm lips to her nape then moved to the side. One large hand came around her front and spread over her belly. "I want you again."

He really didn't have to say it. She could feel the rush of endorphins through the tether of their link. That and his erection rode the seam of her butt cheeks.

With deft fingers he plucked the string on her pants then pushed them down. "Bend over."

Excitement shot through her. "What?"

"Bend over the vanity and spread your legs a little." He put words to action and gently pushed her forward. "I've never made love to a redhead before."

An instant heat filled her.

Damien slid his hand lower on her mound, petting her before finding her clit.

"You're already wet and ready for me."

With his other hand he opened her wide and shoved into her. Jade gasped. They'd made love so many times she felt sore and swollen inside. Multiple times in a night was definitely not the norm for her. She and Quenton were lucky if they managed to sneak their sessions in once every two weeks.

Damien put his mouth near her ear. "I'm sorry, babe. I'm sorry."

She reached behind her and caressed his bare hip, telling him with a touch that she was fine.

She let her eyes slide closed. Couldn't bear to look at herself in the mirror. It wasn't that she felt guilty, or as if she was cheating on Quenton. He'd been dead a few years. He would have wanted her to be happy. And God in heaven Damien made her happy. With him she could soar as she had never been allowed. With him, she didn't have to worry about being herself.

He'd bought her an LCD screen for her poetry.

"Open to me, Jade." He thrust into her hard and fast. His balls slapped her bottom with every movement.

Each plunge drove her forward. The corner of the vanity ate into her belly. Her breasts were mashed against the cold title. The lovemaking wasn't tender as it was before, this time Damien seemed driven by other forces.

"Please, open your mind."

She dropped the shields and let him in. Immediately her body and mind were caught on the razor sharp edge of Damien's love. Pleasure curled around the sides of her brain and enfolded her in a hazy swirl of need.

"Come with me, babe."

If he held her just that way, pressing his thumb against her, working slow circles around her entrance where their bodies joined, he'd have his wish.

He picked up speed, going at her like a man out of control. Putting more pressure on her clit, she started to come.

He threw back his head and let out a cry as he came in response. Jade watched him in the mirror, struck by his perfect masculine beauty and the power that radiated—essential as air and blood.

What divine miracle had bound them together?

He leaned over her, his breath harsh in her ear. His skin was burning to the touch.

Standing with her back to him, his arms around her, she felt safe and content, ready to face any challenge as long as he was beside her.

Was it possible to fall in love with someone after so short a time?

"Let's grab a shower and a few more hours sleep then we need to blow this joint."

Jade nodded, not willing to disrupt the thoughts rumbling around in her brain. Thoughts she tucked away lest she broadcast them again. There would be time to let Damien know how she felt, but not now. Now, if she ever lost him like she did Quenton, she'd never survive. She'd been down that rocky road before. The grief of losing a loved one crippled until the only way to survive was to keep moving forward until you finally outran the pain, or let it pull you under into despair and live in a husk of your former self. Losing Damien would completely eviscerate her. She knew that based on past experience.

Chapter 12

The Black Hills rose up before them, an endless expanse of untamed beauty. The urban sprawl ended where the national forest began, a sad testimony to the country's overpopulation. With over a billion and a half people living on her shores, the good old US of A had to put all those people somewhere.

Now, the only places with a discernable natural landscape were inside the protected borders of national parks.

When Damien and Sam were children, their parents took them on a countrywide tour to visit all the parks and landmarks. His father, Jesse, had been convinced that one day the government would find a way to take even those protected sites away and build housing or strip malls to provide for the overabundance of citizens.

Despite the melancholy reason for the trip, it had proven to be one of Damien's best childhood memories. It had seemed that everywhere they stopped people knew his father and were eager to let the Storms stay with them.

"I've never seen anything like this." Awe had Jade's voice lowered to nothing but a whisper. "Pictures on the web doesn't do it justice."

He turned and smiled at her. "The first time I saw them I had my face pressed to the glass in Clare's backseat. I couldn't believe the mountains were real."

"Your parents brought you here?"

He nodded and looked to the winding highway that led up the side of a mountain. They'd be leaving the paved road soon, but needed to wait until nightfall for that. In the two days since they'd left Sam's they had only traveled at night, until today.

News feeds coming over the glider's comm system mentioned that Jade Tanner and her abductor had vanished from sight. Of course there was the possibility that the authorities were sitting back and watching, waiting for Damien to show them to the Vartek safe haven.

Jade sat in the seat beside him, twirling a long piece of coppery hair around a finger. She looked out of the windows staring wide-eyed at the unspoiled landscape that spread out on the near horizon.

After a moment of silence she turned her attention away from the mountains and back on her project. Her LCD screen lay on her knees. The stylus made a slight popping sound as it glided across the smooth plasticine surface.

She'd been making notes most of the morning. Every once in a while he'd catch her trying out a phrase by whispering it to the air. Over the low hum of the glider's thrusters he could barely hear her. He wouldn't have even known what she was doing but her lips were moving. The first time he'd asked her to repeat herself, thinking she'd spoken to him.

Watching her create a poem as they drove through the country filled him with such pride, he wanted to shout. Every person who passed them on the highway he wanted to hail and tell them how clever and incredible his woman was.

His woman.

Not just his Vartek partner. Not just his lover. His woman. His other self. The other half of his life force.

A bleep on the nav screen caught his eye.

Behind them about a half mile and gaining fast was the unmistakable blue flashing lights of a police glider. Damien took a deep breath and tried to stay calm. It was possible that the siren was in response to an emergency on the highway ahead of them and had absolutely nothing to do with him and Jade.

They'd just have to wait and see.

He kept his speed steady and for once since their journey began he refrained from making any fancy maneuvers. The last thing he wanted was to call attention to them if the police were after someone else. It wasn't worth blowing the rest of the trip. They'd come too far.

A rest area rose up in the center island of the roadway. There was a several story structure there with restaurants and shopping mall, so Damien pulled off to the left sided exit and climbed to the third tier parking and stopped the glider.

Jade gave him a skeptical look. "Hide in plain sight?"

"You might say that. No sense in letting him know he *should* be chasing us just in case he isn't." Damien let the pneumatic hinges up and the doors lifted. Hot summer air filled the car.

"Are you getting out?"

"We might as well." He took a glance at the busy rest area. "It'll be harder to find us if we're out of the glider."

The police cruiser in question flew by with sirens wailing and lights flashing. Two more pulled out of the rest area lot and hit lights and sirens as they sped in the same direction of the first cruiser.

"Something bad must have happened." Jade followed the speeding cruisers with a worried look. "I hope we don't run into it later."

"No, we'll try and stay here for a while. Hopefully, by the time we leave whatever it is will be taken care of." Even saying it out loud he didn't believe it. The hair on the back of his neck tingled, and he didn't think it was from the heat. Something big was about to go down somewhere.

God, he hoped it wasn't the Varti facility.

With the powerful surveillance equipment owned by the government, it would only be a matter of time before authorities found the hideout. Talks were underway to relocate to a new place, perhaps up in Vancouver since the Canadian authorities tended to turn a blind eye to psychic powers.

But Damien took a stubborn stance. He was born in this country. His parents had risked their lives to free the people from the yoke of tyranny and he'd be damned before he would surrender his rights to live in the country of his birth.

"Come on, let's grab some dinner while we're here."

He walked around the front of the glider and waited for Jade to get out. As they entered the service complex, he put his arm around her, holding her close to his side.

Her hair smelled like apples from the hotel shampoo and Damien couldn't resist the urge to bury his nose in the glossy strands.

"I promise you, we won't always have to run," he whispered against her temple.

Jade looked up at him with nothing but love in her eyes. "I know."

The shopping center section of the complex was busy for the time of day. People moved from one kiosk to the next in no great hurry. If they were road-weary travelers, they certainly didn't appear so. Damien would have been happier had everyone been rushing about trying to maintain an impossible schedule—it was easier to overlook two people in a crowd if you were too busy with your own thoughts to notice—as it was he'd have to hope their altered appearances disguised them enough that the casual observer wouldn't notice them.

The offerings at the food court weren't promising and the prices were steep. Damien looked up at the brightly lit menus hanging over the counters. "I think we should share a meal."

Jade nodded. "I wish I could get to my money, but I'm afraid if I try..." The words trailed off. She didn't need to say more. They both knew her father probably had people watching her accounts for activity.

"We have enough to get us where we're going." He placed his hand under her hair at the nape of her neck. "But these prices."

Jade turned to steer him away from the restaurant fronts. "Let's see if there's a small grocery here. We can stock up and save money."

Damien pivoted and started for the other end of the complex. Most rest areas near national parks had some form of grocery for those going into the park to camp. There would be plenty of food where they were headed, but bringing some of their own supplies along to help out wouldn't be taken amiss.

They moved through the crowd, indistinguishable from all the other vacationers wending their way through the pedestrian traffic.

A communication's kiosk had a display of various screens all tuned to a local station. As they passed, a vid feed began with breaking news.

Two bodies flashed on the screen horribly disfigured. Half of the bodies were burnt by what looked like a small flash-fire. Long blonde hair was painted with thick dark blood. Only the ends remained untouched.

"The bodies, though resembling the physical descriptions of kidnap victim, Jade Tanner, and her abductor, Damien Storm, have been confirmed by officials to be that of two persons living in the west side housing project. Police are working on the theory that Storm may have killed the couple in order to call off the three-day manhunt which has stretched across the entire country and involved multiple state and government agencies." The reporter looked into the camera as if she were pronouncing judgment on Damien.

Damien shook his head and pulled her away from the screens. He lowered his face to her head. *"Your father probably had them killed in order to flush us out."*

"How could anyone believe you'd do such a thing?" Pain and worry shimmered through the tenuous thread of their link.

"People will believe it all right. We have to find a way to clear my name while we're trying to free the other Varti."

"But they have no proof you and I were even there."

Damien shook his head in disbelief of her innocence. Sometimes he really had to remind himself that he had grown up in a very different world than Jade. Her parents sheltered her, though she'd admitted she knew the depth of her father's machinations.

"They can fabricate that proof. Lie about it. No one's going to call your father on it."

Jade stopped and turned to him. Her eyes blazed with conviction. "I will."

Chapter 13

After hearing the news feeds, neither of them felt like eating. They found the grocery and bought a few supplies then got back on the road. The sooner they arrived at the facility the better Damien would feel. It just wasn't a good time to be out wandering about the country.

By now the manhunt had intensified, especially with murder charges hanging over his head. The irony wasn't lost on him. The man accusing him of murder was the most vicious prick to ever sit a seat in government. Not even the mainframe computer that had tried to take over the country thirty years before had been as treacherous what Jade's father proved to be.

They moved along the highway to the small town of Shiloh Mission, where they'd pick up the ramp that led directly to the park.

Traffic stalled ahead of them. Police gliders spread across the lanes. They were checking every vehicle and checking identification. Damien rubbed his thumb over his fingers. He'd never had alterations done to his prints. Once they scanned his hands, he'd be caught.

A side road jutted out from the main expressway. Damien slowed and put on his signal indicator, as if that had been the turn he'd wanted all along. They would have to get to the facility by a circuitous route.

The sun had set by the time they made the facility, nestled in the shadows of the Black Hills. Externally it didn't appear to be a large structure, more of a sturdy building used to house utility junctions. At least that's what the warnings on the outside read. Inside, however, the base spread and sprawled inside the earth. Every year more of the mountain was hollowed out to afford more living space to those who sought shelter from the long arm of government.

It was safe, but no way to live.

Damien brought the glider up to the security gate. He raised the pneumatic doors and punched the code into the key pad. Fencing rose from about the twelve foot level then ran parallel to the ground, preventing intruders from lifting their conveyances high enough to breach security.

The effect made Damien feel as if he were trapped inside an aluminum butterfly net. This butterfly net bit with an electric charge that would fry the mother board on any glider that would try to smash through. Varti were nothing if not resourceful and highly protective of their own.

The gate swung open and Damien closed the glider doors and started through the opening. A bright spotlight lit the front of the building, tracing their progress across the drive. When they rolled around to the back parking lot, a few people stood outside waiting to see who had just rolled through their security gates behind the toggle of a very expensive ride.

Damien recognized one of the women, a tall stunning lady with slate gray hair and high cheekbones that suggested a strong Native American heritage.

Evangeline Donner smiled and held her hands under her chin when she recognized Damien. "We were really starting to worry about you."

"I didn't want to contact you in case someone was listening. I thought we should maintain communications silence." He walked around the back of the glider and held out his arms for the woman who had trained him in the use of his Varti gifts. She'd been as close to him in childhood as his own mother. And still was.

She met him halfway and enfolded him in a motherly embrace. When she pulled away, she placed long elegant fingers on either side of his face and studied him closely. "Despite the poor hair color choice, you look good. All things considered."

He smiled and kissed her soundly on the cheek.

Jade climbed out of the glider and stood a little behind and to the side of him. Her anxiety fissured through their link. Her hands opened and closed nervously before her.

Stepping back to her, he placed an arm around her waist and brought her to meet Evangeline. "Evangeline, I want you to meet my partner, Jade Tanner. Jade this is Evangeline. She taught me everything I know about being a Varti."

Jade nodded and held out her hand.

She'd gotten so quiet. So unsure.

He tried to touch her mind, just a tiny brush to reassure, and came up against shield thicker and sturdier than the side of the mountain where they stood.

He slid an arm around her waist. If she wouldn't allow him to comfort her mentally, he'd have to do it physically.

Studying the faces of the other Varti, he didn't recognize any of them. Their curiosity tinged with resentment put an odd taste in the air. Not everyone at the facility was glad to have them come here for help. Evangeline would never turn him away, no matter what.

Had they heard the news feeds and believed he'd killed those poor people to cover his tracks? He'd had enough with "normal" people thinking he meant harm, having suspicion fall on him from his own kind was too much.

"I'm sorry, maybe we should go."

Evangeline turned an angry glance on the people behind her. "No. You stay. They don't like it—they can go. But we do need to talk." When he started to say something in his defense she shook her head. "Not out here."

So, she suspected government surveillance this far into the foothills. It was a wonder they hadn't moved on the inhabitants.

Evangeline put a loving hand on his shoulder and steered him into the building. Damien in turn kept his hand on Jade.

"Have you eaten?"

When Damien indicated they hadn't, Evangeline showed them down a long hallway lit by small globes, but had no windows. They were heading into the hill.

As they walked, his ears began to build pressure, though from the floor he couldn't tell they were moving downward.

The hall ended in a large living area where a huge screen took up one wall and comfortable furniture was grouped in varying sized arrangements around the room. It was most likely the communal entertainment room. It was a recent addition that he didn't remember from his last visit.

They moved through the living area without stopping and out a door on the left of the room that led to a short hallway. This one opened into a large comfortable dining area.

"Have a seat and I'll send someone to bring you some plates. We ate a few hours ago, but there's always something that can be heated up on a moment's notice."

Jade took a seat next to Damien and started to shake her head. He thought to tell her not to bother, but Evangeline overrode her with a look.

They didn't talk about anything of import until after the food arrived. Evangeline had a steaming cup of coffee in her hand. She blew across the top and took a sip. "I'll be up the rest of the night after I drink this, but I can't help myself." She set the cup back down and folded her hands in front of her. "Now, what do you know about the murders today?"

The food Damien had just swallowed was in danger of coming back up. He set his fork down and stared at Evangeline. "You don't…"

Quickly, she held up her hand. "No. Never. I just wanted to know if you heard anything out on the road about the victims. You had to pass right through the town where the murders occurred to get here."

Damien had known that, but he didn't want Jade to know. She shot him a look of betrayal. Under the table he placed a hand on her knee and squeezed it, begging her with his touch to hold on and understand.

Though they had said nothing, nor even exchanged thoughts, Evangeline easily read their body language. "Ah, you didn't tell her. I'd be mad too if I were her." She waved the comment away with a graceful hand. "But we'll get to that in a moment. The victims were a Vartek pair, known very well by this safe house. Aislinn and Conner Merritt were making strides with a local Senator to make South Dakota a haven for all Varti. There is a bill up for consideration in the state legislature called the Inclusion Bill. That bill, though not specific to only Varti, would mean that all persons exhibiting psychic talents could not be prosecuted solely for possessing such gifts."

Damien had heard that there were groups trying to break down the concrete wall of fear against his kind, but he had no idea it had gotten as far as a state legislature. Even a single state would be progress.

Somehow the bill didn't seem to make Evangeline as excited as it did him. "Is there a problem with that?"

She nodded and suddenly looked wearier than he'd ever seen her. "It had its problems before, but now." She threw her hands up. "The murders of Aislinn and Conner and the fact the authorities in all their stupidity pinned the act on you— another Varti. I have no doubt in my mind those murders were staged to garner two-prong results."

For once since arriving at the compound Jade spoke up. "Oh, God. My father had them killed not only to discredit all Varti and attempt to flush us out, but to kill the bill as well. Who is going to back legislation that would make it unlawful to prosecute a Varti?"

Evangeline nodded. "You know your father well."

"Unfortunately, I do." Her hand crept into Damien's where it still rested on her knee. She squeezed it. "No one is going to dispute him. If Farroll Tanner tells the world that Damien Storm killed those people, then he killed them. The authorities won't look any further into the story, or even look to see if any evidence corroborates their findings. No one will question it."

Evangeline gave a half smile. "Don't be too sure."

Damien had no idea what that meant, but he'd bet his last dime that Varti had been gaining positions of power, infiltrating the government in an attempt to overthrow their subjugators. It was what people like Farroll Tanner feared most, and the thing he could have avoided had he let the Varti live in peace.

Tipping her cup up, Evangeline drained the last of coffee. "We'll talk more in the morning. When you finish eating, I'll show you to your room. You're probably exhausted after the last few days."

Damien couldn't seem to do more than pick at his food after that. How could things have gotten so screwed up? He knew contacting Jade came with risks, but he'd stepped in some deep shit this time. Having an angry father after him that was willing to kill and frame him didn't exactly bring comfort or a positive outlook for the future.

And Jade.

She'd been so quiet since they arrived at the hideout. If he only picked at his food, Jade had done nothing more than rearrange hers.

Damien stood and pushed his chair in. "Come on. Let's go get settled in."

She wiped her mouth and placed her napkin on her plate. As they walked behind Evangeline to their room, Jade wouldn't look at him, nor did she let her shields down long enough to let him know how she felt or what she thought of the situation.

Their room was small and utilitarian. Only the basic amenities were contained within the four plain beige walls.

"We're in the process of renovations, so I apologize for the barren room, but there have been several new arrivals the last few weeks and space is at a premium." Evangeline stood at the door, allowing Damien and Jade to step through and investigate their surroundings.

Damien turned a three-sixty and nodded. "It's fine. We appreciate the risk you're taking by letting us stay here. With any luck it won't be too long. Jade seems to be a quick study."

"Jade seems like she doesn't need much help. Her shields are strong."

He turned a knowing smile to Jade. "Yeah, but on occasion she broadcasts. It's very distracting."

Jade frowned at him and excused herself to the small bathroom.

The door gave a quiet click and he ran a hand through his hair and blew out a long breath. "It's been a long day." The apology sounded lame, even to him but he didn't want Evangeline thinking badly of Jade.

He should have known better.

"Give her time, Damien. It's only been a few days since you took her from everything she's ever known. Not only that, but she's dealing with heavy issues right now. Her father is a cold-blooded murderer, and her Vartek partner is being accused of it."

If Jade dropped her shields he'd be able to feel her thoughts, he wouldn't have to rely on assumptions. He hated assumptions. They had a way of being inaccurate.

Evangeline said good night and closed the door behind her. Damien took the time that Jade sequestered herself in the bathroom and went back to the glider to bring their meager possessions to their room.

When he returned, Jade lay in bed with the sheet pulled up and tucked under her arms. Her shoulders were bare, suggesting she had nothing else on. Damien's blood ignited.

"Come to bed, Damien."

"Are you going to talk to me before we make love?" He sat down on the bed and took her into his arms. "Why don't you tell me what's wrong instead of letting me guess?"

"I don't know if I can. These are friends of yours and I don't want to say anything against them. They've given us a place to stay…"

Damien pulled away from her and ran a thumb over her full bottom lip. "You might not believe this because we haven't known each other long, but I love you, Jade. Yes, I've known Evangeline a very long time—hell, she practically raised me, but if I ever had to choose between you and her, you'd win. No question."

Her breath hitched and she took his hands in hers. "You may not have felt it when we first arrived, but as soon as you introduced me as Jade Tanner, the rest of the Varti wanted nothing more than to see me a million miles from here. My father's the reason these people are in hiding. They may say we're welcome to stay here, but deep down they want me gone."

"I guarantee they'll leave you alone. If they turn us in they all go down. You're father wouldn't let even one Varti walk out of here alive. You know that." He lifted her chin with a knuckle then brushed his mouth against hers. "Enough of this for now, I seem to remember you invited me to bed."

Her lips parted beneath his. The soft slide of her tongue against his melted him. Fire leapt from the point of contact down his body, hardening him in an instant. Just the act of kissing Jade made him long to push inside the wet silk of her.

He pushed her back against the pillows, crawling over the bed as he did. She lifted her arms to wrap around his shoulders and the sheet slipped down to reveal her breasts.

Damien tore his mouth away from hers and moved down her neck, kissing her skin with teeth and tongue before finding the hard point of her nipple and teasing it until she whimpered.

Her thighs parted and radiant heat warmed his cock through both sheet and pants. Christ, if she was much hotter he'd start crying like a baby. No man deserved to have such a woman want him. Especially not him. How did he luck out and have a psychic link with Jade? To have her go supernova in his arms.

She moved under him, bringing the hot center of her sex to nudge against him.

"Not yet, babe. Not yet. Let me take my time and love you like you should be loved."

"When you're touching me, I don't want to wait. I want you inside me."

Determined to slow down their lovemaking this time, Damien moved to her other breast and began the sensual assault there. She'd just have to wait. They needed to learn control, and the only way to do that was to force each session to last a little longer. To not give into the overwhelming need to plunge inside as if life depended on the strength and ferocity of the act.

He drew his tongue around her puckered areola. The nipple jutted out, diamond hard, needy. He used small nips of his teeth followed by long gentle strokes to prolong her torture.

Her hands came down on his face and held him there. Tremors moved though her body. Her legs grew restless under his.

He moved lower, dragging the sheet down her belly. With both hands cradling her ribcage, he used his mouth to nip and lick as he went. He circled her navel, dipping just the tip of his tongue inside before moving lower.

He rubbed his cheeks against the soft hair covering her. Women's musk filled his nostrils and head. Wet and inviting, she drew him like a man crossing the desert in search of water. Bracing his hands on her hips he brought her up to his mouth.

Her hand gripped his hair. Her back arched as he began to lick and suck her the way he had her nipples. There were no words to describe her taste. No way to verbalize the way it felt to love her so intimately. To know he gave her such mind-blowing pleasure.

Spreading her wider, he parted her lips and kissed the taut peak of her clit as it protruded outward.

Jade moaned and writhed under him.

He did it again, drawing it into his mouth this time. Her hips rolled forward.

"Damien." The word came out more sigh than name.

Paying attention to the clues of her body, he ran his thumb over the seam of her cunt, pushing in just enough to watch her bare down on his thumb and take him partway inside. He pulled it back, teasing her with the sensation.

He sent his mind brushing against hers again then retreated. Staying linked while they made love was too overwhelming. Pushed him too close to the edge too fast. In order to control the pace, he had to limit the amount of psychic contact, even while he increased the physical.

Slowly, he trailed his thumb down the length of her, coating her with wetness as he moved. When he reached the ring of her anus, he pushed inside, never once letting up on the attention to her clit.

"Ahhhh…"

"Not yet."

He wanted to think the command and feel the irresistible pull of pleasure as it moved through her, but he didn't want to open the channel. To do so would invite disaster at this moment. They'd be back to square one. He'd come in reaction to her and they'd have to wait until he was ready to make love to her again.

In all his training as a Varti, he'd never been told that holding onto control with his lover would be akin to pulling on a greased rope. Just when he thought he'd make it to safety, the line tugged out of his hands and control rushed outward.

He continued to work her, letting his tongue slip inside her passage, tasting her to the fullest.

Her back arched up like a contortionist's.

"Damien… love… ahhh… so good…"

Brief words flashed through his mind, leaking from her thoughts.

The woman picked a hell of a time to start broadcasting.

His erection stood painful beneath his fly. With shaking fingers he undid his pants and pushed his underwear down enough to let his cock get some breathing room before he strangled.

"More… unbelievable… right there…"

A smile touched his lips. Sometimes broadcasting wasn't a bad thing.

"Quenton."

And sometimes it was like a bucket of cold water.

Damien moved away from her, trying not to let his hurt show. Their lovemaking was remarkable and here she lay with her legs spread and his face in her pussy, thinking of another man. He didn't know what to say or how to act.

He blinked a few times. His heart went to lead in his chest.

Jade looked up at him in confusion. "Why'd you stop?"

Damien slid off the bed and headed for the bathroom. He wouldn't be able to talk to her with her juices all over his face. The smell and taste of her haunting his senses. Besides, if he stayed in the room with her she'd see the look on his face, and he was sure she'd be able to see his broken heart in his eyes.

"Damien?"

The bed squeaked as if she were getting up to follow him.

Bracing himself for her questions, he buried his face in a handful of water. He let the water splash over him. With dripping face, he looked up and caught her reflection in the mirror.

"Did I do something wrong?" Her eyes were large and full of vulnerability.

Only a real shit heel would knowingly break her heart or hurt her for any reason. Damien didn't want to hurt her, but whoever Quenton was would stand between them until they resolved it. He didn't want to think he'd pulled her away from a lover. And yet, he could probably safely say he hadn't. Jade didn't strike him as the type to cheat on a man whom she loved. And for whatever else Quenton was, Jade had loved him. That much Damien knew without her telling him. She didn't have to. Damien had felt it as sure as if he'd experienced that love himself.

He picked a towel off the rack and dried his face. "Before we do anything else, we need to talk."

"I *did* do something wrong." She bit her lip and turned to leave the bathroom. "I'm sorry. I told you I don't have much experience."

Damien gave a pained laugh as he followed her out of the bathroom. "Your lack of experience isn't a problem. You're a naturally sensuous woman. I don't think you could help but turn me on, even without trying." He sat down on the bed and pulled her to him. He wrapped her in his arms, laying her face against his chest. The topic would be easier to discuss if they didn't have to look at each other. "We need to talk about Quenton."

Her body stiffened in his arms for a moment before deflating. "I was broadcasting again, wasn't I?"

"Yeah." He kissed her hair to soften the moment. "Like I said, I don't mind the fact you've had lovers before me, there's nothing I can do about the fact. I just don't want them in bed with us. I'm just selfish enough to want the woman I'm making love to thinking about me when I'm going down on her."

She turned her face more fully into his chest. Her voice muffled against his skin. "I didn't mean to think about him. I couldn't help it."

"I don't blame you. He probably never made you a fugitive from your own father, or made it dangerous for you to show your face in public." Pain seared him like an arrow. The words almost choked him. "Maybe you should go back to him."

Jade's arms slid around his waist and she shook her head. "Don't send me away."

Just the thought of doing something like that tore through him. He'd kill to have her with him forever. He tightened his hold on her. "No. Not if you want to stay with me. But you have to be sure you want to. I don't want you with me and thinking about the 'what ifs'."

She pulled away and looked up at him. Tears leaked from the corners of her eyes and slid into her hair. Seeing her stark pain almost undid him.

Leaning forward, he kissed her eyes, tasting her tears on his tongue. "Don't cry, babe. I'm sorry. I didn't mean to hurt you."

"I didn't mean to hurt you either. I can't help but think of Quenton sometimes. I don't want you to end up like him." More tears ran down her face. A small catch in her breathing sounded like she tried to keep from sobbing on him again.

There was so much pain inside her it was a wonder she had trusted him enough to run away with him.

It took a moment before her words sank in. "How did Quenton 'end up'?"

She pressed her trembling lips together and leaned forward against him again. "My father had him killed."

Cold spread throughout Damien's body. Christ in heaven! Why hadn't he seen that one coming? No wonder she worried about Damien and left home without looking back.

Damien kissed her again and brushed his hands up and down her bare back. "I had no idea."

"Do you want to see it?"

"See what?" But he already knew and the thought turned his stomach. She wanted to show him what she'd seen. It would be much easier than telling him. He let his shields down and brushed against her mind. *"Show me."*

The scenes filled his mind like some drama edited by a psychotic director. The memories unfolded in Jade's point of view.

She bent over a man's body. Blood made a cruel red puddle under his head. A shaky hand reached out and stroked flaxen hair away from a wide brow. Sightless blue eyes stared ahead, focused on the afterlife.

A pair of expensive shoes entered her field of vision. She looked up into her father's face. Instead of sympathy for his daughter, there was only cruel disdain.

"See what happens when you break my rules?" Farroll Tanner motioned for two other men who had entered the room. *"I've proved my point. Dispose of him."*

Jade threw herself across her lover's body and held on. When her father's men tried to pry her off the body, she lashed out at them with punching and kicking.

Her father grabbed her off the body, pulling her up by her hair. *"Stop this outrageous behavior this minute."*

"How could you? I loved him."

"You'll love who I tell you to love." He shook her until her teeth rattled. *"He wasn't good enough for you."*

The men took the opportunity to subdue her. Then the sharp prick of a needle stung her upper arm. Vision faded to a pinpoint then vanished into the darkness.

Farroll Tanner had drugged her.

The scene changed.

Light returned. Starting with only a small nimbus then radiating outward.

Jade was now in what looked like a very feminine bedroom. It was a place familiar to Damien. He'd seen it many times before as he'd slipped into her mind as she sat writing poetry.

She lay on the bed on her side, staring off at the wall. Loss opened like a deep gorge inside her. Quenton had been the only person to ever extend a hand of friendship to her. The only person to see her as a wholly lovable and special being.

Just the night before he'd asked her to run away with him and they would be married. She'd said yes. Now, it was all gone.

Damien blinked back tears of his own. So much sorrow and helplessness lived inside Jade. As he dug deeper into her memories, he found it hadn't always been that way. There were places where her father had actually doted on his only child and praised her for her cleverness. Pride had shone from Farroll Tanner like a spotlight.

Then the day had come when his smiles turned to suspicion. About the time she started to feel the compulsion to connect with her Vartek partner.

Had Farroll Tanner known all along his own daughter was a Varti?

Damien kissed her head again then lifted her face away from his chest. "I'm so sorry, Jade. Sorry I didn't find you sooner and steal you away from your father. Sorry I didn't let you know that there was hope somewhere outside that house of horrors."

"You have me now."

"And I'll never give you up to him. You're mine."

A sad smile lifted the corners of her mouth. She nodded. "I'm yours."

He rolled them over so he cradled her under his body. "I meant what I said before. I do love you." When she would have interrupted him, he covered her mouth.

"I understand if you don't feel the same for me. Maybe one day." He removed his hand and kissed her mouth. When he pulled back he said, "Maybe one day you'll even consider marrying *me*."

Looking deeply into his eyes, she raised a hand and stroked it down his face. Damien closed his eyes and pressed his face into her palm. "I want you so much, but I don't want Quenton's memory between us."

"It's not. At least not like you're thinking it is."

"Then what, Jade? You're going to have to explain it to me, because all I see in your mind is an endless loop of your dead lover and how much he meant to you."

She dropped her hand and looked away from him. "You would see that, but it's out of context. Without reference the images are meaningless."

He turned her face back to him, wanting desperately to see what was in her eyes. "Give me the context then. Don't leave me hanging."

She blew out a shaky breath. "I don't want you to end up like Quenton. I don't know what I'd do if I lost you, too. I can't go through that again. I can't imagine..."

"Shhh." He brushed his lips against hers, silencing the words before they had a chance to breathe life. The intent was there in the air between them: Jade couldn't face a future without Damien.

She opened her mouth for him, accepting him and all it meant to be with him. She may fear the fact their lives were in danger, but she didn't shy away from the physical side of their relationship. Only the emotional.

The thing about indulging in a sexual relationship with a Vartek partner, it couldn't remain purely physical for long. Sooner or later the shields would fall for good and she would welcome the intrusion of his mind when they made love. Not that she'd shied away before.

His heart lifted. By then he'd have learned control and would be able to bring them hours of pleasure while they were melded together body and mind.

He skimmed his hand up her side, cupping the sweet roundness of her breast. Her tight nipple poked his palm. Damn, but he loved her breasts. He could spend all night making love to them alone.

His pants were still unzipped. His quickly hardening erection pressed painfully against the zipper teeth. "Wait a minute."

Damien stood and shed his pants and underwear then came back down on top of Jade, nestling between her legs. She spread her thighs, wrapping them around his hips. The wet hot center of her called to him. There was no way in hell he could lay where he was, with no clothes as barriers between them, and not push into her.

Before doing so, he moved against the soft seam of her lips, lubricating himself with her liquid heat. He rolled his hips forward, penetrating the tight vice of her pussy. When he sat seated all the way in her, he stopped moving.

Jade's incredible eyes were half mast. Sexy little slivers of green that stared at him as if any moment she'd come undone. He loved the way she went from zero to meltdown at supersonic speed. One night he'd send her into orgasm over and over just to watch the beautiful look on her face when she came.

She lifted her hips a fraction, driving him deeper still.

"Take it easy, babe. We'll get there."

"How can you stand to be inside me and not move?"

Damien gave her a grim smile. "It's either that or I fuck you senseless right now."

"Is that a problem for you?" She tilted her hips again, forcing him to move.

"Not really." He pulled out just a bit and lunged back in, giving her what she craved. "I just want it to last all night."

She raised a brow in challenge. "Can you?"

Once more he stroked deeply. "Not when I'm making love to you."

"That's incredibly sexy, knowing I have so much power over you."

He threaded his arm under her leg and lifted her thigh. Pumping his hips a few times he whispered, "You do."

All words fled as he concentrated on giving her pleasure. Little by little he let his shield drop, reaching out to her. Not enough to incite the pleasure loop they created the first time they made love, only the merest hint in order to feel the bond.

He was learning that Jade never did anything in halves.

The moment his mind brushed hers, she reached out and held on. The most erotic thing about it was the fact she tended to stroke his thoughts with the same loving devotion he stroked her pussy.

Talk about the most exquisite torture ever given. If he were holding onto nuclear secrets, he'd have spilled them all to her.

The need to have her say she loved him too burned a path down his body and lodged in his heart. He had to clamp his jaws together to keep from begging her to say the words. As it was he didn't know if his shields kept her from feeling the need.

Jade's eyes closed and she arched back one last time before her mouth opened and a long slow moan rose from her quaking body. Damien sank into the sound, letting it roll through his body like a thunderstorm.

"Let go." The words floated through his mind, a call to him on the most primitive level. But he wanted more from her. Much more. The lovemaking hadn't lasted nearly long enough for him.

He pulled out amid Jade's protests.

"It's all right, babe, I'm not going anywhere." He gently tugged on her hips and rolled her over onto her stomach. He placed a pillow under her belly and spread her thighs. Looking at her from behind captured his complete attention. Plump pink lips were open and glistening with wetness.   Damien ran his finger down the inviting tunnel, flicking her clit when he reached the front.

Immediately, her head went down lower into the mattress, her hips rising. She began to ride his finger, asking with her body movements to bring her to orgasm again. He planned to.

Rotating his hand, he slid the rest of his fingers into her welcoming core while retaining the friction to her clit. At the first shuddery sighs she fell over the edge, he removed his fingers and plunged his cock into her.

Over and over he slammed into her, driving her up further the bed. His hands dug into the tender flesh at her hips, bringing her back to meet his thrusts.

Small shrieks erupted from Jade again. She buried her face in a pillow and screamed. Monitoring her via their link was paramount. He wanted only to show her how much he needed her, how desperately he wanted her. His intentions were not to hurt her. So far, he could feel nothing but unbearable pleasure coming from her.

The sounds of their bodies connecting began a slow tribal beat in Damien's chest. He felt both conqueror and conquered by Jade. There was nothing he wouldn't do, no line he wouldn't cross to protect her. Even if it meant in the end he'd have to kill her father and spend the rest of his life in prison.

"No, Damien." Jade raised her head and sobbed.

He must have broadcasted his thoughts. It had been a long time since he'd done that.

But it was too late. He'd already committed himself to her protection the first time he'd connected with her, the first time he'd made love to her.

He bent over her, circling his arms around her body and holding her close as he continued to pump her.

"I'll do what I have to, Jade," he whispered the words against the side of her face. "Anything for you. *Anything*."

He sent one hand questing downward and pressed her clit like an "on" button. The spasms started deep, sending a charge through the tip of his cock and rocketing up the length of his shaft. No longer able to hold back, he came in long hot spurts, filling her with his essence.

He hid his face in the long fall of her hair, brushing his lips along the back of her neck.

After rolling them over onto their sides, he drifted off to a deep sleep, still embedded in her wet heat with the word "anything" echoing through his mind.

Chapter 14

Artificial sunlight poured through the faux windows, giving the illusion that the Varti at the facility lived above ground. It was an attempt to ward off depression and promote positive energy. At that particular moment, Jade would have gladly forgone the positive energy for more sleep.

She blinked a few times and rubbed at her eyes.

Damien's arm tightened around her waist and pulled her closer to him. His breathing changed from deep and even to slightly ragged. His cock hardened against her butt cheeks.

"Good morning, babe."

After the emotions of the night before, she doubted it would be a good morning, but waking up to Damien definitely improved the prospects.

"Morning."

"You feel good in the mornings. You're skin is all warm and soft and pliant." His hands began to move on her as if exploring his discovery.

She smiled and rolled over to face him, wrapping her hand around his cock. *"And you're all hard and hot and horny."*

His eyes closed and a low moan came from his throat. *"That feels good."*

She pumped her hand up and down a few times, enjoying the look of ecstasy on his face. Lowering herself to a level with his erection, Jade held him firm while teasing her tongue around the edges of the domed head.

"That feels even better."

She looked up at him to see his eyes open just enough to watch her. The startling blue of his irises were accented by the dark fringe of his lashes. God, the man was gorgeous and was all hers.

As their gazes locked and held, she took him into her mouth.

His hands sank into her hair, holding her head. "Christ, Jade."

He tasted amazing. Salty and hot with an overtone of her own musky flavor.

"Turn around and let me eat your pussy."

Desire shot through her like a rocket launch. She turned and straddled his face, bringing herself down on his mouth. Immediately his tongue filled her. She lost focus as he worked her ravenously from below.

Inching up a bit, she rubbed her throbbing clit against his chin as he worked. Hanging on the edge of orgasm, she bent to take him back into her mouth. Time for him to catch up with her, but she doubted he could. She was too far ahead of him.

There was just something about Damien that made her want to come from the moment he placed his hands on her.

She took him deeply into her mouth, sucking him hard and keeping pressure on the base of his cock with a tight handhold that she bounced only a few millimeters at a time.

Vibrations from his moans tickled her excited femininity.

His body went tight under hers. She opened her mind to him knowing in the next breath he'd begin to spasm.

Jade wasn't disappointed. He came, pouring his seed down her throat as she greedily swallowed him. But his orgasm was so intense it set off a chain reaction and she bucked up and down on his face as her own shot through her, feeding off him.

Soft kisses rained over her open pussy. The action tickling.

She rolled off him and smiled. *"Now*, it's a good morning."

Damien smiled in agreement.

As he reached for her, a knock on the door interrupted their morning love making.

"Storm, get out here. There's something on the vid feeds you really need to see." It was one of the Varti males, but a voice Jade couldn't identify.

"I'll be right there." He kicked the covers off that had slid to his feet in the night and stood. Instead of bending to find his discarded jeans to put on before answering the door, he headed toward the bathroom.

"Aren't you going to see what's on the feeds?" She spoke into his mind so the Varti at the door wouldn't hear her.

"If it's important, they'll replay it and I can get it from the beginning."

The tap turned on and Jade heard the sounds of Damien washing his face and brushing his teeth. She hoped he shaved. Her thighs and pussy were a little raw from the rasp of his beard stubble as he'd worked her over. At the time, she hadn't cared too much, but now it burned a bit.

She ran her hand down her body and petted her sore lips in a soothing manner. Damien came out of the bathroom and watched her for a moment. *"You keep that up and I won't be going anywhere but back to bed with you."*

She smiled at him and closed her legs as if to keep him at bay. *"Before you do, you'll have to shave."*

He rasped a hand over his chin. *"Sorry about that, babe. I should have thought of that, but you tasted so good."*

Jade sat up and pushed off the bed. "So did you." She blew him a kiss as she walked past him and took her turn in the bathroom.

A little later they came into the common room where most of the Varti congregated around the large vid screen.

A voice came from the feed. Deep, resonant and familiar, Damien stopped in his tracks and Jade almost plowed into him.

"No." The word came out of him in a pained whisper.

The Varti moved out of the way to give them room. An extremely handsome man with intense hazel eyes and an intimidating set to his square jaw spoke before a bevy of microphones.

"My son may have assisted Ms. Tanner in the flight from her home, but if she is with him it is of her own free will."

Now Jade realized why the man looked and sounded familiar, he was Jesse Storm, Damien's father and savior of the United States some thirty years before.

"The government would have you believe my son killed two innocent people in order to cover a crime he didn't commit. I tell you the government is using him to further their agenda against a disenfranchised segment of the population known as Varti. And I know first hand the lengths the government will go to keep her citizens in the dark on their activities."

Damien stiffened beside Jade. "No, dad. Don't do it." But the man on the screen didn't listen.

"I freely admit my beloved son is a Varti. He's a good man. An innocent man. A man I'm very proud of.

"I am in possession of information that proves the identities of the bodies found in Shiloh Mission yesterday were that of Aislinn and Conner Merritt, a Vartek pair who gained a champion and voice in political circles to ensure equal protection under the law for all Varti. It is my belief, and that of my colleagues, that the Merritts were murdered by Farroll Tanner and his agents at the DEP to discredit my son and kill the bill now up for vote in the South Dakota legislature."

Damien's hands were fisted at his sides. His face had gone red with anger. Jade sent out a tentative tendril of her mind to him.

He promptly latched on, holding her tightly.

Love for his father was tempered by worry and traveled through their link. He wanted to stop his father, but from the time stamp on the footage it had been taped earlier in the morning.

"Statistics show that every year hundreds of productive law-abiding citizens are sent to their deaths just because they are born with an innate ability to speak mind to mind with that of one special person." Jesse Storm paused and looked directly into the camera before him. "One."

The word hung on the air. Flash cameras went off around him, dedicating the moment to history.

"There is no evidence to support the government's theory that Varti can converse telepathically with anyone who is not their partner. The frequencies Vartek partners use to communicate are unique only to those partners. Farroll Tanner knows this—intimately."

Jade drew in a breath. What was Damien's father implying? Were her parents Vartek partners? And if so why would he try so hard to kill off his own kind? Wouldn't it make sense to protect them instead? She knew her father held onto a bevy of secrets but the thought he'd seek to destroy his own kind was too out there for even him.

"Those Varti who have not met their deaths at the hands of Tanner's goons have been institutionalized in government facilities to discover ways in which the Varti telepaths can be used as military tools.

"If this sounds like the ramblings of a paranoid man out to save his only son,

I assure you it can and will be verified. Each reporter here will receive a copy of the information I reference in order to get the truth to the public."

Jesse Storm looked into the camera again. "Farroll Tanner, make no mistake, when you attacked my son, you attacked me. And unlike you, I protect my own."

The feed changed and returned to an in-studio reporter. "That was folk hero and inventor, Jesse Storm, at a press conference held at his South Carolina home earlier this morning. Storm is responding to charges his son murdered two people yesterday in the small town of Shiloh Mission, South Dakota, in an effort to stage his own death and that of DEP Director Farroll Tanner's daughter, Jade."

The vid feed split screen. The right continued to show the news anchor as she reported on the press conference. On the left, a still picture of Jesse Storm filled half the screen.

Jealousy stuck in Jade's throat. Damien had been so lucky in his birth. His parents loved him so much. His father had just gone on the national news declaring war on her father in order to protect his son. Jade was sure her father only hunted her because she'd done the unthinkable and ran from him. Perhaps Jade should contact the Senator who had helped the Merritts and ask to have her own press conference. She could tell the world about Quenton's death and how Damien had saved her from a lifetime of emotional abuse and conditional love.

Damien remained planted before the vid screen. No one spoke to him. An uneasy tension hung in the air. The Varti worried of the repercussions of Jesse Storm's press conference. That much Jade guessed without having to possess the ability to read *their* minds.

The studio scene changed as the anchor welcomed an expert guest via vid feed from a remote location. The name on the screen read, Onslow Ruskin, M.D. Jade tensed. The last time he'd eaten dinner at the Tanner estate, he'd cornered her in the library, pressing her between his body and the wall. He had leaned in as if he meant to kiss her, but she'd managed to duck away in time.

Damien bristled and let out a low growl. He obviously knew Ruskin as well.

"Why are they even giving that man camera time?" A woman asked as she put her hand on a man's back who stood beside her. Her partner, Jade thought. The woman began to rub him in a soothing manner as he too reacted negatively to Dr. Ruskin's presence on the news.

"The government probably told the station manager they *had* to have him on or else the FCC would pull the plug on them," Evangeline said as she came into the room and moved to stand beside Jade. "He's in Tanner's back pocket anyhow."

Again she felt the attention of the Varti shift to her. An uncomfortable tension surrounded her. She shifted a little where she stood, moving closer to Damien.

"…a birth defect that can be modified and sufferers can live out normal, healthy lives," Dr. Ruskin explained, but Jade hadn't been concentrating on him, she'd been listening to Evangeline so she missed what he said prior to implying that the Varti gift was a birth defect. Funny, he hadn't acted like it was such a defect when he'd tried to cop a feel and pretend it was an accident.

"The man's an asshole," someone from the back of the room said.

"Do Varti not live normal healthy lives now?" The anchor narrowed her eyes at her guest on the monitor.

"They live a shadow existence, no more than how the homeless lived in the twentieth century. Not really a part of society, but opposed to it."

"Typical bureaucratic puppet, blame the victim," another man said. With a disgusted grunt, he left the room.

"By your own admission, you feel the Varti should be rounded up and placed in interment camps like the Japanese-Americans during World War II."

Dr. Ruskin gave an uneasy laugh. "When said that way it sounds so cold. I merely suggested in my book, *Minds Without Borders*, that it would be easier to study and control the Varti if they lived in a central location rather than spread across the globe."

"That's an interesting point you bring up." She pointed at the monitor with her LCD stylus. "Most other countries have integrated the Varti into their mainstream society, with huge success. Why hasn't the United States done the same?"

The doctor flapped for a moment, seeming to go off balance by the anchor's openly hostile attack.

She did not let up. "Doesn't the Declaration of Independence state, 'all men are created equal, that they are endowed by their Creator with certain unalienable Rights, that among these are Life, Liberty and the pursuit of Happiness'? Rights that are guaranteed by the Constitution." She tapped on the screen before her with her stylus. "Let me read directly from the Fourteenth Amendment. 'No State shall make or enforce any law which shall abridge the privileges or immunities of citizens of the United States; nor shall any State deprive any person of life, liberty or property, without due process of law; nor deny to any person within its jurisdiction the equal protection of the laws.'"

Dr. Ruskin gave the anchor a cocky smile as if he had her nailed to the wall. "State being the operative word. We're talking a federal body that was established to protect her citizens against the ungodly scourge of the Varti."

The anchor frowned at Ruskin's image. "At this point we can assume that Jade Tanner is most likely the Vartek partner of Damien Storm, and yet you sit there and call the Varti a scourge when you've had close personal relations with the Tanner family, and Miss Tanner in particular."

Jade was going to be sick. Damien sent her a questioning vibe.

Ruskin had an odd look on his face. "Jade Tanner is an unfortunate victim of Damien Storm's desperate need to discredit the DEP. Nothing more."

"So, despite what Jesse Storm stated in his press conference, you believe that Jade Tanner is with the younger Storm against her will."

"I do. Jade would never leave those who love her. She's a delicate and gentle woman."

Jade turned away from the vid screen unable to watch anymore of the unfolding controversy. It didn't matter what Ruskin said. No amount of water could put the fire out now. The scandal Damien's father had hinted to would fan the flames of distrust for the DEP and bring them under suspicion.

For years, the Varti had hid in fear of their very lives, and it seemed only now that the public began to question the validity and fairness of the DEP's activities.

Why hadn't people sent up the hue and cry when the agency had first been established? Surely they knew what it meant to create an agency dedicated to eradicate a segment of the population. Or had the fear factor against Varti been too strong?

In the long run, it didn't matter. It happened and no amount of back peddling would resurrect those poor souls lost to her father's wrath. However, they could be avenged.

Jade already vowed to stand up to her father. Now, it was time to make plans to that end. But what could she do to bring him down? He was a powerful man and had proven his ruthlessness time and again. He was just as likely to kill her and tell the world Damien did it as take her back into the fold. Not that she wanted back in the fold, but it may be the only way to find something on him. Or she could join forces with Damien's father.

Her gaze slid to her lover. His attention hadn't wavered from the vid feed. He drank in the spectacle as if it were his only sustenance. "Who is the Senator that the Merritts were in contact with?" He turned to Evangeline who had taken up a post on the sofa.

It was only a matter of time before he raised that question. Jade had thought of that angle herself.

"Thomas Grayhawk. He's a physician by profession and a human rights activist by passion."

Damien jabbed a finger at the vid screen. "Where was that passion when people like Dr. Rush-to-Judgment spread his vicious rumors about Varti?"

Evangeline held up her hands to ward off Damien's anger. "In the dark like most of society. From the way I understand it, he began doing tests and interviewing Varti to conduct his own research."

"Could you get me a meeting with him?"

"I can do that." Evangeline stood and straightened her caftan. "But I would advise against it until the fervor over Aislinn and Conner's deaths dies down."

"Why's that? Seems to me it's the perfect time. He could help my dad sway others over to our side."

Jade didn't like the bent of the conversation.

In order to meet with Senator Grayhawk, Damien would have to leave the safety of the facility. She doubted the Varti would welcome an outsider in their midst in order for Senator Grayhawk to come to them, no matter his good intensions. All it would take would be one of her father's agents keeping tabs on the Senator to follow him to the mountain location. It was too much to risk.

"Let me go," Jade offered.

Damien lurched forward as if the very thought had been a kick to the gut. Shock and fear shot through their link at lightning speed.

She had no choice but to explain her reason for offering to go in his stead. "It makes more sense to send me. You'll be an easy target out there. So far all the media has said about me is that I'm an unwilling participant in all this. At least where the accusations from my father are concerned."

Damien shook his head. He cradled shaking hands around her face and stared down at her. "There's no way in hell I'm letting you go out there alone."

She pulled her face from his grip. "Same goes. I'm not going to sit here worrying while you're out there going into God knows what danger."

"Then we're at a stalemate." He bent and placed his forehead against hers. "I love you so much. If anything ever happened…"

Jade brushed her lips against his. She spoke into the link, rather than let the rest of the Varti assembled into what promised to be a heated debate. *"I know, but that doesn't change the fact that out of the two of us, I'm the best one to send."*

"How do you figure that?" Even in his mind, his tone was sharp, incredulous.

She refrained from saying that her father had less of a reason to kill her than he did Damien, but that was in no way assured.

He pounced on her hesitation. *"Yeah. See? You can't come up with a reason."*

"Guarantee me that you won't do something rash, and I'll consider letting you go." She crossed her arms under her breasts and raised a brow at him, trying to look intimidating.

Evangeline pushed to her feet. "It's obvious there's a discussion under way about who should go to meet with the Senator. It may be more advantageous to have him meet with Jade." When Damien looked as if he'd explode on the spot, Evangeline held up her hand to hush him. "The Senator may want to ask specific questions about Farroll Tanner that only someone who has lived with him and under his thumb would know the answers to."

"And if that happens, I can relay the questions to her and she can answer from the safety of this room."

"No." Jade shook her head. "I won't allow it. If anyone meets with Grayhawk, it's going to be me. If you keep insisting you're going to go, I'll pack it in now and leave."

His want to come back with a stinging retort burned into her, but he refrained in both thinking and speaking the words. Instead he let out a long breath and put his hands up to lock behind his head.

Taking a slow walk around the room, he finally came back to her and let his hands drop in something close to defeat. *"I don't want to fight with you over this. I've searched so hard and waited too long to find you to lose you over something that's supposed to ensure we can stay together. It's ridiculous."*

Jade reached out and took her hands in his. *"A compromise then?"*

"Yeah, but I don't know what it could be."

"Whatever it is, I don't think we should both leave the hideout until it's safe. At least not together." She took a step toward him, bringing her body close enough that her breasts brushed against him.

"Agreed." He released her hands and slid his arms around her waist, pulling her closer. *"But the link stays open if we're apart."*

"Agreed." She looked into his eyes, getting lost in the blue pools. *"You want to go back to the room and discuss this in greater detail? We'll let Evangeline make the contact and ask for a meeting with one of us. It might be that he has his preferences on who he'd like to speak with."*

"Or maybe neither of us."

Jade hated to admit it, but there was that possibility too.

Damien gave her a little squeeze before releasing her. There was no mistaking the hard-on hiding behind his fly. The man must have been sexually deprived for a long time to need it as often as he did.

"No, it's just being near you after so long. You wouldn't believe the dreams I had of you before we were together. And in every one of them we'd end up making love."

Heat rose to her face. She really needed to learn how to control her broadcasting.

He gave her a knowing wink and turned to Evangeline. "Could you call the Senator and set something up. We'll decide which one of us goes after you speak to him. No sense in getting all stirred up if he doesn't agree to a meeting."

"Oh, he'll agree all right." She turned and left the room, presumably to contact the Senator, leaving the reasons hanging on the air.

Chapter 15

Back in their room, Damien wasted no time stripping Jade down to her skin and diving in. Her thighs were thrown over his shoulders as he lost himself in the powerful strokes that would bring them both to orgasm.

She writhed under him, bringing her body up to meet his thrusts. He watched in dizzying desire as her small breasts bounced. The hard peaks showing how turned on she was by his lovemaking.

In every way, she amazed him.

Of all the women he could have had a Vartek pairing with, he lucked out to have the most beautiful woman he'd ever laid eyes on. Everything about Jade was sweet and sensuous. She moved under him, offering him the sweetest of sensations all along his length. It didn't take much for him to get hard and ready for her, but at least his control improved every time they made love.

He gazed down into her face, awestruck by the erotic picture she made. Her hair lay fanned out on the pillow around her like a silken cloud. Her lips were parted as she breathed in the scent of their lovemaking. Cords in her neck stood out as she pushed her body closer to the edge.

And for all her sexual strength, she was a delicate soul.

Protectiveness for Jade roared to life whenever Damien thought of her. His father told him he'd felt the same way about Damien's mother the first time he'd met her, and they hadn't been Varti. Damien supposed love would do that to a man. Take over all his common sense and make him agree to things he knew deep down weren't right, like letting her go to meet with Senator Grayhawk if the good senator decided he wanted to speak with Jade instead of Damien.

He'd lost his damn mind and heart to her. Every last brain and blood cell. Everything that made him a man, right down to his very soul.

"Tell me you love me, Jade." He hadn't intended to think the words. Hadn't meant for them to travel across the link. Her broadcasting was a bad habit he'd picked up.

Damn.

Jade smiled at him and touched his face. She didn't think or say the words he wanted to hear, but they were there in her touch, in the way her pussy milked him as he continued to move inside her. He could practically hear it on her sighs. Or was it just wishful thinking on his part?

Though Vartek partners felt an undeniable need to be together and to mate, it didn't necessarily follow that they fell in love. They usually did, but it wasn't in any way a certainty.

Sweat broke out on his brow and body. Rivulets rolled down his back and chest. Sexy little tremors fluttered Jade's lower abdomen. He knew what that meant: total and complete bliss was only moments away.

On cue, Jade threw her head back and yelled his name. He'd have had to be superhuman to hold back after seeing her do that.

Even the knock on the door didn't stop him from enjoying the orgasm that ripped through him.

The persistent visitor continued to pound on the door—or was that his heart knocking against his ribs? Could be, Jade wore him out, but he just didn't want to stop loving her.

"Damien! Jade! Senator Grayhawk is on the comm waiting to speak with you." It was Elliot. Damien had met him a few times in the past. He seemed a good man, if a bit more conservative than the rest of the Varti.

Damien tried to get his breath back. The words came out like he hadn't drawn a good breath in a month. "We'll... be... right... there."

Jade contracted around his still-hard cock, making him lose his train of thought again.

After a moment of languishing in her, Damien reluctantly pulled out. "We should get cleaned up and go speak to the Senator."

She nodded and started to roll off the bed. "We are being rude."

They hurried through their clean up and redressed. The comm in question was located in Evangeline's quarters. The high-quality gel screen was filled with the image of a Native American man dressed in a nice sports shirt and tie. His hair was slightly longer than one would imagine on a politician, but it looked right with his high cheekbones and hawkish nose. On top of all that, there was something about the man that looked oddly familiar.

He gave a warm smile when Jade and Damien took a place before the monitor. "Damien, it's nice to finally see you again, though I'd hoped it would have been under better circumstances"

Momentarily confused, Damien sorted through his memories and came up with nothing of Grayhawk. "I'm sorry, I don't remember meeting you."

Grayhawk laughed. "I'm not surprised. I was dressed in native attire at the time and you were only a small boy. You were with your parents on a vacation at the time."

Suddenly a scene unfolded in his mind. His family watched a traditional Native American dance. He didn't remember what tribe, only that all the beautiful costumes and colors kept him spellbound. The drums beat straight to his gut. He had stood there speechless. Sam had held onto his hand bouncing up and down, imitating the dancers

"I remember now. You came over later and hugged my father and picked him up off the ground."

"I'd known your father for years." His expression sobered. "Which makes me even more worried that you've incited Tanner's wrath. And why I've decided the best course of action is for Jade to meet with me here at my office and for you to stay hidden."

Immediate and eviscerating panic shot through Damien. He'd promised Jade if Grayhawk wanted to meet with her, he'd let her go out, but now that it was a certainty Damien wanted nothing to do with it.

Jade slipped her hand in his and squeezed. *"I'll be fine, Damien."*

"How can I let you out of my sight?"

"At the first sign of trouble, I'll call for you. I promise."

"There are several things I want to go over with Jade before we proceed, and I'd like to do that in person." Seeming to read Damien's anxiety over the comm screen, Grayhawk continued. "Damien, she'll be well protected here. I'll have her back to you before sunset. Besides, Jade will be traveling to my office with Evangeline. She'll be less conspicuous than you are."

Damien laughed, tortured by the thought. "How can you say that? Look at her. She's going to attract attention no matter where she is."

Grayhawk smiled like an indulgent father. "Will it help if I tell you your parents are on the way here? They took the express shuttle after the press conference this morning. They should be landing soon."

No. If anything it made him more anxious. He loved his parents, but sometimes they put themselves into danger to protect their offspring. He supposed he'd do the same thing when he and Jade had children. Just the thought made him bow his chest out.

Jade's hand tightened around his. "When do you want to meet?"

"As soon as you can get here."

"We'll leave in the next few minutes." Evangeline stood. "Come, Jade. Let's go. It's a about an hour's ride to the Senator's office."

Damien stood to go with them, but Evangeline motioned for him to stay. "You finish your conversation with the Senator."

"At least let me say goodbye to her." He hurried around the chair and cut them off at the door. He took Jade by the shoulders and kissed her long and hard. *"Be careful, babe. And keep the link open."*

"I will. Don't worry. I'll be fine. You'll see me in a couple of hours." She backed away and ran her thumb over his jaw.

He clenched it so tightly he thought it would crack.

"Is there anything you want me to relay to your parents? I have a feeling I'm going to be seeing them shortly."

"Just tell them I love them and to save a date for the wedding."

Red filled Jade's face. She kissed him a quick buss and turned away, following Evangeline out the door and into the world.

Chapter 16

Jade didn't speak with Damien the entire way to the office, but she could feel him there just as she had in those early days when he'd first contacted her. He hovered somewhere near her temporal lobe, brushing against her essence like a feather on the wind. It tickled, but it no longer disturbed her.

She loved him.

How could she not?

But she couldn't seem to open her mind or mouth to tell him the words he wanted and deserved to hear. Jesus, it hurt too much to love someone so completely and lose them. She'd die before she declared her heart again and have it crushed, especially with her father still a major threat hanging over them.

Turning her head, she looked out the glider window as they set down at the public parking adjacent to the government buildings where Senator Grayhawk kept his local office.

The mall was busy with people moving to and from the various buildings in the complex. The federal courthouse stood off to the right. A crowd was gathered there on the steps.

"I wonder what that's all about?" She waited for the pneumatic doors to open before she unlocked her harness, her attention riveted on the scene unfolding across the street.

"I don't know, but it can't be good." Evangeline bent over and pulled a pair of binoculars out from under her seat. After a few minutes she said, "Protestors."

"Can you read their signs?"

Evangeline gave a crack of laughter. "They're calling for your father's immediate resignation and the disbandment of the DEP. I guess Jesse finally got people stirred up today."

Cold dread seeped into Jade's veins. If her father felt threatened, he'd be even worse. He'd do something drastic to prove he and the DEP were right and those opposed were wrong. Farroll Tanner was dangerous before, now he'd be unstoppable.

"What's wrong?" Damien's voice came through the link.

"Protestors at the court house. They're calling for my father's resignation. He'll be on the offensive."

"Or it could curb his ambition for a while. People will watch him very closely now. One false move and his little empire will crumble." Though the words were meant to be reassuring, Jade felt anything but.

"I think we're going inside now. I'll see you in a little while."

"Yes you will." He cut off the words with a caress.

They started out of the parking lot and to the subterranean crosswalk that would take them to the office buildings. From the corner of her eye, Jade swore she saw her father's driver. Afraid to turn her head to verify the man's identity, she kept walking, looking straight ahead. His gaze followed her all the way to the stairs like a hungry ghost. She knew it did, she felt his cold hands as if he touched her.

Chills ran up the back of her neck. Static filled her brain.

"Damien?"

No answer.

"Damien!"

Jade stopped on the stairs. Evangeline was near the bottom when Jade yelled down to her.

"I can't feel him!" She sat down on the steps as agony tore through her. A part of her soul had been severed. And not cleanly. Ragged pieces of emotion dangled on the breeze, pounding an angry beat through her body like the exposed nerve of a broken tooth.

Evangeline turned and ran back up the stairs. She took Jade into her arms. "Come on let's get to the Senator's office."

"No. I want to go back. I have to find him."

"Listen to me. Grayhawk knows people who can help. He's our best bet at the moment."

"But Damien... he was there just a second ago... and now nothing..." Jade heard the sounds of her sobs, but became disconnected from the action. She'd lost control somehow and didn't quite know how to get it back.

Lights flashed by beneath the blur of her tears. Evangeline had her arm around Jade, guiding her through the tunnel and out into the bright sunlight of the plaza.

Deep male voices grew closer. Heavy footsteps slapped against the pavement. Jade looked up to see the outline of a man dressed in a dark suit, his face mostly hidden behind opaque shades. He spoke into the comm disk clipped to his lapel.

"We have a situation."

Even though Jade's mind screamed to be strong for Damien, her body refused to comply. Her knees buckled.

Strong arms scooped her up and held her against a muscular chest. "We're coming upstairs."

Her feeble attempts to be put down went unheeded. She rested her head against the stranger's shoulder. There was no choice in the matter. All her strength seemed to flee with the loss of her link with her Vartek partner.

"Damien, where are you?" The only thing that answered was the lonely pop of static that had replaced his voice in her head. How could she not hear him? Was he dead, or incapacitated in some way?

And if so, did he leave the hideout or was there a traitor in the Varti's midst?

Whispers filtered in the space around her, dying on a gasp as the party left open-mouthed bystanders in their wake.

They came to an elevator and stepped inside after the second guard cleared the car for them.

"He's gone," Jade whimpered.

Evangeline reached out and stroked her hair. "No, I'm sure he's not. We'll contact the facility when we get to the Senator's office. You'll see. There's some other explanation for the silence."

A door whooshed open and they were moving again. Then cool air surrounded her.

"Put her in that chair."

Senator Grayhawk.

God, she hoped he could help Damien—wherever he was.

"What happened?" Grayhawk bent down in front of her and pushed the hair from her face.

"She can't—" Evangeline started to answer but Jade wouldn't let her. This was her tale to tell.

"Damien's gone. All I hear is static where he used to be." She gripped Grayhawk's hand in both of hers, imploring him to understand. "We have to find him."

His deep sable gaze slid from hers to look at someone she hadn't noticed before. A couple stood against the far wall. The woman had her arms around the man, a panicked look on her face. Her eyes were the same incredible blue of Damien's. She had to be his mother. Of course, she was. Who else could she be? Fear for her child radiated out of her and added to the ambient tension.

Jesse Storm spoke quietly to Damien's mother then kissed her hands and came to lean against Grayhawk's desk facing Jade. "Hello, Jade. I'm Jesse Storm, Damien's father."

Jade nodded. "I know."

"It's very important that you tell me everything that happened before you lost contact with Damien." Looking into his eyes, Jade would never conceive of doing anything but following his every word. The elder Storm radiated an intense power and confidence. Damien may have his mother's liquid blue eyes, but he'd inherited his father's spirit and strength.

She choked back the emotions, trying to state only the facts. She told them about the crowd out front and how Damien knew something was wrong. He was there with her as they made their way to the crosswalk. "Then I thought I saw my father's driver. I promised Damien I'd contact him at the first sign of trouble. I started to tell him about the driver, when I got nothing. I can't even feel him now. He's…"

Jesse Storm put his hand up. "I think I know what happened, but we have to verify it before we can act." He turned to Evangeline. "Get in touch with the facility and find out if Damien is still with them."

Evangeline nodded and seated herself at Grayhawk's communication station.

"Jade, I want you to give me anything you can that will allow me to gain a backdoor entrance to your father's private records."

Finally, something she could do, but as she sat there she wondered if it wouldn't be more prudent to send her back to Glendown and access the records while her father remained out west thinking she remained with the Varti.

The only obstacles would be her mother and the house staff.

Evangeline turned from the console. Her face white with shock. "Elliot said Damien ran out of the hideout about twenty minutes ago. Before anyone could stop him or before he could tell them where he was going."

He was coming for her. She knew it, just as sure as she knew he headed straight into a trap.

Chapter 17

The last emotion he'd felt from Jade was panic. Then nothing.

A black hole had more filling it than his link with Jade now held.

What had happened between the last time she'd spoken to him and going into the office building? Or had she even made it there? Could they have been jumped on the way from the parking area to the Senator's office?

He maneuvered through lunch hour traffic, trying to navigate and call up the comm system at the same time. Generally, he didn't have a hard time with such things, but his hands were shaking so hard he kept missing the pads on the touch screen. And Jade had disabled the voice command days before.

"Damn!"

He beat the dashboard with his fist. He never should have agreed to let her go with Evangeline all the way to the government multiplex. His gut had warned him it was a bad idea, and his gut had been right.

Red dots lit up the nav screen. Police gliders were closing in fast. He didn't have time for another chase. Jade's life could very well be in danger.

He abandoned his attempts to contact Grayhawk's office and concentrated on outrunning his shadows.

Pushing the toggle forward, he shot forward like a bullet, putting much needed distance between himself and the police. They had new gliders with super-thrusters underneath. Out here in the mountains they probably needed them to get enough lift to get where they no doubt had to go sometimes.

As the police closed the gap, Damien gave himself over to the chase.

Traffic in front of him stalled on all three levels. Something blocked the flow in all lanes. He craned his neck, but couldn't see far enough ahead to figure out what it was. A quick glance at the nav system made his heart drop to his stomach. Red dots filled the screen on all lanes and levels. A road block.

There had to be a way around it.

There was no way in hell he was going to accept defeat. No way he'd let Farroll Tanner win.

He pulled the toggle a hard left and went sideways. The new glider performed the maneuver with more ease than poor Clare ever had. And it definitely had more power.

He rode through the long lanes of traffic. The damn police were imitating his fancy driving skills. Sirens blared behind and in front of him. Lights flashed. Their reflections bounced off the closed windows and shiny paint jobs of the other vehicles.

Once again he lifted the toggle and changed positions. He shot up out of the aeroplastic-coated cavern and over the top, riding above the jam.

Police gliders at the head of the road block rose to intercept him. The nav screen showed them closing in behind him and on both sides.

They were getting too close. Way too close.

He was surrounded.

A gap between two of the police gliders on the right opened up. Damien turned his vehicle sideways again and squeezed through.

Then impact.

"Jade."

Nothing.

The only sound was the whistle of wind as he started to fall from the sky. Air bags deployed all around him, cocooning him in parachute-like safety. The dust from the bags coated his lungs and started him coughing. Blackness engulfed him, either from the air bags blocking out the windows or the loss of oxygen from the dust they deployed, he couldn't be sure. What he did know was that it was bad.

"I'm so sorry, Jade. It may take me longer, but I'll find you again. I promise."

Chapter 18

Jade shook her head. The words didn't make sense. She knew advances in technology accomplished amazing feats, but this had passed from the realm of possible science to science fiction.

Her father and Dr. Ruskin had brought the horror to a whole new level.

"We weren't even sure they had the technology up and working until about a month ago when larger than normal numbers of Varti began to disappear." Grayhawk explained. "In a few cases, the friends and family of the missing persons reported that right before the disappearance they would lose complete contact with their partners. They heard 'nothing but static'."

Jade put her head down. How could she live in a home with the modern day equivalent of Joseph Mengele and not realize the depths of his depravity? Didn't that make her guilty by association? After Quenton's death she'd simply shut down so tightly she refused to see anymore of the terrible things going on around her. But she should have. She owed it to Quenton. She owed it to Damien and the Merritts.

"So how does this device work?" Maybe if she understood its mechanism she'd be able to wrap her mind around the improbability of the thing.

Jesse slid off the desk where he'd been sitting and took a chair beside her. "The specs we were able to obtain imply that it searches out the frequency Vartek partners use to communicate and then scrambles the signals. It's actually a new twist on old technology—as in twentieth century old. So far, we believe it's only been effective on detecting signals on those Varti who have problems with broadcasting."

Blood rushed from Jade's head. Black spots curled in from the sides of her eyes to cover her vision. Someone grabbed the back of her head and pushed it between her knees.

"Take nice, slow deep breaths, sweetheart." Jesse held the base of her neck in a gentle grip. "Good girl. That's the way. Nice and slow."

A scent like a spring bouquet filled her senses. Jade took in a deep breath. The person slid their arm around her shoulder and bent down over her. "It's not your fault, Jade. Don't you dare blame yourself for this."

She wiped a hand across her eyes. Her fingers came away wet. She didn't remember crying.

Jade straightened up and looked at first Damien's father, then his mother. How could they not hate or blame her for bringing their son into danger? "I… I broadcast. Damien teased me about it, but he never told me how much danger we were in from it."

Soran Storm brushed the hair back from Jade's face. "I know. He didn't want you to worry. Believe me, my son is scared enough for the both of you."

That made Jade smile. "He never acts afraid. He tells me he is, and I can sometimes feel it, but he hides it."

Soran shifted her gaze to her husband and gave him a loving smile. "He's like his father in that respect."

One of the guards came into the room then. His face was pulled into a serious frown.

"What is it, Branigan?" Grayhawk came to his feet.

Branigan studied those in the room as if weighing his words before he said them. "Storm has been captured by the DEP. Our men tried to intercept, but the government swooped in. He's on his way to the detainment facility for reprogramming."

A pit opened up inside Jade. "What's 'reprogramming' mean?"

Soran's arm tightened around her shoulder. "He means they're going to permanently sever his link with you."

Jade shot to her feet, no longer able to sit idly by in terrified paralysis. "Take me home."

Everyone in the room looked to her as if her head had spun backwards and she spoke in tongues.

"Take me back to Glendown. It's the only way. I can access my father's files from there. I know his system, and I know some of the backdoors and overrides." She turned her attention to Jesse. "Plant a comm disk on me so you can guide me through what I don't know." When they still didn't respond to her, she said, "Look, the only way to beat the devil is to meet him in hell. There's no hell worse than the one I came from."

When the answer came, it wasn't from Damien's father, but from the Senator himself. He looked to his guard and then Jesse. "Make it happen."

Chapter 19

The glider hit the ground with enough force to open a crater under him. Blood ran into his eyes from a gash above his eyebrow he had no memory of getting. Otherwise, Damien felt all right. At least he wasn't dead. Yet.

The air bags began to deflate in a slow descent.

Uniformed police surrounded the glider with their weapons drawn and trained on him. Any sudden moves would see him fried to the spot like an insect zapped by a bug light.

"Put your hands up where we can see them."

Damien complied, but only because he had to live through this is order to save Jade. If he had only himself to consider, he would have come up swinging. Maybe not the wisest course of action, but it would sure as hell make him feel better.

"Now, exit the vehicle slowly."

Damien gave the cop a look meant to convey the impossibility of the command. He wiggled his hands that were still in the air. How did the man expect him to operate the doors with his hands in the surrender position? He was good with his dick, but not that good.

The cop jerked his head toward one of his colleagues, indicating him to operate the doors from the outside.

When the doors were up, Damien was pulled from the glider and slammed against the body of it. He was given a thorough pat down and his arms were jerked behind his back and electronic cuffs were placed on his wrists.

"You have the right to remain silent…" the cop began.

Damien frowned. Did they still read the Miranda rights this far out west? The irony of having it at all didn't escape him. All right so he'd broken traffic laws too numerous to count. He'd committed grand theft of more than one glider. But he hadn't killed the Merritts, and he damn sure hadn't kidnapped Jade.

Jade!

No matter how much he wanted to fight and protest, he'd have to sit tight for now and let things unfold the way they would or risk being shoved through the system and placed up for execution before he could even mount a credible defense against his accusers. In this case, Farroll Tanner.

Fucker.

God, he hated that man. Hated him with everything inside.

Damien was led to an awaiting glider for transportation to the local jail. A long black vehicle with government registration eased up to the knot of police congregated on the hot South Dakota tarmac.

The doors eased up and Tanner stepped out, pulling his suit jacket down. "I'll take it from here, Captain."

"I'm sorry, sir, but you'll have to have nothing short of a Presidential Writ to take custody of this prisoner."

Damien looked from the police captain to Jade's father. What kind of pissing contest had he gotten himself into the middle of? Personally, he'd rather take his chances with the local law enforcement officials than Tanner's DEP posse any day, but no one was likely to give him a vote on the matter.

Hot summer sun poured down on them. The blood dried and baked on his forehead. It itched, driving him crazy. He tried to bend his head to scratch it on his shoulder, but with the cuffs on he couldn't reach.

The cop started to nudge Damien into the police glider once again. At that moment, the sky darkened with black government vehicles. The scene was about to get real ugly, real quick.

Damien looked over his shoulder at the cop. "Maybe you should let me go with them. I'd hate to see your boys get shot up by Tanner's personal army. I'm not that big a prick to want that on my conscious."

The captain looked him in the eyes and said under his breath so no one else could hear him. "Your father will kill me if I let you out of my sight."

Damien tried not to react, even as the chance for a clean escape slipped through his fingers. The cops had been a ruse. They were trying to take him into protective custody, not throw him into the system. Damn it. Why didn't anyone ever tell him these things ahead of time? They'd probably been called the moment he'd left the facility alone.

He heard the unmistakable sounds of windows lowering on the gliders that hovered above them. "Tanner will kill you if you don't let me go." He swallowed hard. "Save Jade."

The captain nodded once. He called to Tanner, "Storm has agreed to go with you."

Was it just his imagination, or did the temperature drop twenty degrees when Farroll Tanner smiled in victory.

Chapter 20

On one of the large shuttle transports, it took only a few hours to touch down on the landing strip outside Glendown. Coming in, she'd seen the State Hospital and knew now what it was—not a place where poor individuals cut off from reality went to get treatment and reintegrate into society, but a carnival ride house of horrors where Varti went and were never seen again.

How could she have lived so close to the place all her life and never known exactly what went on there. That her father had a hand in all the deaths and heinous experiments that went on there. If she had the ability to open the window and spit on the place she would have. Anger roiled low in her belly.

When they came in low over the rolling grounds of the hospital, she noticed crowds of people stood outside the gates, looking as if they meant to push inside and rescue those held within.

Society had been stupid to believe all the lies propagated by her father and his henchmen. Just because Farroll Tanner and Dr. Onslow Ruskin thought the Varti were dangerous didn't make it true.

She rubbed her forehead. The beginnings of a tension headache started to throb.

Damien's parents, along with Grayhawk and two of his guards rode in a separate shuttle. The idea was to make it look as if Jade traveled home under her own steam. When they landed, they would head straight for the hospital to try and gain entrance, while Jesse guided Jade's activity via remote access.

It had been a desperate plan sending Jade on the transport alone. A few extra creds given under the counter to the ticket clerk had ensured she was left alone during the entirety of the trip. Jade explained that after everything that happened she just wanted to get home as quietly and quickly as possible. The woman behind the counter had nodded and slid the credits into her uniform pocket.

Jade touched the hair jewelry at her temple and heard Jesse Storm speak into her ear.

"There will be a cab waiting at the curb for you as you exit the terminal. The driver will be wearing a straw hat and look like a tourist. His name is Mickey."

She didn't acknowledge Jesse. It was best if she just kept walking and drew no attention to herself by answering.

There was a line in front of the exit. People pulled luggage behind them as they shuffled through the revolving door. More than once someone misjudged the width of the opening and got caught in the door, backing the line up even farther into the terminal.

She swallowed down the anxiousness. No telling how much of a head start her father and his goons had on them. Damien could already be undergoing some terrible procedure to cleave the psychic pathways from his brain.

The thought was too horrific to even imagine.

"Damien?"

The same static that plagued her since earlier in the day filled the void.

Finally she made it out the door and into the oppressive heat and humidity of late afternoon.

The driver was stationed near a glider cab. He leaned against the frame as if he had all the time in the world. Several people approached him before Jade made it across the busy passenger pick-up lane. When he spotted her, he swept his hat off and gave a deep bow before opening the cab door for her. He was a robust, older man that looked as if someone had spent years using his face as a punching bag.

"Mickey?"

"At your service."

When she was in and settled in the back seat, she said, "Change of plans. Take me straight to the detainment facility."

He shook his head. "Mr. Storm will have my ass if I do that."

"And I'll turn you in to my father and the DEP if you don't." She wouldn't of course, but he didn't know that.

She watched his shoulders stiffen. "It's bad enough Mr. Storm and Grayhawk are over there. Do you know how hard it's going to be for you to get into that place? They have tighter security over there than the Pentagon."

That would be a problem. She changed tactics. "Tell you what, drop me off a few blocks from home and wait for me. I'll find the security access codes as fast as I can and get out of there. I have this awful feeling Damien doesn't have much time before they lobotomize him." She turned her head to look out the window at the passing neighborhoods. All of them familiar, and yet alien. She never felt so far away from home in her life. "My father won't take a chance and keep him whole or alive."

"Fucking Christ," the driver mumbled. He turned the toggle a hard left and up, shooting forward in traffic.

The hair on Jade's arms and neck stood up. At first she'd thought the epitaph was for the danger Damien was in, but when she turned, she saw the black government gliders bearing down on them.

"Go! Go!" She screamed and climbed over the seat and into the front of the glider, taking the navigator position. She'd done this before with Damien, she could do it with his father's man.

She started to grab the toggle from him, when suddenly the other gliders turned off to go into the city proper. Leaning back against the seat she let out a long breath. "False alarm."

"Maybe, not." He looked at the nav screen. "They were federal prison transport, and they were bookin' it."

Neither of them said what they were both thinking.

"Then maybe we aren't too late. Hurry and get me home."

A few minutes later, Mickey put the glider cab down at a street level curb two blocks from her house. "Now, wait for me."

"I can't say I like the idea of you going into that house unprotected." His bull doggish face creased more as he frowned. He reached into the small of his back and pulled out a handgun. The thing was an antique.

"Does it still work?" She turned it over and inspected it.

"It will still kill if that's what you mean? Besides, there are some newer technologies that can disrupt the flow of a laser pistol. Your father and his guards are less likely to own anything that can stop a lead slug."

She nodded. It made sense.

"To shoot, just flip this button down. That's the safety. Then point it at your target. Your sight is here." He pointed to a little v-shaped notch on the top of the black barrel. "Look down that and squeeze the trigger."

Before he let her go off with the gun, he put the safety back on. "Remember, Jade, don't touch the trigger unless you're about to shoot. You might end up hurting someone you don't mean to."

She swallowed.

"Now get out of here before we draw a crowd and the local PD starts nosing around."

Jade didn't quite know where to stash the gun. Her sundress didn't afford too many hiding places. She'd just have to hope no one saw her with it.

Rather than taking the direct route and being seen by her neighbors, she crossed through backyards and down the cannel that ran between properties. By the time she reached her parent's lot, she was drenched in sweat, her hair lank in the humidity. She worried the comm device in her hair would short out and she'd lose contact with Jesse.

On the south side of the yard was a small gap in the fencing, where stone met wire. Using the back gate onto the property like she did when she'd escaped would probably see her caught. She squeezed through the space, catching her dress and ripping the hem. Too bad. She was breaking into her parents' house, not entering the Miss Glendown pageant.

With no way to avoid the security cameras if had they been realigned in the days since she'd fled, she stayed to the shade in hopes it would disguise her arrival a little bit.

She touched the hair jewelry again. "I'm almost there," she whispered.

"Let me know when you're on the terminal and give me the codes. I can break in remotely."

"You got it."

She stood at the edge of the tree line, looking at the patio doors. Jesus, it seemed like such a long way to go. Sick inside, she closed the space.

This time of day the doors might actually be unlocked. Her mother would have already been out for her daily swim and afternoon drink on the patio. Hopefully the servants hadn't locked the doors when her mother came back inside.

Taking a deep breath, Jade kept low and moved as quickly as she could to the doors. The handle turned easily in her hand. Thank God, at least a few of the planets were in alignment.

Jade slipped inside and hurried to her father's office, careful to keep off the squeaky boards and stairs as she moved. She knew every tell-tale one in the house, having avoided them for the years she'd lived there.

Emotion curled her hands into fists.

Her father's office stood at the end of a long hallway. Chances are it would be locked since he was out terrorizing Varti and not home to keep his eyes on his personal fiefdom. The lock wouldn't be a problem, she knew the override codes. The problem was the security guards, Dale and Reis, who were always stationed downstairs. All it would take was the sight of the indicator panel lighting up to tell them someone was trying to access the door to bring them upstairs.

Jade held the gun in her right hand and wiped her left one down her dress to dry it off. She tapped in the override code and waited for the green light to flash.

It stayed red.

No. It wasn't possible.

She entered the numbers again and waited.

The light remained red.

Voices on the stairs had her ducking into an adjacent room, hiding behind the door.

Pressing the communications disk in her hairclip she said, "The override codes for the office door have been changed. I can't get inside."

"Damn it." Jesse paused for a moment, but his words were cut off as Dale and Reis moved down the hall. Oh, these were the worst of her father's lackeys. No life was sacred as far as they were concerned. They had been the ones ordered to kill Quenton. She knew. She'd seen them do it.

An idea came to her then. They just gave her what she needed to get into the office.

"Who's with you?" Jesse tried to gain her attention. She didn't answer but left the channel open so he could hear everything that was about to go down.

Chapter 21

Blinding pain attacked Damien's temporal lobes. Bright stars of color flashed before his eyes whenever he tried to open them. Dizziness brought bile to the back of his throat. He just wanted the world to stop moving so he could get off.

Two flesh-eating beetles were busily consuming the skin on his temples. The way his hands were locked to the gurney where he lay he couldn't raise them to pull the fucking bugs off.

He screamed his voice raw.

He thought his mind raw.

"Jade."

The name went nowhere. The single syllable rattled around in his broken brain and died before ever going anywhere.

No one came to help him from his mindless prison. Tears slid down his face and gathered in his hair. They weren't tears of pain or anger, but of strain. Pushing with every bit of energy he could muster, he tried to break through the artificial walls his captors placed on his psychic pathways. He had to escape before they returned. And he doubted very much he'd be left alone for long.

He settled back down and took a deep breath.

Relax. He had to relax or he'd get nowhere.

Opening his eyes despite the vertigo, he gauged his surroundings. They'd left him in a stark white room with one bright light posed directly above his eyes to blind and disorient him.

If he sat up and bent over, he might be able to pull the gnawing beetles from his head. With much care, he sat up. Looking through only one eye to keep the world from tilting up on its axis again, he bent over at the waist, forcing himself lower and lower. He thought he was limber, but nothing doing. Even turning his hand up it was too far out of his reach.

No. He wouldn't give up that easily.

He surged backward and let momentum carry him farther. Still empty air, but he did feel the brush of his hair on his fingertips that time. The problem with the way they had his hands secured, he couldn't moved them. The restraints were like the electronic handcuffs he been brought to this hellhole in, holding tight to his wrists and allowing very little movement.

He leaned forward on his tailbone as far as he could manage. Then he bent back fast and rocked forward. His hand grabbed the thing on his head and tugged. Pain seared his temple as flesh tore away and blood ran down his face.

He held the thing away from him to see what had been placed on his head to torment him. It wasn't an insect after all, but an electronic device of some kind.

It looked like a large silver lima bean, with red and green lights that flashed intermittently. "What the fuck?"

His face continued to bleed, but he didn't care. He'd rather be scarred and whole then some neuro-veggie-servant to Tanner and his black-suited circus clowns. Then he realized the purpose of the device. It was a God-damned disruptor. Instead of using it as a remote frequency, they'd found a way to implant part of the device under the skin. Butchers.

Repeating the maneuver he ripped the other disruptor from his opposite temple.

Now, if he only had a way to smash them.

There wasn't enough room for him to pull back his hand and hit the device against the bed, so he worried it in his hand for a moment, turning it over and over trying to find a vulnerable spot.

A small seam ran down the side of it. Damien tried to pry the edge of his thumbnail under it, but it didn't work. He ran his hand over the claws that had adhered to his skin. Nothing. The lights were probably just little glass bulbs, but wanting to be thorough in his examination, he pressed on them.

Was that just his imagination, or did the red one move?

He pressed it again and sure enough there was a slight clicking sound when he did. It didn't do anything. Maybe just a loose bulb.

He twisted the device he still held in his other hand until he could see the red light and pressed it. The same click occurred.

A design flaw?

He pressed them both at the same time and was caught off guard when the rush of emotions swirled in him. His link with Jade flowed back to him with tsunami strength.

"Jade?"

"Damien? Oh God, Damien. Are you all right? I'm coming for you, just hold on, sweetheart, until I can get there."

"Don't you dare! Send someone else. Stay away from here, babe. Please."

Her mind wrapped around his in a loving embrace. *"I love you so much, Damien. Do you hear me? So, don't do anything rash."*

Laying back on the gurney he let her declaration feed through him. She loved him. Jade Tanner loved him.

He wanted to shout out his triumph. To tell his captors they could all go to hell in a hovercar.

His heart pounded in his chest and throbbed in his injured temples.

Now more than ever he needed to break the restraints on his arms. If he found a way through the static soup of the link, he could find a way out of this godforsaken place—*wherever* it was. The important fact was he had to escape before Jade came anywhere near.

Chapter 22

She wanted desperately to tell Jesse her link with Damien had returned, but didn't dare alert the guards to her whereabouts. Surprise was her greatest ally. Sliding her thumb up, she clicked the gun safety off.

Jade stepped out of the room and held the antique weapon up to Reis's face. She braced her arms so they wouldn't shake. Despite the pitch and roll of her stomach, she had to look competent and confident or her plan would never work.

When Dale went for his laser, she shook her head. "Go for your gun to do anything other than throw it on the ground and your boyfriend here gets a face full of lead."

"Don't do this Miss Tanner. You're making a big mistake."

"No, you made the mistake when you killed my lover."

"We were doing our jobs."

"You're murderers, just like that bastard you work for." She placed her finger on the trigger. "Drop your weapons now! I won't say it again."

She knew they'd try something so she was ready for it. Dale went for his gun and turned it to fire. She lunged out of the way and shot wild as she went down. The report made her ears ring. A large wet stain filled Reis's upper left breast. He looked down and touched his chest, then fell to his knees. His gaze said he couldn't believe she'd done such a thing.

Jesse screamed in her ear. Damien screamed in her head.

She ignored them both for now. Her hands shook so badly she didn't think she'd be able to function.

Dale leaned over to help his colleague.

Jade took the time to stand. With his attention turned, Jade walked up and put the gun in the base of his skull. "Drop your weapon or you'll die, too."

God, how could she say those words and sound so cool, when she was in truth about to throw up?

He dropped the weapon.

"Now push it away, and do the same with his." When he hesitated, she pressed the gun tighter to his skin. "Now, not tomorrow. I'm on a tight schedule here."

He did as told. "He's still alive. Let me call for help."

"Are you kidding me? What kind of help did you give Quenton? He was your friend and you betrayed him. For money. Nothing more than that." She looked down at Reis. He probably wouldn't last much longer, but she wasn't a murderer. She wasn't her father. In fact, she hadn't meant to shoot him at all.

The sound of people on the stairs heralded help was on the way. "Here comes the cavalry. Now up."

Dale stood, holding his hands up by his head. "Are you going to shoot me, too?"

"I'm iffy on that right now. What I want is for you to open my father's office door for me. I know you have the new override codes."

"Miss Tanner…"

"If my father hurts Damien like he did Quenton, I swear to God there'll be no mercy from me. Open the fucking door!"

"Jade!"

Her mother rushed down the hallway with some of the house staff.

"You people fail to understand just how serious a situation we have here." Jade never took her gaze from Dale. She raised her voice to be heard down the hallway. "Stay where you are, mother, or I start shooting at random."

"Jade—"

She held her hand up to stop her mother's protest. "Not another word." Her gaze continued to bore into Dale's. "Open the door."

He clenched his jaw and tapped in a sequence of codes. The door clicked open. Jade slid inside, closing the door behind her. She locked the mechanism then aimed and shot out the control panel so on one could get in.

"I never knew quite how determined you were to disobey me."

Slowly, Jade turned around. How did he manage to make it home before she did?

Chapter 23

He'd seen it all through her eyes.

She'd had to kill a man and now she faced her lover's murderer. Why did she have to shoot out the door locks? Damn it, even the guards had been trying to warn her that Farroll Tanner was in residence.

Damien didn't blame her for not listening. He probably would have done exactly the same thing in that situation. The compulsion to close off the link and not watch what came next was strong. It was like going to a movie and closing your eyes when the scary part came onscreen. He didn't want to give her advice either. Nothing that would distract her in any way. But he was scared. Christ, he'd never been so scared in all his life.

The best he could do was to feed her strength and courage, and try to free himself in the meantime.

Several times he tried to fold his hand, bringing his thumb inward to attempt and slip his hands from the manacles. The snug fit around his wrists made that a losing proposition. The controls were off to the side, along the bed of the gurney. He didn't even think he could manage to reach it if he turned as far as he could on his side.

He sat up again to get a better look at the situation. Removing his hands from the restraints would be impossible, but what if he removed the restraints from the gurney?

They weren't bolted so much as they were attached by a lip and groove system. Granted the pieces fit flush together, but if he bent the gurney frame enough, the restraint base could be pulled out.

With his right being his dominant hand and therefore stronger, Damien worked on that one first. Rocking the restraint from side to side proved to have very little give, so he lifted up as hard as he could, using the restraint itself as leverage against the gurney frame. Little by little the frame began to give way. He only needed enough room to be able to slip out one side of the base at time, not pass them both through at once.

His right restraint came loose of the bed as the door locks hissed a protest and someone entered the room.

Glendown's answer to Dr. Frankenstein came into the room and stood over Damien. "Impressive. I didn't think you'd manage to get the disruptors off so soon. Well, no mind. In a few moments, you won't need them anymore."

That didn't sound good.

There were only three reasons on the planet why he wouldn't need the disruptors: one, if they let him go; two, if they lobotomized him; or three, if they killed him. He prayed it wasn't number two or three.

Dr. Ruskin leaned closer. "You know your journey ends here. You might as well say goodbye to your lover while you still have the link intact."

Damien spared the man a bland expression. "If my journey were truly ending, Tanner would have just had me killed on the highway. Don't even pretend you're not going to run some hideous experiment on me."

The doctor gave him a smile that held all the warmth of a snake. "Jade will forget you in time. Especially after she and I have our first few children. I'll breed the dirty Varti gene out of them myself. But, as I'm sure you well know by now, Jade's one tasty bit of pussy. I'd be willing to put up with quite a bit to keep her under me every night."

Damien didn't even think about what he did next. Blind rage and jealousy welled up from some great pit inside him. How dare the filthy-assed fucker talk about Jade that way? As if she would even have anything to do with him.

He brought his arm up with such speed and force that when he connected with the side of the doctor's head it snapped sideways. Ruskin crumpled to the ground.

Damien didn't wait around to see if the man was dead or just out cold. Quickly, he worked on the other restraint and freed himself. He jumped off the gurney and hurried out of the room.

A long sterile white hallway opened up in either direction. Not knowing which way to go, he turned right just to keep moving. As he moved down the hall, he could see through the slim windows on the doors he passed by.

Most of the people were dressed in bright white medical gowns. Disruptors were linked to their temples. Jesus, how many Varti were they holding in this fucking prison?

He stopped in front of one of the doors where a big man sat rocking back and forth on the bed. The door was locked from the outside via a code panel connected to the pneumatic locks. Damien tapped on the glass to get the man's attention. The man looked up and squinted at the door.

"I'm going to get you out of here, but you have to agree to help me free the others."

The man nodded and stood with his hands behind his back. Damien didn't know why until the man turned and showed him his hands were in electronic cuffs behind his back.

Damien nodded and held his hand up to let the man know he'd be back. He hurried to find the junction box. It was down the hall and built into the wall like part of the ornate decorations.

Pneumatic locks never held if the air lines were cut. He opened the box and since he had no cutters, simply pulled the pressure hoses from their ports. Klaxons screamed overhead. Red lights flashed, and all up and down the hall doors opened.

The guards would have a hell of a time restoring order with so much chaos about.

Damien ran back down to where he'd seen the man sitting on the bed. He stood there by the door and when he saw Damien, he turned around to have the cuffs removed.

"I don't have anything to cut them with, but I can probably disable them."

"Good enough. You do that, they'll fall off." He looked over his shoulder at Damien. "Name's John Holder by the way. Who the hell are you, the Angel of Mercy?"

"Damien Storm." He went to work disabling the cuffs and in short order they fell to the ground with a clink.

Holder turned a smile on Damien. "Should have known. It's kind of hard to keep a Storm at bay."

Damien gave a brief nod. "You got that right."

As they started out of the room, Damien stopped John. "Take the disruptors off your head and hit the red buttons at the same time. You'll be able to connect with your partner."

Holder looked as if he'd weep. He hurried to do as Damien told him.

By now the halls were filling with Varti, answering the Klaxon's call and running for freedom. Damien stopped as many as he could to disable their cuffs and remove their disruptors. Facility personnel and guards chased the Varti through the halls.

An arm reached out and grabbed him around the neck. Damien turned his head enough to see Dr. Ruskin with eyes wild and hair mussed. He tightened his hold around Damien's neck, cutting off his air.

Something hit them hard from the side, knocking them both to the ground. Then Dr. Ruskin was off him and being attacked by a mob of Varti out for vengeance. Fists flew and legs kicked, everyone trying to get a piece of the man who'd turned them into lab rats.

Guards started firing laser shots into the crowd, but more Varti came up behind them and overpowered the guards, disarming them.

The crowd continued to surge forward like frothy river rapids, taking down everything in its path that wasn't dressed in hospital white. Damien let himself be moved along with the crowd. Then finally the surge came to the front lobby and broke like a wave out into the sunlight.

Pain seared his chest. He looked down expecting to see something sticking out of him, but there was nothing but the internal sound of Jade's scream.

Chapter 24

Jade knew Damien was there, but not what he did. Love and strength poured through her from him, making her feel like an Amazon warrior.

She faced her father. There was no way in hell she was going to let this pustule of humanity intimidate her anymore. The life of the man she loved hung in the balance.

She pointed the gun at him. "I've already shot one man and unless you want to be number two for today, I suggest you hand over your computer codes."

"You'd do anything for him, wouldn't you?"

"Is that so hard to believe?" She inched towards the computer, while waving the gun for him to move away from it. "But then again you'd have to have a capacity to love someone in order to understand the length you'd go to for those you care for."

Farroll Tanner clenched his jaw. He slid his hands into his trouser pockets.

"Get your hands where I can see them."

"You know nothing about me, Jade."

"Nor do I want to. You made sure of that yourself. You're the most heartless creature I've ever had the unfortunate honor of meeting, and to think you're my father…"

The private comm station buzzed. All lines lit simultaneously. Something big was going down and Jade didn't want to lose focus on the immediate task in order to find out what was going on.

"I need to answer that. My agents will wonder what's taking me so long."

"They'll also wonder why there were shots from an antique gun fired inside the house, and why one of your personal guards is lying dead in the hallway, but that's too damn bad." She took another step closer to the computer. "Give me the codes before I lose patience."

"I don't believe you'll do it, Jade. You don't have the heart or the guts. If you killed Reis, it was an accident."

Jade pointed the gun at the floor and shot between his feet.

Her father screamed and bent down.

She hadn't lined up the shot properly and instead of hitting the floor as she'd intended, she shot him in the foot. Handling guns wasn't as easy as what they appeared in old movies.

Her stomach roiled again. Three days ago, she would have never conceived of shooting anyone, now she'd not only shot Reis, but her own father. Somehow, though, she didn't feel near the guilt she thought she should. Her father had hurt too many people and for so long that walking with a limp was probably going to be the least of his problems when Jesse Storm and Senator Grayhawk got a hold of him.

"The. Codes. Father."

He looked up at her with hate in his eyes. "You're just like your whore of a mother. God damn it how I prayed you wouldn't take after her."

"My mother is a whore?" Somehow she couldn't picture Glenda Tanner letting a man touch her in passion, let alone often enough to be considered a whore.

He gave a haughty laugh. Tears ran down his red face. His eyes were bloodshot with pain. "You showed your Varti side much later than most girls. I held out hope. I thought you'd be normal. I thought it would skip you entirely and we could be a happy family, the three of us."

"We would have been if you hadn't been a monster." She waved the gun at him again. "Are you going to give me the codes?"

"No."

"Fine." She sat down at the keyboard and proceeded to type in a series of numbers that would link her to Jesse by remote.

The comm link continued to buzz. She leaned over and ripped the wires from the wall. The sound died.

"I have access to the backdoor. You'll have to find the codes by remote. My father is being slightly uncooperative." She looked over the top of the monitor as Farroll rose and limped closer.

"Come just one step closer and you'll have a whole in your chest to match your foot."

He held on to the back of the visitor's chair on the other side of the desk from her. "You even look like her sitting there, turning my world upside down again."

Jade had lost the thread of the conversation. Her mother wasn't likely to turn anyone's world upside down. She was the perfect Agency Director's wife. Prim, understated arm candy with class and pedigree. "You really are demented."

"You aren't going to leave me, Jade. I didn't let Isabelle leave me, and I sure as hell won't let you."

Isabelle? Who the hell was Isabelle?

The door exploded off the hinges, showering the room with wood particles and hardware fragments. Jade tried to duck. She raised her hand to try and protect her face. A large piece of wood struck her in the chest, between the ribs. She looked down at it protruding from her body. She must have made a sound, but didn't remember uttering one.

"Jade! Jade!" Jesse screamed in her ear. She could hear him yell something else, but lost the words as people rushed into the office.

Her father limped around the desk and took her in his arms. "Jade, speak to me."

She tried to fight his hands from holding her. If she was going to die, she didn't want the last moments of her life to be in the arms of the Varti butcher.

"Damien? Damien..."

Epilogue

Six months later.

Warm sea air blew in through the open window, caressing her bare shoulders and bringing her up from the dark realm of sleep.

Jade opened her eyes. She hurt like hell. All over, too. Not just in spots. Damien had been insatiable the night before. Who would have thought making an honest man of him would turn him on so much. She was almost positive that she'd pulled a muscle or two and probably cracked a few ribs.

Her hand slid under the sheet and rubbed at the scar beside her breast that still shone purple. It hadn't been long enough for it to fade. The memory of that horrible day still made her shiver.

Damien rolled over and took her into his arms. His body was warm from sleep. His cock hard and insistent behind her.

He kissed her neck then moved slowly down her shoulder. Large hands caressed her breasts and belly. "Don't think about it, babe. Think about me and how much I love you."

"I almost died, Damien. If Mickey hadn't heard the shots and come to investigate, they would have let me die."

He brushed the hair back from her face. "Shhh. No they wouldn't have. Mickey had to pry you out of your father's arms."

That was the most disturbing thing about that day, the fact her father had been nearly inconsolable thinking she was dying. Then she learned after her long hospital stay exactly who Isabelle was and what part she'd played in the entire Varti/DEP fiasco.

Isabelle had been her father's lover. She was beautiful, ethereal and a Varti. Farroll and Isabelle had been very much in love, and delighted with their new baby girl. Until the day Isabelle's Vartek partner showed up.

Isabelle promised to stay with Farroll and Jade, but in the end she'd left them both. Farroll retaliated by having both Isabelle and her partner killed and started a movement that caused distrust and suspicions against the Varti. She had known that her father harbored a dark secret, but not the extent. Everything she'd believed about her life had been a lie.

Jade let out a sigh. The woman she'd always thought was her mother, had been a political match, nothing more, which explained the affectionately sterile environment she'd grown up in. What wasn't so easily explained was how one man's hate for a genetic quirk had turned into a nationwide movement to eradicate the Varti from the gene pool. Sometimes it only took one powerful person to start a movement. In this case it had been a destructive and hateful one. In the six months since that day, the DEP had turned from accepted government agency to a dark blot on American history. And once her father's files had hit the public news feeds he'd been indicated. And so had his main henchman, Dr. Ruskin.

Jade had been promised to Dr. Ruskin in exchange for his help in finding ways to separate Vartek pairs and wipe the gene from human DNA. The man had been so obsessed with Jade he had let Farroll lead him by the nose.

Damien moved his hand lower, strumming through her curls and into her folds. He circled her clit again and again. "I'm trying to distract you from your dark thoughts."

"I know." She rolled over in his arms to face him. He'd let his hair grow back and the blond highlights were long gone.

She brushed her hand over his forehead, moving the hair from his eyes. Because of him, she'd been able to pick up the pieces and start a new life. One full of love and joy, something she'd only thought of in distant dreams and poetry. "I love you so much, Damien. I don't think there are enough words or thoughts to let you know how much."

"That's good because I'm pretty much over the moon with you, too." He pulled her to his chest. Her breasts pushed flat against him. "Now that's settled, let me make love to you again Mrs. Storm."

She laughed at him and his adolescent horniness.

The dark thoughts lifted, scattering to the stratosphere as Jade opened her mind and body to the one man who had claim on both.

About the Author:

Kathleen Scott weaned her sci-fi teeth on the original Star Trek *series,* Twilight Zone *and* Outer Limits. *Now, eating a steady diet of SciFi Channel programs, she enjoys creating her own science fiction and futuristic realities out of thin air. She lives and writes from rural NJ, where she shares her life with her own superhero husband, Dave, and their rocket-powered dog, Lilly. You can find her daydreaming, stargazing or dreaming of far-off destinations. Or visit her at* www.MysticKat.com.

Seducing Serena

by Jennifer Lynne

To My Reader:

My love affair with romance began when I discovered others out there had the same dream as I, that one day we might be swept off our feet by the perfect hero—someone to cut a swathe through the emotional pain that ties up our hearts, and set us free to love and live more fully. Nick is my perfect hero, and Serena so much in need of his unique brand of rescue that I couldn't help but give him to her. I love their story, and I hope you do too!

Chapter 1

Serena Hewitt stared at the perfectly proportioned man and wondered at the cruel fate that had given this black-haired, green-eyed, bronze-skinned Adonis a brain the size of a pea.

"Why bother reading books when you can wait for the movie to come out?" he'd asked in that delectable voice, lifting his shoulders in a shrug. Just one more in a long line of opinions that had her head shaking in disbelief.

"Surely you're joking," she said. "Everybody reads *something*!"

The disappointment sat in her stomach like a lead balloon. How many men had she interviewed over the past three days? Seventeen? She'd thought, when he walked in… but no. Nicholas Wade was not the one for whom she'd been searching.

Not even when that quirk at the corner of his mouth and the gleam of amusement in his eyes caused a curl of anticipation deep down in her belly.

"Why would I joke about it?" he asked. "That's what today's about, isn't it? Get to know each other a little and see whether we wanna hook up. And with me, honey," he spread his hands wide and grinned, "what you see is what you get."

Her eyes narrowed, even as she felt herself responding physically to the charm of his grin. *See whether we wanna hook up*? For a second she wondered whether he was teasing, but why would he do that in these circumstances? "Well, thanks for your time, Nicholas—"

"Please, not so formal. Make it Nick." He leaned forward and the flash of a diamond in his left earlobe winked, as if mocking her attempt to categorise him.

"All right, er, Nick." She crossed her arms, then uncrossed them when she realised the action highlighted her cleavage. "I've heard enough to be able to make my decision. I'll be in touch soon."

Liar, liar, pants are definitely aflame. She leaned back in her chair as he stood up and dwarfed the normally spacious room. Late afternoon sun, rare in mid-winter Melbourne, slanted through the window of her city office, casting odd shadows across his face.

"So business-like." His teasing tone deepened into curiosity. "Let me ask you something, Serena. Do you really expect to find Mister Right this way? Where's the passion? The excitement? Don't you ever let your hair down and just have fun?"

"Of course." Unexpectedly stung, she sat up and removed her glasses to glare at him. "I'm thirty two years old, Nick, and its taken me the best part of my life to discover there's no such thing as Mister Right. Romance is well and truly over-rated."

"If you believe that," he said slowly, "then perhaps you've never been well and truly romanced."

"Maybe, maybe not." She held up a hand to still his response and continued, "I'm not looking for excitement, okay?" *I had that and it didn't work.* "I just want someone I can be comfortable with. Besides," she frowned, "if you're just after a bit of fun, why on earth did you respond to my advertisement?"

He shrugged, blank faced, then leant over the desk towards her. She detected the faint aroma of an expensive aftershave and had to fight the urge to inhale more deeply. "Let's call it a whim," he said. "I saw your ad in the paper and it was so serious. Even the wording of the ad—"

"What was wrong with it?" *Wanted,* she'd written. *A suitable man for the job.* Nothing unreasonable about that!

He chuckled, a slow rumble as contagious as a child's laugh. Her pulse quickened. "It stood out from the others for its lack of emotion, Serena. It made me curious. I wanted to hear your voice, get a feel for the *real* you." He moved into a patch of sunlight and his eyes blazed. "And when I accessed your voice mail..."

He reached out a long finger to caress the line of her jaw. The touch, so slow, feather-light, sent unwanted tremors coursing through her system. "Your voice intrigues me. It's totally unexpected. Deep. A little bit husky. Your voice gave out a completely different message to the business-like words of your ad. I couldn't resist its sexy appeal."

"I—well!" No one had ever commented on her voice like *that.* She tried to avoid moving back in her seat, out of the reach of his gentle touch. It was hard to concentrate with the almost hypnotic whisper of skin on skin. But she didn't want that knowing look in his eyes to deepen, the one that said, *I know what effect my touch has on you.*

"And then I came here today and found a curious contradiction," he continued. "A buttoned-up accountant with solemn grey eyes all set for business rather than pleasure." His words were like ice water in her face. She suddenly had no trouble breaking away from his touch. Then she scowled uncertainly as he added, "But there's one thing that tells me you might not be quite as straight-laced as you seem."

"Oh?" She spoke through gritted teeth.

"That tiny red rose on your left ankle."

"What? How did you—?"

"If you want to hide it you should wear trousers, Serena. Not that I'm complaining about the skirt." He grinned at her obvious discomfort and waved an arm as he said, "It was like a tiny flash of passion amongst all this grey common sense."

"No," she said after a considered pause in which she too, looked around the room. It *was* grey. But she liked it that way. "More like a tiny flash of rebellious madness amongst a mostly mundane teenage existence." Her dry words elicited a glance of appreciation.

"Quick witted, I'll give you that."

"Gee, thanks!" There was no doubt about it. He made her feel about as far from comfortable as you could get. She tried a light laugh. "Like I said, Nick, I'll be in touch soon."

"No you won't!" His quiet voice carried a thread of amused irony. "Did you know your face is an open book, sweetheart? And that's one book I *can* read!" He leaned over and flicked her nose with a gentle finger. "You have no intention of calling me again, have you? Pity. It'd be interesting to see if the promise of that rose could be fulfilled. And it's been fun baiting you today." His teeth flashed in a quick grin, then he was gone and she was left staring open-mouthed at the door.

Baiting? Her movements were jerky as she paced around the desk and across plush carpet to stare into the mirror above the couch. Startled eyes stared back at her from a pale face framed by a halo of riotous brown curls. Let her hair down? She didn't even have it *up*, for God's sake!

But she knew what he'd meant. And it wasn't a fair assumption.

Just because she'd decided to advertise and interview for a potential relationship didn't make her a passionless bore. It meant that past hurts would stay in the past, while the future would be hers to mould as she saw fit. On her terms. Without pain and suffering.

For once in her life *she* would have control.

She nodded decisively and straightened the white shirt she had chosen to wear with her favourite charcoal skirt. No—grey. Grey skirt. I *like* grey, she thought. And if Nicholas Wade is looking for a bit of fun then he'll just have to find it elsewhere.

Nick stood outside the building, looking up at the tall mirrored wall. His first thought when he left her office had been relief that she was more interested in whether he read Shakespeare than in who he really was and what he did for a living.

She was a strange one, Serena Hewitt, giving out signals that he suspected were mixed even in her own mind. Very prim and proper, she'd seemed, sitting there behind that enormous desk surrounded by grey walls and carpet. But there had been that glimpse of the rose, and the promise of something more in the fullness of her lips and the spark of defiance in those beautiful, dark-lashed eyes.

And her hair—he hadn't been able to resist that taunt about letting down her hair. It was gorgeous, a rich chestnut that fell to her shoulders in wild kinks and waves. He'd seen a couple of barrettes flung carelessly on the desk and guessed that at some point she'd tried and failed to contain the wayward locks. He was glad. It had given him several minutes of intense pleasure to imagine leaning across the desk and running his fingers through her hair, and further, to imagine her heated response if he'd done so.

For the first time in ages he felt his interest seriously piqued. She was an enigma, and one he intended to plumb until he found what made her tick. That was his specialty after all, or one of them at least, digging deep until every piece of the puzzle was in place and the mystery revealed. She might have no intention of calling him again—and that in itself was an unusual yet exciting challenge—but the ambiguous Serena was in for a surprise.

He caught sight of his reflection in the mirrored wall of the building, saw that he was grinning wolfishly and cautioned himself, "Down, boy, down. Remember its a job, and she's just one of many." But as he strode down the bustling city street his veins pulsed with an unexpected vitality, almost as if he'd been pumped with a shot of adrenalin.

And he found that of all the women he'd met over the past fortnight, there was only one face, one voice, one generously curved body, monopolising his thoughts.

"Serena? He was *gorgeous*! You can hardly go wrong with someone who looks like *that*!" Excitement threaded Vanessa's voice as she came through the doorway.

Serena shifted her shoulders to release the tension in her body and smiled at her sister. "Sorry, Ness. The man was impossible!"

Vanessa's jaw dropped as she stared at Serena. "What do you mean, impossible? He was the sexiest person I've ever seen. Well, in real life, anyway."

"Nicholas Wade probably thinks *Hamlet* is a baby pig!"

Even Vanessa faltered for a second. Then she grinned. "So what? Not everyone knows their Shakespeare as well as you. Just get him into bed as fast as possible and try not to let him speak too much. With a body like that…"

Her voice trailed off reverently and Serena found herself staring towards the door. Could will alone conjure him back? Truth be told, there *was* something about him strangely appealing. He'd arrived at her office twenty minutes late and completely unrepentant. She'd studied him in amazement, from the dark hair pulled back in a sleek ponytail and the flashing diamond stud, down that splendid physique encased in black T-shirt and jeans, to the slightly dusty and extremely well-worn boots.

Serena had struggled to breathe evenly. He hadn't dressed to impress, but he'd still looked like a movie star version of an undercover cop, with an aura of self-confidence that had shaken her to the core. Virile, was the word that had come to mind as she sank into a chair and gestured him to do the same.

Even so, it hadn't been his amazing looks, but the undisguised challenge she saw in those sea-green eyes, and the incredible energy that seemed to emanate from his body, that had caused a quiver of excitement to skate across her skin. Excitement. And fear.

Let him go, she thought, looking back at Vanessa and releasing her pent-up breath in a sigh. "Not everything is about sex," she said, in answer to her sister's flippancy. "Relationships should be about communication. Being friends."

"Well, I guess so."

Serena grinned at the doubt in her sister's voice. "You don't sound convinced."

"To be perfectly honest, I'm not. If you don't have the initial spark, Serena, the chemistry, then none of the rest matters, does it?" Vanessa frowned. "And I don't see how you're going to find the ultimate passion by going about this in such a *business-like* way."

She stiffened. There it was again. "I'm not looking for the ultimate passion! I just want compatibility. What *is* it about that idea that people can't seem to accept?"

Vanessa rolled her eyes. "Apart from being boring? All right, forget it. It's just…" She hesitated, then said with a rush, "Not all men are like Alex, you know."

Serena's heart skipped a beat at the shock of his name. "Don't—" she began, but Vanessa didn't heed the warning.

"I know you were hurt. Remember? I'm the one who had to help pick up the pieces after he and Kelly moved out."

"I know. And I'm grateful. But please, Ness, please don't say any more." Serena glanced at the calendar on her desk and realised that the little girl who had won her heart as a toddler would be eight years old next week. The pain of loss and betrayal had dimmed slightly over time. But not enough. Not nearly enough.

"Let's just leave the past *in* the past, shall we?" Never had she been more aware of the huskiness in her own voice. *Damn Nicholas Wade*, she thought, and had to clear her throat before continuing. "Ness, I admit it. He was sexy, that last candidate. *Very* sexy! But," she shook her head defiantly, "Nick's not the one for me. Comfortable is the last thing I feel when I'm near him. In fact, to be honest he makes me downright *un*comfortable."

"Maybe that's a good thing."

"No. It isn't."

She couldn't define exactly how she'd felt when Nick was in the room. All she knew was that her body seemed to respond to his raw sensuality as if it were waking from a long sleep, while her mind skittered away in fright.

She snatched up the list off her desk and frowned. "Right," she said. "Three left, I think. I wonder if Joe Crofton is here yet?"

"Well, there was *someone* sitting out there when I came in," Vanessa said doubtfully, "and if its *comfortable* you're looking for, then my guess is he fits the bill quite well. But—"

"Don't, Ness."

"All right, I'm going. But maybe you should think about this, while you interview the nice comfortable Joe Whatsit. When it comes to relationships you've got to *feel* it, Serena, not *think* it. Alex may have dented your heart, but he didn't break it. It still works, somewhere in there behind that wall you've managed to put up around your emotions."

Vanessa, you owe me, Serena thought several hours later as she found a seat in the lounge area of the bar and waited for her sister to bring a refill of their drinks. Those parting words had ruined the remaining three interviews and now she was back to square one. Alone.

Joe Crofton had been nice, but there wasn't any real spark of attraction. She might have chanced following up their initial meeting with a proper date, if it hadn't been for Vanessa's voice replaying itself in the back of her mind. Feel it, don't think it.

Why couldn't Joe have had a little of Nick's raw sensuality? Just an ounce would have done. But he hadn't.

She glanced around to see how her sister was faring at the bar. This Irish pub was owned by a client of Serena's, and the two girls sometimes met here for a drink after work or a bite to eat at the small but good quality restaurant next door. It was more crowded than usual, and she wished yet again that she was at home with her cat and a really good book. At this time of year there was nothing nicer than lounging by an open fire. Indeed, one of the reasons she had bought the tiny weatherboard cottage on the outskirts of the city was the double-sided fireplace it offered in both lounge and main bedroom.

That, and the fact that it was far from the ultra-modern urban apartment she'd shared with Alex, both in distance and style.

She sighed and turned away from the bar, then did a double take as her gaze clashed with a pair of green eyes that registered surprise and then a calculated kind of amusement.

"Damn," she said, then a further expletive left her lips as she saw Nick change stride and head across towards her. The fact that her heart started pounding almost painfully in her chest was due purely to embarrassment, she told herself. Ditto the struggle she had to catch her breath. "Hi," she managed as he sat down beside her, aware that almost every female head in the place had swivelled to gauge his destination.

"Guess I'm the lucky one, then," she said, indicating the envious looks of a group of young women at the next table.

His smile was slow and full of promise. Somehow he acknowledged his effect on the other women without taking his eyes off her, and the control she'd been scrabbling for disappeared in a wave of desire as deep as it was unexpected. She grabbed for her glass and drained the last of her wine in one big gulp, replacing it on the tabletop with a clumsy click as he spoke.

"You look lovely tonight. Different." His gaze raked across her top, admiring the deep red camisole that had replaced the white shirt. She'd had no choice in the matter, Vanessa having spilt coffee on her earlier and immediately pulling this trashy top out of her bag as a replacement. An obvious ploy, but she'd had nothing else to wear.

Automatically she tried to hike it up a little, aware that her plump curves were well and truly on display and wishing for the millionth time for a figure as sleek and svelte as... well... probably three quarters of the women in this room. Did any of them ever eat?

He watched her efforts with interest. "Matches the rose," he said at last, and in spite of her discomfort she felt as if she could listen to his mellow voice for hours.

"Let's see if I can get this right." He leaned back and thoughtfully studied her face, feature by feature. His gaze felt like a caress on her skin and she felt the heat of a blush creeping up from her neck. "A rose by any other name would smell as sweet."

"I... *what*?"

He grinned. "You hang upon the night like a rich jewel in an Ethiop's ear. Not quite verbatim, but near enough, don't you think?"

"I… I don't know—"

"*Romeo and Juliet*, sweetheart. When he first meets her and is swept away by her beauty."

"I know *that*!" Now she was aware of what he'd meant about baiting her. "I didn't know *you* knew, that's all. Why did you deliberately give me the impression that you were… less than well read, shall we say? Were you trying to make a fool of me? Was it all just some kind of game to you?"

"Life's a game, don't you think?" His pose was relaxed, one arm resting along the top of the couch, fingers drumming lightly on the burgundy leather. She shook her head as he added, "It just seemed so serious, so impersonal, you sitting there behind your big desk with a whole list of prepared questions. What do I do for a living? What are my interests and hobbies? Selection criteria." He grinned again. "I wanted to shake you up a little. Like I said today, where's the romance? The passion?"

She was quiet for a minute. "Like *I* said today, romance is over-rated. Expectations are rarely met. And ultimately, people get hurt."

Nick sat forward. The grin was gone now, but even so she could see a lurking trace of amusement as he said softly, "I think you're wrong, Serena. And you know what? It might be fun for both of us if I try and prove that to you."

Chapter 2

His audacity shocked her into silence, but at the same time she felt a quiver race like wildfire through her veins. Everyone else in the room faded away and it was just the two of them, staring at each other, not touching and yet connecting in a way she had never felt before. Not even with Alex.

She wanted to reach out, feel his skin, cement this strange unity in a physical way.

"What do you think, Serena?" he whispered. "Are you up to the challenge?"

She couldn't breathe, couldn't think beyond the possibility of this moment. "I—I don't know."

"Yes, you do," he said. "Let's dance." He laced his fingers through hers and drew her to her feet, and she found herself complying as if in a dream. She hadn't noticed the music until now except as a faintly annoying background hum, but she realised the tempo had changed to a slow, pulsing beat that trembled through her limbs and called to her inner essence with a strength that couldn't be ignored.

It's the music, she told herself, that's making my blood hum like this. Not the touch of his hand on mine.

He turned when they reached the dance floor and drew her into the circle of his arms, the heels of her black shoes giving her the necessary height to fit comfortably into the long length of his body.

Too comfortably.

She felt a gut wrenching ache deep down in her belly, felt her nipples go taut beneath the silken camisole as his torso brushed against hers. How did it come to this? she wondered, fighting the urge to undo his shirt and inhale the delicious scent of his skin. One moment I'm rejecting him as a potential suitor, the next I'm melting against him as if... as if...

"Mmm." The groan left her lips involuntarily as Nick cupped her buttocks and pressed her against the solid core of him. She couldn't think, just wanted to feel him, touch him, *taste* him... The heady musk scent of him rose around her, encasing them like a private cocoon. Her head dropped back and she felt him swoop in to claim the open expanse of her neck with his lips and tongue. A ribbon of warmth spread outwards from the contact point. Her pulse danced crazily as he followed the line of her throat upwards and began to tease her earlobe with a gentle nibble. Then she realised he was swelling against her, the hard flesh pressing into her belly with almost frightening dimensions, and she moaned her desire and shifted to better accommodate him.

"I wanted you naked the minute I set eyes on you," he whispered, warm breath tickling her ear.

The words should have raised alarm bells in her mind. Should have. But didn't.

"I thought I was too business-like for your taste," she murmured.

"You are! But that's the ultimate challenge... to break down those barriers and find the sensual woman beneath. And there *is* passion under the surface, isn't there, Serena? I can read the promise in those smoky grey eyes of yours, see the unconscious grace every time you move."

"I—I don't know." Her heart was fluttering like a mad thing in her chest. Nobody had ever spoken to her like this before. "Maybe there was, once. But now..." She shook her head, then squealed as his teeth grabbed briefly in a gentle crescent on her neck.

"Open yourself up to the possibility of passion, Serena. Let yourself feel how right this is." His lips followed where his teeth had gone, caressing the line of her neck and up to her jaw, then she was staring into eyes that had darkened to an emerald hue, eyes framed by faint laughter lines that deepened just a little as he smiled at her. The amusement was always there, she realised, as much a part of him as the desire that currently softened the strong lines of his face.

That's what desire does to you, she thought dreamily. Blurs the edges until you don't know your own mind. Until you don't know where one person ends and the other begins.

Until you don't know wrong from right.

Thirty-two years of life had not prepared her for his kiss. It started with a caress of his lips across hers, a warm exploratory quest that became instantly demanding as she yielded to the heat of their twined bodies and opened herself to him with a moan. Thought faded as urgent need took over. His lips and tongue met hers in a sensual dance she had never expected to learn again.

Heat, moist and musky, the divine taste of him, the sound of his ragged breathing intermingling with her own as they broke apart for an instant then reformed as one. Her fingers found their way into his hair, revelling in the strangeness of the long silken strands, then quested lower, over shoulders and back that offered up both soft heat and muscular hardness. The kiss went on and on, deeper and deeper, until she felt the very depths of her soul had been plundered.

She wanted him. It was that simple. She wanted him with every fibre of her being. Pressed against him, limbs trembling madly, aching and unfulfilled, she wanted to sink herself onto the shaft of his desire and chase away the ghosts of the past. Then he groaned, a deep guttural sound, and she discovered the true extent of her need in the heavy moistness between her thighs.

"Serena, if you don't stop grinding your hips against me I can't speak for the consequences." His voice was raw with need. "More than anything else right now I want to lose myself in your gorgeous body, but—" his chuckle was a trifle hoarse, "—this probably isn't the right time or place."

"No, of course not! I—*no*!" The blood rushed to her face as reality intruded. Looking wildly for signs of censure in the faces of those around them, she tried to step back out of his arms.

"Whoa, not so fast." He grinned wickedly and her blush deepened as he explained, "Just give me a minute before you expose my... er... need to public view."

She went super-still in his arms, trying not to incite further arousal in either one of them, grateful that no one seemed to be paying particular attention. After a pause she said shakily, "This wasn't a very good idea, was it?"

"Why not? I can't think of anywhere I'd rather be right now than holding you in my arms." She felt the brush of his lips on the top of her head, a gesture more tender than erotic, as he continued musingly, "Except perhaps my bedroom upstairs."

"You're staying *here*?"

"Next door. I keep an apartment for when I'm in town on business. It comes in very handy sometimes."

"I'll bet it does!" She was torn between outrage at his implied suggestion and laughter at the hopeful tone in his voice. Laughter won. "Sorry, Nick. I know you don't seriously expect me to sleep with you. And *before* the first date, too!"

"I guess not." The voice was glum, but his eyes twinkled. "But maybe there's something we can do about that. I meant what I said about proving you wrong. Romance does exist, you know. Shhh." He placed a gentle finger on her lips as she opened her mouth to protest. "Give me the chance to prove my argument and come out with me tomorrow. A proper first date."

She considered his words as he ushered her from the dance floor. What harm could one date do? Lots, was the cynical response. Logic screamed at her to say no, but her body ached from his nearness. "What did you have in mind? Dinner? A movie?"

"How about a picnic breakfast? You don't work Saturdays, do you?"

"Well, not usually, but—"

"Good. I'll pick you up about half past eight. Dress warmly. And Serena..."

"Y—yes?"

He leaned over to whisper in her ear, "This'll be the best first date you ever had. I guarantee it."

His teeth captured her earlobe and pulled gently, then he turned and left.

Leaving Serena host to an internal war between exhilaration, and dread.

❦

Bad idea, she kept telling herself the following morning as she waited for Nick to arrive. Nervous tension flooded her stomach and she doubted she'd be able to eat any breakfast at all. Except a packet of antacid tablets.

She replaced her glasses and studied herself in the tiny bathroom mirror, adding a final touch of gloss to her lips and pleased that for once she'd managed to capture her thick hair into a reasonably neat ponytail. Her denim jeans, brown leather boots and camel-coloured woollen pullover were, she hoped, practical enough for a picnic in July without being dowdy.

Today she was going to be sensible. She was not going to kiss him. She was not going to lose her head and try to rip his clothes off. And she was definitely not going to grind her hips against his like a lust-struck teenager.

"Maybe it'll rain," she muttered half-hopefully to her cat as he sat calmly watching her. "Or maybe he won't turn up."

The doorbell rang. Her heart thudded painfully, once, twice, then settled back as she wiped nervous hands on her jeans and went to greet him.

"Hi, Nick," she said, and if her voice was breathless she put it down to almost tripping over the cat rather than her visitor's deliciously sexy appeal. Again in jeans and boots, today he'd exchanged the T-shirt for a cream wool pullover under a well-worn black leather jacket. His hair gleamed in the sunlight and his eyes danced with mischief, and she acknowledged resignedly that Nick Wade, in appearance at least, could probably go head to head with Brad Pitt and come out on top.

He grinned as if aware of her mixed emotions. "Beautiful morning for a picnic, don't you think?"

She peered past him at the clear blue sky and felt the truth of his words in the cool, crisp air on her face. Melbourne weather was inconsistent at best, but if you did happen to get one of those rare sunny days without the treacherous southerly wind, then there was nothing nicer than being outdoors.

A reluctant smile tugged at her lips. "What did you do, Nick? Bribe the powers that be?"

"Something like that. Ah, hello puss. What's your name?"

Serena looked down in shock to see her cat rubbing madly against Nick's jeans-clad leg and purring like a recently tuned lawn mower. "Lancelot," she said gruffly.

He raised an eyebrow. "For someone who doesn't believe in romance that's an unusual choice of name."

"Yes, well…" She cleared her throat, ignoring his probing look. "He doesn't normally like strangers."

"He's using his animal instincts, Serena. Maybe you could learn something from old Lancelot here."

"Hmm. Let's go." She grabbed her bag and a thick lambs-wool coat from the rack in the hallway and stepped outside, momentarily face to face with Nick until, with a faint grin, he moved back to give her room. She locked the door carefully behind her.

He leant forward and kissed her cheek, a light caress more promise than reality. "By tonight you'll invite me inside, you know," he said, and she raised an eyebrow at the matter-of-fact confidence in his voice.

"We'll see about that," she murmured. *I'm definitely not ready to invite you into my home, Nicholas Wade.*

His hand encasing hers felt decidedly warm as he guided her down the pathway to his car. A wry smile curved her lips when she saw the BMW roadster.

"Tell me," she asked, "why is it that men like you always drive black, sporty-looking things and not, say, a little white Mazda?"

"Wouldn't fit in a little car, sweetheart. And besides, not as much fun!"

As she settled into the comfortable leather seat and watched Nick fold his six-foot plus frame inside the car, she had to conclude that in this case, he was probably right.

Nick didn't want to admit to nerves, but it was hard to find another explanation for the accelerated pumping of his heart and the unfamiliar sensation of butterflies in the stomach. At thirty-seven he was hardly a stranger to the dating game, but there was something about Serena that had truly caught his interest and for her sake even more than his own he wanted today to go well.

More than well. He wanted to introduce her to all the fun and passion that she seemed to have missed out on up to now. She had an air that spoke of shattered self-confidence. If it was in his power, he wanted to help rebuild that confidence. And if he got the information he was seeking, and had a little fun along the way, it would be a win-win situation for them both.

And so here he was, pulling up at the yacht club and waiting with bated breath for her reaction when she realised their picnic would not be land-based. "Well?" he barked impatiently as she just sat there, staring across the car park towards the state's largest floating marina. An impressive sight, with over two hundred boats currently berthed in the green-tinted water. Yet she wasn't reacting quite as he expected. The churning in his stomach intensified. "I thought I'd take you out on the bay in my yacht."

"You have a yacht." There must be something going on behind that bland expression, but damned if he could figure out what it was. She closed her eyes and he saw, magnified by her glasses, the network of tiny blue veins that laced across her eyelids. It reinforced the impression of fragility and he had to fight the urge to reach over and scoop her into his arms. Then she opened her eyes and smiled, a sudden wide grin that caught him like a blow to the solar plexus.

Who am I kidding? he thought. *This woman is more than just a job. Or a bit of fun.*

Sitting in the car, watching her gather up her things, Nick's interest crystallised into a fierce determination to seduce the thick woollen socks right off Serena Hewitt. Until her fear of the chemistry between them was blasted away in the heat of their burning passion.

Until, together, they fulfilled the promise of her delicious, sexy red rose.

Chapter 3

When Nick cast off and motored out of the marina Serena found the gentle rocking strangely therapeutic. Even more so when they reached the open waters of the bay and picked up speed. Nothing wrong with her stomach, then. Except a bad case of nerves.

Trepidation at the thought of being truly alone with him warred with an underlying sense of excitement. Excitement that grew until she felt the unfamiliar force as a buzzing beneath her skin.

He slanted a quick glance her way as if he sensed the burst of energy. "You're going to be fine," he said, and it seemed as if there were a double meaning attached to his words.

She felt a shiver run down her spine at the ease with which he appeared to read her. "We'll see."

She sat quietly in the passenger seat as he piloted, watching with interest as he consulted the many electronic instruments that surrounded them. Radar, depth sounder, GPS system – she could only guess at the function of each piece of equipment. But Nick's calm confidence spoke of familiarity and she felt the tension in her body begin to dissipate as they followed the ragged coastline.

"I didn't realise yachts could be piloted by one person," she said, as a yellow ribbon of sand stretched and curved into the distance. When she looked back towards Melbourne she could see the receding cluster of high rise buildings making up the city skyline and the arc of the West Gate Bridge. She let out a shuddering sigh that was quickly carried away on the breeze, and swivelled back to face Nick, lean and tanned and framed by the blue-green ocean.

"How big *is* this thing, anyway?"

"Sixteen point eight meters, just over fifty-five feet." He flashed her a quick grin, then refocused on his task. "Top speed thirty-two Knots, if you're interested. And its true, a lot of yachts need more than one crew member, but not this one."

She studied the aquiline features alight with concentration. He was obviously enjoying himself, but with a capable edge that made her feel safe in this less than typical environment. The feeling of safety was ironic, though, given how little she really knew about him. "What *do* you do for a living, Nick? You never actually told me."

"Didn't I?" His features became guarded. "I suppose you could say I'm a jack-of-all-trades. I have interests in a variety of businesses."

"Such as?"

He hesitated. "A vineyard in the Yarra Valley, for one," he said at last. "Boutique reds, mostly. I'm also part owner of a small sheep station in western Victoria, though I don't get over there as often as I'd like. My sister lives there, with her husband and six children."

"*Six?*"

"Mmm. How do *you* feel about children?"

The question hit her out of the blue and something within her tightened painfully. *Oh, Kelly.*

"I... I can't imagine the chaos of a household with six young people." She smiled, and it was almost a real one. "I'd love to have children one day, but probably only two or three."

Strange, she thought, how much warmth one could extract from another person's smile. And Nick's was very warm indeed.

When they headed into the shelter of a picturesque cove and he turned off the motor, the silence was absolute. She stepped down onto the deck and turned full circle, searching for movement of some kind, and saw nothing. Not another living soul. Save Nick.

Her heart bumped unevenly in her chest at the realisation that she had deliberately chosen to step onto this boat – and in doing so, had probably sent a message to Nick that she wanted to be alone with him. But she still wasn't sure if that were true.

She tried to concentrate on the feel of the sun as it warmed the top of her head, the soft fleece against her skin as she curled shaking fingers up into the sleeves of her coat. Then she heard the clunking, splashing sound as the anchor went into the water, and for some reason the sound calmed her. Like an anchor for my emotions, she thought. Such a responsible, purposeful action. Designed to stop us drifting into dangerous territory.

She had a moment's reprieve as he disappeared below deck, and she took the time for a few deep breaths, then he was back with an ice chest and a large white tablecloth.

She strove for normality. "So, a vigneur? Wine must be doing well." She gestured around, aware from the quality of the fittings that the sleek white vessel was a top-of-the-range craft.

He reached into a locker and pulled out a folding table that he proceeded to erect on the deck near the built-in padded seating. "Viniculturist, actually. And I've had the yacht a lot longer than the vineyard. I got her when I was twenty-two, just out of uni and in need of somewhere to live." She watched, strangely shy, as he set the table with the cloth and cutlery from the ice chest.

What would he expect from her today? Would she be able to resist if he asked more than she was willing to give? Would she *want* to resist?

"You're standing on the balcony of my first home, Serena. Here, try this." He handed her a plate stacked with smoked salmon, crusty white bread and a selection of ripe fruit and she sat down feeling an odd disconnection with reality.

As they ate, a salty breeze swept across the deck in playful gusts, tearing at her ponytail. She tried in vain to push back loosened strands of hair. Why didn't *his* hair come loose from its neat tie? He shot her an amused look as if he could read her thoughts and she gave up the lost cause and settled back to enjoy the spectacular view.

And spectacular it was. She looked across the water towards the still-distant shore lined with green scrub and felt a curious sense of contentment steal over her. "Tell me, how does anyone afford a boat like this straight out of university? My memories of that time are a grungy one-bedroom apartment in need of new carpet." She shook her head. "I remember my parents begging me to come home, but I was very proud of my newfound independence."

His chuckle was deep and throaty, his eyes glinting merrily like twin emeralds. Originally she'd thought they were the colour of the sea, but now that she had the water to compare with she realised they were a darker, richer green. "Just lucky, I guess," he said. "My grandfather set up a trust fund for me and my sister. He practically raised us while my parents travelled overseas." His face softened and he said huskily, "He died not long after Charlotte's high school graduation."

"You loved him very much."

"Yes," he said simply. "He and Charlotte – and now of course her six kids – mean everything to me."

She shook her head, smiling. "I still can't get over that. Six!"

"And little devils they are, too, sometimes. But they're great. I love 'em."

The obvious closeness with his family surprised and intrigued her. She thought of Alex, of their once-a-month duty visits to his mother, of the countless times she'd approached him about providing Kelly with a half-brother or sister. Funny, she hadn't realised until today just how much she would have liked to start a family of her own.

"Serena? Hey, where have you gone, sweetheart?" Nick put down his plate and slid into place beside her on the bench seat, thigh against thigh. She felt the instant warmth even through two layers of denim. He reached up to cup her chin, turning her towards him. "Everything okay?"

"Sure," she lied. "It's just… well… nothing. Tell me about your parents, Nick. Why did your grandfather have to look after you?"

He waited as if to let her know that he was aware of her ploy to change the subject, then gave in gracefully. "Dad's a diplomat and my mother—" he grinned wryly, "—she's a good diplomat's wife. They decided early on that it'd be more stable for Charlotte and I to grow up in one place, so my grandfather volunteered. And to be honest, I'm glad. To grow up in the country, while still being close enough to the city and the bay to enjoy all of this…"

He waved his arm, encompassing the view, and she marvelled at his ability to find happiness where others might harbour filial resentment at being offloaded onto someone else.

For several minutes they ate in a kind of silent companionship that she had never thought possible when she first met him… was it only yesterday? She even accepted a fluted glass filled with light golden champagne, with only the briefest of protests about the time of day.

"Only on special occasions," he answered, eyes crinkling at the corners.

"*Is* this a special occasion?"

"What do you think?"

She found herself, glass in hand, leaning back into the circle of his arm. Above them she could see a pair of seagulls gracefully riding the breeze, the same breeze that whispered through her hair and across cheeks tingling with vitality.

"I think maybe it is," she admitted, and was rewarded with a brief tightening of his embrace. "I had no idea when you said a picnic that *this* is what you had in mind."

"Almost... romantic, would you say?" His teasing tone brought the blush fully to her cheeks.

"Maybe, just a little. But that doesn't mean you've won me over. Yet."

"Give me time, Serena."

She pushed against him playfully and he grabbed her wrist, then somehow her torso was up against his and he was removing the glass from her hand. "Do you know how badly I want to kiss you right now?"

She shook her head, suddenly mute. Part of her had been waiting for this moment ever since she'd opened her door to him this morning.

The sweet ache in her belly flared instantly as he took her hand and guided it downwards where her trembling fingers touched denim material straining across his abdomen. "*This* is what you do to me," he said gruffly, "with your air of self-possession and your achingly full lips. I want those lips wrapped around me, Serena. I want *you* wrapped around me, and then I want to pleasure you until you can't take any more."

Her intake of breath was sharp. She tried to think of a reason to say no, but the nerve endings in every inch of her skin were clamouring their own alternative response.

"Wh—what do you want from me?" she asked as her breath escaped in a shaky sigh. "We both know you could have any woman you wanted. Why me? Is this part of your game?"

"I don't want any woman. I want you. As to why... the honest answer is I don't really know. There's something about you that makes me want to ravish you and protect you at the same time." He shrugged as if embarrassed by his words. "All I know is, for the past twenty-four hours I haven't been able to get you out of my head."

She gasped as he slipped a cold hand beneath her pullover to tease around the edge of her bra. A nice serviceable bra that she had no intention of revealing... that is, she *hadn't* had any intention..."That tickles," she managed as he raised a querying eyebrow.

"Oh?" His fingers dipped beneath her bra to brush across one erect nipple and she shivered at the intense sensation. "How about this? Does this tickle, Serena?" His thumb and forefinger gripped the nub and pulled gently, then began to massage in slow circles that raised goosebumps across her skin.

"No," she gasped. "That doesn't tickle. It—*aches*." The last word came out as a moan and even with half-closed eyes she saw his face harden with desire.

"Good," he growled. "As to what I want from you..."

"Yes?"

"I want *this*," he said, then his lips came down on hers in a kiss so new and exciting, yet so achingly familiar, that she surrendered to him without further thought.

He tasted of champagne, and salty sea air, and the sexy sweet flavour that she was beginning to know was uniquely Nick. His tongue thrust against hers with an arrogant mastery and she heard the guttural protest deep down in his throat as they parted for a moment, then reformed as if he couldn't get enough. This time the kiss was so long and so deep that her head began to swim. But when his lips left hers to nuzzle at her earlobe she whimpered at the desertion.

The sound incited him further and with a violent movement he yanked out the tie holding back her hair. "Better," he grated. "Now take off your coat."

"But—"

"Take it off!"

The savagery in his voice required instant compliance.

Then as the long strands blew across his face and hers she found herself lifted up and over his lap until she was poised above him.

"Fair's fair," she whispered, and reached up with a trembling hand to loosen his hair from its confines. She touched her fingertips to the silken locks, prolonging the moment before their flesh made contact, feeling the unfamiliar power as she looked down into his blazing eyes and waited, waited… Then her hips came down to explore his hard heat in the valley of her own body with a slow and hesitant rhythm.

His hands cupped her buttocks, wordlessly encouraging her sinuous movements, then slid up her back in a trail of heat to find and release the rear snap of her bra. As her breasts swung free beneath her clothing she heard him growl, "I want to see you better."

"Yes," she breathed, and lifted her arms to assist as he jerked her top up and over her head. The bra followed. For a moment, as cold air blasted across her torso and naked breasts, she froze in indecision.

There had been only one man in her life. Until now.

This is madness, she thought. I'm about to make love to a near stranger on a boat in the middle of the ocean.

As if he sensed her hesitation Nick shifted a little beneath her. The movement emphasised his huge proportions and sent the ache in her womb spiralling again. "As much as it pains me to say this," he said breathlessly, "we don't have to go any further if it doesn't feel right for you."

She stared down at him in shock, saw the sincerity in his eyes and was even further confused. He was like Alex in so many ways. The good looks, the easy charm, the arrogant assumption that things would go his way, and also, she knew, the potential to wound if she let herself feel too deeply. It was the latter that scared her most of all. But maybe there were differences, too. Differences that would allow her to set the pace, to back off if she felt unbearably threatened.

But did she want to back off? Right this minute, feeling the power of his arousal beneath her, feeling this overwhelming need to lose herself in him, to obliterate Alex from her head and her heart…

There was something about Nick so utterly compelling that the simple act of being offered a choice enabled her to choose him. She reached up to caress his angular cheek, captivated by the smoothness of recently shaved skin. "I want you, Nick," she admitted. *Do or die.* "And I want to make love with you, right here on this boat. I want us *both* to lose control."

She felt his fingers tighten convulsively on her hips and her heart leapt in response. She bent her head to meet his lips in a sizzling union before he twisted away to explore her throbbing breasts. He took one exposed peak into his mouth and suckled, and she moaned as the warm moistness competed with the cold sea air. "Nick," she managed as his tongue circled her nipple playfully, "please…"

"Please what, Serena?" he teased as his fingers continued where his tongue had left off. "Do you want more of this? Do you want more, here?" With the tip of a finger he left a warm trail from her breasts down across her stomach to rest, feather-light, at the button of her jeans.

"Yes," she whispered, "I want more." How had she ever thought she could live without this? Her head dropped back and her spine arched as he popped the button and slowly undid the zipper. She heard his breath catch in his throat and felt the trembling of his fingers as he caressed the tiny scrap of lace covering her sex.

"So this is where you've been hiding your passion. I just love red on you. Though its a toss up between this little piece of material," he slipped his finger beneath her panties, "and the rose."

Even through the haze of desire she had to laugh. "You don't give up, do you?"

"In the game of love? Never."

The words hardly registered as his fingers teased her lightly. Wild sensations spread outward from his touch and her breath quickened. Then he slid her off his lap until she stood shivering before him. "Let me show you the state room," he whispered, lacing his fingers through hers. Wordless, she let him lead her through a tiny salon and down to the bedroom. They stood together as she stared with wide eyes at the neatly made bed.

"Are you sure about this?" he queried again, and she smiled crookedly.

No! "Yes. Where were we, Nick?"

"I think," he dropped to his knees in front of her, "we might have been about… here."

She held her breath as he shimmied her trousers down, then released it shakily as his fingers unerringly found their mark. "You're gorgeous," he said with an almost reverent tone. "So deliciously curvy."

"Plump I think is the wor—*Oh*!" The exclamation turned into a moan as he ripped the lace in one quick movement and leaned forward to taste her with his lips and tongue.

Serena had never felt such exquisite agony. She wanted to scream her need aloud but found herself whimpering instead as her fingers tangled in his hair and her body shuddered beneath his ministrations. The world closed in until there was nothing beyond this moment, this person, this wet slickness between her legs that was better than anything she had felt before. Fear was forgotten, everything was forgotten but the need, the desire, the excruciating hunger for blessed, climactic release.

"Yes," she breathed, "yes, Nick, don't… stop… *please…*"

She was pleading for him to continue, pleading for him to stop, couldn't think, could only feel, as his tongue flicked aside the folds of her flesh to find and stroke her swollen, throbbing clitoris. She felt the scream welling inside her but she fought to hold it in, to hold *on* just that little bit longer…

Feeling her body writhe under his lips and tongue, inhaling her sweet scent and hearing her tiny cries as he guided her to the edge of reason, Nick felt his own body trembling with the effort of holding on. Just a little longer…

This was no game.

This woman meant something to him.

But what that something was, he had yet to discover.

He loved the taste of her. Couldn't get enough. Pure woman, but with a hint of her own unique perfume wafting into his nostrils. So sweet, so slick, so… *wet* and ready to be fucked.

He lifted his mouth from its intimate embrace and looked up, along the feminine curves of her body. The rapture transforming her features was almost his undoing. With a shuddering groan he drew her down onto the coverlet where she lay panting, arms and legs spreadeagled in unconscious invitation while she watched him undress. And there on her ankle was the rose, that symbol of everything she had to offer, a bright splash of colour against her milk-white skin. He wanted to press his lips to it, then travel up her leg to the dark inviting triangle at her core.

He heard her gasp and saw her eyes widen as he released himself from the prison of his jeans, and revelled in the cool air across his hot, blood-engorged skin. Then she sat up and, with a sweet yet knowing look in those amazing grey eyes, leaned across to take him into her mouth.

And he was gone.

Nothing existed but the moist warmth of her lips and tongue as he shuddered and pulsed inside her. His cry strangled in his throat and he fought to hold on just that little bit longer. "I can't, my love, I'm… going… to…" He twisted away, fumbled quickly in his jeans for the foil packet, then her hands, her smiling lips, were there again and he was sheathed and ready to plunge inside her as she lay back on the bed and opened herself to him like a glorious flower to the sun.

When his body became one with hers they both cried out, then he was riding her, plunging, deeper and harder, fucking her so hard he thought he would die. He felt the exquisite tightening of her body and for a millisecond everything stopped. He stared down into her beautiful grey eyes, holding the moment, burning it into his memory, and felt rather than heard the scream burst out of her as her muscles began to contract around his cock. He tried to wait, to watch her as she came, but the pressure was too intense and he released himself into her with his own triumphant cry of possession.

Chapter 4

"Tell me again why you were looking for a partner through the personals, Nick."

She lay snug beneath the comforter on the bed, curled against the silky smoothness of his long form. He had one arm beneath her, the other tracing aimless patterns along the line of her collarbone, circling around the gold heart locket she always wore.

Even sated she could feel the power in his fingertips, with the potential to send her spiralling out of control once again. The thought sent a thread of unease through her system and despite the cocooning closeness she shivered. How could he affect her so intensely? Leaning up on one elbow she stared down into laughing green eyes that gave away nothing. Except perhaps a certain smug contentment. But then, she conceded, feeling the pleasurable ache through her limbs, I've probably got the same look right now, too. Except my contentment is tempered with a huge dose of doubt.

"Well?" she demanded when he didn't answer straight away. "I'm sure you know you could give Brad Pitt a run for his money." She grinned at his snort of laughter, but persisted with her question. "Why would you even need to *look* in the personals, let alone actually respond?"

"Why would you?" he countered. "Does it have something to do with… this?" He flicked the gold locket and she instinctively raised a protective hand to cover it. "Are you looking for someone to replace the person in here?"

"No! Don't be silly. You don't know anything about it."

"Then tell me." His voice was persuasive.

She sat up and looked away from him. Through the tiny window set high in the teak panelled wall she could see blue sky and fairy floss clouds. If she squinted, one of the clouds looked like a heart. She frowned as the shape stretched and broke apart. "I don't know if I can," she said. "It's very personal. And I hardly know you."

She felt the shaking as he tried unsuccessfully to contain his laughter, then he flicked back the blanket to expose their nakedness and said, "Really!"

For a moment she hesitated, not sure whether to take offence, then she was laughing with him. "Okay," she admitted. "So maybe we do know each other to a certain degree. But that's different. That's physical. I'm talking about, well, emotional closeness. That's something I doubt you and I will ever have." She hugged her knees tightly into her chest, certain of the truth of her words even as a wave of guilt swamped her.

"Why the hell not?" His voice was rough with anger. "You and I just shared the most intense sexual experience I've ever had. I hoped you felt the same way. But now you're saying... that's it? Game over?"

"Its not a game, Nick." Her voice was fierce, but inside her heart flip-flopped painfully. The most intense sexual experience of his life? "What we just had was wonderful," she admitted more softly. "But that's precisely why I can't let this go any further. I—" She took a deep breath. "This isn't me, Nick. This... impulsiveness. I usually think everything out very carefully before I act. Weigh up the pros and cons. And so far with you, I seem to have done the exact opposite. I feel as if meeting you has forced me to take leave of my senses!"

His eyes narrowed. "If I didn't know better, I'd say you're deliberately trying to make me angry in order to create a distance between us."

"No!" Then she considered his insight and realised she owed him – and herself – the truth. "Well, maybe." How could she explain her fear? "If I let myself, Nick, I think I could fall in love with you." She felt his start of surprise and added, "But I can't. *I just can't*! There's nothing left inside me to deal with it if I get hurt again. *Nothing!*"

For a minute or so there was silence, punctuated only by the lapping of waves against the side of the boat. Then in the distance she heard the faint thrum of another motor, someone else out on the water enjoying the weekend winter sunshine. It was as if their circle of intimacy was breaking up. She wasn't sure that was such a bad thing.

Nick sighed and put his hand under her chin, forcing her to meet the unusually serious look in his eyes. "If I could promise not to hurt you, Serena, I would," he said. "But I can't. All I *can* say is that when I met you I wanted to have a bit of fun, but now it's gone beyond that." He shook his head and amusement flared again. "To be honest, you're taking me into new territory. New and damn confusing! But please believe me when I say I'll do everything in my power to avoid hurting you. Everything!"

"I know you will. But—"

"Stop!" He placed a warm finger over her lips. "Don't say any more. Just let today run its course and see how you feel later. Right now, I think we should get dressed."

"Why? I mean... yes... of course." She leant forward, glad for once that her hair was thick enough to hide behind as he got up to retrieve their mingled pieces of clothing.

"I have something else to show you," he explained. "But—" his eyes crinkled at the corners before disappearing beneath his thick pullover, "—we won't be alone this time, so it might pay to put your clothes on first."

"Oh! All right." Her blush deepened as she fumbled for her underwear, feeling even more awkward when she remembered he'd torn her lace panties right off her body. Another first.

His lack of embarrassment at being naked only served to emphasise her sudden reticence. As if aware of her inner turmoil, Nick left her alone to finish dressing, appearing again with two mugs of steaming coffee as she was zipping up her boots.

"There's milk and sugar in the galley," he said, but she shook her head.

"Black's fine." She took a sip of the fragrant liquid and felt its heat travel right down to her stomach. Maybe he's right, she thought, following him up on to the deck. Maybe I should just see what happens. At least for today.

He pulled anchor and started the engine and they continued along the coast. Serena sat quietly, fully aware of every move Nick made. She didn't need to turn her head to see the angular planes of his face, the tanned skin, the dark hair flowing out behind him as he sat beside her. She *felt* him. Felt his essence even as she tried to concentrate on the view.

It was some time before the scenery worked its magic and taut muscles began to relax. Once Nick pointed ahead and to the right, and she saw two dolphins burst from the water in a perfectly synchronised arc, disappearing beneath the waves in a splash of white spray.

"Beautiful," she breathed, and her vision blurred as tears threatened.

"Yes, beautiful," he agreed, and when she blinked the tears away and looked at him he was watching her with a tiny smile lifting the corners of his mouth.

At last they slowed and headed towards the shore, pulling in at a small jetty near the seaside village of Sorrento. Nick worked with impressive efficiency to secure the boat and offered his hand to help her alight on the jetty.

"Where are we going?" she asked as he led her from the sandy beach up a dirt walking track cut into the hill.

"To a friend's place. After our meeting yesterday I thought you might be interested in some of his wares. There," he said, pointing to a two-storey building as they crossed the road at the top of the hill.

"A bookshop," she said, unable to hide the delight in her voice. She'd assumed he was going to show her a view of some kind, but this was a wholly unexpected pleasure. Especially when they stepped inside and she realised *Lotus*, as the business was called, contained a cafe upstairs with huge floor-to-ceiling windows overlooking the bay. "A bookshop, food, *and* a view. This is my kind of surprise." She smiled at Nick and saw the pleasure he took in her response.

On impulse she reached across and grabbed one of his hands, pressing it tightly between her own. "Thank you," she said. "You're doing all you can to please me and I'm being very prickly in return, aren't I?"

"I wouldn't quite say that." He pulled on her hand and it seemed completely natural to move into the circle of his arms. He leaned down and pressed a gentle kiss on her forehead. "You felt remarkably soft and supple on the boat," he whispered. "No prickles in sight." Warmth filled her, then he was releasing her to greet his friend who had appeared with an exclamation of delight.

"Nick! I can't believe its you. Annie's going to be so disappointed she missed you. She's gone to an antique auction. We haven't seen you here for six months."

"It has been awhile." Nick turned to introduce Serena.

"Ben Harper, an old school friend of mine. We've known each other since we were… what… seven?"

"Something like that. Pleased to meet you, Serena."

She felt unaccountably shy as she shook Ben's hand, hoping she didn't look like a woman who'd just made love. She could tell he was curious, and she didn't want to fan the flames. Nick, she noted wryly, looked just the same as ever. Devastatingly sexy, and totally in control.

Once the introductions had been completed Ben asked, "So, how have you been? How's the vineyard? And what else are you working on these days? Still writ—"

"Yes, yes." Nick cut across the other man. "So, Ben, if we have a look down here first, have you got a table for a late lunch?"

Ben gave Nick a strange look, then turned to Serena and grinned. "Have I got room for a beautiful woman? Any time." He was as tall and well built as Nick, but his brown hair and freckled face gave him a boyish air that was friendly rather than sexy. She smiled back, instinctively liking him.

Then found herself wondering why it was so hard to find the same simple liking for Nick. She moved away to browse through the shop, but her thoughts were not on books. It wasn't that she didn't like Nick. But what she was beginning to feel for him was far more confusing. And frightening.

Nick couldn't explain the impulse that had led him to bring Serena here. *Lotus* was one of his few refuges from an intensely busy life, and until now he'd never thought to bring one of his women friends over. They belonged in the city, where he could wine, dine and bed them in glamorous surroundings. Ben and Annie, and this peaceful little pocket of south-eastern Australia, were different. They were… special.

So why was he standing here, grinning like an idiot as he watched Serena avidly browsing the extensive bookshelves and exclaiming over some rare little tome she'd managed to discover?

And why was he so nervous about Serena finding out the truth of what he did for a living? About why he'd responded to her advertisement in the first place? I *have* told her the truth, as far as it goes, he thought. But I haven't told her the whole truth. Yet.

Lunch was simple but delicious, a seafood pasta with yet more wine to accompany it, followed by cake and a refreshing pot of tea. Serena felt warm and replete, basking in the glow of Nick's vivid eyes as he stared at her over the rim of his teacup.

"You look almost civilised with that thing in your hands," she teased, deciding not to question the momentary happiness.

"Almost?" One eyebrow raised itself suggestively and she chuckled.

"It's the earring, I think," she said. "Maybe the long hair. Not quite boy-next-door."

He replaced the cup in its saucer and leaned forward. "And if I were the boy-next-door, would you be sitting here with me today, Serena? Would you have surrendered yourself so completely on the yacht this morning?"

The events of the morning had been central in her thoughts, but she felt her cheeks begin to burn at his unexpected reference. "That's not something I make a habit of, you know."

"Yes, sweetheart, I did figure that bit out." His voice was gentle as he folded his hands over her clenching fingers. "And I want you to know that I didn't plan it that way. Hoped, of course, but I didn't plan it."

"Really!"

Her dry tone brought forth a chuckle, then he sobered. "I'm also hoping that it won't be a one-time thing. That there could be something more between us."

"I don't know, Nick. I just don't know!"

He immediately pulled back. "I'm sorry. We'll leave it for now. Besides, I think it might be time to head home."

She could tell by the set of his face and hunched shoulders that she'd hurt him, but didn't know how to make him feel better. Then she followed his frowning gaze out the window and saw dark clouds gathering in the distance. It seemed ridiculously appropriate.

Their trip back was conducted in near silence, Nick grim-faced with the effort of manoeuvring through increasingly choppy waters, Serena thoughtful but queasy as the wind picked up strength and the day turned dark. The first drops of rain began to fall as they reached the marina. By the time they got to the car it was a full-on downpour, and she wondered if this was a portent of worse to come.

It was.

When they arrived at her cottage the rain had turned to hail and she was shivering violently as she searched for her door key. "Why don't you come in, Nick," she said, "and wait till the worst of the storm has passed. I make a mean hot chocolate."

He smoothed dripping hair from her face "I don't think that's a good idea right now. Maybe we need to slow things down." He shook himself and droplets of water sprayed in all directions. "When I see something I want I push hard for it, and today on the yacht, I didn't give you much choice, did I?"

"Of course you did!" She was shocked. "Today was my decision as much as yours and I don't regret it one bit." As she spoke she realised it was true. Whatever her motivation had been, she knew that her decision today had been the right one. And she wanted more. "Please," she coaxed with a gentle smile. "Come inside, Nick, and let me prove that to you."

She moved sinuously against him and for an instant he held her tight. Then he groaned and stepped back, giving her a gentle push towards the door. "Go, before I lose my gentlemanly self-control! I'll call you tomorrow."

She watched wordlessly as he disappeared into the driving rain, her body awash with aching desire and her mind swirling with confusion.

Nick slammed his fist against the steering wheel, his whole body thrumming with need. What he wanted to do more than anything in the world was take her right there and then on the threshold of her home, half in and half out of this blasted storm. A cynical grin twisted his lips as he imagined her reaction. How would she have felt if he'd succumbed to the impulse and ravished her as hot and hard as his body was screaming out for?

"Damn it," he muttered, starting the car and heading back to his apartment for a quick shower. Serena had invaded his every thought. His senses were fully attuned to her. But he knew that for tonight at least he had to put her out of his head. He had to forget the feel of her soft silky skin beneath his fingers, forget the sultry sweep of her lashes as her eyes closed in the midst of their passion. He had to pretend he couldn't hear the echo of her mindless cries mingling with his as he drove himself into her moistly accommodating body.

If he didn't clear her from his mind - if he couldn't wash her sweet perfume out of his hair and clothes - he wouldn't be able to do his job properly, and that's where he needed to be right now, out doing his job. Gathering the facts. Dating the others.

Chapter 5

Serena felt remarkably better after a long bath filled with perfumed bubbles. She wrapped herself in her favourite old bathrobe and used firelighters and kindling to establish a cosy blaze in the lounge room hearth. "Do you think there's any such thing as a knight in shining armour, Lancelot?" she mused, scratching her cat under the chin as he curled up beside her on the couch. "Is Nick right? Or are you the closest thing I'm going to get to that?"

As she stared into the flames Nick's face stared back at her, that ever-present grin threatening at the edges of his mouth. She frowned and blinked, but it was no use. Even the thought of him caused a throbbing ache to start up in her womb, as her body relived the sensuous feel of hands and lips in intimate places.

She shifted, trying to forget the incredibly full feeling as her body struggled to accommodate his enormous size.

Tried to forget the triumphant glint in his eyes as he moved over her, slowly at first, then faster until he took her with him into the place where thought ended and sensation was everything.

And his murmured endearments as he held her afterwards, the gentleness in his touch that was an unfamiliar counterpoint to the previous force of his passion.

The flames in the fireplace moved and shimmered as tears threatened to spill. Would she ever find the happiness she sought? In Nick's arms, with his body joined to hers, it had seemed possible. Then they parted and all her fears came crashing back.

Who *was* Nicholas Wade?

"What do you think, cat? Am I too uptight, with a wall around my emotions, as Vanessa says? Or am I just... sensibly cautious?"

The cat said nothing, but the doorbell spoke volumes. She glanced at the clock on her mantelpiece and frowned. Who would be calling at a quarter past ten at night?

With some trepidation she put on the safety chain and opened the door to find Nick leaning against the wall with a look of determination on his face.

"What are you doing here?" *I'm not wearing any makeup. And I haven't brushed my hair and... oh, God, I'm wearing the oldest bathrobe in the history of the world!* "I don't think this is such a good idea, Nick. Maybe you should come back tomorrow."

"No!" His voice vibrated with emotion. "Let me in, Serena. We need to talk."

She hesitated. "What happened to taking it more slowly?"

"Guess I'm not a slow-paced kind of guy," he murmured. "Please?" The plea was accompanied by a crooked grin.

She released the safety chain.

As he entered she was struck anew by his physical magnificence. He was dressed for what seemed to be a night on the town in dark trousers, a light shirt and yet another leather jacket, this one markedly less worn and dusty than the other. His hair was neatly drawn back, showcasing his winking diamond earring. She pulled her bathrobe more tightly around her.

"I hope you're not expecting me to come out with you now?"

"What? Oh, no." He frowned as she gestured him into the lounge room. "I've been out already. I had an appointment I couldn't change but," he looked around the room with interest before collapsing onto the couch next to Lancelot, "I found that I couldn't stop thinking about you. About us."

"Oh!" He seemed too big for the tiny room. She sat carefully in the armchair opposite, taking time to arrange her bathrobe neatly over her legs, and began picking at a loose thread near one of the buttonholes. Her fingers were trembling too hard to get a proper grip. "I must admit to having certain thoughts along those lines myself," she said.

"Really?" He lifted his head and she saw his gaze sharpen as if noticing her attire for the first time. "I love those slippers. Very sexy."

She looked at her feet, encased in big balls of pink fluff, and her cheeks darkened. Then she was laughing with him and the awkwardness began to evaporate.

When he lifted a hand and said, "Come here," she obeyed with only a moment's hesitation, as if an invisible cord connected them and she was powerless to resist.

Let's hope it's a bungy cord and I can bounce back afterwards.

As the cautionary thought raced through her mind she found herself half on and half off his lap in a tangle of limbs. There was no more time for regret. His mouth swooped down to claim hers in a kiss that had nothing to do with gentleness and everything to do with hunger.

Insatiable hunger.

When Lancelot yowled at being crushed beneath their bodies, they parted for an instant, laughing as the cat stalked off with a twitching tail. Then Nick pressed her down into the soft cushions again. "You look all fresh and clean, and you smell like rose petals," he said. "I want to sink myself into your niceness."

"I've never heard it called *that* before."

He chuckled briefly, then sobered. "You're different to what I was expecting when I responded to your ad."

She shifted beneath him and he moved so that his weight was not pressing her down. "What were you expecting, then?"

His eyes glittered. "Not you, that's for sure. Not this… *power* you seem to hold over me."

"Well, um—" she wriggled her hips suggestively, "—I think its me under *your* power at the moment. And very powerful it is, too. Nick, kiss me again, please."

"Serena!" His groan ended as their lips met in another ferocious kiss.

The sound of the telephone, shrill and jarring, took several seconds to penetrate the sensual fog in which they were encased.

"Leave it," he muttered, making a grab for her as she hurried to answer the summons.

"No, it's kind of late. It might be an emergency. Hello?"

"Serena, its Ness." The voice on the other end held a note of tension.

"What? Is something wrong?"

She felt rather than saw Nick sit up at her words. She gestured at him to relax as her sister answered, "No, everything's fine. At least—" Vanessa paused, as if unsure how to proceed, then said softly, "I was at *Velvet* tonight, and—"

"*Velvet*? You mean the nightclub? Are *you* okay?" Vaguely she was aware of Nick moving towards her, but she was concerned at the strange tone in her sister's voice.

"I'm fine. No, its something I saw tonight. I think you were right yesterday about… *what was that*?"

Nick had wrapped his arms around her from behind and nipped Serena gently on the neck. She had let out a muffled gasp as Nick murmured against her skin, "What's going on?"

"Um, I actually have… company at the moment, Ness. You remember Nicholas Wade?"

There was a silence, then Vanessa said stiffly, "I remember."

Why did she sound so odd? Serena took a deep breath. "Its hard for me to admit that I was wrong, but in this case, maybe I was. You'll be pleased to know I took your advice, Ness."

"Oh!"

Serena frowned. "You don't sound pleased. You sound as if you're about to choke."

"No, I… damn it!" This time the pause was several seconds long, and Serena's heart skipped a beat.

"What *is* it?"

"Nothing. Maybe. Look, I'll see you tomorrow, sis. Just… enjoy tonight, will you?"

I intend to, Serena thought grimly as she hung up the phone. What on earth was that all about? Vanessa could sometimes be a bit flaky, but this was out of the ordinary even for her.

She turned to face Nick but now he too was frowning. It threw her further off balance. "Was your sister at *Velvet* tonight?" he asked. The tone was neutral, but there was an edge to his voice she didn't understand.

"Apparently," she said. "What's the matter with *you*?"

"Nothing. What did she say?"

She let a couple of beats pass before she answered. "To be honest she didn't really say much of anything. It was kind of odd, really." *Like your reaction.*

His fists were clenched at his sides and she wondered if he was annoyed at the intrusion. Annoyed that she'd answered the phone when he'd specifically asked her not to. *Sorry, Nick,* she thought. *I won't kow-tow to any man again. Not like*

I did before.

"Don't worry about it," she said, reaching out to touch his arm as he turned to look at the fire.

He sighed, then touched his fingers to hers. "There are so many things we don't know about each other. Yet."

She smiled. "I like the yet. It implies a future—*hey*, steady on," she gasped as he clutched at her arms and dragged her down onto the rug in front of the fireplace.

"I want you, Serena. I *need* you." There was desperation in his voice, in his touch, and she felt her body respond with a primal surge of passion.

"I'm not going anywhere," she whispered.

"Good." And with that he swept aside her bathrobe and her misgivings and attacked the buttons on her cotton nightgown. Vanessa was completely forgotten.

His fingers whispered against her skin and she held her breath as the liquid warmth spread outwards from his touch. Her lips felt full and lush and her breasts ached with a heavy throbbing that echoed deep in her belly as he slid the nightgown down from her shoulders to pool in a heap at her waist. "You're so beautiful," he said, and she looked down at herself to see firelight dancing across her torso and bathing the peaks of her breasts in an orange glow. For the first time in her life she actually *felt* beautiful.

With a gentle smile she reached out and helped him shrug off his leather jacket, then it was her turn to undo the buttons on his shirt before he too, was naked to the waist. Now it was she who marvelled at the smoothly tanned beauty before her, she who reached out to flick his puckered nipples and inhale the intensely male aroma that was Nick.

"I want to feel you against me," she whispered, and he obliged with a quick movement that pinned her to the floor beneath his warm, pulsing body.

"Like this?" he asked, moving against her with a slow and steady pressure. A moan escaped her at the feel of his arousal. He was huge, and hard, and she yearned for the completeness that would come when their bodies joined together.

"No," she whispered huskily. "Too many clothes."

With a guttural groan he shifted away and she saw through eyes half-closed with desire the trembling of his hands as he removed the rest of his clothing. Then her nightclothes were gone too, and he was back with her again, skin against skin as they wrapped themselves around each other and fused their lips together.

But this time when they kissed the urgency was gone. In its place was a slow burning fire that echoed the smouldering logs in the fireplace. The kiss was long and deep and the incredible tenderness of his lips and tongue as he teased a response made her feel the wonder as if it were her very first time.

The wonder only increased when Nick's lips left hers and descended to leave a trail of tiny kisses along her collarbone and down to her breasts. She arched towards him as he took one sensitised peak into his mouth and teased it with his tongue. She felt a trembling deep within her body as he suckled first at one breast, then the other, until the desire burst from her in a husky cry of pleasure.

Then she was pushing against him, rolling him backwards until he lay on his back and she was straddling him, cradling his arousal between her swollen vulva lips. She smiled down at him, revelling in her moment of power, basking in the glittering fire of his gaze and the faint pressure of his touch as he urged her to move her hips along his length in a slow, rocking rhythm.

"Do you like this?" she queried huskily. "Or this?" She reached down and cupped the tip of him in her hands, massaging gently, and his breathing grew increasingly ragged.

"Yes," he muttered hoarsely. "Its incredible. *You're* incredible. I wanted to take you places you've never been before, but," he groaned again and reached for her gently swinging breasts, "instead you're taking *me*."

"Good," she managed, "then you have some idea of how I feel—*oh*!" Her gasp ended in an incoherent moan as Nick lifted her up until she was kneeling above him, his head cradled between her thighs. His fingers slipped into her moist opening and her hips began to rock convulsively as he explored her innermost sanctuary. She felt his breath against her pubic hair, ragged and hot, felt her clitoris swelling in response, as if it had a mind of its own and was reaching out to meet his flicking tongue. This is heaven, her mind repeated, over and over, while her body screamed for release from the delicate torture. "Please," she sobbed, "I need you, Nick. With me… inside me… now…*please*—"

"I *am* with you, sweetheart," he growled, then he was pulling her down and back towards him, impaling her on his enormous pulsing shaft. She screamed at the impact, then her body settled around him, absorbing, embracing the pain… She began to circle in frenzied haste and he groaned his assent. "Go, baby, as fast as you want." She felt the pressure of his hands on her buttocks, kneading the flesh, egging her on, faster, faster…

She looked down at his face with its rictus of concentration, heard the gasping of her own breath and knew she was spiralling toward madness, not control.

But control was all-important. She needed it, to protect herself.

With an effort of will she stopped mid thrust, then lifted herself up until the very tip of his arousal was just grazing the entrance of her womanhood. Then slowly, oh so slowly, she lowered herself back onto his shaft, slipping down the hot flesh with powerful precision as it began to fill her core.

"Serena, are you trying to kill me?" A guttural groan followed his words as she leaned forward to taste his lips with a playful grin.

"I'm in charge, now, am I not? Slave?"

She ran her fingertips down his chest, revelling in the hard-soft feel of him, like steel sheathed in silk. Her fingers continued down to the juncture of their joining, stroked briefly across her own belly as she marvelled at his fullness within. Then her head dropped back and she began to move again, slowly this time, the shivering of his body beneath hers, his ragged breath, the moans escaping her own lips, adding to the moment, fuelling the movements until the frenzy returned and she was riding him like she'd never ridden before.

His hips thrust madly to meet hers and their mingled cries filled the room as dominance gave way to a blaze of sensation so intense she almost blacked out as they exploded together in an extended, shuddering climax.

She fell forward over his body and his arms gripped her hard as she shook and sobbed from the force of her release.

It was some minutes before she realised that he was shaking almost as much as she, and that his heart was only now beginning to slow its racing beat beneath her cheek.

"Wow," she whispered, collapsing off him to lie spent in the circle of his arms.

"Wow indeed!" The amused irony caused a smile to curve her slightly bruised lips.

"That was…" She stopped, searching for the appropriate word.

"Extraordinary? Breathtaking? Magical?"

"All of the above."

He propped himself up on one elbow and stared down at her, and she revelled in the slightly predatory look as his gaze raked her body. "Serena, there's such a thing as good sex, but you must know this is more than that."

"Yes." She reached up to trace the curve of his lips, then turned to look at the slowly dying fire. "But as you said before, there are things we should discuss."

She felt the tremor that ran through his body. "Yes." His voice was heavy. "There are things that… have to be said."

She turned to face him again. "I want to tell you about this." She touched the gold locket around her neck.

"Oh… er… all right." He cleared his throat. "Only if you're comfortable."

"I am." She opened the locket and leaned forward so that he could see the picture inside. "This was my stepdaughter, Kelly," she said. "She was four when this was taken, on the swings at our local playground. She had the most infectious laugh."

Nick studied the photo gravely. "She looks happy. But… stepdaughter? I didn't realise you'd been married."

"Well, I guess technically she's not, but I always thought of her that way. I was with her father, Alex, for more than ten years and Kel lived with us for most of that time."

"So how old is she now? And where is she?"

"She'll be eight this coming week. And she lives in Sydney now, with Alex and her mother. They're both investment bankers. They… er… got together again over a year ago and decided to start a new life thousands of kilometres away from me. Taking Kelly with them, of course." She felt the familiar ache in her heart as she spoke, but strangely, sitting here in her cosy nest with Nick, firelight dancing across their naked bodies, the ache was not as piercing as usual.

Nick was frowning. "Kelly is eight?" he asked slowly. "But… if you were with Alex for ten years that doesn't make sense, unless…"

The bitter laugh bubbled up before she got herself under control. "Oh, it made perfect sense to Alex. He had an affair with his boss about eighteen months into our relationship, but the first I knew of it was when Kelly came to live with us just before her first birthday."

"Christ!" Nick's eyes were very green as he gently placed the locket back against her chest. "You must have been devastated. Why the hell did you stay with the bastard?"

"Ah, that's a question my family and friends have been asking for years. Partly it was because I was so young and Alex was very… authoritarian." *An out-and-out bully, according to Vanessa.* "But I think, mostly, it was because of Kel. Her mother had just abandoned her in favour of a huge promotion and this tiny, helpless little baby needed… someone… to love her."

Despite her resolve a sob escaped and she dashed away the tears that threatened to fall. "I'm not used to talking about it," she said gruffly.

"Maybe its time you did." Nick got up to throw a couple more logs on the fire, then reached across to retrieve the quilted blanket she kept on the back of her couch. She leaned against the seat of the couch, loathe to move from the rug and the fire but needing the solid feel of furniture behind her. She had the feeling he was giving her time to compose herself, and she was grateful.

When he covered her with the blanket and slid in she instinctively curled towards him, feeling safe as his arms came around to hold her.

"Thank you," she whispered.

"Pleasure, my love," he murmured, stroking her hair. She felt his lips touch her forehead in a light caress, and was glad she had shared this piece of herself, however painful.

"I really loved her, you know," she said.

She felt his nod. "That's obvious," he said. "But, it also makes me wonder…"

"What?"

He cleared his throat before continuing. "I wonder why you don't have a photo of *him* in this locket. After all, there's space for two photos, not one."

She hesitated, then let out her breath in a slow sigh. "There *were* two photos, Nick. Until this evening. After you dropped me home today I… well… I removed the photo of Alex." The decision had come out of nowhere, as she stripped down for her bath. She remembered staring into the tiny mirror above the basin, still feeling the ache from their lovemaking, and the sudden realisation that she didn't want to carry Alex around next to her heart any more. "Not that it means anything, mind you," she teased, and was rewarded with his shake of laughter.

"Of course not!" Then he shifted and she found herself looking up into his craggy face. "But what about this?" he asked, and bent his head to graze her lips with his own. Feather-light. Sizzling. "Does this mean anything?"

"Hmm." She frowned. "Not sure. You'd better try again."

When his mouth descended she was ready, putting all her pent-up emotion into the kiss until she felt his body stir into hardness against her. She moaned deep in her throat as the heat seared between her legs. This time there was no foreplay. With a rough growl he shrugged aside the blanket and propelled her back onto the floor, then grasped her left leg and lifted it up to hook over his shoulder. With unimpeded access he positioned himself just millimetres above her.

"What about this?" he asked huskily. "Does this mean anything, Serena?" He turned his head to her ankle and traced the outline of her tattoo with his tongue.

"Yes," she moaned, "yes. It does."

"And this?"

With one hand on his erection he used his own body to stroke her, up, down, then up again, until she was pulsing and panting with need.

"Oh, Nick, please... oh, God, I can't bear it—"

She clutched at his hips, unable to believe how quickly he could ignite her. Nothing mattered but the feel of Nick and his hot, swollen length cocooned inside her. This time the desperation was hers as she pulled him into her body. She cried out as he thrust, furiously fast, until she heard his hoarse cries in her ear and felt herself following him over the edge into their own little piece of heaven.

Nick watched her sleep.

The light and shadow of the flickering fire played across her somnolent features as he sat in the dark and debated. He should have told her the truth from the beginning. Especially now that he knew about that stupid bastard Alex.

God, what she must have been through!

Coward, he thought. You have to tell her. But what then?

The fear, always present, rarely acknowledged, held his tongue.

He knew where that fear came from. It was the reason he avoided emotional entanglements. If you loved them and left them, then they couldn't leave you.

Like his parents had.

Chapter 6

Serena slept more soundly than she had in over a year, so soundly that when Lancelot meowed for breakfast it took several seconds before she realised the firm surface beneath her was not her prized mattress but the rug on her lounge room floor.

With eyes still closed she smiled and stretched luxuriously. "Soon pussy cat, soon," she murmured, and turned to snuggle more closely into Nick. But he was gone.

The shock jerked her more fully awake and she opened her eyes and sat up. The only other living thing in the room was Lancelot, sitting in front of the fireplace, which now held a pile of grey-black ash. At some point during the night Nick must have collected her quilt and a couple of pillows from the bedroom. Funny, but she hadn't heard that either.

As she sat in contemplation the cat meowed again and galvanised her into action. "Okay," she grumbled good-naturedly. "At least I can rely on *you* not to leave me. As long as I keep up with food, eh?" It wasn't until she threw back the quilt and reached for her bathrobe that she realised Nick had left something. The branch of a hydrangea bush lay on the pillow, sporting two clusters of budding blue-purple. There was a tiny piece of paper tucked underneath.

I'd have preferred to leave a rose, but you don't seem to have any in your tiny little garden! Call you later – there's something important we need to discuss. N.

The "N" was a large dashing swirl that echoed the flamboyance of his character. She grinned at his words. No one could ever accuse her of having a green thumb, as much as she'd have liked one. Her garden was very basic and filled with plants that needed little or no maintenance. Like the hydrangea bush outside her front door. Cut it back to a stick once a year and watch the new growth bloom.

A bit like me, she thought, opening a can of cat food. I've been paring back my life, trying to avoid love and passion, running a mile from anything that might remind me of the past. And in the emptiness something new is growing.

She hummed as she showered, dressed and flung herself into the housework. Even cleaning the bathroom only dimmed her smile for a minute or two.

I wonder when he'll call, she kept asking herself as the morning wore on. I wonder where he is. What he's doing. Why he had to leave so suddenly.

"Maybe he has family commitments, like me," she pondered aloud to Lancelot. It was a Sunday tradition in her family, that she, Vanessa and their younger brother

Liam had a roast lunch at their parents' house. Since her mum had been ill it was even more important than ever, and looking at the clock, Serena realised she'd have to get a move on if she wanted to arrive on time.

"Maybe he has a Sunday roast with his sister and her six children."

Lancelot looked at her.

"No, you're right," she laughed. "I can't quite imagine the seductive Nick surrounded by the chaos of six kids." But even as she said the words aloud she realised there was a tiny part of her that *could* imagine it. He had a capacity for laughter that would appeal to a child, and vice versa.

"The perfect catch, eh? So what's wrong with him, then, Lancelot? Nobody's perfect, are they? What's Nick's secret fault?"

It was a question she hadn't answered by the time she arrived at her parent's place an hour later.

They still lived in the same house in which she and her siblings had grown up, a small square brick residence on an eighth of an acre in Melbourne's outer suburbs. It was a house filled with love and a quiet contentment, where she and Vanessa had shared a bedroom and their dreams for the future.

Then she had met Alex and her dreams came crashing down. Not at first. She'd been a complete innocent at nineteen. When suave, sophisticated Alex had shown an interest it seemed too good to be true. She'd lain everything on the line – her feelings, her heart, her life – in the naive hope that this man was the one she'd been dreaming about.

But reality had become a world full of mistrust, betrayal and shattered expectations. Until she met Nick, Serena hadn't realised she still harboured remnants of those childhood dreams of being swept off her feet and living as the fairytales did… happily ever after.

A smile curved her lips as she acknowledged the speed with which Nick had captured her heart. Her heart? The thought sent her pulse into overdrive and she froze. Surely she wasn't falling in love with him? Lust, certainly – who wouldn't lust after Nick with his looks and overt sensuality? But love?

She sat at the kitchen bench and studied her mother as the older woman pulled a roasting pan from the oven to check sizzling meat and vegetables. According to Eva, she had met her husband at a town hall dance when she was seventeen, and immediately known he was the man she would marry.

"Mum, do you believe in love at first sight?"

Startled grey eyes stared at her. Eyes very similar to her own, or so she'd been told. "Of course I do," Eva answered. "You know how your father and I met."

"Well, yes, but—"

"But nothing!" Eva's cheeks darkened. "As clichéd as it sounds, our eyes locked across the room and I couldn't breathe. The connection was immediate. Your father told me he felt the same way."

Serena shivered as she recalled her first meeting with Nick. An immediate connection? Definitely. But that wasn't love. That was just… pheromones. And there was fear mixed in with the attraction, the fear of opening herself up and getting unbearably hurt in the process.

Maybe fear was blinding her to the truth.

Maybe love at first sight *was* possible.

She realised her mother was speaking and tried to focus on the task she'd been given. Shelling peas. In this house, as always, frozen peas were not an option. "Sorry?" she asked. "I was worlds away, mum."

"You were indeed. I was asking if we're going to meet the man who's given you that dreamy look."

Serena reached across to pick a crunchy bit of potato from the pan and was rewarded with a gentle smack across the fingers. "Ouch!" She rubbed her hand gingerly. "How do you know there's a man?" she prevaricated. "Maybe I'm just feeling happy. Maybe I'm hungry and I know your roast will taste good."

Her mother laughed. "Because I know you, darling," she said. "And because I know that look. It tells me you've met someone."

She felt a sudden shyness, ridiculous at thirty-two, but in some ways Nick made her feel like a romantic teenager. "I hope so," she admitted. "And if things keep going the way they have, maybe you will get to meet Nick. Perhaps sooner rather than later."

"Nick, eh? Nice name at least."

"Cheeky!" Chuckling, she grabbed a handful of peas and threw them at her mum, but they sailed past and hit Vanessa as she came through the kitchen door.

"Bloody hell," said her sister, brushing herself off. "A food fight?" She sounded surprisingly grumpy, and Serena raised her eyebrows at the uncharacteristic mood.

As their mother returned the pan to the oven and bustled into the lounge to wrest their dad from his television sports show, Vanessa planted herself on the stool next to Serena and reached across to grab a handful of pea pods. "So," she asked, "how was last night?"

The blush crept across her cheeks. "Wonderful," she said at last. "I was too quick to judge the other day. Nick's not like anyone I've ever met before. And he's definitely not like Alex."

"Isn't he?" Her sister frowned. "I'm not so sure, Serena."

"What do you mean?" she demanded. "You don't even know him!"

"All right! Don't jump down my throat! All I mean is… well…" Vanessa hesitated, then asked with a rush, "How well do *you* really know him? After all, its only been a couple of days."

"I know that!" Her eyes narrowed. "Where's the attitude coming from, Ness? I don't get it. Or you – and I've known *you* for all your twenty-nine years."

Her sister opened her mouth to retaliate but Serena added accusingly, "And it was *you* who told me to go with the flow and not be afraid of getting involved again. You who said I should just get him into bed and not worry about the rest."

"I know. What a stupid thing to say." Vanessa glumly threw her peas into the pot and put her head in her hands.

Serena took a deep breath. "Does this have anything to do with your phone call last night? What is it? Something happened at *Velvet*, didn't it?"

"You could say that." Vanessa sighed. "I'm just finding it difficult to figure out how to tell you, especially…"

"Tell me *what*?"

"Nick was at *Velvet* last night, Serena."

"Oh." *I don't think I want to hear any more.*

"It must have been before he came around to your place. I'm sorry. I saw him there… and he wasn't alone."

She didn't know she was holding her breath until the air escaped with a hiss. *There'll be a simple explanation. There* must *be.*

"What do you mean, he wasn't alone?" She asked the question slowly, as a signal to Vanessa to be sure of her facts. This was *Nick* she was talking about! The man with whom she might possibly be falling in love.

Vanessa stared at Serena. "He was with another woman. I'm sorry, love, I don't want to hurt you, but they looked to be getting rather… intimate."

She flinched. She couldn't help it. There was a long pause before she felt competent to answer. "I see. So, what exactly do you mean by… intimate?"

Funny, she thought. I sound almost normal. But I feel kind of frozen inside.

"Well, you know, holding hands, staring into each other's eyes, that kind of thing. Like they were on a date. Serena, are you all right?" Now Vanessa's voice seemed to be coming from far away. And there were black spots dancing in front of her eyes. Why did she feel so… weird? "Damn it! Quick, Serena, put your head down between your knees. Take deep breaths."

She felt a hand shove hard at the back of her head, then she was bent double, staring at the tiles on her mother's kitchen floor and wondering why the hell she kept making the same mistakes over and over. *Alex. Nick. I should have known. Deep down, maybe I did.*

At last she felt the dizziness receding. "I'm okay," she gasped, and felt her sister's hand release her. She sat up slowly. "Why didn't you tell me last night?" *Before I gave away my heart?*

Vanessa looked guilty. "I probably should have," she admitted. "But when I rang and he was there, I thought… well, hoped, I guess… that I'd got it wrong. And I thought you needed to experience passion again, to remind you that you're not dead from the neck down."

Serena clenched her fists so tightly her nails dug into her palms. "Well, thank you for allowing me my one night of passion with… *him*. So kind of you."

Unexpectedly Vanessa's eyes filled with tears. "Its not my fault, Serena. I wish to hell I'd never gone to *Velvet*. Never seen what I did. Do you think I *want* to hurt you? I'm sorry!"

"No. You're right. Its not your fault." Her skin felt clammy and she wanted to vomit, couldn't seem to get enough air into her lungs, either.

Lunch was a nightmare of stilted conversation and concerned looks from both her sister and mother, the latter having noticed the abrupt change in her demeanour. Thank goodness her brother Liam and her dad didn't seem to pick up on anything unusual. They kept the conversation going with talk of various weekend sports events.

At last she was able to say her goodbyes and return home, only to find a huge bunch of red roses sitting on her front doorstep. There was a note attached. *Matches the one on your delectable ankle. See you soon. Love N.*

Love? Tears filled her eyes as confusion swirled inside. How could anyone appear so kind, so loving, so… goddamn *sexy*, and yet none of it really mean anything?

Inside she threw the flowers furiously onto her kitchen bench, then found herself rescuing them as they fell towards the floor. She wanted so much to believe there could be a proper explanation. That tiny kernel of hope in the corner of her heart said she should give him another chance. For now. She hefted the flowers, looking at the trash can, but after a few seconds stood the flowers in the sink instead.

Then she pushed the button on her answering machine and heard Nick's mellow voice fill the room. "Hi, sweetheart. Unfortunately I had an urgent message on the mobile this morning. I have to go out of town on business for a couple of days, but I should be back Wednesday, so I'll give you a call then. Last night was *incredible*, Serena. I… look, there's something I want to talk to you about, but not over the phone. Take care, love."

She replayed the message twice more, hearing the unusual note in his voice and trying to identify what it was. Guilt? No, she decided. It wasn't guilt, but uncertainty. Not something she identified as part of Nick's make-up. Thoughtfully she went to her cupboard and pulled out a crystal vase, taking several minutes to arrange the roses to her satisfaction. She would give him the benefit of the doubt. Until Wednesday.

The day he would tell her the truth about why he'd come to her bed straight from another woman's arms.

The enormity of his betrayal suddenly hit home. With a violent gesture she grabbed the roses from the vase and stuffed them into the trash, then had to reach for a tissue to stem the bleeding from where one of the thorns cut her thumb. Then she slumped down at the kitchen table, as the tears welled over and painful sobs racked her body.

"How could you, Nick?" she whispered. "How could you?"

Nick ordered dinner from room service and flopped onto the bed with a weary sigh. The chance to attend this wine festival in Adelaide was important for the future of his winery, but it was supposed to be his manager sitting here waiting for a club sandwich to be sent up to the room. A bout of influenza at the last minute meant it was Nick who'd had to take up the invitation instead.

A week ago he'd have jumped at the chance. But not now. There was only one place he wanted to be, and it wasn't here in this luxuriously appointed hotel. Thoughts of Serena's tiny cottage and its welcoming country appeal filled his head. He wondered what she was doing right now. Wondered if she was curled up in front of her fireplace, on the rug where they'd spent so much of last night making incredible, passionate love.

He felt his body stir and shifted uncomfortably. Wouldn't do to start thinking of her deliciously generous curves, her wild hair, her shy smile. He grimaced as the tightness in his groin intensified. At this rate he'd either have to take things into his own hands, or experience the joy of a cold shower.

Irritably he grabbed the TV remote and channel-surfed aimlessly until the knock at his door signalled dinner.

He pictured Serena at her table, his roses a colourful centrepiece, her delectable mouth wrapped around some exotic piece of food, her smoky eyes dreamy as she recalled the previous night... how his hands had explored every inch of her satiny skin... how his lips and tongue had eagerly followed...

"Hell!" He threw the remote across the room and heard it smash against the opposite wall. Terrific!

What was it about her that had crept inside his head? Why couldn't he go five minutes – make that *one* minute – without thinking about her, wanting her, wanting to be with her? She wasn't the most beautiful woman he'd ever met, or the most obviously sexy, but that didn't seem to matter. She was like a drug he couldn't do without.

Was this love? He wasn't sure. But it was different to anything he'd experienced before. And whatever it was, he sure as hell wanted more of it.

Cold shower be damned!

He lay back and took things into his own hands.

Chapter 7

It seemed like forever before Wednesday rolled around. Serena worked with a vengeance, pleased to have a complicated tax return that needed detailed client visits to sort out. She tried desperately not to think about Nick but her mind refused to cooperate.

When the phone rang at a quarter to five that afternoon, she felt the hairs on the back of her neck stand up. Nick. Carefully she pressed the save button on her laptop before answering.

"Hi, sweetheart. Miss me?" A shiver traversed her skin.

"Not much," she managed. "Hardly knew you were gone, to be honest. I've been too busy."

There was a pause before he said, "What's the matter? You sound different."

"Different to what?"

"Different to how you were the other day. You sound distant. Sexy as hell, mind you, with that gorgeous huskiness, but there's a definite hint of something else. Do you want to talk about it?"

"Not over the phone."

"All right. I'm coming over."

"*No!*" She took a deep breath. *Try it without the panic this time.* "No. I really am busy, Nick." She thought quickly. "We could meet for a drink around seven, if you like, at that pub where we met the first night."

"If that's what you really want…" His voice trailed off, and she knew what was in his mind. Because she was thinking the same thing. How easy it would be to have him come around to her office or home. How deliciously easy to fold herself into his arms, feel his mouth on hers, tasting, demanding, until the heat in their bodies would not be denied and she surrendered… willingly…

"It is." She hung up before the pounding of her heart became audible over the phone.

Nick replaced the receiver thoughtfully. What was going on? Serena's voice carried an edge that he hadn't heard since their first meeting. Surely a few days without him hadn't changed her mind? The thought sent a wave of panic through his body, a feeling all the more frightening for its unfamiliarity.

How the hell had this happened? He couldn't imagine not being with her. The past few days had been like torture, as he'd met and talked with and smiled at countless men and women who shared his passion for good wine and food.

But none of them had been Serena.

It was all he could do not to jump on a plane and fly back to Melbourne every evening, just to see her again, hear her gorgeous voice, kiss that rose tattoo, and more besides…

I *need* her, he realised with a shock. And looking into the future, I can't imagine a time when I *won't* need her. Until now he'd always skittered away from the idea of marriage and children. But now…

I've known her less than a week, but I can imagine her as the mother of my children.

I can imagine us growing old together.

Happily.

The bar was a lot quieter tonight than it had been last Friday. Serena watched a lone guitarist on the small corner stage, crooning about lost love and sadness. She didn't know whether to laugh or cry at the seemingly appropriate ambience for her meeting with Nick.

She'd dressed for containment of emotion more than anything else. The suit was her most severe, a dark pinstripe reserved for meetings with conservative clients. Her hair was scraped back tightly into a bun, though how long it would stay that way was anybody's guess. Long enough to get through this meeting, she hoped.

Her stomach was churning with acid, and her heart felt all fluttery and light. Her gaze darted around the room, searching for Nick. And then she saw him, coming through the door, and her already pounding heart rate raised itself another notch.

I'd forgotten how potent he is, in the flesh.

When he saw her his face lit up with such pleasure that her breath caught in her throat. He *can't* be like Alex, she thought. I couldn't bear it.

When he slid into place beside her on the couch she managed a tight smile. "How was the trip?" she asked.

"Adelaide? Fine," he said dismissively, then leaned forward to pull a stray lock of hair free of its confines. She flinched slightly and he frowned. "But it wasn't where I wanted to be. I missed you, Serena."

Why did his voice have to sound like warm honey? she wondered. Why not fingernails on a blackboard?

"I'm glad it went well," she began stiffly, then blew out her breath in an explosive sigh. "Sod this! I can't do it!"

"Do what?" Uncertainty flickered across his features and for a moment she was mesmerised. It felt as if she were looking at the bare bones of him.

Like most people, his core probably contained a wealth of vulnerability, but it wasn't something she usually associated with Nick.

I bet not many people see the real Nicholas Wade.

Maybe she had the power to hurt Nick as much as the other way round.

This was a situation she'd never had to face with Alex, and there, she realised, was the fundamental difference between the two. Nick cared. Alex had not.

"I missed you too," she admitted, and found herself enveloped in a tight embrace before his mouth swooped down over hers in a kiss so profoundly sweet it brought tears to her eyes.

For precious seconds she allowed herself to forget the uncertainty. Instead she went with what she felt. And it felt right.

So right.

Instant heat, the luscious ache of desire throbbing in her breasts and womb. His tongue, thrusting against hers, teased a response and tasted divinely of Nick. She settled in with a tiny moan of pleasure.

She felt the urgency beneath his kiss and it echoed her own. God, how she'd missed him these past few days. In spite of everything, the doubt, the betrayal, the fear of too much hurt to bear, she just couldn't deny herself this last little piece of him. Her hands whispered across his chest, crept beneath his jacket to feel the hard muscle of his back. His responding groan incited her further and she pressed against him, inviting his touch.

He popped the buttons on her jacket and cupped one hand around her breast through the silk shirt, his thumb rubbing back and forth across the already taut nipple. His mouth left hers to trail along her jaw and nuzzle at her earlobe.

"I need you," he whispered, and she shuddered at the raw desire in his voice.

"Not here," she gasped, trying in vain to twist away from his questing lips. She'd never known how arousing it could be to have one's ear laved by a willing tongue. "Oh, Nick, stop! You have to stop!"

"Why?" he murmured. "Your skin feels so soft and you taste so sweet. I won't go too far; I know we're in a public place. Which reminds me…" His lips explored the frantic pulse point in her neck.

"Y-yes?"

"Why here, Serena? Why not somewhere more private? Where I can fulfil all the fantasies I've been creating in my mind since the last time I saw you?"

"*Oh!*" His words suddenly brought back all the pent-up emotion of the past three days and with a violent shove she pushed him away. "You want to know why? I'll tell you why. Because my sister was at *Velvet* last Saturday night and she saw you there. With someone else. Being… *intimate*. Right before you came round to my place and we… we…"

She couldn't finish. Since Sunday she had felt battered by vacillating emotions, from numbness to hope to abject fear. Saying the words aloud, watching his shocked look as he sat back and lifted a hand to rub the sudden furrow between his brows, broke through the numb feeling to the raw hurt beneath.

You're supposed to say Vanessa got it wrong.

She clenched her hands in her lap and waited for his denial, knowing deep down that she would wait in vain. His reaction told her the truth, the way he let out his breath in a slow sigh, the look of profound regret that crossed his face.

She was already nodding, her lips twisted cynically, as he said, "I'm sorry, Serena. I wanted to tell you the other night but… I was *going* to tell you—"

"Are you married?"

"God, no!" His laugh was brief but genuine. She felt a flash of panic at the desire that washed over her. "I'm not the marrying kind. At least, I haven't been, up to this point."

Her heart seemed to miss a beat, and then resumed pumping double time. Ignore it, she thought. It's a diversion. "Who was she?"

At least he didn't pretend to misunderstand. "A date."

"I see." She nodded again. Couldn't stop nodding. "Did you sleep with her too? Are there others?"

"Don't be ridiculous."

"*I'm* ridiculous? You're the two timing rat. I can't do this, Nick. I can't go through it again."

She made to rise but his panicked, "*Wait!*" stopped her. "I'm handling this all wrong. Its not what you think, Serena. That woman I met at the club… it was research."

She laughed, a brittle sound. "That's a new one."

"Please, just listen," he said. "One of my business interests… the one I didn't mention… I also freelance for a newspaper. The one where you placed your lonely hearts ad. There's been a significant increase in the number of people using the personals to meet and I was asked to write a story about it. Find out why."

Her mouth dropped open in shock. "So… so—" She took a deep breath and tried again. "So you've been… undercover? Researching your story? And all that stuff about a vineyard in the Yarra Valley, and all the rest – everything – was just a *lie*?" Nausea swirled, threatened to overtake her, but she couldn't move to save her life.

"No!" His eyes flashed as he caught and held her stricken gaze. "Everything I've told you is true. *Everything*. I do have a vineyard, in fact I live there most of the time. I never actually lied to you, except about why I responded to your ad. And even then, it *was* your voice that drew me in. I could've chosen any number of ads but there was something about yours that intrigued me. And when I met you," he shook his head, "it was like I'd been sucker punched. I've never met anyone with such a powerful effect on my senses. Or my mind."

I know what you mean.

It was too much to take in, particularly in his presence, which threatened at every moment to topple her hastily rebuilt defences. "How many ads did you follow up?" Her voice came out so low he had to lean forward to hear. She shrank from his nearness.

"Fifteen."

She blinked furiously. *I will* not *cry.* "So I'm one of *fifteen* women you've been dating these past few weeks? How do you even get time to sleep?" She felt like she was going to choke on the words, but she had to ask, "And have you been… having sex… with them all?"

"No." His eyes darkened. "I want to be very clear about this. I haven't made love with, kissed, or even *thought* about anyone except you since the day we met."

"Great! Wonderful!" She was like a moth attacking the light. She knew the danger, but couldn't seem to stop. "So what's your explanation for last Saturday?

Nessa *saw* you—"

"Then Vanessa was mistaken in what she saw. There was no intimacy in that date. Except for some hand holding. On her part, not mine." For the first time she heard a hint of steel in his voice. It confused her. He sounded sincere, but…

"How can you expect me to believe anything you say from now on?" Despite her resolve she felt tears pricking and swallowed hard. "It's just like Alex all over again," she whispered.

"*It's nothing like that!*" She jumped at the shouted words and looked around to see several people staring at them. "Sorry." He hunched his shoulders and scowled. "I'm not Alex, Serena. I'd like to teach that bastard a lesson or two for what he did to you." He took a deep breath. "I haven't betrayed your trust, except in one way. Not telling you why I responded to your ad was wrong. I know that, and I'm sincerely sorry. But that's the *only* thing I haven't been truthful about. Everything else, including how I feel about you, is true."

"I don't know what to think." She sat there staring down at her clenched hands—numb. Serena wasn't aware she was crying until Nick leaned over to wipe a tear from her cheek.

"Sweetheart, all the other women knew who I was and what I was doing. It was my job, but with you it was different. I didn't want to tell you because I couldn't bear the thought of losing you."

She shook her head. "Don't."

Her whispered command didn't discourage Nick. His arm slipped around behind her shoulders. She fought the urge to sink back into warm comfort.

"Serena, look at me. Look," he commanded, lifting her chin with one hand. "I think I might be falling in love with you, and I'd like to believe you feel the same way. But love can't exist without trust, and we need to trust each other."

I think I might be falling in love with you.

A few days ago she'd have been delirious with joy to hear those words. But now – hell, a few days ago she didn't even know him! A tiny sob escaped. "You're right, Nick. Love can't exist without trust. But I don't know if it's in me to trust again." She tried to look away but his gaze continued to mesmerize her. "If you want the truth, *that's* the truth. And as to how I feel about you…" She shrugged helplessly. "I don't know that either. I thought I knew but… this… it's too much."

Abruptly she stood and he leaned back to stare up at her, his face unusually pale. If he weren't so intensely masculine she'd swear he was close to tears. "I didn't want to lose you before you had a chance to get to know me properly," he said. "You were so judgemental at the beginning."

She looked down at him sadly. "Maybe," she conceded. "But you never gave me the chance to get to know you, did you?"

"Then let me give you that chance, if that's what you need. Come with me next weekend to see where I live, see the place I love most. I want to show you the vineyard, and the Yarra Valley. It's *real*, Serena, and its a huge part of me. More than my work with the newspaper."

"I don't think—"

"Please?"

Serena felt like she was drowning in the depths of his green eyes. "Will I be the centre of a lonely hearts story if I agree?"

"No! I promise you that!" He took a deep breath. "If you want me to I'll give it up. The whole idea. If that's what it takes to make it right, Serena—"

"It'll take more than that, Nick. A lot more."

"But its a start, isn't it? Say yes. Say you'll come with me next weekend, and I'll show you who I am. No secrets, no lies, just… truth."

She found herself nodding even as logic screamed she was crazy. She needed to escape her past, not relive it, not make the same mistake with Nick that she had with Alex But a tiny kernel of hope at the centre of her being kept telling her the two men were different.

And if she just gave Nick this one last chance he might prove it.

She grabbed for her satchel bag and fled before completely falling apart and bawling like a baby in public.

Nick let out a shaky breath and grabbed for his drink, taking several large gulps before setting the glass back on the table with a fumbling click. Christ, he felt as if he'd been through a wringer, like the one on the farm that his grandparents claimed to have used for the washing before he went to live with them.

The idea of losing Serena was incomprehensible. The idea that he'd never really had her in the first place even more so. Bloody hell! Women threw themselves at him, always had, ever since he turned eight and Chrissy Macbeth gave him his first kiss on the school playground at lunchtime.

If this is love, then it's damn hard work.

But Serena was special and she deserved better from him. Hell, she deserved the best. She made him feel more alive than he'd ever felt before, happier than he could remember, and more aroused than any man had a right to expect.

She was worth fighting for, and this time, if she'd give him a second chance, he was going to do it right.

Chapter 8

Serena held tightly to the rope in the early morning darkness, feeling the flare of gas-generated heat above her head as the balloon carried their basket into the silent sky.

I must be mad!

"Ever heard of dinner and a movie, Nick? When you said you'd show me the Yarra Valley I didn't think you meant hot-air ballooning."

His chuckle was as contagious – and as potent – as it had been the first time they met.

"There's no better way to experience it, sweetheart." He moved to stand behind her, one arm coming around each side of her to grip the edge of the basket. "And there's no need to be frightened. Pete's the best pilot in the business."

She glanced at the taciturn, middle-aged man in charge of their flight. "I'm not frightened," she said. "Unless I look straight down." *Or turn around and gaze into your eyes.*

"Just look over there," he murmured in her ear, pointing briefly to the east.

She caught her breath in wonder. The sun was in the process of cresting the horizon and the rolling hills were ablaze with a mixture of gold, orange and pink. The dark pre-dawn shadows were being driven back to reveal a vista of striking emerald beauty, shrouded in random pockets with a white, swirling mist. Through it all the Yarra River wound like a long brown snake.

"Its gorgeous," she breathed. "I've seen the sun come up over Uluru in Central Australia – people come from all over the world to see that – but sometimes we only need to look in our own backyards."

"Beats dinner and a movie, doesn't it?"

"I guess it does. But Nick, this doesn't change anything. I'm reserving judgement on us."

"Better than a straight-out rejection." His quiet chuckle tickled her temple. She fought the instinct to relax back into his arms, fought the need to take comfort from his solidity in this less-than-secure environment.

For a few minutes they stayed quiet, marvelling at the view. Looking west, she could see the tiny cluster of high-rise buildings that marked the city, and a strip of darker blue along the horizon that indicated Port Phillip Bay.

Somewhere out there in the endless blue, she and Nick had first made love.

A shiver ran through her at the thought of how far they had come since that moment. In such a short space of time. Yet the question remained – how far still to go? Lust was a heady experience, love even more so, but without trust…

As if he could hear her thoughts she felt Nick tense. Then he leaned forward and she realised the source of his tension came from far below them. "There, Serena," he said. "That's where my vineyard begins. Across those hills and up to that collection of buildings on the rise."

The note of pride was blatantly obvious. So he hadn't been lying about this part—at least. She looked down upon rolling hills covered in neat rows of grape vines, but from this height could not distinguish any more than the enormous breadth of his venture. "You said boutique wines," she accused. "I assumed something small."

"I never go in for half measures," he said. "You should know that by now." She felt him press hard against her and she caught her breath, then he was shifting away to give his attention to their landing. "You know where to take us down, Pete."

"If I can, Mister Wade. Its not guaranteed." The pilot began manoeuvring to begin their floating descent. Serena realised they must be going to land somewhere on Nick's property, and became conscious of an immense curiosity about the vineyard. This place was obviously special to Nick.

"Do I get the grand tour?" she asked, turning to face him at last.

He was watching her steadily, a tiny smile hovering on his lips. "After breakfast."

"I hardly need fattening up, and yet you always seem to be feeding me." Her smile was self-deprecating.

"Just maintaining the status quo." His gaze travelled the length of her body and back up again, and she could see the flare of temptation in his darkening eyes. "Your curves are just right. I want to keep them that way."

"Don't," she warned, and was rewarded for her caution by the light going out of his face.

"I'm not going to pretend I'm immune." His tone was impatient. "You wanted truth, I'm giving it to you."

Her hand went to her throat and she shot a nervous look at Pete. "Trouble is, I can't tell what's truth and what's just plain blarney," she murmured.

His eyes narrowed and she hurried to head off his response. "What about your car? How will you get it back from the launching place?"

The tightness in his features acknowledged her change of subject, but he answered readily enough. "I'll send someone for it later," he said. "Hold on now, we're in for a ride."

You're telling me, she thought as they descended at what seemed an alarming rate. Several people on the ground were there to help as they bumped to a halt. When her feet touched firm ground again she realised her legs were trembling.

They were in a grassy clearing, bounded on two sides by grapevines and on the third by a slowly trickling creek. Up on the hill ahead of them were the vineyard buildings. She could see now that they were a mixture of sandstone and western red cedar, clustered together in cosy fashion and surrounded by a tiered garden.

She didn't question how they'd managed to land so close to Nick's intended destination. He just seemed to have a way of getting what he wanted. No matter how difficult.

On a further rise behind the vineyard buildings, she could see a sprawling single-storey house, its grandiose nature softened by a wooden-post veranda on at least three sides. She could see that the house, like the other buildings, was made primarily of sandstone, but was too far away to discern the finer details. Yet she got a strange, tingly feeling when she stared at it, and knew even before he confirmed it that she was looking at Nick's home.

"I'll show you later," he said softly. "For now, the restaurant doesn't open until eleven, but I got the chef in to prepare us a special breakfast." He pulled gently at her hand.

"You got the chef in—Nick, I don't mean to sound rude, but, is cost ever a factor in your decision-making?"

"Spoken like a true tax agent." He grinned. "Seriously, Serena, you don't have to worry about money. I have enough."

She felt the blush spreading up from her neck. "I – I didn't mean—"

"It's okay, I know what you meant. I've been pushing pretty hard since we met, what with yachts, balloons, and now the vineyard but," he grinned, "you have to admit, it has been fun, hasn't it?"

As he led her into the building and across a stone-flagged floor to a linen-covered table by the window, she had to agree that these past couple of weeks with Nick had been one roller-coaster ride of excitement.

The exact opposite of what she'd had in mind when she placed the personal advertisement.

"This is stunning," she admitted as they took their seats. She looked out across a manicured lawn to the brightly flowering shrubs beyond. In the distance, rows of grapevines stretched neatly away towards the emerald hills and valleys of the Yarra Ranges. From Nick's home, she thought, higher up on the hill behind them, the view must be even more spectacular.

"It must have taken a lot of effort to get this up and running. How did you manage it, with your…" she hesitated a moment before finishing, "your newspaper commitments as well?"

His quick look acknowledged the tension behind her hesitation. "Lots of hard work, a fair bit of swearing, and a damn good manager," he said. "I'll introduce you to her later."

"Her?" Serena raised her eyebrows.

"Yes, Helen's one of the best in the business. What – you think I'm some kind of chauvinist now as well? I date women but I don't respect them enough to work in equal partnership? Or…" He paused a moment, then said slowly, "I'm not sleeping with her, if that's what you think."

Amusement threaded his words, but she could sense the lurking hurt. Was this the start of it – a wedge driven between them by her lack of trust? By his economy with the truth?

"No," she said. "I'm just not used to men who acknowledge a woman's professional skills so readily." *Put that down to Alex's legacy.* "I'd love to meet Helen, she must be pretty amazing to have helped you achieve all of this."

Her arm swept out and almost collided with the waiter who had arrived to take their order. With a smile of apology she chose the smoked salmon omelette with bacon and toast on the side and a freshly squeezed grapefruit juice, while Nick opted for a full cooked breakfast – sausages, eggs, tomatoes and mushrooms.

"I love the way you eat, as if you really enjoy your food," Nick commented as they finished the last of their coffee in quiet contemplation.

"Of course I do," she said, surprised. "I've tried dieting in the past, but quite frankly I can never stick with it. If you have to eat you might as well do it properly and enjoy it."

Nick grinned wickedly. "You make love the same way, you know. With your heart and soul. Total concentration. Its… quite riveting."

"Oh!" When he came out with comments like this she never quite knew how to respond. She felt the blush heating her cheeks and looked down, grateful that her hair had blown loose on the hot air balloon ride. "I'm ready for that tour now," she mumbled.

He laughed suddenly, the sound rich and warm, and she felt the heat like molten lava cascade through her system. Not the heat of embarrassment, this time. The kind of heat that sent a thrumming to the far reaches of her body, and reminded her of all the reasons why being in love could be so exhilarating.

And it *is* love I feel for him, she realised. Otherwise I wouldn't be here, giving him a second chance. But that only raises the stakes. In the game of love, to use Nick's parlance, when you give someone your heart, it's so much easier to have it broken.

The tour was a revelation for Serena, not so much for what she learnt about wine, than for what it revealed about Nick. In her job she had audited many businesses, some successful, others not, and she knew what it took to succeed. It took vision and drive, and true commitment. Nick had that in spades. But he had something more, too. He had *passion*, a genuine love for what he was doing. As he showed her through the crushing room, where the fermenting process took place and then the storage facility filled with wooden barrels, he made her *feel* his passion.

And that made Nick unique.

Helen had joined them for the last part of the tour, and made no attempt to hide her curiosity about Serena. "Other than family and people directly related to the business, he's never shown anyone through here before," she said. Tall, blonde and elegant in an ice-blue trouser suit, despite the blocked nose left over from her bout of the flu, she had a friendly smile to which Serena couldn't help but respond. Her momentary flare of jealousy at the sight of the beautiful woman who worked side by side with Nick dissipated as she spent more time with them both. She sensed a deep liking and friendship between the two, but no real sexual chemistry.

That's reserved for me, she realised with a flare of excitement, as Nick shot her yet another smouldering look and suggested he show her the house. "I'll catch up with you later, Helen," he said to his manager, and with a friendly wave in Serena's direction, the blonde woman departed.

Once they were alone Nick drew her into his arms with a faint smile. "You asked for some time and I've given you nearly six hours," he said. "I've been wanting to do this ever since I first saw you at five o'clock this morning."

His mouth came down over hers, gently at first, making his point but allowing her the opportunity to draw back. But she didn't want to. Instead she pressed her body closer against him, their breath mingling as he deepened the kiss, urgency growing as the moan caught and held in her throat.

Her lips parted to allow his tongue inside where it danced with her own until she felt faint with dizziness. He released her mouth briefly and they were both breathing hard, then he captured her again. The sensuality was so strong she stopped breathing altogether. The exquisite taste of him, the feel of his slightly rough skin against her face, the power of his growing erection surging against her stomach, assaulted Serena's very soul.

This was her reality.

This was her truth.

Her knees buckled and she sank into him, his arms taking her weight almost effortlessly as her body cried out for more. When they parted this time her mouth felt bruised, aching, her lips throbbing in tandem with her breasts. "I want you," she said.

"I know."

For a moment longer they stared at one another.

"Show me where you live, Nicholas Wade," she said, and wordlessly he led her out of the vineyard building and up a curving pathway to his home.

They paused on the threshold before a double-sided leadlight door. "You don't have to do this today," he said.

"Yes," she answered. "I do."

Without warning he swept her off her feet and carried her over the threshold. They were both laughing when he put her down in the slate-tiled entrance. "Couldn't resist," he admitted, and she could have sworn, before he turned away, that his cheeks were stained with pink.

The lounge was enormous, a long low room with thick scattered rugs to break up the tiled floor and artistically arranged groupings of luxuriously comfortable-looking furniture. Along one side of the room were a series of windows that opened out onto the wooden veranda with a stunning view of the landscape beyond.

She could see an archway that led off into a formal dining area, but what interested her most was the far wall that had been converted into a huge bookcase. It was completely covered from floor to ceiling with books, as were the built-in shelves on either side of the open fireplace. Despite its vast proportions, the room felt solid and immensely welcoming. It was a rare room that would shine in both hot and cold weather, and Serena smiled her approval.

"A lot of these books came from Annie and Ben. I've spent plenty of time with them over the years," he said.

She remembered his words at their first meeting and shook her head in self-disgust. *Why bother reading books when you can wait for the movie*? And she'd taken him at face value, judged and condemned him without knowing the facts. She deserved all the teasing he'd given her.

"I don't suppose you've got any Shakespeare in this collection?" she murmured.

"A few."

She began to laugh, a bubbling noise that she could neither understand nor control. Then she realised she was laughing at herself.

"Did you know Alex only ever read the *Financial Review* and investment magazines?" she asked.

He scowled. "Don't compare me to him. *I'm not like Alex!*"

She walked over and linked her arm through his. "I know," she said gently. "Show me the rest of your home, Nick. I love what I've seen so far."

The kitchen and meals area was pure country, yellow and blue and full of sunshine. The only thing missing, in Serena's opinion, were bunches of herbs drying on a rack over the bench. That's what I'd do if I lived here, she decided. Start an herb garden in that patch of sun outside and bring the aroma of lavender and oregano inside.

The study too was large, so large that two desks could fit comfortably without compromising the space. And the view... There was a lot to be said for working from home, if your home was as magnificent as Nick's.

As he led her down a passageway to the spare bedrooms her heart gave a sudden jolt as she realised the direction of her thoughts. It was so easy to imagine living here that she couldn't seem to help herself.

And it added an extra layer of meaning when they reached the end of the hall and she looked into the master bedroom. Once again the room was exceptionally large, but this time thickly carpeted for warmth. He had taken advantage of the incredible view with floor to ceiling windows across one of the walls, but it was the king-size four-poster bed that dominated both the room and her attention. "Wow," she managed after a moment. "So this is where you sleep when you're not... hanging out in the city." She tried to keep the tone light, but her imagination ran riot at the thought of Nick alone in this enormous bed.

He cleared his throat and she managed to tear her eyes away from his bed, only to meet a blaze of green when she turned. "Ever made love in a four-poster before?" he asked.

"No." Funny, she was having trouble breathing properly. Her heart felt all fluttery and her stomach was twisting itself into strange aching knots.

He stepped closer. One step. Two. Then stopped. "Would you like to?"

There was only one answer that made sense.

"Yes," she whispered. "Take me to your bed, Nick."

Chapter 9

She stepped into the room of her own free will. No being carried over the threshold this time. She slipped off her jacket and let it fall to the floor, then walked over to the bed. Raising one trembling hand she slowly, oh, so slowly, ran it up and down the heavy wooden post. "God help you if you betray me again, Nick."

"I won't."

Her breath came out in a tiny sigh. "I've never seen a four-poster before."

As if it would make any difference. If Nick was with her, location was moot.

"Then you're in for a treat." She heard him step up behind her, felt strong arms slide around her waist, the heat and thrust of his arousal pressing into her back, urging her lower body relentlessly forward until the cleft of her thighs was hard against the bedpost. She let out a tiny whimper as he began to rock her gently from side to side.

"Do you like that?" he asked, voice husky in her ear, and her head fell back against his shoulder, exposing the line of her neck to his lips.

"Yes," she groaned, "oh, yes."

Luscious agony rippled through her body where the carved ridges of wood rubbed against her. She clutched at the bedpost as his hands left her waist and travelled up beneath her sweater to cup her aching breasts. His fingers massaged gently, slipping beneath the bra to find the jutting point of her nipples.

She felt as if she might faint from the strength of the need inside. And he was fighting a battle too. She could feel his shuddering chest against her back as he drew in ragged breaths, heard the lack of control in his voice as he whispered against her neck, "I can taste the desire on your skin."

Then he bit her, once, twice, and over again along the exposed ligament in her neck. Pleasure and pain merged and she dropped her head even further, encouraging the contact with a moan of assent. She'd have a bruise there tomorrow, for sure, but it didn't matter, she wanted, *needed*, more.

Imprisoned against the bedpost she was helpless to move, but when he finally lifted his lips from her neck and released the pressure against her buttocks she was free to turn and kiss him properly, connecting with his mouth in a desperate lunge that momentarily stunned them both.

"Do that again and we won't make it onto the bed," he warned gruffly.

"I don't care," she sobbed. "Just… tell me how this damn belt buckle works!"

His laughter was edged with roughness. Warm fingers came down over shaking hands that were tugging vainly at his clothing. "Let me," he said. Within moments, he was standing before her wearing nothing but his diamond earring, the long tanned body taut with anticipation and his massive arousal begging for attention.

She couldn't help but comply. With a smile that was part shy, part promise, she knelt down and tasted him, revelling in the surge of hard heat between her lips and enjoying the sound of his groans above her. "Wait," he commanded hoarsely, and lifted her up again to face the urgent need in his eyes. "I want to see you, too."

She allowed him to remove her clothing, piece by slow piece, the wool of her pullover and the denim of her jeans rustling across sensitised skin like an extension of his fingertips. When she too, stood bare in front of him, he raised a hand and traced around first one aching nipple, then the other, before bending his head to suckle at the nub as his fingers continued in light circles around her flesh.

She moaned at the feel of his lips on her skin, flinched at the playful flick of his tongue and blindly reached out to clasp his erection in her hands. She felt his jerk as she stroked the length of him and then concentrated on the tip, heard his breathing mirror her own, shallow and fast.

When his mouth left her breast she cried out, but then he was lifting her up, onto the bed, the pressure of his hand urging her legs wide. She was damp and throbbing and primed for his entry, but he didn't comply.

Not yet.

Instead he turned himself counterpoint and bent his head to dip into the core of her with his mouth. "Oh," she cried out as his tongue grazed across the swollen bud of her sex, then slipped inside to taste her innermost secrets. She was lost in a haze of sensation that grew and grew until she wanted to explode against his lips.

Then she was reaching up with her hands, dragging him towards her and laving him with her own lips and tongue as, together, they used their mouths to bring each other to the edge of control. And beyond.

He thrust hard in the warm cocoon of her mouth as she bucked and twisted beneath his, until she couldn't hold on any longer and cried out for release.

He lifted himself away and reached for the drawer in the bedside table as she lay panting and slick with arousal. He fumbled with the foil packet, swore, then he was back with her again, turning her over this time until she was kneeling on all fours.

"Okay?" he queried.

"Yes," she said fiercely. "*Yes!*"

She felt him behind her, felt the tip of him pressing against her, and gasped as his sheathed body filled her almost to bursting point.

When he moved it was going to hurt.

And she couldn't think of anything she needed more.

"God, Serena," he groaned, "I need to fuck you hard this time."

"*Yes*, Nick. Love me as hard as you want."

With a primal noise part groan, part yell, he thrust. She felt as if she were being torn apart, the pain exquisite, edged with rapture, like nothing she'd ever felt before, her body impaled on his sex, clenching around him, sucking him in until they were not two but one entity, rutting and moaning and screaming for release.

Need. Pure need.

The need for sensual oblivion grew and grew until a mutual, pulsing explosion drew from them both a shuddering, throaty cry.

She came back to earth slowly, her body tangled up with his, so heavily replete it was difficult to move. In fact, she realised, it was getting a bit difficult to breathe, as well. "Nick, could you… do you think…"

"Sorry!" He shifted his weight then turned to lean up on one elbow. "Better?" he asked softly.

"Oh, yes!" She stretched luxuriously and turned to meet his quizzical grin. "Much better!"

She stared up at him with a kind of fascination. His eyes at this moment were a clear green, ringed by dark lashes even longer than her own. Never in her life had she ever thought to make love with a man as markedly good-looking as Nick, and yet, he didn't seem particularly aware of his looks, or the sensuality underlying them.

His free hand dropped to caress the line of her collarbone. "Serena, do you realise," he asked, "that I'm completely and utterly in love with you?"

The words, apropos of nothing, shocked the grin from her face. She sat up and drew her knees to her chest, averting her gaze from his naked magnificence. Instead she concentrated on the brightly coloured artwork on his bedroom wall. Contemporary. Expensive. A perfect offset for the heavy antique furniture.

"I don't know how to answer that, Nick," she said.

The bed shifted beneath her as he too, sat up. "How about, I love you too?" he asked, and she frowned at the laughter in his tone.

"Why is everything a joke to you?"

He put a gentle hand on her chin. "Do I look like I'm joking?"

"No," she admitted. "Who knows, maybe I want an excuse to get mad at you again. It's very confusing in here." She tapped her chest lightly.

"Are you sure it's your heart that's confused, and not your head?"

She shrugged. "With me it might as well be one and the same. Alex hurt me. He hurt me more than I can ever truly explain. I – no, wait—" She held up a hand to still his protest. "I want to finish. I was practically a child when I met Alex. And I gave him *all* of me, Nick. Everything I had. When he threw it back in my face… I don't know if I can open myself up to that again. Not completely."

"Its okay, Serena."

"No," she said fiercely. "Its *not* okay. You don't deserve second best, and I honestly can't say if that's all you're going to get with me."

Nick shook his head, the dark hair loose and luxuriously thick. She stifled the impulse to run her fingers through it as he said, "If what you're giving me right now is second best, then it's better than anything I've had in thirty seven years of living, and that's good enough for me. Come here."

His arm slid around her back and pulled her towards him. His skin felt warm against her own, and despite her confusion she felt a flare of heat renew itself somewhere deep inside. She hadn't known her body was capable of such a strong physical response.

If only she could be sure that he would always tell her the truth.

"I've spent the best part of my life chasing fun and avoiding commitment," he said as his lips curved against her temple, "but when I look at you I see a future filled with both."

"Really?" She tried for lightness. "So why will it be different with me? A lifetime avoiding commitment is a big habit to try and break."

His lips left her temple and travelled down to nibble at an earlobe. "I've never loved anyone before. Not like this. You see, Serena, that's the effect you have on me. That – and *this*!" With a sudden move he pushed her back against the covers and left her in no doubt about her physical effect on him.

Nor did she have any doubt about the strength of his effect on her.

She wrapped arms and legs tightly around his long hard body and responded to his kiss with everything she had. She wanted to lose herself in him, in their lovemaking, until logic disappeared and instinct took over. Until fear and doubt were transcended and the blaze of passion became all-consuming.

When Serena woke it was late afternoon, the sky outside grey and heavy with the threat of rain. She turned to Nick and found him gone from the bed, but as she sat up he emerged from the connecting bathroom clad only in trousers, towelling his dark hair dry. Her nostrils flared in appreciation as a clean, soapy smell wafted out with him.

"Is it time for Cinderella to go home from the ball?" she asked, and was rewarded with a grin as he peeped out from beneath the towel.

"Don't know if I have the stamina to last until midnight, but we could give it a try," he said.

The hopeful tone made her laugh. "As enticing as that sounds I think I'll have to pass," she said. "I'm not used to getting up before dawn."

"Was it worth the early start?"

"Definitely! The whole day has been wonderful, Nick. Thank you."

She stood and stretched, her body slightly sore.

"Feel free to have a shower," he offered, pointing the way, "or a soak in the clawfoot tub. Fresh towels are in the cupboard."

"Thanks." She stepped forward with a hint of shyness, unwarranted given the afternoon they'd just spent together. "Would you… like to join me?"

"I'd love to, but I can't." He seemed genuinely regretful. "I need to get some work done. Make a few phone calls."

"Oh. Okay." A few minutes later, as she soaped herself clean under the shower and let the warm water wash down over her shoulders and back, a tiny kernel of distrust grew. Was he working on vineyard business? Or the newspaper article? Was he right this minute sitting in his study writing notes about their afternoon together? Revisiting his research about other women he'd been dating?

Stop! she told herself. *Stop now*!

He says he loves me. He says he can see a future with me. Hold onto that. And don't run away from it. Don't sabotage it with these crazy thoughts.

She squealed in shock as the shower door rattled open. "I changed my mind, sweetheart," he said, stepping in and pulling her purposefully into his arms. "Your invitation was too good to refuse."

His mouth came down over hers with a forcefulness that swept away all doubt and brought the pounding of her heart into tandem with his as their warm wet bodies slipped and slid against each other in the steamy cubicle.

His hands cupped her buttocks and pressed her into him and she gasped as the folds of her skin yielded to his hardness. "So, Prince Charming," she teased breathlessly, "you don't think you can keep this up until midnight?"

"I can give it a try, Cinders," he murmured against her lips. Then he was lifting her, arm and thigh muscles flexing with the strain as he took her weight, then slowly, excruciatingly slowly, lowered her down onto his arousal, until he filled her completely. Serena moaned and dug her heels into his back.

"It looks a damn sight easier in the movies," he grumbled, then she was laughing and gasping and moaning with pleasure as his lips found her breasts and his arms lifted and dropped, urging her body into an age-old rhythm that had her quivering at the painful pressure inside.

Nick groaned and buried his face in her glorious hair. The tension in his loins built to an unbearable level. "Yes," he urged her hoarsely as she slipped up and down him like a whisper of silk. It felt so right to be inside her. She was so tight, her muscles clutching his cock like a vise. He wanted to fuck her like she'd never been fucked before, but he held back, waiting. "Let yourself go, my love. I want to feel you climax around me. I want to watch your face as you lose control."

"I... don't... like... losing control."

"I know."

He felt the clenching of her muscles even before the whimpering cry tore out of her. "Go baby, go for it!" He struggled to hold on. She shuddered around him in a pulsing frenzy that went on and on until he could wait no longer.

"*Yes!*" he cried out, surging further into her.

Her body began yet another climactic wave and her groans of delirium mingled with his before washing slowly, inexorably, away.

Night had fallen and a gentle mist of rain wafted over them as Nick led her down the lamp-lit pathway to the car park. It was empty save for his car, which had been brought back during the day – no doubt by one of his faithful staff.

Only several kilometres away from where their journey had begun but it might have been a million miles for the distance they had travelled today, she thought. So much had happened since the balloon ride. So much more of Nick had been revealed to her.

And yet, a little part of her mind insisted, there are still parts of him I don't understand, parts he hasn't allowed me to share. Like his newspaper work.

"When is your lonely hearts article due?" she asked as the car purred into the night.

He flicked her a cautious glance, then shrugged. "I'm hoping to have all the research done in the next three or four days, then it's a matter of sitting down and writing."

"So, these other women you've been seeing... are they anything like me? What were their reasons for placing an ad? Did they agonise over the whole process as much as I did?"

"Serena, I don't think—"

"I wouldn't ask if I didn't want to know."

She saw his hands clench on the steering wheel, but he answered calmly enough. "Okay. Well firstly, none of them are like you. You're one of a kind." His grin faded at her stony look.

"Actually, each of the women I spoke to had their own individual story, so it's a bit hard to generalise. Some were coming out of a long-term relationship and didn't like the idea of entering the singles scene again."

He paused, then added thoughtfully, "And I think for many people – men and women – the idea of being able to screen potential partners, at least to a certain extent, is appealing."

Serena nodded. "I went to a nightclub once, with Nessa," she admitted after a few minutes silence. "It was a month or so after Alex left. The experience was degrading. All those men looking you over like a choice cut of meat. Ugh!"

Nick let out a long, low chuckle. "Please tell me I don't make you feel that way."

She looked at him, relaxed yet alert as he drove, and shook her head. "No, you make me feel quite different."

"Good." She could see in the glare of passing headlights that he was serious behind his smile. "I won't betray your trust, Serena. Not again."

"Nick..." What could she say that hadn't already been said? She let out her breath in a quiet sigh and instead of speaking, reached across to rest her hand on his thigh. She felt the ripple of muscle beneath her fingers, then he took one of his hands off the steering wheel to cover hers.

Warmth. Security. Awareness. All contained in that simple connection of skin to skin. She left her hand where it was for the remainder of the trip home.

When they pulled up in front of her cottage there was a car already parked out front, a dark sedan she didn't recognise. She shrugged as Nick looked at her questioningly. "Maybe one of the neighbours has visitors?" she guessed, and didn't think any more of it until they were walking up the front path and she felt Nick stiffen at her side.

"Looks like you have company," he said. "Is that your brother, Liam?"

She looked towards the front door to see an immaculately dressed man standing on her porch. His expensive-looking grey suit and neatly styled brown hair immediately put her and Nick's day-old casual clothing to shame. She came to an abrupt stop and felt the blood drain away from her face.

It was not her brother.

Chapter 10

"Hello, Serena."

"Alex! What are you doing here?" She stared at the man who had been the centre of her adult life for so many years, felt Nick's arm tighten instinctively around her, but couldn't tear her eyes away from Alex. He looked exactly the same as he had the day he left.

"What do you want?" She could only manage a whisper.

There was that little smile she knew so well, the tiny shake of his head as if she'd said something exasperating. "We need to talk, Sassy," he said.

Her heart bumped painfully at the sound of the old nickname. Then a sudden thought struck her and she raised a horrified hand to her mouth. "Oh my God, its not... Kelly? Is something wrong with—"

"Relax. Kel's fine. She's still in Sydney with her mother. No, we need to talk, but I'd prefer a bit of privacy if possible." His flat gaze flicked across to Nick. She felt the tension in Nick's arm, as if he were vibrating with controlled anger.

Alex's look sharpened with sudden interest and he stared at Nick as if trying to gauge his measure. With his attention momentarily diverted, Serena was able to break the feeling of being mesmerised and glance up at Nick, only to encounter an unusually pale face and emerald eyes glittering with suppressed emotion as he glared at the man who had hurt her.

She was struck by the enormous difference between the two, even on a purely superficial level. Nick seemed all vibrant passion to Alex's cool sophistication.

Heat and ice, she thought. Either way, you get burnt.

"Its all right, Nick," she murmured, touching his hand gently. He flinched beneath her fingers, but the movement was quickly controlled. "I don't need protecting," she said.

"Are you sure... Sassy?" His repetition of her nickname was cruel, but even as she shot him a reproachful look she had a flash of understanding.

He was scared of losing her.

The thought filled her with a strange exultation and she turned back to Alex with a renewed show of strength. "Just give me a minute, please." She dragged at Nick's arm, pulling him towards the car. "I need to do this, Nick. I need to face him. On my own."

"I don't think you should be alone with him."

"Please!" Her head felt light with the shock of seeing Alex again. The last thing she needed was to deal with Nick and that stubbornly arrogant set to his jaw. "Nick,

I'll be fine. He can't hurt me, not anymore. Please, just go. You keep asking me to trust you. Now I'm asking you in return… trust me on this. I'll deal with whatever it is that Alex wants, and then I'll call you. I promise."

"I…" He seemed to swell with the effort of holding himself in.

"I want to fight my own battles, Nick," she said. "I don't want – or need – you to fight them for me. Please."

She watched the clenching and unclenching of his fists as he debated within himself, then finally he said roughly, "Fine. I'll be at the apartment in town. You know how to reach me there. If you want me." He slammed into the car and roared off, and even as anxiety about the coming confrontation made her tremble, a tiny part of her felt the urge to laugh at his display of testosterone. All men were boys at heart.

Even her beloved Nick.

Nick fumed as he drove, a guilty conscience forcing him to ease off the accelerator after a few minutes to a slightly less dangerous speed. It had gone against everything he stood for to leave her alone with that *bastard*.

Serena wanted to hear what Alex had to say That wasn't so bad, was it? But how could she face him so easily, so *calmly*, after all he'd done to hurt her? Was she secretly still in love with Alex? Was that why she'd found it hard to commit herself?

When he realised who was standing on her doorstep it was all he could do not to race up the path and punch the guy's lights out. Not once but twenty times over. It was a feeling he'd never had before and the intensity of it scared him.

But Serena had been the opposite. As he filled with rage she'd been remarkably calm. She'd lived up to her name all right. Serene.

So what if her voice had a shaky note in it, if the hands touching his arm were trembling as she urged him to leave? Didn't mean anything either way.

He punched the steering wheel, then jumped and scowled as the horn accidentally went off. Who knew what they were doing right now. Whether they were talking. Whether he was asking for – and receiving – forgiveness. Whether the son-of-a-bitch was using his daughter to persuade soft-hearted Serena to do whatever it was he wanted.

Whether he'd taken her in his arms and she was melting for *him* the way she melted for… *Stop*! He told himself with a sense of self-disgust.

If that's what she wants, then so be it. There's nothing I can do about it. I've lain my heart on the line for her, shown her how I feel.

And if she doesn't want it, I could always place a lonely hearts ad of my own.

"Aren't you going to invite me in, Sassy?" Alex's voice still had that slight edge of sarcasm that had always made her feel as if she'd done something stupid.

She gritted her teeth. "Will this take long?"

"I'd rather talk inside," he said. "If that's okay with you, of course?"

After a moment she nodded, then stepped carefully past him. And if it took three tries for her door key to fit into the hole then at least she could blame the cold evening air laced with misting rain.

"Come in, then." She removed her wet coat and saw Lancelot start down the hallway towards her, then stop suddenly when he saw she was not alone. He sat down and began to wash his face with sharp agitated movements.

She led Alex into the lounge room and gestured to a chair, trying not to look at the rug where she and Nick had made love. "Well?" she asked, when he made no move to be seated.

His blue eyes assessed her carefully. "You're looking good, Sass. Better than I remember, actually."

"Don't call me Sassy, please." She couldn't stand hearing the name that had symbolised their closeness.

He raised an eyebrow at her tone, and she decided that if he wasn't going to sit, then she sure as hell wasn't, either. She gripped the back of the couch. "You look well, too," she admitted with a grudging air. It was true. But when it came to Alex she'd learnt her lesson well. Appearances could be deceptive.

She took a deep breath, grateful for the polo neck that hid the racing pulse in her throat. "Alex, I haven't seen or heard from you in over a year. If its not about Kelly, then why…?"

"I'm here because things haven't been going too well in Sydney and, quite frankly, I'm moving back to Melbourne again. On my own."

Serena blinked. "Oh. But what about Kelly?"

He shrugged. "She seems happy enough in school and all that. Got some little friends now. She's doing ballet, and she loves her swimming lessons. And Deb seems reconciled to being a mum too, so we think its best to leave Kel where she is."

Reconciled to being a mum? As if Kelly were anything but a joy! "Really. How nice for you all."

Alex seemed oblivious to her disgust as he continued, "Deborah and I were doing okay for a while, then this big promotion came up and we both went for it. I got it."

She read the smug self-satisfaction in his face and knew in a blinding moment of clarity that she was truly over Alex. She hardly heard him as he added, "Deb was spitting chips, of course, and after a while I got sick of her carrying on about how I only got the job over her because I'm a man."

Oh, Nick, she thought. *You're worth a million of Alex. How could I ever have compared you?*

"So what does any of this have to do with me?" she asked, guessing full well where this was heading, but perversely, needing him to spell it out just the same.

"Well, you know. I'm back. I thought you might want to show me around town again, for old time's—"

"*No!*"

"What?" He looked genuinely shocked at her vehemence, and Serena almost laughed at the absurdity. What a doormat I must have been in the past, she thought.

No wonder my family couldn't understand me.

She took a deep breath. "What do you take me for, Alex?"

"Nothing! I—"

"Let me make this crystal clear," she said. "There is no way in *hell* you and I are *ever* going to get back together, not in any way, shape or form. I don't love you, I don't want you, I don't need you or miss you. I don't even like you. And even if I hadn't met someone else, my answer would still be the same. No."

Alex's blue eyes narrowed. "So that guy who was with you—"

"That guy, as you call him, is the best thing that's ever happened to me, with the possible exception of my time with Kelly. He... never mind, you don't need to know any more about him. Its none of your business." *And what Nick and I have together is too special to discuss with the likes of you!*

"Now," she added, "if that's all you came to say, then I think its time for you to leave."

"You're making a mistake, Sass." He paused, then said in a persuasive tone, "What if I were to bring Kelly back to Melbourne?"

"Oh, Alex." Her heart broke for the little girl with parents like Alex and Deborah. But it sounded as if she were making a reasonable life for herself in Sydney. She clung to that thought, even as her lip curled in bitter disgust at the man standing before her. Willing to use his daughter in order to get what he wanted. "Get out," she said. "Now."

Alex hesitated, opened his mouth as if to argue, then closed it again when she shook her head and pointed towards the street. But it seemed he couldn't help himself. As he crossed the threshold he stopped and turned to face her, a knowing smile on his lips. "It won't work, you know," he said. "You weren't woman enough for me. Why would you think you'd be woman enough for anyone else?"

Her mouth opened in shock.

"And especially someone like your new boyfriend." His lip curled. "He's a player, like me. I saw it in his face. Poor Sass, doomed to fail in love."

Then he was gone, and she slammed the front door and leant against it, feeling the dual heat and cold in her face and fighting the urge to vomit.

"He's scum," she whispered. "Don't let him win." Gradually the nausea receded, and she sank to the floor as the weakness in her legs made itself felt.

Just as he'd always been able to do, Alex had managed to shoot his vitriolic arrow straight to the heart of her most deep-seated insecurity.

Nick's a player, like me.

And yet I managed to surprise him, she thought. Remember that. I stood up to him this time and he wasn't expecting it. Those parting words were pure spite. I rejected him and he wanted to hurt me. That's all. It isn't true.

Nick and Alex couldn't be more different.

She smiled grimly as she realised how much she must have changed in recent months. And the change had been occurring without her even realising it.

Absent-mindedly she began to pat Lancelet when he darted forward to rub against her knee.

Vanessa was right. *My heart still works. Creaky, but its working.*

And I'm finally willing to lay it on the line. For Nick.

She lifted her chin, feeling a huge weight drop from her shoulders. With a light laugh she jumped up and ran to the phone, determined to tell him how she felt. Her enthusiasm was only slightly dimmed when she got his answering machine. He said he'd be at the apartment and she believed him.

On impulse she grabbed her coat and bag and headed out, stopping only long enough to dump some cat food into Lancelot's bowl when he grabbed her protestingly around the ankle. She left him gulping contentedly and raced out to the garage, oblivious to the heavier rain now falling in the darkness.

Her purple VW beetle was practically a vintage car, or so she told her friends when they teased her about it, but she kept it meticulously maintained and as always it started first time. Nick's city apartment was a suite of rooms in the building next to her client's pub, the place they'd had their first real taste of the sexual chemistry between them.

She remembered that kiss with Nick in every detail, the heat, the taste of him, the hidden depths of desire, the hint of fear at the ferocity of her own response. She felt the ache as her body relived the memory. She hadn't known then that she would love him. She'd fought it with her mind, but her body knew. Her body felt the connection before she understood what it meant.

And it was as real for Nick as it was for her. She was sure of it. Nothing to do with research for a newspaper article. And she was ready to give herself to him. *All* of herself – not just her body but her heart as well. Anticipation fizzed through her veins at the thought of his response.

The magic of love. It really *did* exist. There *was* such a thing as Mister Right. For her, it was Nick.

His apartment was a short distance from her workplace and she knew the area well, so it took her only a few minutes to find parking nearby. But when she entered the building and spoke to the man at reception, she found Nick had been in briefly, then gone out again.

"He said he might not be back until late," the man said, looking curiously at Serena as she hunched deeper into her coat. "Would you like to leave a message, ma'am?"

"No thank you," she mumbled. Where had he gone? The vineyard?

She tried not to think about the other Nick Wade, the newspaper man with a hidden agenda. There would be a good explanation. She'd just have to curb her curiosity until morning. She exited the building and headed back towards her car, determined to give him the trust he had asked for. Just as she had asked for it in return.

As she passed the pub where they'd met the door opened and a blast of happy voices washed over her as a man and woman, entwined in each other's arms, exited into the street.

She smiled. Why not? The old Serena Hewitt would never have dared enter a pub alone at this time of night. But that person was gone, and in its place was a woman with backbone! She exchanged a grin with the couple as they made their way past her, then stepped out of the night and into a room full of warmth and laughter.

Shaking her head free of water droplets and removing her coat, she made her way towards the bar.

Then stopped short. Her mouth dropped open as the bottom fell out of her world. Nick raised his startled green gaze towards her over the head of the woman he embraced.

Chapter 11

A fog of blackness obscured her vision, then it cleared and she stared at Alex and the dark-haired woman beside him.

Alex? No. She shook her head, confused.

Nick. It was Nick in front of her. Not Alex.

What difference does it make?

She wanted to turn and run but instead stood as if frozen while he turned his now-stricken gaze towards the woman, then back to Serena. Somehow that made it worse, that he could be caught between the two of them, not knowing who to support.

And it was clear that the other woman needed support. Her face was an unhealthy white, her hands clutching at a crumpled handkerchief, and she was leaning into the curve of Nick's arm in a familiar way, as if used to drawing energy or comfort from his touch. It was obvious they knew each other.

Maybe he's just told her she's going to be the centre of a lonely hearts story, she thought. Maybe she's just discovered the real Nicholas Wade. It was strange that she could feel nothing at all, not even a pang of pity for this other woman.

Nothing but the curl of rage starting as a flicker of warmth in her stomach. Nothing but the heat spreading through her body, supplanting the cold shock, growing, consuming her, until nothing else existed but this white-hot blaze of fury.

She stood still a moment longer, deliberately allowing the animosity to take hold She needed the strength of it to stand and face him. And when the kindling was well alight, her cheeks burning with the heat of it, she moved.

Forward.

To face Nick and her fears head-on, as she had already faced Alex tonight.

"Hello, Nick." Her slap knocked his head sideways. She heard a gasp of shock from the other woman, but from him there was nothing but a narrowing of the eyes as he straightened and raised a slow hand to his cheek.

The mark of her fingers showed already as an ugly red welt and a flare of guilt filled her. She had never hit anyone in her life. Not even Alex.

"Nicky, are you all right? What the heck—?"

"*Stay out of this!*" His tone silenced the other woman, who sat back with a raised eyebrow and neatly folded arms.

"All yours, bro!"

Bro? To Serena's heightened senses the word had an ominous ring, but she had no time to digest the feeling, or to clarify what it meant. Nick's eyes were glittering with a savage intensity, made all the more sinister by his seeming calmness.

"And that was for...?" The voice was silky smooth, but she'd have to be deaf not to hear the undertone beneath. Not calm. Anything but.

She swallowed. "Betrayal of trust... *Nicky*." He moved sharply at her parody of the other woman and she took an involuntary step backwards. Then her chin jutted forward and she crossed her arms tightly as if to hold her emotions in check. "Its not going to work between us, is it?"

Her heart pounded as she waited through eons of silence. She could read nothing in the harshly etched lines of his face. She wanted to hear... *something*, but she wasn't sure what. Agreement? A heated denial? A declaration of true love?

"No," he said at last, and it was the finality in his tone that brought sudden tears to her eyes. "I don't think it *is* going to work, Serena, but not for the reasons *you* believe."

"Wh—what do you mean by that?" Why did her heart *ache* so?

His laugh was brittle. "Love without trust, Serena. You can't have it."

He shook his head and turned to the woman staring curiously at them both. "This is my sister, Charlotte. Sis, meet Serena, the woman I was telling you about. Though I guess its all moot now, isn't it?"

"Your... your..." She felt as if she'd been punched in the stomach, couldn't seem to get enough air. "Your... sister?" Yes, she could see the resemblance now, though Charlotte's face was somewhat softer, less vital than her brother's. And you wouldn't lose yourself in Charlotte's green eyes, whereas Nick...

"Oh!"

"Oh, indeed." Now it was his voice thrumming with emotion. She met his gaze and saw the hurt etched deep. And in that moment she faced the awful truth.

He was right. It would never work between them, but not because of Nick.

Because of me, you stupid fool! Because of my own stupid fear, the fear of heartbreak. The fear of opening up to the possibility of passion. The fear of *living*.

"I'm so sorry, Nick, I..." Her throat closed over and she couldn't finish. Just shook her head at him, nodded stiffly to Charlotte, and left.

"Well, aren't you going to go after her?" Charlotte disengaged her arm from Nick's and frowned as her brother just sat there.

"No." He couldn't explain the hurt. It went deeper than anything he'd felt before.

"Nicky, its your life, but if I were you—"

"I said *no!*"

"Fine!"

Brother and sister glared at each other in a momentary stand-off, then suddenly he was up and racing for the door, adrenalin suffusing his movements with desperate precision. He slipped past someone without knowing who it was, all his focus on Serena and what she must be thinking right now... what she must be feeling...

The look on her face when she saw me here...

Shock, then utter despair, then a strange blankness. It was like seeing someone you knew disappear before your very eyes. Impossible, and yet it had happened, right there in the pub. Was this too much for her to bear? He had to get to her before it was too late.

I need you, Serena. I need your love. I need your sweetness.

He felt like a knife stabbing through his heart at the thought of never seeing her again. But it was still working… must be… it was racing now, pumping the blood so loudly in his ears that he couldn't hear the traffic in the street.

Which way had she gone?

There, ahead in the driving rain. Disappearing around the corner. Fast.

He sprinted in that direction and rounded the bend, but when he got there she was gone. He let out a strangled cry.

Too late.

Serena had no idea how she got home. It was incredible how calm she felt, now that the anger had gone. Maybe a little part of her had been expecting the worst since she first met Nick, and now that the worst had arrived it was almost a relief.

Heartbreak.

She didn't have to guard against it any more. It was there, with her, and it was all her own fault.

She felt the warmth as Lancelot rubbed against her shin and realised for the first time that she was wet through. Maybe that's why her teeth were chattering. For some reason the thought struck her as funny and she began to laugh, then found she couldn't stop. When the cat skittered away in fright she laughed even harder, then suddenly the laughter turned to sobs and she was crying like she hadn't cried since childhood.

Eventually the river subsided and she made her way to the bathroom. No, she thought. A few tears won't stop the heartache. Nothing will.

I let Nick into my heart, and he's still there. When Alex hurt me, he destroyed any love I might have felt for him. I only stayed because of Kelly.

But with Nick…

How do I get *him* out of my heart?

It was hours before she finally sank into a restless, dream-filled sleep. And then in the darkest hours near dawn, when the weight of her error seemed to press most heavily, it was as if something broke inside her chest and all the love she'd been holding onto came tumbling out.

This is as real as it gets, she thought. To imagine a future without Nick is unthinkable. Forget my stupid business-like plans. Nick loves me, and I love him.

It's as simple as that.

And that's worth risking everything.

She sat up and stared at the muted blue curtains covering her window. In the dark they looked black. But appearances could be deceptive. Alex had taught her that.

And Nick had taught her that opening up to love and passion was far better than staying in the grey, emotionless world she'd inhabited up to now.

How am I going to make this right? How can I make it up to him?

As if on cue Lancelot jumped onto the bed and reached over to gently lick her hand, then rub the side of his jaw along her thumb joint. As Serena looked down at his display of affection a slow smile began to spread across her face.

"Of course," she said. Since the moment they'd met – well, she amended, not the first moment, but pretty soon after – he'd seduced her with wine and roses and talk of the importance of passion and romance. Where was it written that she couldn't do the same for him?

She would woo Nicholas Wade until that long luscious hair of his was standing on end. Maybe a few other parts of him as well.

And she would prove to him once and for all that she was over Alex and ready for love. And all the baggage that came with it.

Including trust.

Nick felt as if he could sleep for a week.

He replaced the phone in its recharging cradle and rubbed his eyes wearily. Charlotte had called to say she was home again, the problems with her husband still there, but at least they were seeing a counsellor now. He thought he'd be glad to have the place to himself again, but instead he felt drained and empty, strangely depressed.

Despite the stress of the past few days he'd found it impossible to get Serena out of his head. He kept wondering where she was, what she was doing, how she was feeling. But the initial urge to chase after her had been obliterated by hurt. They could have had so much. If only it weren't for that bastard Alex who'd destroyed her trust in others.

And then his anger would grow all over again until he felt like he had to punch something to relieve it.

When he first met Serena he'd had no idea of the impact she would have on his life. Or his heart.

But now…

He moved into the study and sat, waiting listlessly for his laptop to power up before opening the document he'd called "lonely hearts". His mouth twisted at the irony.

Who knew, when I first began this project, that the loneliest heart of all would end up being my own?

He began to type.

Serena knew what it meant now when people talked about having their heart in their mouth. Her pulse was racing so hard that her throat and even the inside of her mouth seemed to be pulsing with the beat.

You'd think with all this blood racing through my system that I'd at least be warm. But I'm not. I can't stop shivering.

What if he says no?

She couldn't afford negative thoughts. Not now. Not if she wanted this to succeed.

And she wanted it to succeed more than anything she'd ever wanted in her life.

She should have called first. He might not even be there. Most likely he was still at his apartment in town and she'd have wasted a journey out to the vineyard. But some deep-rooted instinct she couldn't explain had her heading out on this dark, cold night towards the Yarra Ranges, and the vineyard that Nick called home.

He was there.

She could see the lights as she drove the last couple of hundred metres up the hill towards the sprawling homestead. She parked the car and took a few deep breaths before climbing the steps to the veranda. Here goes nothing, she thought. But before she could knock the door opened and he was there, a large dark shape silhouetted against the golden light spilling out from inside.

"Hello, Nick." Her voice was shaking. She cleared her throat awkwardly, and they stood in silence a few moments before he made an impatient noise and shifted back from the doorway.

"Come in, Serena."

She frowned at the carefully neutral tone, but followed him into the lounge without comment. There was a roaring fire in the grate, a half-drunk glass of red wine and an upturned book on the coffee table next to one of the armchairs. *Moby Dick.* Despite her nervous tension she felt her body relax a notch as the cosy warmth of the room stole around her.

"Look, I'm sorry—"

"How did you know I was here?"

They spoke together, then laughed awkwardly and as she looked into his eyes she saw a faint spark of humour. It gave her hope.

"I didn't," she answered. "I just knew I had to see you and found myself driving out here."

"You're lucky. I only arrived an hour ago."

"Oh." God, this was awful! Two strangers making polite, meaningless conversation.

She moved nearer to the fire and held out her hands to the heat. Then jumped as his voice came from directly behind her. "How did your meeting go with Alex?"

She turned and found him inches away. Felt the heat from his body almost as strongly as the fire now at her back. "It went out the door and far away, never to return. I hope."

The corner of his mouth twitched. "Really?" His tone was distinctly softer, and encouraged by this, she drew a deep breath.

"Nick, even if I hadn't met you, there would never have been anything again between me and Alex." She grimaced. "What I felt for him, while real enough, wasn't exactly love. And whatever it was between us is long gone."

"I know that." He smiled. "I have to admit to a moment or two of jealousy when I realised who was standing on your porch, but once I got back to the apartment I knew you were too smart to fall for his tricks again. I trusted you."

Implicit in his last three words was a wealth of accusation. She made to reach for him but he moved away and sat down in the chair he'd obviously been occupying before her arrival. Disconcerted, she stood for a moment longer, then lowered her arms to her sides and sat on the couch opposite.

"I'm so sorry, Nick," she said. "The only thing I can say in my defence is that it really threw me seeing Alex again. And when I saw you with Charlotte, well, maybe I was seeing what I'd expected to see all along. The theory being, of course, that if you expect the worst, then it can't hurt you as much." She laughed bitterly. "Only it doesn't work that way, does it? I ended up creating more hurt, and not only for me this time but for you as well."

He nodded slowly. "I was sitting there listening to Charlotte talk about her problems, and all I could think about was how much I wanted you there with me. That's what I was thinking when you walked in and nearly knocked my head off my shoulders. How much I missed you."

"I'm so sorry, Nick. Believe me." Quickly she closed the distance between them, knelt beside him and placed a gentle hand on his knee. "I love you, Nick. With all my heart. It's taken me a little while to figure out exactly what that means, but… well… maybe I can show you."

Slowly she got to her feet and stood before him, trembling slightly at what she was about to do. "You taught me the meaning of passion… of love… even trust, the hardest lesson of all. Now I want to show you how much I've learnt."

With a self-conscious gesture she loosened the black chiffon scarf around her neck and watched his eyes widen in shocked understanding as she let the end of the material swish across his lap and fall to the floor in a delicate pool of darkness.

"Serena, I—"

"No," she whispered, "don't speak." She leant forward and touched her lips to his. His hands came up as if to catch hold of her but she twisted out of his grasp. "Not yet, Nick." And she stepped back before taking off her jacket to reveal the dark red camisole beneath. She felt the smile play around her lips as she watched the awakening of desire in his features. Wondered at the rush of excitement in her own body as she saw the evidence of his arousal growing before her very eyes.

"Desire begets desire," she murmured, and began to undo the buttons at the front of the camisole, one, then the next, in a slow yet steady action.

Nick was leaning back now in the chair, seemingly relaxed. Yet his eyes watched hungrily as she flicked open the last button and slid the straps of the camisole off her shoulders, one at a time, until the silken material slithered down to join the pool of black chiffon on the floor.

"Do you like what you see, Nick?" she asked huskily, and heard his answer in the hiss of breath as she leaned forward to place one hand on each arm of the chair. Her breasts swung slightly in the new red bra. "Its see-through, isn't it?"

"Serena," he groaned, "are you trying to give me a stroke?"

"If you say so," she murmured, deliberately misunderstanding him, and lightly ran her hands over his lap until her questing fingers found his hardening centre. "A stroke like this?"

She dragged her fingernails up the length of him, revelling in his instinctive flinch as she reached the pulsing tip. Even through the material of his trousers she could feel the radiant heat, and it was all she could do not to rip at the zipper and be done with it. But not yet, Nick, she thought. Not yet.

Once again she stepped back, and this time it was her trousers that fell to the floor, revealing the red garters and black stockings hidden beneath. "Oh, Serena," he breathed, staring at her in awe. "No panties?"

Still in black high heels, she kicked the trousers away, feeling as if she were symbolically removing the last trace of her conservative self. "This is not about sex, Nick," she said. "This is about trust. And love."

Her hands went up to cup her own breasts, the thumb of each hand flicking across the raised nub of her nipples, then moved downwards, gliding over her stomach and the garter belt to reach the hair shielding her aching sex. Reticence threatened, but she forced it out of her head as her fingers found their mark and she watched Nick's eyes avidly following every stroking move.

She groaned, and saw his hands tighten convulsively on the arms of the chair.

"*Serena…*"

"Do you want to touch me, Nick, like this…?"

"*Yes!*" He held out a beseeching hand. "Come here before I explode."

"No." She parted the triangle of hair, exposing the already swollen nub of her clitoris. "You can have this," she whispered, "but not yet."

She bent down to retrieve her scarf from the tangle of clothes on the floor, then reached up to remove her glasses, dropping them onto the coffee table with a tiny click. She brought the wisp of chiffon up to her face, stopping for a moment to inhale her own perfume on the material, then shivered as she heard his intake of breath. "The ultimate test of trust, Nick. For me, at least. Putting someone else in control."

She hesitated, but only for a moment. Nick needed this, needed to know that she could place her trust in him. Quickly she tied the material across her eyes, then waited with a sense of exhilaration for whatever would come next. "I'm yours, Nick, if you want me," she whispered, and felt his fingertips graze her stomach.

"Oh, I want you, my love. Make no mistake." The purpose in his tone was an aphrodisiac, causing her body to thrum with anticipation.

With her eyesight hobbled she found other senses strangely heightened. She could feel his presence like a magnetic charge, and was reminded of the first time they'd met, when she experienced that quickening in her body as soon as he entered the room. His breathing, as hoarse and ragged as her own, was underlined by the crackle and pop of wood in the nearby fireplace, and the creak of leather as he shifted in the chair. His scent was heavy in her nostrils, the spicy aftershave, muted now by several hours of wear, the smell of arousal coming from both of them. And his touch on her skin…

She shivered at the feel of questing fingers trailing over her body, felt her nipples pucker more as he unclipped the bra and it slithered off. "I'm going to taste you," he said, and pulled her towards him. Using instinct to guide her she climbed awkwardly onto his lap, one knee each side of his thighs. Then she arched her breasts toward him and shuddered when his lips made contact. Moaned at the moist warmth when he took her deep into his mouth. Clutched at his shoulders as he explored each of the heavy, aching lobes   on the brink of climax already but not wanting to get there on her own.

And without sight she was more aware of what he felt like beneath her own exploring fingers. The satiny smoothness of his skin as she slid her hands beneath his shirt, the prickle of body hair, the hard muscle, the raw heat.

"You're gorgeous, my love, so gorgeous," he growled against her neck. His lips were feather-light against her skin. His hands were shaking as they slid down over her hips to cup her buttocks. Unlike last time his touch was gentle, not squeezing her but stroking, probing bruised flesh that had been punished by teeth and lips during their last bout of lovemaking, then...

"Oh!" His tongue had followed his fingertips, the moist warmth an electrifying shock, the trail of wetness moving down from her waist and across her hip as he lifted and turned her to reach her buttocks. "No... I..." She felt a shyness as his tongue dipped into the crevice of her behind, but the yearning in her womb intensified and without thought she bent forward to give him whatever he desired. "I'm yours, Nicholas Wade," she whispered.

He ceased his ministrations. "You've always been mine, darling Serena. Now sshh."

He turned her toward him and then guided her hips downward. Her aching sex touched his erection as he moved her body to stroke his arousal. The spiral of heat spread outwards until her whole body shook with the force of it. He groaned as the undulations of her body increased in pressure and intensity, and she felt his hand caress the scarf still blinding her. "I love you, Serena. Like I've never loved anyone before."

"I know." She fumbled her way to his hand and pressed a kiss to the palm. "And I love you, Nick. With all my heart and soul. Please believe me."

"I do."

Awkward in the self-imposed darkness she undid the buttons of his shirt, then shifted lower until she felt the rough edge of his zipper and freed his pulsing organ from its material constraint. "Serena, I can't take much more of this," he murmured, but she just smiled and bent her head, again using instinct as a guide, inhaling that primal male smell, feeling the heat and the hardness in her mouth, enjoying his bucking movements and the almost animal moans coming from his throat.

With a convulsive movement he pulled her upwards and ripped away the chiffon. "I have to see the look in your eyes when I fill you with my cock," he growled.

She blinked in the shifting light. "You're all golden," she whispered, "just like when I first met you. A bronze-skinned Adonis, I thought then, but I was too afraid to admit it."

"A bronze Adonis? That's a lot to live up to." His grin faded. "Are you afraid now?"

"No."

Their lips met and she felt a rush of something through her body, bigger than desire. Stronger. Sweeter. This is love, she thought. Real love. She moaned against his mouth, overwhelmed with feelings too strong to explain, and he deepened the kiss before breaking off to wipe a trembling tear from her lashes.

"I know," he whispered. "I know."

And she saw that his eyes, too, were brilliant with unshed tears. For a second she tensed, primed by the past to shrink from inner exposure, from allowing him to see the raw emotion within, from the knowledge that if she let him in they would be entering a new phase in their relationship.

Then she gathered her courage and kissed the corner of his mouth where it curled up in that quirky way. "I'm trusting you with everything I have," she said, and from that simple sentence she saw joy flow across his face, felt the weight of unhappiness disappear from her shoulders as she handed over her heart to his safekeeping.

She smiled and lifted herself up, and he slipped into her easily as if they were made for each other. Again she felt that rush of something strange, like desire but different. Better. Then instinct took over and their bodies rocked gently in a rhythm so intense she found tears running down her cheeks as they climaxed together.

Minutes... eons... later, she turned to look at the fire, lower now, but still putting out a delightful orange glow that created an interesting play of light and shadow across the room. "You showed me how to love again, Nick," she said. "You made me whole. I'm going to do everything in my power to give you the same happiness."

"You already have, darling."

She continued to gaze at the glowing embers, secure at last in her knowledge of how the future would unfold. Knowing that he would treasure her gift, as she intended to treasure his. Knowing that at last, in the cradle of Nick's arms, she had finally found her shining knight.

About the Author:

Jennifer Lynne lives in Melbourne, Australia with her two beautiful daughters and the best cat in the world. She discovered romance—and writing—at the age of 12 and couldn't understand why that first novel never saw light of day. Many years on, she is thrilled to be writing for Red Sage and sharing her belief that there is power in love to change our lives for the better. Even if our own heroes are imperfect!

Pirate's Possession

by Juliet Burns

To My Reader:

I must confess, dear readers, my pirate was inspired, not by Johnny Depp, but by a true Scotsman, Gerard Butler, as he appeared in the movie *Beowulf & Grendel*. Ooh, those intense green eyes… Who wouldn't want to be taken to his cabin and… possessed. But my pirate needed a woman whose spirit and stubbornness matched his own. I hope you'll agree Lady Gertrude possesses a quiet strength and a cool head to anchor this pirate's heart and free his soul.

Chapter 1

London Docks, September, 1649

The raucous dockside tavern quieted as a woman in a rich hooded cloak strode purposefully in and searched the pub. Her gaze must have landed on Ewan, because she approached his table and took a seat.

Och, this didna bode well.

"Are you the captain of the *True*?" she asked in a cultured voice.

How did she know him? He'd a bloody price on his head, and the woman walked in here as bold as she pleased? From beneath his wide-brimmed hat, Ewan MacGowan studied her. She wore no wig, powder, or patch. Still, her fine dress and manner declared her a lady. Damned English nobles.

"Ye've got the wrong man."

Dismissing her, he tipped back his ale, his mind returning to the fooking disaster his life had become since he'd dropped anchor twelve hours past.

"I can pay you."

He looked up sharply, set down his mug, and took a closer look under the shadows cast by the hood, noting the angular nose and severe lips. Despite a pair of fine brown eyes, she wasna a bonny woman. He could think of only two reasons a lady would venture to the docks at this time of night. And he would neither kill nor swive for money.

"Just what do ye think to get for your shillin'?" He let his gaze roam down to the small expanse of bosom peeking above her corseted bodice.

She glanced around, but then daringly met his gaze. "I need passage to Ireland. Tonight."

Ireland? What kind of trap was this? He'd sailed into London this morn to find King Charles executed and the Queen and her Royalists fled to France for their lives. He needed coin, aye, but he was nae fool.

"I canna help ye."

"But I must get home!" Her gaze faltered a moment, then rose back to his with renewed determination. "Since my father's death, 'tis no longer my home, but I must see it once more before my cousin takes residence." She spat the word *cousin* as if it were putrid meat.

Ewan narrowed his eyes. 'Twas an old trick, the helpless woman bit. Did she nae ken he was called *Merciless* MacGowan?

"I've told ye, I canna help ye. Ye must apply to your husband or this cousin for passage."

She hesitated. "I've no husband. And I've no wish to be indebted to my cousin. I plan to join the sisters at the convent of Saint-Martin-aux-Bois."

He didn't believe a word of it. "Your cousin must be truly loathsome for ye to prefer the cloistered life. Or, willna he wed ye, then? Has he nodged ye and refused to do right by ye?"

She jumped from her chair, her gloved hands clenched into fists at her sides. "I wouldn't marry that toad even if he—" Her voice trembled. Flushing down to her neck, she glanced nervously at the door and back to him before taking her seat again.

Either she truly despised her cousin, or she'd trod the stage all her life. Mayhap the lady was on the run, and this cousin of hers would pay dearly to get her back. Had the answer to his troubles fallen into his lap?

"What's your name, lass?" He glanced at his quartermaster, Tate, who'd been listening behind a post, flintlock ready.

"'Twould do you no good to know who I am. My cousin can't pay you a ransom. He's penniless."

Ewan growled. Perhaps he'd underestimated her. "And what's to stop me from haulin' ye to the public square as a runaway?"

A wee smile crossed her lips. "You're a wanted man, Captain MacGowan. From what I hear, Lord Cromwell's lieutenant didn't appreciate having a dagger at his throat."

"Who are ye, and how do ye know me?"

"I am—was, a lady-in-waiting to the Queen."

Queen Henrietta? He'd made sure to encourage her favor in years past by bringing her jewels and fine lace to keep himself in her good graces. He supposed this woman could have seen him at court. But why hadn't she escaped to France with the rest of the royal court?

And, more worrisome, how had she known to find him here?

"Like you, Captain, I'm an enemy of Lord Cromwell."

Cromwell! The scurvy bastard! Ewan wanted to spit just at the mention of his name.

"Careful, milady." He leaned across the table. "'Tis treason to claim the new *Lord Protector* as enemy."

"Let us speak plainly, Captain. I know Lord Cromwell confiscated your entire cargo. And when you refused to sign an oath of loyalty, he revoked your letter of marque. Now you're wanted for treason. If you stay in London much longer, you'll be arrested." She drew a deep breath. "Therefore, I believe we can help each other. I am willing to pay for passage. You are in need of funds. All we need agree upon is your price."

The rudder in his mind turned to change course yet again, calculating her worth. She was no young maiden. Past bedding age, surely. Mayhap she was widowed, or some lord's mistress. She wore no jewels. What if she'd sold them? What if she *could* pay him?

He needed provisions for a crew of thirty. Six weeks to cross the Atlantic....

"Fifty pieces of eight."

Her face went as pale as the sails on the *True*, and she swallowed. But she let out a deep breath, raised her chin and stuck out her hand.

"Very well. But we must leave immediately."

Stunned, he stared at the satin grey glove. Were his problems solved that easily? But life had never handed him something for nothing. He folded his arms.

"Let's see it, then."

She blinked. "Well, I don't have it with me, of course. I'll pay you once we reach—what is so amusing, sir?"

Ewan couldn't help his hearty laugh. It was either that or grab the lady by the scruff of her neck and throw her out. He sobered and leaned toward her menacingly.

"Ye've wasted enough o' me time, your ladyship. Now get ye gone, before I decide to take your fine lady's body as me payment."

Instead of flinching in terror as he'd expected, her expression hardened. She leaned in and met him nose to nose. "Better *your* possession for one night than Reginald's for a lifetime."

His insides flared and his cock twitched. *Your possession.* He'd only meant to frighten her. But hot blood coursed through his veins and pooled in his hardening rod at the thought of making an English lady his *possession.*

She straightened and folded her gloved hands on the table. Soft, scented lady's hands, he'd wager.

Ewan swallowed. The ladies at court had amused themselves with him from time to time, dallying in a corridor, getting his blood up, then laughing at him. Treating him like the scum on the bottom of their fine slippers when next they saw him.

He'd learned to save his cock for bedding tavern wenches. They might have work-roughened palms and stinking bodies, but a man got a good honest drabbing for his coin.

"You see," she said, "I'm not so easily frightened off. I can and *will* pay you your fifty pounds once you take me to Galway. So there's no need for other forms of payment."

His gaze snapped to her bosom for a closer study before wandering down her body. He could almost taste the clean, creamy skin of her breasts and imagined possessing her all through the long night. Her lips were thin, but claret red, and her wide mouth would surround his shaft—

"Well?" The lady shifted in her seat and Ewan brought his attention back to her determined brown eyes. "What say you, sir?"

The door to the tavern burst open and a handful of Cromwell's men shoved through the crowd, muskets aimed.

"Ewan MacGowan, you're under arrest!"

The traitorous harlot! She must have somehow signaled the waiting soldiers that he was within. Ewan's flintlock lay ready on his lap. Quick as a cannon's boom, he raised it and shot the lieutenant in the shoulder.

As the officer dropped his musket, Tate shot another soldier and the tavern erupted into chaos. Muskets fired. A ball grazed Ewan's arm as he drew his cutlass and leaped into the scuffle.

Rowdy sailors took that as their cue. The pub echoed with the crack of knuckles meeting noses and pain-filled grunts as rough sailors and disgruntled dockworkers joined in the fight, swinging chairs and fists.

The soldiers' sabers were no match for Ewan's wide blade. Once he'd sent the last of Cromwell's men to hell, he searched the room until he found the lady hiding beneath a table. Leaving the sailors and workers still brawling, he clamped his hand around her wrist and dragged her with him out the back door. Tate was behind him, reloading his pistol. They raced down a winding maze of alleys before the lady finally struggled free of Ewan's grasp.

"You're taking me to Ireland?" Her breath came in gasps and her hood had fallen back. Strands of hair had loosened from a knot at her nape. Thick, rich tresses of mahogany fell around her shoulders. They softened her face, and the color enhanced the smoky sable of her eyes.

Aye, he'd take her right enough. He grabbed a handful of her hair, pulled her head back, and set his mouth on hers. He was daft to stop for a kiss, but fighting always got his blood up.

And he'd been cheating death for a decade or more.

Still, he would have pulled away, had she not slid her arm around his neck and opened her lips to him.

She kissed him back and he felt her passion, along with a will that matched his own.

The taste of tooth powder reminded him this was no tavern wench he kissed. He pulled away.

"Ye'll regret betrayin' me to Cromwell's men." Before she could protest, he bent, hoisted her over his shoulder, and headed for the river.

"Sir, there has been a misunderstanding," she replied between labored breaths. "I most certainly did not inform Cromwell's men of your whereabouts."

When he ignored her, the lady began to struggle. "You must put me down. I can't breathe."

She was no match for his strength. For all her spirit, she was a wee thing. He'd not given up hope of ransom, or mayhap she had told the truth about paying him in Ireland. Either way, it was time to flee London. But she'd pay for the trouble she'd caused. She was his until they reached Galway.

"Release me!" Her incessant demands grew in volume as she pounded his back and kicked his front, only just missing his culls. Already the militia was giving chase. He needed stealth.

"Tate, shut her up, will ye?"

"Aye, Captain."

Ewan felt a jolt, heard fist meet jawbone, and his captive went limp in his arms.

He stopped in his tracks and swung around. "Are ye daft, man? I only meant for ye to stuff a kerchief in her mouth."

"And how was I to know?"

"Cursed, I am," Ewan mumbled as he hefted the unconscious woman higher on his shoulder and continued down the dark, grimy alley.

They raced between buildings, not stopping until they'd crept down the ladder to the river. His mouth a grim line, he lowered the lady into Tate's arms, then stepped into the dinghy and lifted her to his lap while Tate rowed them out to the *True*.

When the pirate with the lady in his arms turned to scan the dockyard, the dockworker scuttled behind a stack of crates. He watched between the cracks until the dinghy had disappeared into the fog, then raced away to the lodgings of the gent what spread word of a reward.

The dockhand would be ten shillings richer for his spywork this night.

Lady Gertrude Fitzpatrick slowly awakened, her head splitting, her mouth dry. She tried to remember where she was. The place was dark save for weak moonlight seeping through a round window. She smelled the briny odor of the sea. Waves crashed and wood creaked. The room pitched and rolled. She was on a ship—

It must be the *True*! She was safe!

From Reginald, at least.

She sat up, a sharp pain stabbing along her jaw and temple. Her cheek felt swollen and hot to the touch. That pirate had hit her!

Perhaps she had miscalculated her chances with the infamous Merciless MacGowan. But what choice had she? How could she have conceived that her mother would betray her so? That she would lure her into Reginald's hired coach and expect her to marry that pompous, powdered popinjay?

No sense dwelling on the past, Tru. Better to take stock of her situation.

In the dim moonlight from a small round window, she could barely make out her surroundings. She'd been swathed in a silk coverlet on a large bunk with a thick mattress. Pirates lived well, it seemed.

The cabin was small but well appointed, with a thick Persian rug covering the planking. A large oak desk and chair were bolted to the floor. The wall behind it formed built-in shelves that stored books and scrolls held by leather strips across the framing. The shelves were crammed with books.

Pirates could read?

The door flew open and there he stood. Merciless MacGowan. The feared pirate.

And the most handsome man Tru had ever beheld.

Captain MacGowan was breathing heavily, his long legs spread wide. From one large hand swung a lantern, and in the other lay a brass mariner's quadrant. He wore no waistcoat or coat. Blood and soot stained his shirt, open at the collar to reveal a swirl of brown hair. The same shade of brown fell in thick, tangled hair to his shoulders. His lighter short beard enhanced pale green eyes that cut into her as though he wanted to flay her alive.

She stood, smoothed back her hair and brushed nervous hands down her wrinkled skirt. "I must insist you knock before entering this cabin from now on, sir." Pride kept her voice steady.

His lip curled, and his laugh sounded more like a disbelieving grunt. Hanging the lantern, he strode to the desk and reached behind him for a chart. He unrolled it and placed the quadrant on it, then pulled a log book, quill, and ink from a drawer and began making notations.

Tru cleared her throat. "Sir, I—"

"Wheesht!" He slammed a palm on his desk and Tru jumped. His eyes glittered in irritation. Her silence assured, he returned his attention to the book.

Reading? Writing? Navigation? For a moment, the man seemed more merchant than pirate.

She'd spied him once at court, elegantly dressed, on one knee before Queen Henrietta. A force had burned in him, just beneath the surface. As if he had to restrain a constant urge to attack someone. She'd never forgotten him, and in her girlish fantasies, she pretended he'd named his ship, the *True,* for her.

Shamefully, her vivid fantasy life had nearly always featured the dashing privateer in quite improper scenarios. But s'truth! His kiss had been more sensual than any of her imaginings.

As she watched him, head bent over his notebook, the arousing sensations she'd felt upon seeing him in the tavern came rushing back. The shortness of breath, the ache in her stomach, the longing that had assailed her when his mouth had swept over hers—

A knock sounded at the door.

"You're my possession now." He waved a hand. "Answer the door."

Possession? He thought he owned her? Terror slammed into her chest. Then they weren't headed for Galway? Was she being taken across the sea? How would she help her people now? She'd heard of captives walking a plank, or merchant crews left adrift to die of thirst. Tales of women ravaged. Sold into slavery.

Use your brain, Tru.

Why would he be wantin' to ravage ye, ye silly girl? And what man would pay good money for the likes of ye?

And wouldn't her mother cringe to hear her even thinking with an Irish lilt? Her wits had gone begging. In the presence of a dangerous pirate, she was worrying what her mother thought of her thoughts.

But 'twas a fact she'd never inspired lust in a man. Unmarried after eight years at court was proof of that. How oft had her own mother called her plain at best and ugly if she were in a nasty mood? Even her cousin had said bedding her would be a loathsome duty done only to force her into marriage.

"Well, woman? Doona jus' stand there!"

Tru flinched and hurried to open the door. A boy of about fourteen years carried a tray with a gold goblet and a bottle. And a wet kerchief.

"Evenin', Miss." He eyed her up and down, his gaze resting on her bosom. Her cheeks heated as he shoved the tray into her hands and turned to the pirate. "Cap'n, Mr. Tate reports we're clear of the harbor."

"Tell him to set the rudder at thirty degrees waest by nor'waest, Henry. And don't knock again."

The boy grinned and nodded, tugging his cap brim, and shut the door.

Tru stood holding the tray while Captain MacGowan continued to make notes in his book.

Fear tightened her stomach. Had she fled her cousin's clutches only to be sold into slavery by a cold-blooded pirate?

It mattered not. 'Twas too late to lament her choice.

She would honor her Da's last wishes. His cryptic note could only be interpreted one way. She must get home to *Baile an Chláir* and give her people the means to be free of Reginald's tyranny. And she was determined to see it done. Whatever the price.

She delicately cleared her throat. "Are you taking me to Ireland, sir?"

"Bolt the door," he ordered without looking up.

Her body began to quiver and her lungs couldn't take in air. Her palms dampened. Was this her last day on earth?

Don't go borrowin' trouble, girl, she heard Da's voice advise.

Straightening her spine, she lodged the tray on her hip and slid the bolt home, feeling the heavy wood lock her fate.

The pirate began rolling up the chart and clearing the desk. "Set the tray here and pour me a dram." Slipping the map into its slot, he stood and watched her, hands on hips.

Perchance he only planned to keep her as a servant? She trudged to the desk and did as he asked, removing her gloves before pouring. Her hand shook so badly the liquid splashed over the goblet. When she glanced up at him, he was scowling at her, and she noticed a crescent-shaped scar creasing his left temple and another on his right cheek, slashing across his beard. How many more scars lay beneath his clothes?

Gertrude Fitzpatrick!

"The rag's for your ding." He gestured to her jaw and tossed the wet kerchief to her.

Tru caught it and held it to her throbbing cheek. The cold relieved the ache and his concern relieved her fear. Still, her heart pounded.

"I don't hit women, or allow my crew to do so. 'Twas a misunderstanding."

She smiled and heaved a deep sigh of relief.

He took up the goblet and drank deeply, studying her person as if estimating her worth.

"Take off your clothes."

Chapter 2

Tru gasped. "I beg your pardon?"

"You're my possession now." The pirate raised a brow. "Ye said better me than your cousin, did ye nae?"

S'truth! She had! A lump of dismay formed in her throat. "But, sir, I thought you bluffed. And I promise you, I will pay you the fifty pounds as soon as we reach Galway."

"And what good is your word to me? Thanks to ye, my crew sails without food or fresh water, trustin' me to find a way to purchase supplies."

"I swear I did not betray you to Cromwell! You would punish an innocent?"

"Punish? Nae." He folded his arms across his chest. "If you're bound for the convent as ye claim, ye'll thank me someday for givin' you a woman's pleasure afore you're shut away for the rest o' your life."

Tru swallowed the lump. "A-a woman's pleasure?"

She remembered his kiss in the alley and shivered. The way his warm lips had moved over hers, strong and demanding. Her body shook on the inside, as if her veins rippled.

"Aye, I'm thinkin' your cousin didna pleasure you none."

"My cousin?" He certainly had not. Just the memory of Reginald's kiss repulsed her. His lips had been cold and wet on her neck.

"Are ye a parrot, woman? Off with your clothes!"

But she just couldn't. She couldn't undress in front of a complete stranger. Even her maid had never seen her naked.

As if that's all ye need worry about, ye daft girl!

"If I have to strip ye, 'twill be with my dirk," he growled, glaring at her.

Tru blinked. He would *cut* her clothes off? What would she wear the rest of the voyage, then? Clamping her lips together, she set the kerchief on the desk and began unbuttoning her bodice at the back. Was this it, then? Was she to be ravished? She dropped the bodice onto the bed and worked at loosening the laces of her skirt and petticoat. Her breathing grew ragged, her heartbeat unsteady.

She knew what happened between men and women. Mostly. She'd lived at court since she was fifteen and 'twas not uncommon to happen upon a couple *in flagrante*. On the contrary, she'd had many a restless night of erotic dreams after catching sight of a lady bent over a table with her skirts raised and the courtier's bare bottom flexing as he pumped into her from behind. She'd awakened from those dreams burning, wondering what it must be like to feel a man's thrusts.

Remembering the dreams now brought a hot flush to her cheeks. The reality was not like the fantasy. She was terrified. Though she kept her eyes cast down, she could feel the heat of his gaze as he watched her unlace her corset.

Did he wish to inspect the merchandise he would sell? She shuddered. She'd heard of the horrors of Barbary Coast slave blocks. Would he hurt her first? Would he keep her prisoner and then kill her? Or worse, would he take one look at her unappealing body and laugh in repugnance? Her fingers trembled as she slipped off the corset.

"Take down your hair."

She lifted her arms and her breasts tilted upward. She became distinctly aware of her nipples brushing against her chemise. How mortifying to be so attracted to the man and know he would feel only disgust.

As she pulled out pins and her hair dropped down her back, he came around the desk and reached a hand to the ribbons of her shift. She instinctively swatted it away.

He glowered. "'Tis fine linen and lace ye be wearin'. I'd hate to see it torn."

Tru blinked back horrified tears. Where was the dashing captain who had kissed her outside the tavern? She wanted more kisses.

He reached out again and Tru forced herself to hold still as he untied each ribbon slowly, his knuckles grazing her skin beneath.

At the brief touch, her nipples puckered and, by the time he reached the last tie, tightened to the point of pain. She fought to keep her hands at her sides, digging her nails into her palms.

With one hand, he spread her shift open one side at a time and looked his fill at what her mother had always called her indiscernible bosom.

Shaking, anxious, and wanting nothing more than to cover herself, Tru stood before him.

"Your tits are bigger than they seem with your clothes on, milady. Almost a handful."

The observation felt absurdly like a compliment, but fear kept her from enjoying it as such. When his warm hand covered one breast and caressed it, she gasped and realized she'd been holding her breath. She couldn't draw in enough air, and her chest rose and fell as she gulped in breaths.

"Shh, now. Doona fash yourself about it. I'll be sweet and gentle as a lamb. Ye'll enjoy yourself, ye will." He cupped her other breast as he spoke and began fondling and pinching her nipples.

Streaks of pleasure shot to her stomach and lower, in her woman's parts between her legs. The pleasing ache melted her strength, putting truth to his words. She squeezed her eyes closed, feeling ashamed and frightened. And yet at the same time she felt an urgent desire for more. She wasn't sure what kind of more. Just more.

She felt him drawing the shift up her body and raised her arms at his command so he could pull it off. Now she stood in only her stockings, garters and shoes. She thought for a crazy moment of looking the fool, naked save for her satin slippers, and kicked them off. Witless. She'd gone witless.

"Open your eyes, milady. I'll have ye ken 'tis Ewan MacGowan taken you, not some hated cousin," he said quietly, seductively.

She looked up in surprise to meet his gaze, just as his mouth lowered to her breast. He cupped it from beneath and took her nipple between his lips.

Sweet, tormenting aches shot straight between her legs as he suckled and tongued her taut peak. Holy Mary, mother of God! How could something so wicked feel so good?

He let go with a pop and moved to the other one, exactly what she would have begged for if she'd been able to speak. She could only cry out and make embarrassing little mewling sounds.

Sinful feelings of desire swept over her. He hadn't hurt her so far. Was ravishment not a painful experience?

"I like ye with your stockings on. 'Tis silky and fine they are," he murmured. "Just like your skin, here." He slid a gentle hand down to her stomach. "And you're even softer here." His fingers crept through her dark nether curls and between her thighs, which she immediately clamped together.

He raised his gaze from her breast. "Open your legs to me." His voice had hardened to a gravelly command.

With a whimper, Tru spread her feet.

His fingers delved between her thighs and began massaging her and rubbing a particular spot that provoked a sensation of pleasure akin to pain. As he stroked her, the pleasure grew into a powerful throbbing that set her hips to rolling.

"Aye, ye like this, don't ye, milady?"

In answer she put her hands to his brawny shoulders to steady herself and pushed against his fingers, trying to relieve the building pressure.

He moaned and cupped her bottom with his other hand, pulling her against him.

"Tell me ye like it, milady. Tell me your cousin never made ye feel so," he whispered against her temple.

"Yes," she rasped. "Yes." It was all she could manage, incoherent with wanting, with reaching. She buried her face in his neck, clutching his shoulders until her knuckles were white.

His fingers moved faster, rubbing at that center part of her that screamed its need. Her hips kept pace, rocking with abandon until he grabbed her thigh and lifted it around his waist.

"Please," she begged on a moan, not knowing what she asked for.

"Say my name," he growled. "Say, 'Please, Ewan.'"

Anything to end this torture, to gain the release she sought. "Please, Ewan."

The moment she said his name, he slipped a long finger deep inside her and pumped it in and out while wiggling his thumb over the little hard nub. Her body exploded in spasms of quaking bliss. With a loud cry, she threw her head back and rode out the tremors until they slowly calmed.

Finally she opened her eyes and became aware of him watching her intently, of her breasts crushed against his chest, of his hot hand clutching her thigh. Of his fingers still cupped between her legs.

Mortified, she dropped her arms and slid her leg down.

Supporting her around the waist, he raised the hand that had caused her such wild abandon, brought the wet fingers to his nose, and inhaled.

"Jaysus, woman." His tone was filled with awe. "Ye came on my hand like a Edinburra whore."

Her face flamed in humiliation. She had. And she'd begged for it. Tears stung her eyes. Her Irish temper broke free. She shoved away and slapped him.

Ewan grabbed his cheek. She'd hit him! She was snatching up her clothes, trying to dress. He'd have none of that. She was his, if only for the next thirty hours. And he'd barely gotten a taste of her. Ahhh, but what a taste. He'd never had a woman so responsive to his merest touch, so open in her pleasure he could hear it in her breathing, smell it on her skin.

"Nae!" He snatched the clothes from her hands. "We're nae done yet. I'll keep ye naked as long as I wish, woman."

She covered herself with her arms, as if he hadn't already seen her brown curls and pink-tipped breasts.

"Y-you are a vulgar brute!" Her voice quavered, but she lifted her chin with all the dignity of a queen.

Aye, he liked her spirit. "That may be, but ye'll nae raise a hand to me again or I'll tie them both behind your back!"

Her eyes flared wide and filled with tears. "Please, sir. Allow me to dress. You've had your revenge."

God's teeth! He'd given her pleasure without seeking his own, and she called it revenge? He'd never understand women. They were as changeable as the sea. And just as treacherous. He rubbed his cheek. She'd dinged him in the face, and not only had he not blocked her hit, he still felt tenderness for the lady.

Likely her purpose for the tears.

Her body was so different from other women he'd lain with. Slim and firm, almost boyish, yet soft and white and unmistakably feminine. And her hair was a glory. Thick and straight, with so many colors of brown and red and gold that it seemed to shimmer. And so long, it curled around her arse, those tiny little globes of flesh he'd like to dig his fingers into as he took her from behind.

Jaysus, his cock throbbed with wanting. His breeches pulled tight over his suffering rod.

She'd caused him enough trouble. He'd risked much by bringing a woman aboard the *True*. And for once in his flea-bitten life, he would know what it felt like to lie between the creamy white thighs of a noblewoman.

"Get on the bed!" He scowled and pointed to his bunk.

"I am not a whore."

"Then so be it." He unbuckled the belt from around his breeches and closed the distance between them. He'd not leave her hands free to claw him. Though she struggled, he easily got her hands behind her and the leather tied around her wrists. The wrestling excited him, her wee breasts rubbing against him and her eyes spitting fire. He picked her up and carried her to his bunk and felt her shivering all over. Tears leaked from her eyes.

Goddammit! He wouldna feel guilty for taking her. She'd agreed to be his possession!

He yanked his shirt over his head, pulled off his boots, began unbuttoning the flap on his breeches… and stopped.

Her eyes were wide with fright as she stared at his groin. Had her cousin hurt her when he took her? Mayhap a dram of whiskey would calm her. He strode to the desk and filled the goblet, then took a long swig from the bottle.

He brought the goblet back to the bunk and held it to her lips. "Drink it. 'Twill calm ye."

She glared at him and twisted her head away.

"Ye'll drink it or I'll turn ye over me knee for a spank!"

Instantly she opened her mouth and swallowed it all. Then her brown eyes widened and she turned to the side and coughed and sputtered. He dropped the goblet, sat and held her shoulder and stroked her hair, playing with the strands, gathering bunches into his palms.

"Your hair is glorious. 'Tis like a living thing, and all ye should ever cover yourself with."

She stayed on her side, her eyes squeezed closed. "Please, release my hands."

He began spreading the thick tresses over her hip and pulling locks over her shoulder to drape over her breasts, caressing the breast through the strands. "I've nae wish to fight ye."

"I-I won't fight."

He must be an eejit to even consider letting her loose. She'd led Cromwell's men straight to him!

But she claimed she hadn't. What if she told the truth? Anyone in the tavern could have turned him in for the reward.

"Damnation!" He'd never taken an unwilling woman. He wanted her with her arms about him, and wanting him as well. Grudgingly, he loosened the leather belt, tossed it across the floor, and waited to have his eyes scratched out.

But all she did was rub her wrists and say thank you in a tiny voice that screwed up his stomach.

"Best save your thanks. I still intend to have ye." He lowered himself beside her, throwing one leg over her hip, and kissed her.

She stiffened at first, but he kept moving his lips over hers until she softened against him.

She smelled sweetly of something fresh and clean, and her skin felt so good against his. Desire surged through him and he swept his tongue into her mouth, tasting the whiskey. His cock was straining to be inside her, pulsing for release. When she squirmed under him and touched her tongue to his, he groaned and almost spilled in his breeches. Was he a pulin' boy with his first whore?

He cupped her breast. She'd responded to his caresses before. 'Twas no hardship to stroke her a bit before he took her. He tweaked her nipples between thumb and finger and kissed down her jaw, careful of the bruise. She made a wee sound, almost a sigh, and lifted her hands to his shoulders. But she wasna pushing him away. She was pulling him closer.

Nuzzling her neck, he slowly moved between her thighs, nudging them apart, and reached down to unbutton his breeches. He could hear her ragged breathing and suckled a nipple to distract her as he took his cock in hand and guided it to her entrance. But he hesitated.

"Put your arms about me, woman. Say ye want me." His weight on his elbows, he raised his head to look at her heavy-lidded eyes. "I need to be in ye. But I'll nae have ye cry rape after." He rubbed the tip of his shaft all around her opening, smearing his juices with hers.

"You need me?" she asked breathlessly.

"Aye, I burn with it," he choked out. He kissed her, pouring all his powers of persuasion into the kiss. "Ye burn for me, too, do ye nae?" he mumbled against her lips.

She moaned, pressing her mons against his cock. "Yes."

'Twas all Ewan required. With a rough groan, he surged inside her to the hilt. But he was frozen by her piercing scream and the unmistakable barrier he felt himself rupture.

"Get out! Get off me!" She pounded his chest and wiggled beneath him.

"Jaysus, be still, woman!" He squeezed her to him, willing himself not to move. "'Twill only hurt the once." She sheathed him so tight he might spend even while holding still. "Ye said your cousin had had ye, or I would've took care." Took care? A bloody virgin? He'd have never gone there in the first place.

She wiped her eyes and sniffed. "I never said that."

Had she not? Then why had he assumed...? Be damned! He'd think on it later.

"Are ye all right now?" Christ, he needed to move.

"If you mean am I still in pain, then, no." Her lips trembled and she avoided his gaze. "Are you—is it done?"

Och! If he werna at the edge of control, he'd have smiled. "Nae, lass," he said through gritted teeth. "'Tis gentle I'll be with ye now, though, aye?"

Before she could answer, he placed a soft kiss on her lips, lingering along the surface until she began to respond. Once he felt her body soften beneath him, he took the kiss deeper and slowly began to move in her, sure that one stroke would be all he could take. He squeezed his eyes closed and concentrated on her lips, on not thrusting too hard as he longed to do, and holding off as long as he could. He'd hoped to bring her to pleasure once more, but her fingers crept into his hair, and her tongue ventured out to play with his, and she was so tight.

With each thrust she moaned and moved her hips to meet him. "Ewan, 'tis building again."

Her words made something ache in his chest. He'd taken her virginity and she still responded to him, still wanted him. The sensation of being with this lady was beyond his ken. He thrust again, and once more—

He threw his head back and shuddered while the most powerful pleasure of his life swept over him.

Lost, he was. As a youth, he'd been trimmin' the sails durin' a squall when a giant wave had washed him overboard. That's how he felt now. Lost. He couldna even focus. The world had blurred 'til all he could see was her mouth, her eyes, the one tear tracing a path down her cheek.

Shite!

Still catching his breath, he moved to her side and tried to gather his wits. He smelled the musk of their sex over her lady's scent.

Her fingers began to comb through his hair, and he liked the way she caressed his scalp. Her other hand massaged his back, tracing the paths of his scars. His body relaxed. His eyelids grew heavy. Mayhap, jus a wee nap. And postpone the guilt of takin' a virgin. Ah, well. What was doon was doon.

Snuggling against her breast, he did something he'd not done with a woman before. He drifted to sleep in her arms.

Chapter 3

Dazed, Tru lay staring at the ceiling. Surely this was all a dream and she would wake. But no. This big, brawny man, the handsome privateer of her fantasies, snuggled beside her, snoring lightly, his tanned flesh touching hers, his callused palm cupping her breast. How could he sleep after something so glorious, so stimulating?

And how could she, even now, feel no shame at what she'd allowed?

Shouldn't she be bemoaning the loss of her virtue? Praying for her mortal soul? Why didn't she feel ruined? Soiled?

But all she could think was, *he'd burned for her.*

So, this was what sexual congress was like. To make love. Her body still tingled, the passage between her legs still contracted with little spasms of delight. She'd never felt so attractive, so womanly. So desired. If the carnal act provoked such rapturous sensations, she couldn't regret the experience.

How could she ever have imagined Merciless MacGowan, a coarse, ruthless pirate who'd probably bedded hundreds of women, would want plain, bookish Lady Gertrude Fitzpatrick?

She looked at his breeches, bunched below his knees, and she smiled. She'd welcomed him inside her, had *burned* for his touch. Despite a little soreness, her body felt complete and sated. And she wanted to do it again, to feel that astonishing surge of pleasure once more. It was as if quiet Tru had vanished and a bold wanton had taken her place.

Could she now take vows and remain chaste for the rest of her life?

Her thoughts were a jumble of contradictions, scrambling around in her head like a child lost in the hedge maze at court. Thinking of the events that had led her here—the death of her Da, her mother's betrayal, her greedy cousin—she lay for a long time, wrapped in the captain's arms, listening to his soft snore. And felt, unaccountably, safe.

Eventually she heard his low rumbling groan and realized his member had hardened again and was pushing against her thigh. His scratchy jaw nuzzled behind her ear, and his rough hand moved down, caressed her stomach, and delved through her curls. He pressed the heel of his hand against her mons and pushed her thighs apart.

Tru cried out at the twinge.

The pirate stilled, poised to move between her legs. "Did that hurt ye?"

Her face flamed. How could she speak of the soreness between her legs, the sticky wetness still on her thighs?

"A little," she whispered.

"Well, now. I'll just kiss it and make it better."

Before she could determine what he meant, he rolled her to her side, brushed her hair out of the way, and kissed down her spine.

Ooh, the sensation caused chill bumps to rise all over her body. A pleasured moan escaped her, and she stretched like the queen's cat during a back rub.

"Tha's it, lass. Purr for me," he rumbled against the small of her back. And something in the way the word "lass" rolled off his tongue sounded so intimate and so caring.

Then he left her, returning quickly with the damp cloth. His arm snaked around her waist, lifted her to her knees and began gently cleaning her.

The cool rag rubbing around and between her thighs felt good, and she arched her back. 'Twixt one moment and the next, the rag was replaced by his mouth!

"Sir! What are you doing?" She tried to clamp her legs closed, but he gripped her thighs.

"I promised ye'd thank me someday for givin' ye pleasure, did I nae?" He nuzzled in and began licking the tender folds around her woman's center.

"But this cannot be decent."

The kissing halted. "Ye want me to stop?" He sounded incredulous, like he'd be hurt if she said yes.

Taking her silence as a no, he swirled his tongue all around and inside her. She groaned and wiggled her hips as he suckled and stroked and even his teeth nibbled! It was indescribable. Torture and ecstasy all at once.

He took her hand and guided it between her legs, making her fingers rub her flesh the way he had done earlier. Then he was gone from her. She turned to see him standing beside the bunk. Quick as a flash, he shucked his breeches and bent his mouth to her again.

Tru gasped and jerked as her fingers met his lips. She touched his teeth, felt them as they closed around her fingertips and suckled. As if from far away, she heard herself cry out like a babe as his mouth and her fingers stroked and played in her, like a courtier performing on a lute, thrumming a rhythm that sent a pulse pounding through her.

His lips caught hold of that special nub that was so sensitive and worked it in his mouth until the need to scream overcame her. She clutched the bedclothes as the world became hazy and her body stiffened and spasms shook her again.

"Ah, woman, you're a wonder, ye are." He crawled up her limp body and entered her from behind. The feel of his long, thick member pushing in and filling her started the sweet, sharp aching.

As he pulled out and thrust deep inside her, Tru shuddered and tears welled in her eyes. His hairy thighs rubbed against the backs of hers, and she could even feel the light slap of his seed sac hitting her intimate spot. She was on her knees, accepting a pirate into her body as a mare accepts a stallion. And she relished his attention and took pleasure in his touch.

His hot mouth grazed her shoulder. His body surrounded her, and yet his ragged breath, hot in her ear, told her he was not in complete control of his desire. His hands caressed her everywhere, shoulders, back, stomach, breasts and hips. Down the front of her thigh and back up between her legs.

"Licence my roving hands, and let them go,
Before, behind, between, above, below."

She'd read those words of John Donne's poem and had pictured a man, a husband cherishing her person. But those fantasies seemed innocent and vague now. The reality was so much more. So physical, so passionate, so possessive.

His fingers dug into her hips as he started pumping faster, harder. His organ invaded her very core. Her inner passage seemed to throb and swell, and the more rapidly he moved, the closer she came to… ahh! Abandonment! Ecstasy! Just as she spiraled away, he cried out, thrust hard, wrapped his arms around her.

She felt him shudder. The he relaxed and collapsed beside her, pulling her back against his chest. He was still breathing heavily, and Tru could feel his heart pounding against her spine. Sweat dampened his skin and hers, and his seed ran down her thighs.

"Ye must tell me your name now, milady. Ye must ken I'll nae be asking your cousin for ransom."

Alarm stabbed her chest. Did he mean to keep her with him?

"Milady?" He placed his fingers under her chin and turned her face toward him. "Listen, now." He came up on one elbow. "I dinna ken you were a virgin or I wouldna… You dinna betray me to Cromwell, did ye?"

Such a gentle touch and a soft tone. He was a curious mix of strength and tenderness.

She shook her head.

"Hell and damnation! What an eejit I am." He rolled out of the bed and grabbed his breeches.

She gaped at his nakedness. At his wide, brawny chest and shoulders with scars everywhere. At his long legs and thick, beefy thighs. At his manhood, hanging low from a thatch of black curls. She watched in fascination as it swung back and forth when he stepped into his tattered woolen breeches.

The Greek gods could not have matched such masculine beauty.

He paused in buttoning the flap and placed his hands low on his hips. "Aw, lass. Best you nae look at me so, ere I take you again."

She jerked her gaze to his eyes, caught disapproval lurking there, and hastily drew the sheet over herself. Had her bold perusal of his nude body disgusted him?

"I do not regret our lovemaking." Rather, she believed that in the long, lonely years to come, she'd think on this experience long after the Captain had disappeared from her life.

"But ye will, milady," he promised in an ominous tone. "Ye will."

"Regardless, I still need to reach Galway."

"Why? What awaits ye in Galway?"

Clutching the sheet to her chin, she drew a deep breath. "My name is Lady Gertrude Fitzpatrick. My father was the Earl of Belclare."

She heard him curse again under his breath as he ran a hand through his hair and reached for the whiskey bottle.

"The earl died three—no, four days ago."

The captain stopped mid-swig and looked at her. "I'm sorry for your loss." There was true sympathy in his tone.

"He never trusted my cousin, or any Englishman for that matter."

"A man after my own heart," he mumbled as he took another long swallow.

"He-he put away a bit to care for me and his faithful servants after his death."

"And ye have enow to pay me fifty pieces of eight?"

His mention of the money pricked her pride. But naturally he was most concerned about his payment. She fingered the embroidered silk coverlet. The truth was, she didn't know. After the reading of her Da's will, her cousin Reginald had raged like a candidate for Bethlem Hospital. His tantrum had allowed the solicitor to tuck a note into her palm from her father:

Do not trust your cousin. There's money for you in our safe place. Take care of Baile an Chláir.

*I love you, **a Stóirín. (My little darling)***

But she couldn't tell Captain MacGowan she knew not how much money was there. That she might not have the funds to pay him. He'd refuse to take her then.

"I have no need of money where I'm bound. But I must ensure Da's servants receive their bequests. If my cousin gets his hands on the money, he will drink and gamble it away, then raise the rents to pay for more. My father wished me to protect the people of *Baile an Chláir*."

That much was certainly true.

"And ye were willin' to trade your virtue for a few servants' pensions? Are ye daft, woman?"

"They are more family to me than my mother!"

Muttering something about taking *noblesse oblige* too far, he shook his head as he drank down more whiskey. "What the hell am I to do wi' ye now?"

"You can take me to Galway, sir."

"And after?" he growled. "Am I to leave ye to your cousin's mercies, or will you next be askin' for passage to France?"

"Would you charge me extra for that?" Was that her voice, so timid all of a sudden?

He slammed the goblet on his desk. "Jaysus, woman! Have ye nae sense? I already have a bloody price on my head!"

"Does that mean you're not taking me to Galway?"

"Nae." He sighed and ran a hand through his hair. "I'll see ye to your castle right enow."

"Oh. Well, then. I'm truly grateful, sir."

An awkward silence fell between them while he took another swig of whiskey.

She sat up and wrapped the sheet around her, clearing her throat gently. "I-I'd like to get dressed now."

His gaze cut to hers. "Nae!"

Tru shivered at the heat in his eyes and the fervor that roughened his deep voice. Her stomach clenched, and lower, too. Impossible! How could her body react so powerfully to merely a look and a word?

He crossed to her and cupped her face. "The damage is done, and I've nae had my fill of ye yet." Slowly, he covered her mouth in a deep soft kiss.

That seemed to make sense. Technically, she could not lose her maidenhead more than once. And, truly, he was right. She would like to experience more of his most skillful lovemaking before she took her vows of chastity. As he deepened the kiss, Tru forgot to hold up the sheet in favor of wrapping her arms around his neck.

With a groan, his lips traveled down her jaw and into the hollow of her throat. Delicious pleasure tingled through her. He pushed her back onto the bed and followed her down, tugging the sheet completely away and cupping her breast.

But she noticed the room had filled with daylight. "The-the sun has risen while we've talked, sir. You cannot mean to…."

"Aye," he whispered into her neck. "I do mean to."

"But, 'twould be indecent during the day, surely!"

"Day or night, doesna matter. I read a Latin book once. It said, *Carpe Diem*."

A shocked thrill hit her chest. He'd read Horace, too? In Latin? How many scholars had scoffed at her, a mere woman, wanting to learn to read Latin? "Pluck the day," she interpreted, and the phrase took on a whole new meaning to her.

"Aye," he whispered. "Now call me Ewan like ye did before."

Her skin tingled where his hand caressed the underside of her breast and then he pinched her nipple and she jerked in pleasure-pain. "Ewan!"

He chuckled. "Tha's it, milady," and then he licked the tip and suckled it deep into his mouth.

"Oh," she moaned and wiggled beneath him. "Ewan?"

"Hmm?" His marvelous mouth moved to the poor neglected breast and suckled there as well.

"You may call me Tru."

He lifted his head and met her gaze. "Tru, eh? Like me ship? Aye, it suits ye. Now, kiss me, Tru." His lips moved over hers more playfully this time, nipping at the corners and teasing her with his tongue. Boldly, she ventured hers into his mouth, tasting the bite of the whiskey.

He groaned long and deep. "Unfasten me breeches, Tru."

Just as she untangled her fingers from his hair to do as he asked, a deafening explosion shook the ship.

Chapter 4

"Be damned," Ewan growled.

Tru sat up as Ewan bolted off the bed and tugged on his boots and shirt. Another cannon boomed. The wall behind her shook.

They were under attack!

"Get dressed and stay here!" He raced out the door, shouting, "Beat to quarters, lads!"

Shaking, Tru dressed quickly, missing buttons and ties in her haste. She was in the midst of a sea battle! What if they were sunk? What if—*Calm yourself, Tru.* She dropped to her knees and crossed herself. *Our Father, who art in heaven—*

A thunderous explosion rocked the ship and she could hear men shouting on deck.

Her hands shook as she clasped them under her chin. *Hallowed be thy—*

What French or Spanish ship would attack just hours away from London harbor? She'd never read an account of piracy in the English Channel.

—Thy Kingdom come, Thy will—

But anyone who had heard of the reward money might be after Merciless MacGowan. If they were captured, she'd be taken back to Reginald. And what would they do to Ewan? An image sprang to mind of the beautiful man hanging in a cage, his body drawn and quartered, or his head on a pike along London Road. Her chest hurt to think of it.

She sat back on her feet and pressed her cold palms to her cheeks. Oh, why could she not concentrate on her prayers? The priest at *Baile an Chláir* used to scold her for hurrying through them. She'd always been so anxious to go riding with Da.

But she was grown now. What kind of bride of Christ couldn't say the rosary without getting distracted? And what bride of Christ turned wanton fool for a handsome pirate?

Yet what else would she do if not take the veil? Her mother had ensured that Queen Henrietta thought Tru a traitor, and she couldn't stay in Ireland with Reginald as lord of the manor.

She heard a man shout, "Fire in the hole!" just before a cannon boomed somewhere below her.

Her whole body jolted. She couldn't sit in this cabin while a battle of life and death raged above her. Stay here, indeed. Perhaps there was something she could do to help. She flung open the cabin door, stumbled down the passageway and hiked up her skirts to climb through the hatch.

And stepped into fiery chaos.

Smoke dimmed her vision and waves sprayed over the ship's railing. The stink of sulphur made her cover her nose. Half-naked sailors scrambled everywhere, some climbing the riggings, others hopping over torn sails and tackle. Ropes as thick as her waist snarled on the deck like snakes. The thunderous blast of cannon fire rang in her ears and the ship lurched out of the water, hurling Tru head over heels onto the rolling deck.

She got to her knees and tried to stand, but the wood was slippery with sea-water.

Frantic, Tru crawled to the mast and latched on as another giant wave crashed over the ship. She wiped wet, sticky hair out of her face.

"Can ye make out the ship, Jaime? How many guns has she got?" That was Ewan's voice yelling above the clamor, but she couldn't see him for the smoke and salt in her eyes.

Another blast caused the ship to pitch to the side and the smoke cleared. There! At the back he stood, feet spread, his shirt open to his waist and billowing in the wind as he held a spyglass to his eye. He'd tied his long hair back, defining his angular jaw beneath the short beard.

"Tate!" he yelled down to his man. Then his gaze met hers and his expression darkened to a furious glower. "What the devil are ye doin', ye eejit woman? Get below!"

A cannonball hit the ship. The explosion knocked her over and iron and wood splinters shot everywhere. A man screamed in agony somewhere close by. She made her way over to him on hands and knees. It was the boy, Henry. He lay on the deck, clutching a wood fragment the size of a dirk embedded in his side. Blood seeped from the wound.

"Tru!" Ewan appeared beside her. He dropped to one knee, his arm around her shoulders. "Are ye hit?" Frantically, he searched her person.

"I'm uninjured. Ewan, 'tis Henry!"

Ewan turned to the boy and examined his side. "Henry, 'tis nae but a scratch, lad. Take the lady below and then see what Cookie can do, aye?"

"Aye, Cap'n," Henry gasped between painful breaths. He sat up, his face a grimace of pain. Ewan helped him stand and Tru put her arm around the boy's waist. A head taller, he leaned heavily on her.

"Cap'n, they're dead astern!" a man clinging to the topmast yelled down, terror in his voice.

Ewan's gaze met hers, his eyes deadly serious. "Get to my cabin and bolt the door. I've a pistol in my desk. Use it if ye must." Then he shouted, "Ready aboot, lads!"

The red-haired man who had hit her grabbed Ewan's arm. "That'll bring us right broadside with the bastards!"

Ewan pulled out of his grasp. "The *True's* been damaged. We canna outrun 'em. I want every man not gunnin' to follow me below. We bring up the granadoes."

"But Ewan, didna Cromwell's men take them?"

"Nae." A brilliant smile appeared on his sooty face. "I ordered Henry to stash a few beneath the shite pots before we dropped anchor. Now ready aboot!"

The red-haired man grinned and turned toward the upper deck, shouting, "Every man below with the captain, now!" Then he scrambled up the ladder to the upper deck and began turning the wheel hand over fist. He shoved his arm through the spokes and held it tight in the crook of his elbow.

Ewan strode below, followed by a dozen sailors.

As the ship turned sharply, spraying even more seawater over the deck, Henry slumped against Tru. "I don't feel so well, miss." She looked at the blood saturating her dress and hands. "Try to walk, Henry. You must see the surgeon."

"There's nae surgeon, miss." Henry's voice was weak and his eyes rolled back in his head.

S'truth! What to do? The boy could die! But panic would serve no one. She could do this. Hadn't she assisted Dr. Banyan after the O'Learys' croft caught fire? Her muscles protested as she lowered him to the deck.

Sailors were scrambling back up through the hatch, running past them carrying iron balls the size of pineapples.

The enemy ship appeared out of the smoke so close along their side Tru could have jumped from rail to rail. Grappling hooks flew across and caught in the *True's* balustrade.

Panic seized her by the throat. She froze.

Then Ewan's men sprang up from their hiding places and began pitching the iron balls across to the other ship. The strange balls exploded on the enemy's deck, spreading fire and acrid smoke.

Tru returned her attention to the boy. There was no help for it. If she couldn't get him below, she must see to him here. She yanked up her skirt and ripped part of her petticoat off. She shook so hard her ribs ached.

Biting her lip, she took hold of the jagged splinter and wrenched it out. She staunched the blood, then fashioned a makeshift bandage. The gash required needle and thread, but her undergarments would have to do for now.

At the same time, several cannons shot from the *True's* hull directly into the other ship. Tru heard the piercing screams of men in pain as the other ship rocked away. Even so, some had managed to jump aboard the *True*.

Pistols fired. Pirates fought all around her. There was naught she could do but huddle close to the boy and pray no one noticed them. She saw Ewan in the frenzy of fighting, a blood-rage on his face as he swung his sword. The veins in his neck protruded and his teeth were bared as he stabbed a man in the chest.

The murderous action chilled her to the bone. But why should it shock her? A pirate captain lived his life by violence. Without a blink, he'd shot Cromwell's man. And yet, he'd held her so tenderly.

She became aware of triumphant shouts from the crew. The fighting had stopped. The *True* seemed to be turning again. Her bruised jaw, and now her back and knees too, ached. With the battle over, her body drooped with the weariness of all she'd endured.

When she sat up to wipe her hand across her brow, the coppery scent of blood invaded her nostrils. Blood and death all around her. The world wavered, and she fought a bout of dizziness. Perhaps this was a nightmare. Perhaps she would wake safe in her apartments at court.

But no. Struggling against Reginald and escaping from his coach, then making her way to the docks and hiding with naught but the clothing on her back and the pearls her Da had given her—that had all been real. Her eyes burned from too many nights without sleep.

A large hand reached past her as the pirate captain bent to inspect her handiwork.

"Ye did fine, milady," he said in a tender voice.

His comforting presence and soft words of praise drained the tension from her body.

"Perhaps I should keep ye as my ship's surgeon." He grinned and took her hand, helping her to her feet.

But her knees wouldn't support her. She couldn't keep her eyes open. As exhaustion claimed her, the world faded away and she collapsed into his strong arms.

Ewan gazed down at the limp, wee woman sagging unconscious once again in his arms. Had she lied about being unharmed?

"Tate!" he bellowed. "The wheel is yers. Brendan, see to Henry. Jaime, bring hot water and the tub to my cabin. Quinn, question the prisoners. I want to know what they were after. To stations, men!"

Fear for the lady clutched his heart as he carried her to his cabin and laid her in his bunk. Again.

But this time her clothes were soaked, her hands and brow streaked with blood. Her wet hair, long and loose around her, dripped onto the sheets. Strange how bonny she seemed to him now. She'd taken a clout on the chin, been ravished, and yet she'd managed to doctor one of his crew in the middle of a raging battle. By God, he'd never witnessed such courage in a female!

Cautiously, he stripped her, searching her pale body for injuries, but found none, praise be. Relief swept through him, but he didn't stop to examine the emotion. He wrapped her in the coverlet, pulled her onto his lap and rubbed her cold skin through the silky fabric. Why did she not wake up?

"Milady." He tapped her lightly on her unbruised cheek.

She didn't move.

"Tru," he called, fingering strands of hair away from her face. He took one of her dainty hands, now coated with dried blood, and held it to his cheek. There were shadows beneath her eyes. He traced the tip of his finger along them, then down her nose and over her wide lips.

Mayhap 'twas his fault. He'd been too rough with her. He was a scoundrel! What kind of knave breached a woman's maidenhead and promptly took her again?

"Aw, lass. Ye humble me," he mumbled against her palm. "Wake up now, darlin' Tru."

Mayhap she needed food. His own stomach complained of its emptiness. He cursed Cromwell again for a thief.

Just then she moaned, drew in a deep breath, and turned her face into his chest. Her eyes fluttered. "Ewan." She whispered his name as though she called to her lover.

His cock swelled. Jaysus, he was a bastard to be wanting her again.

"What happened?" She sat up, wide-eyed, looking down and clutching the coverlet to her bosom. "Why am I undressed? Where is Henry?"

Though she struggled to escape his arms, he held tight. "Henry will be fine."

At a knock on the door, Ewan called admission to a pair of crewmenbers carrying the hip tub and pails of hot seawater. "Robbie, tell Tate to open his bottle of rum for everyone. Ye fought well."

"Aye, Cap'n." Robbie grinned, his black teeth showing, and swaggered out.

"And now, milady, into the bath wi' ye." He gently lowered her into the water and she drew up her knees, watching him as he retrieved soap from his shaving mug. He handed her the rough chunk of lye. "I've none o' that sweet-smellin' French soap you're likely accustomed to. Not after Cromwell took all but my ship."

A crinkle appeared at her brow as she began rubbing the soap between her palms.

God help him, even that small action stirred him.

"My Da used to say, 'There is no great loss without some gain.'"

Ewan grunted. "All I remember me Da sayin' was, 'Pump those bellows faster or I'll tan your backside 'til ye bleed!'"

"Your father beat you?" She gripped the edge of the tub and stared at him with dismay in her wide brown eyes.

He crossed his arms and leaned against his desk with a shrug. "'Twas nae worse than I got from the quartermaster on the Mary Aleyne in me youth."

"How old were you?"

"When I ran away to seek me fortune?" He scrubbed a hand over his jaw, thinking. "Minny'd just given birth to a babe. William and Rose were still in nappies." He began counting on his fingers. "Conner and Rupert were old enough to bring wood. There was Terrance and Catriona, then Robert, then Fenella. I wus, mayhap, ten and two?"

"Oh, Ewan! You were but a boy!"

"Nae. T'were old enow to sweat over a blazin' forge all the day. And I wasna goin' down no damned mine!" He shivered. Even now, the thought of crawling down into that black hole in the ground made him want to draw in a deep lungful of air. "Aboard the merchant ship, I was given lessons in reading and arithmetic. Captain Howard saw I was quick, and soon I learned to read a compass and sundial. Cap'n taught me to check log lines for speed and how to read the astrolabe and tide computers. Knowing how to navigate saved my bloody life when the pirates attacked us."

Why was he blatherin' on so? Was he goin' soft over a female? But the lady looked at him as if his life mattered to her.

"Then you were forced into piracy?"

"Nae. Well, only at first." He scowled, remembering that blistering day in the Caribbean. "And we're nae pirates, but privateers. Sailing with letters of marque from King Charles. Or at least, we were. I'll be hoistin' the Jolly Roger now, thanks to that bastard Cromwell! I've nae desire to be hanged a criminal."

"But you'll have my passage money. Surely you've no need to turn pirate."

He grunted and crossed one boot over the other. "Fifty pounds will only get me supplies for the journey across the sea and repay me crew for what Cromwell took. Nae, what I want will take a much larger sum."

The water sloshed against the sides of the tub as she turned toward him. "What do you want, Ewan?"

He looked to the future, to the dream he nursed in his deepest heart. "There's a settlement in the American colony of New Hampshire. Exeter. 'Tis a fine port town where a man can be anything he sets his mind to. Where the people are clamorin' for supplies and a man with his own merchant ship, or two or three, could make a legitimate living."

"And you would be that man?"

Telling his dream to her somehow forged it in the fire of reality. "Aye. I will."

A knock on his door sounded and the hulking Quinn stepped in.

The lady squealed and hunched forward in the water, crossing her arms over her chest. Ewan stepped in front of the tub to block her from view.

Quinn's knuckles were bruised and raw from the interrogation. The only man in his crew bigger and stronger than Ewan, 'twas a good thing Quinn was too slow to learn navigation. There was hate in his eyes when he glanced at Lady Tru. "Cap'n."

"What'd ye learn?"

"'Twas nae that bastard Cromwell. 'Twas the new Laird of Belclare. The bitch's cousin!" He spat.

Ewan lunged for Quinn and pressed the point of his dirk against the giant's throat. "If ye disrespect the lady again, I'll slit your gullet."

Quinn narrowed his eyes. After a tense moment, he lowered his burning gaze. "Aye, Cap'n."

Ewan returned his dirk to his boot. "I've a price on me head. But what's he want wi' her? She must be worth a fortune for him to hire a ship to come after her."

"'Tis not true!" the lady protested from the tub behind him.

Ewan shot her a menacing glare.

"The sailor didna know," Quinn answered.

Ewan slammed a fist into his hand. "How many men did we lose?"

"Three dead. Shorty, Mickey, and Ned. Twice as many wounded."

Ewan nodded, a lump in his throat over the loss of Shorty. The old man had been with him when he'd bought the *True* seven years earlier. He swore the woman would pay. "See to the prisoners and get back to your duties."

"Aye, Cap'n." Quinn strode out, his mouth a grim line.

Ewan looked over at the lady in his tub with her knees drawn up and her shoulders hunched. Her wide eyes filled with guilt.

Fury flared his innards and blurred his vision for a moment with its force. He clenched his fists to keep from grabbin' her up and shaking her.

"Ye'd best tell me the truth now, woman." He ground the words between his teeth. "An English ship doesna attack its own countrymen unless the crew's been promised enow wealth to make it worth their while. The measly price on me head couldna ha' tempted them. Even the fifty pounds ye promised me wouldna be enow."

"I have told you the truth." That little chin of hers went up. "If there is a fortune, I know not of it. My cousin is crazed. He thinks my father hid a coffer filled with gold like some leprechaun from the ancient tales."

"And why would he believe such?"

"My mother. She's convinced Cousin Reginald that my Da hoarded great wealth."

"Your mother would endanger her own daughter?"

"My mother has always hated me. She was forced to wed my father for his title, and the moment she'd recovered from childbirth, she abandoned us for life at the English court. Until I was old enough to be of use to her. On my fifteenth birthday she summoned me to London, to be married off to some lecherous old man. All to gain political power for herself."

Ewan shrugged. 'Twas the lot in life for a well-born lady. Yet the thought of Tru in some drooling old goat's bed filled his stomach with bile. Och, he couldna let this woman make him weak again.

"How did ye escape her scheming?" Then a thought hit him like a pulley swinging onto his temple at high wind. "Or did ye nae?" His chest filled with an icy fog. "Are ye married? Jaysus, Mary and Joseph, did ye kill him on your weddin' night before he could take your maidenhead?"

"No!" She looked truly horrified at the suggestion. "How could you accuse me of such? By God's grace I was befriended by Queen Henrietta. We shared a love of reading, and she persuaded my mother I would serve the Queen best as a companion."

He stepped closer, crossing his arms. "You're still lyin' about something."

The truth of his words was there in her eyes, but she only clamped her lips tight and looked away.

"Even were there nae other lies between us, ye still betrayed me." He grabbed her shoulders and shook her. "Ye knew your cousin would come after ye, yet ye said nothing! Three of my men are dead. My ship is takin' on water. The cost o' the repairs alone—"

The poison of her treachery seethed through his veins. The woman took him for a fool! And the worst was, he'd fallen for her innocent act. Just because she'd been a virgin, he'd let his guilt make him feel tender toward her. But she was no different than any other noblewoman.

What the hell would he do if she refused him his money in Galway? Or if there *was* no money? What if she'd somehow laid an elaborate trap for him and his crew? He'd be taken to London to hang, and she would claim the reward!

He'd make sure she paid for her treachery. And she could start right now.

Hardening his innards, he stripped off his clothes and stepped into the tub to sink down before her.

She gasped and sat up, her mouth forming a perfect shape to slip his cock into. Why hadn't he made her take him in her mouth thus far? Mayhap she'd taken other men that way to save her maidenhead.

"Wash me!" He shoved the chunk of lye beneath her nose.

"Ewan, I'm sorry—"

"Take the soap and be quick about it." He wanted to hurt her. To humiliate her as he'd been humiliated. "I've time to take ye at least once more before we reach Galway."

Her face lost all expression as she reached for the soap, and something shifted inside Ewan. But he wouldn't yield to the weakness. Compassion could get a man killed.

She had to come up on her knees to reach him, and while she scrubbed his shoulders, he took advantage by spreading his knees, clasping her around the waist, and bringing her between his thighs. Her breasts jiggled before his eyes and he lapped at the nipples until they hardened into ripe little berries.

When she stopped soaping him, he shook her. "Keep scrubbin', *milady.*" He slid one hand down her silky wet arse and worked a finger between the tiny white cheeks. Her little hole puckered and tensed in response to his prodding.

She jerked away. "What are you doing?"

He tugged her against him once more. "Whatever I will. You're mine to do with as I please." He cupped the back of her head and captured her lips, purposely taking her harshly, pouring all his anger and frustration into the kiss. "Now, wash me." He took her hand and brought it down to cover his lengthening cock.

She drew in a quick breath and her expression went from anxious to thoughtful as she wrapped her fingers around his shaft. She slid her palm up to the tip and rubbed a finger over the slit.

He leaned his head back, eyes closed, and groaned.

Her hand lifted away. "Did that hurt?"

"Nae!" Reminding himself she must be a grand actress, he put more command in his voice. "Don't stop."

After a moment, he felt her hand circle him once more, traveling the length of him as if she were checking every bump and crevice. Then her fingers moved to his culls. He sat up and grabbed her wrist. "Careful."

Still holding her wrist, he let her explore. Her eyes held his captive as she cupped and gently squeezed them, caressing them around and beneath, then moving back up to his cock. Jaysus, he was hard as stone.

"'Tis so huge, Ewan," she whispered, biting her bottom lip. "I cannot believe it fit inside me." She took her other hand and cupped his culls again. "Yet, 'tis so soft."

She put just the right amount of innocence and wonder in her tone, damn her. Sliding her middle finger further down, she rubbed the sensitive skin between his culls and arsehole. He'd never felt anything so erotic. His cock wept and his hips moved of their own accord.

Surely no innocent would know how to seduce a man that way.

He couldn't take any more. He wanted to feel her mouth on him before he plunged deep inside her. In one move, he wrapped his arms around her waist and arse, lifted her and climbed out of the tub. As he tossed her onto his bunk, he reminded himself again that she was lying to him. She was using him.

"Mayhap if ye tell me the truth o' your plot now, I'll nae take ye like the whore ye are!"

Chapter 5

Tru scrambled to the opposite side of the bed, clutched a sheet to her body and huddled against the wall. Her heart thundered like a cannon inside her chest. Could she blame him for his fury? She'd brought death and danger to him and his crew. But how could she have known Reginald would hire mercenaries? Where had he gotten the funds?

"Ewan, there is no plot." She must convince him of that truth. "My cousin was left nothing in my father's will but the land and castle entailed to the heir. He's been living off his expectations for years, gaming and drinking, and he's deeply in debt. He wants the money my father hid for me. That is all."

And she couldn't and wouldn't tell him more than that, not even to avoid his wrath. He might beat her now. But if he knew she might not have his fifty pounds, he'd throw her overboard and keep sailing.

"Mayhap ye tell the truth." Dripping wet, his organ standing at attention, almost straining toward her, Ewan reached across the bunk, grabbed her ankles and yanked her toward him.

"But trustin' ye got my men killed." He caught her wrist and lifted her to sit on the edge of the mattress. Curling a fist into her hair, he gripped his manhood with the other.

His organ was so close she could see tiny blue veins encircling the thick shaft. Like a sword, the end came to a point, a smooth, strangely shaped head.

"Take me rod inside your lips."

His rod? In her mouth? A quivering panic gripped her. But for a brief moment, she'd experienced only pleasure from it. Would it now be an instrument of pain? Yet she couldn't help but wonder, how would it feel? How would it taste?

"Remember how I pleasured your quim with me mouth and tongue, Tru?" As if he sought to reassure her, his tone softened. "'Tis the same pleasure for a man."

If he received even half the pleasure from her mouth as she'd received from his....

She parted her lips and lapped at the glistening, swollen head.

He moaned. "Tha's it, Tru. Suckle it, sweeting."

Encouraged, she did as he bade and closed her jaws over as much length as she could, drew back, then moved forward to take it deeply inside her mouth again.

A strangled sound broke from his throat. She peeked up to see his head thrown back and his eyes squeezed closed. The sight gave her a thrilling sense of power, and she suckled hard as she pulled away and drew him in again and again, finding a natural rhythm.

A low, rumbling growl rose from his chest. Soon he was clutching her nape and moving his hips. His thrusts grew deeper and harder against the back of her throat. Her jaw and cheeks began to ache. She put her hands to his thighs and pushed away.

He let go, his fists dropping to his sides as he breathed in deep gulps. "Are ye part witch, woman?" His dark eyes glittered with lust and confusion. "How can ye be so innocent and then suck my cock 'til I want to cry for mercy? Blast ye! Why canna I abuse ye as ye deserve?"

He reached behind her and tossed the sheet over her. He dropped to the bunk and bent elbows to knees, clasping his head in his hands.

A sweeping tenderness filled her at the earnest frustration in his voice. He'd fought a battle because of her. Lost men. And believed she lied to him still. Yet he'd not hurt her.

Tru lifted her hand to his shoulder. "I'm sorry for endangering your crew. But I swear on my Da's grave that I have not betrayed you to Cromwell."

He remained still, and she felt his body trembling beneath her palm. In that moment, it seemed to her this rough pirate, this terror of the sea, was but a man in need of womanly sustenance. And 'twas her profound pleasure, for this fleeting time out of time, to fulfill such a womanly role, to give to him, to be his succor.

She leaned over and cupped his cheek, placing soft short kisses at both corners of his mouth beneath the moustache, then across his soft beard and up to his weathered cheekbone.

He grabbed the sides of her head and claimed her mouth with his as he twisted and pushed her down across the bed. His lips moved over hers with passion, not anger, not commanding or insisting, but lifting away and coming back for more as if tasting a fine wine. He used his tongue gently, imploringly. His fingers caressed her temples.

So passionate was his seduction, she barely noticed her hips now cradled his. He'd spread her thighs wide with his knees. Hot masculine skin pressed to her cold nakedness, surrounding her, warming her. The hair of his chest rubbed her breasts, the perfect friction to arouse their interest. His huge organ pushed against her hip in a rhythm to match the warm invasion of his tongue.

With a strangled sound he lifted his hips and pushed into her, stretching her with his long, rigid length. He gathered her in his arms and buried his face against her neck as he moved. Each thrust of his manhood stimulated her woman's parts more and more, the coil in her belly tightening. Instinctively she stirred beneath him to complement his rhythm.

Without missing a stroke he slipped his arms under her thighs and raised her knees over his shoulders. He surged in so deep it felt as if he touched her womb, nay, her very soul. With one last push he shouted, and she felt his hot seed fill her.

As his body relaxed against hers, she knew in her heart that their paths had crossed for a reason, and that being possessed by this rough pirate had changed her forever.

Tru awoke in the bunk feeling sore, disoriented, and alone. Gingerly, she got up and assessed her situation. Ever the pragmatist, she took a deep breath. They must be close to Galway by now. She would dress and be ready for their arrival.

Once there, she would ask Dr. Banyan to see to Henry's wound. But before they disembarked, she would check on the cabin boy herself. She washed, dressed and did her best to comb and pin up her hair. Then she went to find Henry.

After questioning a passing sailor, she learned Ewan was at the ship's wheel and the boy was in a small room off the galley.

Henry lay on a makeshift pad of canvas. Old sails, she realized. His breathing was rapid, and a sheen of sweat covered his face. When she shut the door, he opened his eyes and gave her a weak smile. "Miss!"

She returned his smile. "I've come to see how you're faring, Henry. May I check your wound?" She knelt and placed her palm to his forehead. He burned with fever.

Henry set his jaw and looked away. "I should be up, helpin' with repairs, but the Cap'n says I mus' stay in bed."

"I see."

The boy had ink-black hair and dark eyes. His petulant expression reminded Tru of the Queen when first she'd met the young monarch. Despite his protest, she pulled back the threadbare blanket and began untying her blood-soaked bandaging. "Have you found Captain MacGowan to be a good leader? Knowledgeable? Making fair decisions for his crew and his ship?"

"Aye, miss. You've the right of it. Cap'n's a good man."

Peeling away the sticky dressing, she was encouraged to detect no stench. The wound needed stitches, but 'twas not putrid. She went to the galley and returned with a bucket of hot water. As she bent to set it down and rip off more of her petticoat, she glanced up and caught Henry staring down her bodice. Well, the boy wasn't *too* sick!

"Tell me how you came to be on a pirate ship, Henry." She hoped to distract him while she wiped the wound with the hot salty water.

'Twere the Cap'n." The boy bared his teeth, but bore the pain without a sound. "He bought me."

She stopped folding her torn piece of petticoat. "I beg your pardon? *Brought* you?"

"Nae, he bought me. Off a slave block in Marrakesh, he did. Paid a pretty sum for me too, on account o' I was strong for my age."

"Good heavens!"

"Never been fed so good as here. Never whipped. He gave me my freedom, and all I 'as to do is fetch and carry for him, learn my letters and numbers, and deliver the money to his Mam when we dock in Dumfries."

Tru calmly tied off the new bandage, but a lump of emotion had formed in her throat at what Henry had revealed. She blinked away moisture and sat back on her heels. "You are learning to read?"

"Aye! And writin' and mathematics too!" He beamed as he told her. "The Cap'n teaches me hisself. Every night until—" He broke off and looked away. "Until you, miss." His face was flushed with fever, but now his cheeks reddened even more.

Swallowing her mortification, she folded her hands in her lap and focused on the news of Henry's education. Ewan had taught the boy himself. How gratifying it would be to teach children to read and write. To instruct those young ones who could never afford a tutor or governess. Perhaps that was something to which she could dedicate her life. Perhaps in the New World….

"I'm sure you're a fine student, Henry."

"I want to get up now, miss!" His lips pursed and he glared at her. "I'm a poor excuse for a pirate if I let a tiny piece of wood fell me. The others'll be saying Henry Morgan is nothin' but a pulin' babe!"

"Nonsense, Henry! You're very brave. And you have a perfect pirate's name"

"Ye think so, miss?" He looked at her, eyes full of hope.

"Captain Morgan! The fiercest pirate to ever sail the seas!" She combed his hair back from his forehead.

Just as the sun was beginning to set, Ewan sailed the *True* up the river Connacht and weighed anchor beside a thick stand of trees. He sent Tate and Quinn through the forest on foot to scout for signs of a trap. When sure there were no soldiers waiting for him in town, he rowed Tru upstream to the pier.

The people eyed him suspiciously, but once they recognized Tru, they were all smiles and deference for the "lady of the manor" and even offered a farmer's cart to ride up to the castle.

She sent a boy to fetch the doctor and bid him visit Henry aboard the *True*, and when Ewan's stomach roared like a loch beastie, she stopped in the baker's, calling the man and his wife by name. With a regal air, she bespoke enough bread and meat pies for his entire crew on the ship, charging the purchase to the castle.

Hope began to flicker in his full belly that she would actually pay him his fifty pounds. But he knew full well nobles were extended credit even when they never paid their bills.

He left Tate in charge of loading fresh water and food supplies on the *True* and warned Quinn to keep watch for Belclare or Cromwell's soldiers. Then he climbed in the cart and rode up the craggy mountain still gripping Tru's arm.

If he could flay himself, he would, for being so weak over this woman. He couldn't seem to get enough of her warm, soft flesh. He'd woken to the late afternoon sun pushing its way through his window and the weight of the wee lady on his chest. Tru lay over him, one knee encircling his groin as if to keep him prisoner. Her hair had been wrapped around his fist and his other hand rested on her hip.

He'd watched her sleeping, her breathing slow and even, the fragile skin beneath her eyes feathered with soft brown lashes. Something had wrenched in his chest. And he hated it, whatever it was. It couldn't be good.

When she emerged from his cabin this afternoon, she'd looked the fine lady once again, her hair pinned up and gloves pulled on.

Daylight was fading, casting shadows on the rolling hills. The farmers' crofts seemed well tended, and sheep grazed on the greenest meadows he'd ever seen. Even the lush jungles of the Caribbean islands couldn't compare to the fertile countryside around him.

Once the castle came into sight, Ewan was beset by how far above him this lady was. *A poor blacksmith's son from Dumfries, and the daughter of a fookin' earl.*

He'd taken her maidenhead. He'd done things with her only a whore should know about.

Be damned! As her guardian, the new Lord Belclare had every right to hang him.

As they approached the castle drive, liveried servants poured out, exclaiming and cheering when Tru climbed down from the cart. She hugged them all in turn and strode arm-in-arm with an older lady through the huge wooden doors into a great hall.

Prosperity was evident everywhere he looked. Colorful tapestries hung on the stone walls, three iron chandeliers as large as his ship's wheel lighted the room, and gilded furniture sat beside a hearth massive enough to hold an ox. She'd grown up here? This was the life she was accustomed to?

He seemed to have been forgotten. Tru greeted even more servants, removing her fine cloak and gloves as she spoke with them all. He should stop staring about him like a green lad and listen in case she was plotting against him.

She turned to him. "If you'll wait here, I'll bring your payment," she said, her gaze not quite meeting his. Her voice had taken on an impersonal tone, speaking to him as if he were a lowly supplicant. A beggar.

Fury burned hot in his gut. She was dismissing him. Was eager to be rid of him.

"Nae." He fingered the handle of his cutlass and stared her down. "I'll nae wait here like a servant."

Her brow furrowed briefly before she recovered her haughty expression. "Very well. Come this way."

She lifted her skirts and turned toward an immense staircase of rich oak. As she climbed, her hips swayed and Ewan followed, his blood heating with each step she took. Damn her, she'd not get rid of him this easily. Just hours ago, she'd given herself to him so sweetly, so fully, he'd felt her desire for him in her touch, in the way she'd clung to him and cried out his name as he'd lost himself inside her.

Even now, his body hardened just thinking of her passionate responses. He wanted her again. When would he have his fill of her? Surely he'd grow tired of her after another day or so. Mayhap it was the knowledge that she was his no longer.

She glided down a wide carpeted hallway with brass sconces and silk wall coverings. At the first door on the left she stopped and entered a large bedchamber, obviously the master's. Her Da's.

The bed was almost the size of his entire cabin on the *True*. Soft and inviting it looked, and he imagined laying Tru down on it and stripping away her air of reserve along with her clothes.

Closing the door behind her, she turned to him and gestured to a cushioned chair beside a marble fireplace. "Please have a seat."

"Like hell I will!" In two strides he was close enough to circle his arms about her and lift her against him. She gasped but didn't struggle. Her hands clamped on his shoulders.

"I want ye one last time, Tru."

She stared into his eyes, and in her brown depths he saw a mixture of desire and sadness.

"I cannot." Her breath quivered. "I should not."

She wasna as detached as she pretended. "Ye know ye want me, Tru." He took her to the bed and sat her on the edge.

Her gaze flickered to the door. "Mrs. Murphy could come in."

He cupped her face and kissed her long and deep. With a tug at her nape he pulled her hair from its tight knot and drove his fingers through the thick tresses as they spilled down onto the bedcover.

His lips roamed down her jaw to her neck as he reached beneath her skirts and untied her garter. With a moan he caressed the downy skin of her thigh before rolling her silken stocking down and pulling it off along with her slipper.

"Mmm, Ewan. I do want you. I do." She leaned back on her hands, drew a deep breath and presented her other leg.

He smiled and clasped her right thigh at the juncture to her quim. "Hold your skirts up, Tru. I want to see your legs spread for me."

She closed her eyes and shivered, but obeyed.

The lack of a petticoat reminded him she'd sacrificed it for Henry's wound. The thought made a tender emotion well up inside him.

Her limbs were white as milk and slim, not shapely. But somehow their slenderness only enflamed him more. As he untied the other garter, he brought his mouth to the fleshy inside of her thigh and kissed his way down while he removed the second stocking. He could smell her woman's juices mingled with his seed, and his blood pulsed between his legs at the musky scent. His cock twitched to be inside her, but he would savor their joining this last time.

He studied her a moment, enjoying the sight of her knees raised, her toes curled into the coverlet. With her hands behind her, her breasts were ripe for plucking. He curled his fingers beneath her bodice.

She whimpered when he tugged it down and her tits popped free, pushed up by the tight fabric. Jaysus, Mary and Joseph, he could take her right now. Just as she was. But he was made of sterner stuff. He bent to her and laved his tongue over the tip of one firm nipple until it hardened to a tight peak.

She moaned and shuddered.

"Ye like this, do ye nae?" he asked as he drew the nipple into his mouth and suckled. When she didna answer, he lifted his head and captured her gaze. "Mayhap I shouldna continue?"

"No!" She grabbed his head and pulled his mouth to her breast. "I mean, yes, you should continue."

He chuckled and took the wet, rigid crest between his teeth and teased it with his tongue until she cried out. As he gave the other nipple equal treatment, he leaned on one hand and began untying the laces at her back with the other until her dress was loose enough to strip away with a swift yank.

"Now take off your shift, but keep your legs spread for me."

He watched her fingers trembling as she complied. His own trembled a bit, too, as he ran them over and around the curls at her slit, pulling the folds apart to study her sweet entrance.

"'Tis the secret of a woman's power." He lowered his head and nuzzled her lush flesh, swollen from his attentions the past night and day. "This dark and mysterious passage that beckons man and renders him unable to resist her."

"Oh, Ewan." She leaned forward and cupped his face, tangling her fingers into his hair and tugging it free from the leather tie. "Would that it were so."

"'Tis best ye know not the power ye hold, milady." He mumbled against her, closing his eyes to relish the feel of her supple folds in his mouth, the taste of her on his tongue.

While his lips paid homage to her woman's flesh, he inched a finger inside her and licked and suckled her hidden nub.

Her hips writhed and bucked beneath him while she whimpered and encouraged him with incoherent sounds of pleasure. Her fingers gripped his hair almost to point of pain as she gave a most unladylike groan against the top of his head and stiffened beneath him.

"Ewan," she gasped. "Please." She was pulling up his shirt from the back, pushing him away to wrench it off his arms and over his head. "Give me your— your—"

"Cock?" he supplied.

"Yes! Yes, your cock." Her cheeks reddened and she hid her face against his bare chest.

He chuckled at her blushing cheeks. After all they'd done together, she could still shy away at saying the word.

The utter sweetness of having her in his arms nearly unmanned him. Where the bloody fook was the man known as Merciless MacGowan? He'd been enslaved by a wee lass with a severe nose and no curves to speak of. Shoving the tender feelings away, he shook his head.

"Nae. I'll nae take orders from ye, milady." He retreated a step. "If ye want me cock, ye must work for it. Unfasten me breeches and kiss it."

Tru reared back at Ewan's harsh tone. He sounded angry again. He was the most maddening man! Fine. Let him think he commanded her. Eagerly, she reached for the buttons on the flap of his worn woolen breeches.

His organ sprang free as she pushed his breeches to his ankles. He tugged off his boots, laying his dirk on the bed beside her, and kicked out of his breeches. Before he'd set his feet down, she circled the base of his rigid organ with her fingers and drew her tongue slowly along its length. When she reached the smooth head, she took it into her mouth with a vengeful suction and a light pressure of her teeth.

With a grunt, he clutched her head and pulled away. "I said kiss it, nae bite it off!"

A spark of mischievousness ignited. She shoved him back and turned to crawl away.

"Come back here, woman!" He reached for her ankles, but she kicked at him and by luck managed to reach the headboard without capture.

As he crawled up after her, she smacked him hard in the face with a feather pillow. "Take that, ye beast!"

She giggled. Giggled! Not since her Da had she played and laughed.

"Argh! You're a shrew of a woman, Gertrude Fitzpatrick." His voice was stern, but a wicked smile tugged one corner of his mouth. Just before he lunged for her, his smile disappeared and hot determination shone in his eyes. He wore the same look as when he'd tied her hands.

Suddenly she'd had enough of his possession, of giving in. Rebellion surged within her. She flung herself off the bed and ran toward the dressing room. Let *him* work for it!

As her hand touched the latch, he grabbed her around the waist. She went wild, kicking and fighting in his arms, grunting and growling until he subdued her with his superior strength.

"Shh, Tru. Tru! What the holy hell is goin' on wi' ye, lass? 'Tis but love play, ye crazy woman!" He held her tight against him, his chest rising and falling against her back as she went limp.

Love play?

He swung her into his arms, carried her to the bed and laid her down. Releasing a long breath, he bent to grab his breeches and ran a hand through his hair. "I'll take me pay and be gone." But his organ still stood erect, pointing to the ceiling, stiff and stretched and reddened.

"Ewan!" She sat up, grabbed his hand. What was the matter with her? She'd gone berserk for a moment. *Love play.* "I don't know what came over me. I was overwrought," she finished lamely.

He stared at her, his gaze moving over her body with the same expression he'd given the pastries in Mr. O'Flaherty's bakery. Like a little boy with his nose pressed against the glass, longing for one, but knowing he could never have it.

Her heart twisted, and in that moment she knew it was love she felt for him.

"Please, Ewan." She tugged on his hand. "Be with me."

He fell on her with a passionate cry, kissing her everywhere. "Aw, Tru," he rasped. "Ye've bewitched me body and soul, ye have." He positioned himself between her legs and thrust inside with a powerful lunge. "And I canna let ye go."

Groaning his pleasure, he came up on his knees and elbows to palm her breasts while he worked in her.

"Ye canna still be thinkin' a nun's life will suit ye," he mumbled against her jaw, and then looked into her eyes. "Ye'll coom with me, Tru."

Faster and harder he moved in her while his lips and tongue caressed her skin from throat to breast and everywhere between. "You're mine, Tru. Say it." His words matched the rhythm of his thrusts. "Say you're mine."

She wanted to make all his dreams come true. To be his helpmate, his lover, and his children's mother.

A sob caught in her throat. "Yes. I'm yours."

But in her heart, she knew it could never be. He was headed for a life of piracy in the Caribbean, and she—well, if she couldn't pay him his fifty pounds, he'd hate her forever. A stone of sadness seemed to push on her chest as a bleak future spent she knew not where appeared before her.

Carpe Diem.

She would pluck whatever pleasure she could from the day, and worry about tomorrow when he was gone.

Tru held tight as the pressure built in her, the pulsating feeling more than a physical sensation. She concentrated on memorizing the feel of his shoulder blades, moist with sweat, moving beneath her hands, the softness of his golden brown hair in her fingers, the firmness of his lean hips as they pumped against her.

She would commit to memory the touch of his rough hands cupping her face and the exact shape of his Roman nose as he nuzzled against her chest. The way the veins stood out in his neck as he grimaced and strained and gave her his seed.

Slowly, his body rested. As he laid his head on her breast, she vowed to remember the heat of his breath as it blew against her sensitive nipple.

His hold tightened around her. "I'll take ye with me, I will. Ye nae belong in a convent, Tru. I canna let ye go."

She squeezed her eyes shut. Perhaps it was sinful to give herself to him. But then, she could be lying instead beneath Reginald, used only as a vessel for his greed. Surely there was more sin in fornicating only for wealth and power than choosing to surrender her virtue in the name of passion and desire.

And love.

She could never take the veil now. But neither could she sail the seas with him, knowing every day that Ewan could be killed in battle or hung as a common thief.

The pirate captain craved honest work. When he'd talked of this New Hampshire, she'd heard the hunger in his voice. He wanted to lead a legitimate life.

But even if she had the means to keep him from piracy, she couldn't. Her Da had wanted the money for his tenants and servants. By law, everything in the castle belonged to her cousin now. But Reginald would only squander it on drinking and gambling. The money would help to stave off the hard times to come. Would Ewan understand her obligation to her people, who would surely need protection from Reginald's tyranny?

She knew in her heart Ewan was an honorable man. He plundered, yes, but only from his country's enemies. He'd been loyal to the king and queen. But he'd said he needed a large sum to start a business. If there was a fortune, would he be too tempted? Did she have the right to take that chance?

A light snoring distracted her from her troubled thoughts, and she looked down to see his face, youthful in repose. This was her chance to look for the money.

She quietly slipped from beneath him, rolling him into the feathery softness where he burrowed down with a satisfied moan.

The room was almost full dark as she threw on her dress and took a candle from the mantel. As she crept into Da's dressing room, the scent of his pipe tobacco struck her nostrils and her heart at the same moment. Reverently, she drew off the dustsheet to uncover his armoire. Time dissolved and she was eight years old again, choosing his waistcoat for him as she had done every morning.

"Aw, Tru, me girl, how would I get by without ye," he used to say with a be-whiskered smile.

The daily ritual, she realized with an adult's perspective, had nothing to do with him needing help deciding what to wear.

But he'd sent her off to London without so much as a second glance the moment her mother crooked her finger. And Tru had wasted so many years resenting him for it. Feeling betrayed.

He'd written to her in London to explain he'd done it for her. Written how life in the wilds of West Ireland was no place for a titled young woman. How he hoped she would marry and give him grandchildren.

And now he was gone, and she hadn't even known until he was already buried! A great, wracking sob broke from her chest. She clamped a hand over her mouth and squeezed her eyes closed.

There was no time to indulge her grief. She wiped her cheeks on her sleeve and reached behind the armoire to push on the wall.

The hidden door popped open.

Looking around with a sudden shivery feeling tingling up her spine, she slipped through the gap.

Chapter 6

The narrow passageway was dark and dank and cold. Brushing cobwebs out of the way, Tru stepped cautiously into the secret tunnel. The mustiness reassured her that no one had passed this way in a very long time.

She'd only been inside once before, when Da revealed the hiding place to her, and she'd never gone this far. She'd been twelve, and wars between the Irish and their English landowners had broken out all over Ireland. The Great Rebellion still raged today. And though the castle was positioned for defense, her Da had impressed on her the importance of this route to safety.

She stepped over scuttling mice and shoved away thick cobwebs. Had Da's mind been clear at the end? Perhaps there was no money at all! How would her people survive?

Then the candlelight reflected off a metal object. A brass buckle on a leather strap. She dropped to her knees before the wood-and-leather trunk and unbuckled the clasp with shaking fingers.

At last she raised the dusty lid and lost her breath.

S'truth! She gazed in wonder at the trunk full of silver crowns and half crowns. There must be thousands upon thousands of pounds here!

"So this is what ye've been lyin' aboot."

Tru jumped, almost dropping the candle, and swiveled to find Ewan glowering down at her. His feet were bare and he wore only his breeches and belt. His fists clenched tightly at his sides. Disgust shone in his eyes.

"Ewan! You frightened me half to death!"

"Ye thought I'd steal it from ye, Tru? Think ye I have so little honor?" His lip curled in hatred, but the hurt in his voice struck a knife in her heart.

"I just—I didn't know...." Her voice trailed away.

There was a clamoring outside, someone banging like a banshee on the hallway door. "Lady Tru! Lady Tru! Are ye in there?"

'Twas Mrs. Murphy! The kindly housekeeper who was more mother to her than servant.

"I must see to this." She brushed past him. "Stay hidden here."

"Nae!" He grabbed her arm.

She made herself meet his eyes. "If 'tis Cromwell's men, they can search and search and never find you." Knowing she left him in total darkness, Tru rushed past Ewan to the tunnel's entrance, hearing him curse as he tried to follow blindly.

Once she reached the dressing room, she closed the hidden door on his furious bellow and let her housekeeper in.

"Mrs. Murphy! What's the matter?"

The housekeeper held a kerchief to her mouth as tears spilled from her eyes. If she wondered why Tru stood in a dusty dress in the dark dressing room holding only a small candle, she said naught.

"Eh, me'dear. I wouldn't normally intrude, but 'tis so horrible, I canna believe it!"

"What is it? What has happened?" A knot of terror coiled in her stomach. Had Reginald arrived so quickly?

Mrs. Murphy dabbed at her eyes. "Mrs. O'Brien sent her boy over from Ballinasloe. Her cousin, who lives in Drogheda, appeared at her doorstep in the night. She barely escaped with her life! Cromwell's forces have overtaken the city. He's slaughtered everyone! Women and children, even priests!" She cried out and crossed herself, gulping back tears.

Black horror sank into the pit of Tru's stomach. Cromwell wouldn't stop there. Quashing the Irish rebellion would be just the clout he'd need to gain England's favor.

Tru's world was falling apart before her eyes. "You must calm yourself," she told the housekeeper. "Gather as many people as you can at the church. We must leave Ireland."

"Yes, milady." Mrs. Murphy sniffed, nodded, and hurried out.

Tru dreaded facing Ewan again, but she straightened her spine and entered the tunnel, candle held aloft. The trunk sat close to the entrance now, but he was nowhere in sight. She moved past the trunk, seeking him in the shadows.

"Ewan?"

From behind her, his arm snaked around her throat and squeezed. "I swear I'll snap your neck if ye've betrayed me, woman!"

"There is news of Cromwell," she squeaked.

He loosened his hold bit by bit as she told him the news of Drogheda.

"I believe we must all leave Ireland," she said at the end. "Will you give my people passage to France?"

"Aye," he readily agreed.

Humbleness and relief mingled with respect and love for the honorable man before her. She touched his arm. "Thank you."

"For the entire trunk of gold, I'll take ye wherever ye want." He flung off her hand and stooped to lift the trunk. "I'm a pirate, after all," he sneered as he turned back to her, hefting the strongbox to his chest. "Known far and wide as Merciless MacGowan, aye? Scourge of the Caribbean. Ravisher of innocents. Vile thief and murderer." He leaned in with a menacing snarl. "I even rape nuns."

His eyes sparked with disgust. But she couldn't blame him. She hadn't trusted enough in his honor.

"No." She tried again, bringing her palm to his cheek, but he flinched away. "You're an honorable man. Brave and loyal." She stepped closer. "'Twas not rape, Ewan."

"How nauseatingly romantic, cousin."

Reginald!

Ewan spun on his heels, protecting her with his body.

Her vile cousin blocked the doorway between the tunnel and the dressing room, backlit by a candelabrum on the desk.

Tru heard the click of a flintlock's hammer being pulled back and tried to shove Ewan aside. He was unmovable.

"Don't move, Captain MacGowan. I'd rather return you to London alive." Reginald aimed his pistol at Ewan's head. "But I'll can still collect the reward if I drag your dead body back."

Cursing himself for a fool, Ewan gripped the trunk in front of him. A damned fine time to be caught without pistol or cutlass! Even his dirk lay somewhere on the bed. He'd been a fookin eejit to let his guard down.

Still, the new earl was a head shorter than Ewan and slightly built. If he could disarm him….

"So, Tru." Ewan glanced behind him. "*This* is your cousin? The swaggerin' cockscomb whose prick is so tiny he couldna swive ye proper?" He gave a scornful snicker, hoping the earl would take the bait.

The shorter man's face twisted in mottled rage. "Is that what this bitch told you?" He looked past Ewan to Tru.

The moment's inattention was all Ewan needed. He heaved the weighty trunk straight at the earl, knocking him to his arse. The pistol fired as it hit the ground. Silver coins showered into the dressing room, tinkling like raindrops in moonlight.

"Run, Tru!" Ewan pounced on the earl, drawing the stunned man's sword from its scabbard. Free of the tunnel, he had a fighting chance.

"Now!" the earl shouted behind him.

Ewan heard Tru scream just as the butt of a musket slammed into the back of his head. Sharp pain sliced through his skull. As he sank to his knees, the world faded to black.

"Ewan!" Horror hit Tru like a punch to the belly as he slumped to the floor. She flew to him and dropped to her knees at his side.

"*El pirata lo hace demasiado fácil!*" A well-dressed Spaniard stepped from behind the wall panel door.

Reginald got to his feet, dusted himself off and retrieved his sword. Then he cackled as he stared down at her, his eyes dancing with malice. He grabbed her hair, yanked her to her feet, and backhanded her across the face. The blow would have knocked her to the floor but for his hold on her hair.

"You'll regret running from me."

Her vision blurred. Her cheek burned like it'd been set to flame. Before she could recover from the blow, Reginald dragged her toward the bedroom.

"Well, Captain Ortega, we both have what we want now. If I recall, there are dungeons below." He nodded at Ewan. "Feel free to make use of them."

"No!" Tru fought Reginald's hold, sank her nails into his wrist, but he shook her by her hair until her scalp burned. When she lost her footing, he towed her along on her knees until she managed to regain her feet. Hot tears of fury spilled down her cheeks as he hauled her into the bedchamber.

"You've been most troublesome, whore." He flung her toward the bed. "I presume I won't have the joy of hearing you scream as I tear your maidenhead." He smiled cruelly. "But perhaps I can make you scream some other way."

Nausea swirled in her stomach as she pictured him touching her and coming inside her. Poor Mrs. Murphy stood in the outer doorway with a bloody lip, her grey hair disheveled. Tru wanted to fling herself at Reginald and scratch his eyes out.

Think, Tru! What are ye going to do?

The Spanish pirate dragged Ewan, still unconscious, by his feet out into the hall. Blood trickled from his temple, and she heard each crack as his head hit the wooden stairs. A giant fist clamped her heart. What would the Spaniard do to him? *This was her fault!* The thought echoed in her mind.

"Reginald. You have all the money you'll ever need now." She hated that her breath came in gulping heaves, revealing her fear. "Let Captain MacGowan go." She forced herself to place a hand on his waistcoat. "Save him, and I'll willingly do your bidding."

"How revoltingly noble, cousin." He began unwinding his cravat. "But I think I prefer you *un*willing. 'Twill be my first act as the new lord." He turned to the sobbing Mrs. Murphy. "The people around here will learn not to cross me, eh? Now go downstairs and tell cook I'll want dinner after I'm done here. A prick-scouring always leaves me with an appetite."

Mrs. Murphy glanced from Tru back to Reginald. "Please, milord."

"Do as I say or I'll have the entire household arrested for treason!" His voice and pitch rose with each word. Spittle flew from his mouth.

"It's all right, Mrs. Murphy." Tru nodded to the loyal housekeeper. "Go on, now. See to your duties."

Mrs. Murphy wiped her eyes and blinked at Tru. "Yes, mila—" She cut her gaze to Reginald. "Milord." She curtsied and left.

Reginald came at her, swinging the cravat. "Now, cousin. Take off that dress and let's see if the pirate taught you anything useful."

Her gaze scrambled for anything she could use as a weapon. From the corner of her eye, she spotted Da's blunderbuss above the mantel. If only she could get to it. Was it even loaded?

"Naturally, I can't take a whore as my bride. Not that I'll complain, but your mother will hate losing her means of support. Still, if you please me, perhaps I'll keep you as my mistress for a while."

The thought of being kept and used by Reginald shot a desperate panic through her veins. Somehow, she must get to that gun! All she could think to do for now was distract his thoughts.

With shaking fingers, she began unbuttoning her dress.

Chapter 7

Standing naked before Reginald, Tru couldn't help but compare how she'd felt when Ewan had looked at her body. His words may have been harsh, but his eyes had shone with appreciation. His touch had been erotic.

She knew the opposite to be true with Reginald.

As she straightened her shoulders and kicked the dress aside, her cousin yanked off his wig to reveal thick, wavy blond hair.

"Lie back on the bed and raise your hands above you." He fingered the still-raw scratch marks on his left cheek. "You see, I've learned from our last encounter to be more careful."

Oh, God in heaven. Once he tied her hands, she'd be completely at his mercy. She swallowed the bile in her throat and gingerly sat at the foot of the bed, where only an hour before Ewan had—Ewan! He'd taken off his boots and tossed his knife somewhere on the bedclothes.

"That's it, dove," Reginald cooed, stepping close. "Let's see what the pirate's left for me." He shoved a hand between her legs.

Tru stiffened at first. Then, remembering Ewan's words about a woman's power, she set her jaw and spread her thighs wide. "Is this what you want, my lord?"

"Oh, my dear girl." His eyes flared in lust as he stared at her. "I see he's trained you to be a good little whore." He shoved two fingers in her.

She winced, but met his brutal sneer with chin raised. She would set her mind to thoughts of escape. And Ewan.

While Reginald moved his fingers inside her, her own hands discreetly searched the disheveled coverlet for the knife.

"Still tight." His breath came a little quicker as he cruelly thrust a third finger inside her.

She clenched her teeth, refusing to cry out at the pain. Where was that knife?

"If only you weren't such a scrawny little thing." He withdrew his fingers and unbuttoned the placket on his silk breeches. "Still, we can't be too careful. Roll over and put your hands behind your back."

Now was the time!

Tru rolled to her hands and knees, frantically searching for the knife with shaky hands. *Please. Please let it not have fallen to the floor!*

"Ah, so there's still some fight left in you!" Reginald lunged for her, grabbing at her arms, clamping wiry fingers around her wrists.

As she fought and kicked, he chuckled and fell on top of her, wedging his knees between hers. "By God, you'll not escape me this time." He wrapped his cravat around one of her wrists and yanked her arm behind her back.

Her temples pounding with the pulsing of her blood, she struggled to pull her hand from his grasp and buck him off as she swept her free hand across the bed.

"I think you like it rough, cousin." He clamped his other arm around her waist, dropped his weight on her and whispered against her cheek, "Fight me, little cat. Little scrawny cat."

She felt his organ pushing between the folds of her entrance. Her stomach heaved in disgust. *Block it from your mind, Tru. Think of finding the knife.*

As he shoved against her with a grunt, her palm ran over a hard ivory handle. She grabbed hold of it, twisted beneath him and plunged the knife deep into his left shoulder.

Screaming, he grabbed his arm and jerked away, incredulous eyes fixed on the knife protruding from his shoulder. "You bitch!"

Snatching the cravat from his loosened grip, Tru scrambled off the bed and ran for the blunderbuss above the mantel. She tugged the heavy weapon down, swiveled, and lodged the butt against her hip. With both thumbs she pulled back the hammer, praying her father had kept the weapon loaded.

Taking aim, she fired. The explosion knocked her to her backside and filled the room with smoke.

When air returned to her lungs, she sprang to her feet and snatched up her dress. She was shaking so badly it took three tries to close her fingers around the filthy satin.

Reginald lay on his back, a large gaping hole in his chest, his eyes staring sightlessly at the ceiling.

Her mind numb, she slipped the dress over her head and wiped hair and sweat off her brow with the back of hand. Then she drew back her foot and kicked the bastard hard in the chest.

With a satisfied nod, she walked to the fireplace, took the heavy iron poker from its stand and headed for the dungeons below.

Ewan braced himself for another blow. When it came, his head snapped back. Pain splintered through his cheek and jaw, and he could feel a tooth loosen.

He'd woken up chained in an icy cell. Moisture seeped from the stone wall at his bare back, and a single candle was the only light. His head throbbed like the devil. He tasted a mixture of sweat and blood on his lips.

He fookin hated being underground. But he'd be damned before he'd let the Spaniard see it. He spit blood to the dirt floor, then looked up and grinned. "Is that all ye've got, ye scurvy son of a whore?"

The Spaniard glared at him, drew back his giant fist and landed another blow, this time to Ewan's stomach.

Goddamn it! If his wrists hadn't been shackled above him, he'd have doubled over. As it was, he bent forward as far as his chains allowed, gasping for air and coughing.

Once they unshackled him for the trip to London, he'd stuff this Spaniard's culls down his throat!

When he could finally draw a breath, he straightened and looked up. One eye already swollen shut, Ewan met the Spaniard's gaze once more. "Me Minnie could hit harder than that, ye canker-ridden dog."

He grunted at the blow to his side and heard a distinct crack of a rib as pain shot through his midsection. Gritting his teeth, he affected a sneer. "Never thought to see the day a Spaniard obeyed an Englishman. Do ye suck his cock as well?"

The Spaniard snarled and began using both fists on him. Ewan had no time to recover from one blow to the next.

The beating he could take. He'd suffered worse. But not knowing if Tru was safe might kill him. Was she now at the mercy of that pig-swiving cousin of hers? If that black-hearted toad hurt one hair on her head, he'd slice him up and feed him to the sharks one limb at a time!

He'd give his life if it would bring her happiness. The thought stopped him cold. When had her welfare become so important to him?

But it had.

And he'd done nothing but bring her grief. He remembered the hurt in her eyes when he'd demanded all her coins. Cursed be his blasted temper! Why had he lashed out at her so? It wasn't the money. It was her damned lying to him about it.

But what right did he have to expect she'd trust him? He'd treated her like a whore, not accepting her word that she would pay him.

But she wasn't like other noble folk. He knew that now. He wanted one more chance. One more moment with her, so he could tell her what a fool he'd been.

The thrashing went on. His nose was broken and bleeding. He heard another rib crack. His body would be bruised for weeks, if he lived that long. But he'd learned to deal with pain and sent his mind into familiar dreams, into a different world where he was a successful shipping merchant with vast holdings and a manor house. Only this time in his dream, a wee lass waited for him on the veranda cradling a bairn in the crook of her elbow. He raced up the steps to sweep her into his arms—

"If you do not cease at once, I shall bash your head in."

He must've slipped into delusions. He was imagining he'd heard her voice.

The beating stopped.

Ewan looked up, straining to see through his one good eye. There stood a fierce warrior woman, her hair flowing wild around her, gripping a thick iron poker with both hands, ready to strike.

The Spaniard's attention was on the woman.

Ewan took a chance. Summoning all the strength remaining to him, he kicked the man between his legs.

The Spaniard grabbed his culls and dropped to his knees.

The warrior woman stepped forward and swung the fireplace poker against the back of the man's head. He collapsed with a thud.

Ewan blinked and tried to wipe the blood out of his eye with his shoulder. Tru?

He must have said her name out loud. She dropped the poker, raced to him and cupped his face in her palms.

"Oh, my love, what have they done to you?" She grabbed up her skirt and used it to wipe his temple.

My love?

As her worried gaze and gentle fingers searched his face, inspecting his injuries, her lips brushed his cheek. "Oh, Ewan."

She stilled suddenly, her countenance cleared of all emotion. "Where are the keys?"

"Tru, are ye hurt? Where's your cousin, lass?" He grimaced as his split lip cracked open.

She stepped back and looked about distractedly. "He's dead. I stabbed him with your knife. Then I shot him!"

Stunned, Ewan stared. She could be hanged for murder! When had she become such a bloodthirsty lass? "Remind me ne'er to get on your bad side," he muttered.

"Too late," she snapped. "Now, where are those keys?" She picked up the candle from the stone ledge and began searching the Spaniard's body.

It struck him as he watched her fumble for the keys. She'd killed an earl! And instead of taking the money and leaving him to rot, she'd come down here to fight the Spaniard too? Was there ever a braver woman, more spirited and true, than his Tru?

Ewan's heart constricted as he realized, by God, he loved her!

Aye. He knew it, clear as a Caribbean sky. This deep yearning in his heart for her, this wild desire and supreme respect for her. 'Twas love.

And he didn't deserve her.

"Tru. Milady. Ye shouldna have come down here. The earl is sure to have more men about."

"Aha! Found them." She dangled a set of keys from an iron ring.

"Tru! Are ye listening, woman? Ye shouldna have risked comin' after me."

She heaved an exasperated sigh. "Captain, do you want to be freed or not?"

Ewan set his jaw. "Aye. Unlock me, then, and be quick aboot it, afore the earl's guards appear."

But instead of bringing the key to his shackles, she folded her arms across her chest. "Grant me a little intelligence, Ewan. I saw no other guards about. For Reginald to arrive so swiftly, he couldn't have traveled with a regiment of men."

He ground his teeth. Even now, soldiers could be storming the house, and she wanted to debate? "Tru, unlock me now and we'll discuss it later."

But she merely raised a brow and tapped a bare foot. "Is that all you have to say to me?"

Arrgh! Women. "What is it ye wish to hear? That I've wronged ye and I'm sorry? Verra well. I have and I am. And I don't want your money. I'll take ye and your people wherever ye will."

Now both her brows shot up in a haughty glare. "You say that now. When I hold the keys to your freedom."

He gave her his best ferocious glower. "I was in a temper. Ye insulted me honor.

I don't steal from innocent women. I don't want your blasted money!"

"What *do* you want, Ewan MacGowan?"

"I want ye to unlock these cuffs!"

"Hmm." She put a finger to her adorable chin and cocked her head to the side. Her long hair swayed behind her. "And what would you pay me to unlock you?"

"Pay ye?" he sputtered. "Leave off the games, milady. We've nae time for this."

"As you wish." She spun on her heel. "I hope someone finds you soon."

"Tru!" he shouted, yanking at his shackles. "I've nothin' but me ship."

She stopped and faced him again.

"But 'tis yours," he whispered.

She closed the distance between them with a slow saunter. "What would I do with a ship? No. You have something else I want."

He met her gaze, hoping she'd see the truth in his one good eye. "I'd gi' ye the world if I could, milady, just to be in your sweet company."

"Oh, I had in mind something much more useful." She placed her hand on his battered chest, and her silken touch made him shiver. Tenderly, she ran her palm over his nipple, and then pinched the tip between thumb and finger.

"Tru," he groaned.

She moved upward, combing through the hair under his vulnerable arm. He jerked away, ticklish, and winced as his ribs protested.

Her fingers left a trail of heat as they glided back to his other nipple, rubbing and tweaking it as well. "Ewan, you're so strong and muscular." Then her caress became stronger as her hand slid down over his stomach. And kept going.

He hissed in a breath and stiffened.

She pressed her palm over the front of his breeches and cupped his hardening rod.

"Aw, don't, milady," he rasped.

Ignoring him, she rubbed up and down its length while it stretched and grew. "I want your cock, Captain MacGowan." Her lips moved against his jaw, her breath caressing his battered cheek. "At my disposal until we reach our destination."

He squeezed his eyes closed, biting back a tortured moan. "Tru, unlock these damned irons," he growled through clenched teeth.

"And I want your promise." She unbuckled his belt, opened his breeches and shoved them to his knees. His cock sprang free, hard and aching. She circled the shaft and ran her thumb over the tip. "Swear that you will be *my* possession, serving my needs until I tire of you."

Swallowing past the lump in his throat, he looked down at her. "Aye, milady." He pushed into her hand. "By my troth, I so swear."

"Ewan," she whispered and rose up on tiptoes to open her lips to his.

He returned her kiss, hungry for her. For the smell of her. For the feel of her. His cuts stung, but he moved his mouth over hers, nipping at her soft lips and sweeping his tongue inside for a taste of Tru. His hands itched to be free, to wrap her in his arms and hold her and tell her how he felt.

And all the while she stroked his rigid shaft until it wept, until it had become her quivering, throbbing supplicant. Until she pulled away and his lips and cock were both left alone in the cold, reaching for her.

Every deep breath sent shooting pain to his ribs, but he gulped in air and watched her as she pushed the key into the iron manacle and popped it open. As she moved to unlock the other, her skirt brushed against his straining erection.

With his arms free, he wavered on his feet a moment, then dropped to his knees before his lady. Pinpricks tingled up and down his arms as they came back to life. He took her soft hand, which smelled of gunpowder and smoke, and placed a kiss on her knuckles.

"I'm yours to command, milady." He looked up into her eyes. "My cock. And my heart and soul as well."

Her eyes widened. "Ewan. What are you saying?"

"Aw, lass. I love ye with every breath I take. With my very life."

Her cool composure crumpled. She swayed and slumped forward, sinking to her knees with a soft cry. "I love you too."

"Aw, Tru." He caught her in his arms and held her delicate little body tight against him as she cried.

"Ewan?" She sniffed.

"Aye?" Savoring the feel of her beneath his hands, he cupped the back of her head and buried his face in her neck.

"I don't want to go to France," she said quietly.

"I'll take ye where'er ye want to go, milady. Ye and all your beloved people." He placed a kiss atop her head. "I'm yours to command."

After another sniff, her arms stole around his neck and she nuzzled against his chest. He winced a bit, but he didn't care about the pain. His Tru was in his arms.

"Ewan?"

"Aye?" He kissed her forehead.

"What if I said I wanted you to come with me to the New World? To take our money and our people and go to this New Hampshire and build a great shipping empire together?"

An ache swirled in his chest that had nothing to do with the beating. "Nae, lass. I'll nae take your money. I've caused ye enough grief."

She pushed away from him and sat back on her feet and his arms felt empty. "You said you were mine to command." Her voice hardened. "Well, I command you to use my money to begin your shipping business!" Her mouth thinned and she crossed her arms over her chest.

"Tru." He grabbed her shoulders. "Don't ask me. Ye'll need that money to live."

"Of course we will. And what better way to ensure it will last than to invest in a profitable business venture? You *can* make it profitable, can't you?"

Hope flickered somewhere deep in his heart. Instead of a life of piracy in the Caribbean, years of fighting and killing or being killed, he could establish his own shipping company in the New World.

With blinding clarity, he saw his dream coming true. The house, the veranda, the woman with the bairn.

Catching her up in his arms, he hugged her to him. "Aye, then! We sail for America. A new life. A new beginning." He dug his fingers into her thick hair and kissed her thoroughly, showing her in deed all the feelings his words couldn't express.

Her arms curled around his neck as she met his kiss with willing lips and tongue.

"Marry me, Tru! My love, my heart," he whispered against her mouth.

In answer, she slipped one hand down to wrap around his cock. "You would still be my possession?" She tugged on the shaft and caressed the tip with her finger.

He moaned low in his throat. "Aye, milady. Your servant, your true love, your husband. Your possession forever."

Chapter 8

The Atlantic Ocean, three weeks later

Ewan crashed into their cabin and slammed the door behind him. Tru rose from her seat behind the desk.

He was more handsome than ever, her Ewan. His swollen eye and bruises had healed, though his ribs were still tender. But there was something different about him now. A lightness in his step. And whenever he looked at her, there was a playful curve to his lips and a passionate spark in his eyes that spoke of love as well as lust.

"'Tis colder than a witch's teat out there!" he said as he untied his snow-laden cloak and tossed it across her Da's chest of silver.

A frisson of excitement tingled through her spine. She smoothed her hands down her skirt to hide their trembling. "Bolt the door, Husband."

Ewan froze in the act of warming his hands before the swinging lantern and glanced at her. "Mrs. Murphy will be bringin' tea."

She folded her arms and raised a brow. The last few weeks had been a frenzied blur of escaping Ireland, buying supplies and repairing the ship in the north of Scotland, and a quick marriage over the anvil. Their lovemaking had been wondrously sweet, breathtakingly marvelous. But now that his ribs were mostly healed, Tru meant to test her new husband's promise.

Mumbling under his breath, he finally did as she bade in two quick strides, then waited by the door, watching her with a devilish glint in his light green eyes.

"Now, unbind your hair and take off your clothes."

He glowered. "I'll freeze my arse off!"

Tru grabbed the bread knife from the desk and marched around to stand before him. "You promised to be my possession, Ewan MacGowan. Now, take them off, or I'll cut them off!" She forced a menacing glare.

"You're a hard-hearted woman, Wife," he grumbled, but she saw the tiny quirk to his mouth as he reached up and pulled the leather tie from his hair. When he began unbuttoning his new woolen coat, she had to clench her fists to keep from pulling his face to hers and kissing him until neither of them felt the cold.

Instead, she wandered to the desk and poured a dram of whiskey. When she'd taken a sip, she turned back to find he'd shed his waistcoat and shirt and was yanking off his boots.

She never tired of staring at the hard planes of his chest with its dark swirls of hair and tight little nipples. Took pleasure in watching the band of muscles across his flat stomach ripple as he bent to set his boots down. And waited with anticipation thrumming through her veins as his fingers went to the buttons of his buckskin breeches.

The leather bulged around his masculine parts, and Tru couldn't wait to feel his long thick cock surging inside her.

He peeled off his breeches and stood there, hands low on his hips, legs spread wide, and, poor dear, trying not to shiver. He wore a look that said he'd have his revenge sometime tonight.

How delicious.

"Go lie on the bed and stroke your cock to ready it for me."

He growled. "I'm burstin' with need for ye already, ye daft woman." But he obeyed. Pouncing onto the mattress like a large sleek cat, he turned on his side to face her and rested his head on his hand, one knee bent. Then, his gaze capturing hers, he encircled his shaft and caressed himself with a lazy, practiced finesse.

To torment him, she stood and watched him handle himself. It was a particular pleasure to observe how his manhood darkened to a deep red at the tip and began to secrete the clear fluid. How his throat tightened and his eyes closed until he finally opened them again to glare at her with a fiery gaze.

"Please, Tru," he begged in a strangled voice. But he never stopped stroking. "Come to me."

At his words, liquid heat descended from her passage and wet her thighs. How could she deny him—and herself—the pleasure of touch a moment longer? She undressed quickly and joined him on the bed. With eager hands, she rolled him to his back, straddled his thighs, and took over the pumping of his cock.

He groaned and reached up to cup her breast, but she swatted him away. "Put your hands behind your head. I'll tell you when you can touch me."

He glared at her. "Ye ask too much, Wife. Ye'll be the death o' me, ye will."

Judging from the slippery discharge coming from his slit, 'twas probably true. "Are you my possession or not, Ewan MacGowan?" She played with the reddened tip and rubbed his juices around the shaft and he groaned again.

"Aye, I'm yours!" His green eyes had darkened like the sea during a storm.

"Well, then." Starting at his forehead, she combed back his hair, and then ran a finger down his nose to his lips. She played with his lips and slid a finger inside his mouth, and he suckled it and tickled it with his tongue. After she pulled her finger free, she caressed every rough surface of his naked skin, moving slowly down from his shoulders to his navel. Around his slim hips and up his thighs behind her. And all the while, she stroked his cock until he was bucking beneath her. The muscles in his arms bunched as he fisted his hands behind his head.

"Tru, no more, I beg ye."

"Shall I make you spill on my hand, Husband?"

"Nae!" He grabbed her wrist to stop her stroking, cupped the back of her head, and pulled her down to capture her mouth.

"I need to be inside ye, lass!" he rasped against her lips, then devoured them in a desperate kiss. As he moved his mouth over hers, he flipped her to her back and massaged the soaked opening between her thighs, teasing with his fingers and rubbing his thumb across the swollen, responsive center of her pleasure.

He tasted of sea and salt and Tru raised her hips to his masterful touch. Tears of joy sprang unbidden to her eyes. It took all her strength to blink them back and pull away. "You did not have permission to remove your hands from behind your head. Perhaps I should tie them?"

'Twas a weak attempt, Tru knew. His eyes narrowed and he lifted his hand from her folds.

Oh, why had she not kept quiet?

"As ye wish, milady. I'll nae touch ye with me hands." He planted his palm on the sheet beside her and lowered his head. Slowly, he licked her nipple, teasing it with his tongue, around and around until she was writhing beneath him, whimpering.

"Ewan." She twined her fingers into his long brown locks and guided his mouth to her other breast.

"Aye, milady?" he asked around her other nipple, then flicked his tongue over the very tip and pulled it between his teeth.

"You—" She moaned as he suckled hard. "You may use your hands now."

"But, mistress." He lifted his head and flashed a wicked smile. "My mouth has jus' begun." Bending from the waist, he dove between her legs, pulled her thighs apart, and sank his mouth between her folds.

Heaven. Tru smiled and raised her hips to meet his eager tongue. Surely this was heaven on earth. She gasped as he lapped at her slit and nuzzled deeper for more. But one thing was missing.

"Ewan." She scooted close to his hips.

"Mmm?" His fingers had crept from her thighs to pull her nether lips apart and thrust a middle finger inside her.

"Straddle my shoulders, my love."

A moment's hesitation, then he moved as she requested and she had what she wanted, his cock, stiff against his stomach. She reached up, pulled it down and surrounded the moist tip with her lips.

A long groaned rumbled in his chest and he widened his thighs until the column sank into her mouth. She suckled him and pumped the silky flesh. He moved his hips to her erotic rhythm. But there was one more thing she wished to try. With her free hand she fondled his seed sac, then slid her finger up and pressed it against his puckered hole as he'd once touched her.

His attention to her sensitive nubbin lapsed. "Tru?"

"Mmm?" She pushed in.

"Och!" When he rose off her she let go of his cock with a pop and rolled up to meet him. His breathing fast, he sat beside her, facing her.

"I was merely trying to warm your—your arse." She fluttered her lashes and presumed an innocent look.

He gripped her shoulders and caught her to him. "'Tis enow, Wife!" His lips were shiny with the pungent evidence of her desire and she smelled herself as he swept his kisses over her shoulder and into her neck. "I've been thinkin' on our arrangement." He pushed her down and moved over her, shoving her legs wide as he sank between them. "And it seems to me, ye ne'er paid me my fifty pieces of eight." He took his cock in hand and guided it to her entrance.

"Oh?" She clutched the muscles of his upper arms and squirmed beneath him.

"Nae. Ye didna." He pushed just the tip inside her. "So, you're still my possession!" He thrust deep and Tru cried out at the exquisite ache.

They were one at last.

"I am yours, my beloved pirate." She moved her hands to his buttocks as he pulled out and drove back in.

"Aye." He worked in her, lifting away, then plunging deep again and again until she arched beneath him and cried his name. With a tremulous shudder he followed her into dizzying ecstasy, spurting his seed and collapsing beside her.

"And I'm still yours, my lady Tru."

About the Author:

Having had the good luck to be born in Texas, Juliet can't imagine living anywhere else. She's lucky to share her life with a supportive husband, three rambunctious children, and a sweet Golden Retriever. She likes to think her emotional nature—sometimes referred to as moodiness by those closest to her—has found the perfect outlet in writing passionate stories late at night after the house gets quiet. Juliet loves reading romance novels and believes they have the power to change lives with their eternal message of love and hope.

Men you've been dreaming about!

Secrets

Satisfy your desire for more.

*F*eel the wild adventure, fierce passion and the power of love in every **Secrets** Collection story. Red Sage Publishing's romance authors create richly crafted, sexy, sensual, novella-length stories. Each one is just the right length for reading after a long and hectic day.

Each volume in the **Secrets** Collection has four diverse, ultra-sexy, romantic novellas brimming with adventure, passion and love. More adventurous tales for the adventurous reader. The **Secrets** Collection are a glorious mix of romance genre; numerous historical settings, contemporary, paranormal, science fiction and suspense. We are always looking for new adventures.

Reader response to the **Secrets** volumes has been great! Here's just a small sample:

"I loved the variety of settings. Four completely wonderful time periods, give you four completely wonderful reads."

"Each story was a page-turning tale I hated to put down."

*"I love **Secrets**! When is the next volume coming out? This one was Hot! Loved the heroes!"*

Secrets have won raves and awards. We could go on, but why don't you find out for yourself—order your set of **Secrets** today! See the back for details.

Secrets, Volume 1

A Lady's Quest by Bonnie Hamre
Widowed Lady Antonia Blair-Sutworth searches for a lover to save her from the handsome Duke of Sutherland. The "auditions" may be shocking but utterly tantalizing.

The Spinner's Dream by Alice Gaines
A seductive fantasy that leaves every woman wishing for her own private love slave, desperate and running for his life.

The Proposal by Ivy Landon
This tale is a walk on the wild side of love. *The Proposal* will taunt you, tease you, and shock you. A contemporary erotica for the adventurous woman.

The Gift by Jeanie LeGendre
Immerse yourself in this historic tale of exotic seduction, bondage and a concubine's surrender to the Sultan's desire. Can Alessandra live the life and give the gift the Sultan demands of her?

Secrets, Volume 2

Surrogate Lover by Doreen DeSalvo
Adrian Ross is a surrogate sex therapist who has all the answers and control. He thought he'd seen and done it all, but he'd never met Sarah.

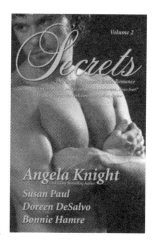

Snowbound by Bonnie Hamre
A delicious, sensuous regency tale. The marriage-shy Earl of Howden is teased and tortured by his own desires and finds there is a woman who can equal his overpowering sensuality.

Roarke's Prisoner by Angela Knight
Elise, a starship captain, remembers the eager animal submission she'd known before at her captor's hands and refuses to become his toy again. However, she has no idea of the delights he's planned for her this time.

Savage Garden by Susan Paul
Raine's been captured by a mysterious and dangerous revolutionary leader in Mexico. At first her only concern is survival, but she quickly finds lush erotic nights in her captor's arms.

Winner of the Fallot Literary Award for Fiction!

Secrets, Volume 3

The Spy Who Loved Me by Jeanie Cesarini
Undercover FBI agent Paige Ellison's sexual appetites
rise to new levels when she works with leading man
Christopher Sharp, the cunning agent who uses all his
training to capture her body and heart.

The Barbarian by Ann Jacobs
Lady Brianna vows not to surrender to the barbaric
Giles, Earl of Harrow. He must use sexual arts
learned in the infidels' harem to conquer his bride. A
word of caution—this is not for the faint of heart.

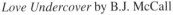

Blood and Kisses by Angela Knight
A vampire assassin is after Beryl St. Cloud. Her only
hope lies with Decker, another vampire and ex-merce-
nary. Broke, she offers herself as payment for his services. Will his seductive powers
take her very soul?

Love Undercover by B.J. McCall
Amanda Forbes is the bait in a strip joint sting operation. While she performs, fellow
detective "Cowboy" Cooper gets to watch. Though he excites her, she must fight the
temptation to surrender to the passion.

Winner of the 1997 Under the Covers Readers Favorite Award

Secrets, Volume 4

An Act of Love by Jeanie Cesarini
Shelby Moran's past left her terrified of sex. International film star Jason Gage must gently coach the young
starlet in the ways of love. He wants more than an act—
he wants Shelby to feel true passion in his arms.

Enslaved by Desirée Lindsey
Lord Nicholas Summer's air of danger, dark passions,
and irresistible charm have brought Lady Crystal's
long-hidden desires to the surface. Will he be able to
give her the one thing she desires before it's too late?

The Bodyguard by Betsy Morgan & Susan Paul
Kaki York is a bodyguard, but watching the wild,
erotic romps of her client's sexual conquests on the
security cameras is getting to her—and her partner, the ruggedly handsome James
Kulick. Can she resist his insistent desire to have her?

The Love Slave by Emma Holly
A woman's ultimate fantasy. For one year, Princess Lily will be attended to by three
delicious men of her choice. While she delights in playing with the first two, it's the
reluctant Grae, with his powerful chest, black eyes and hair, that stirs her desires.

Secrets, Volume 5

Beneath Two Moons by Sandy Fraser
Step into the future and find Conor, rough and masculine like frontiermen of old, on the prowl for a new conquest. In his sights, Dr. Eva Kelsey. She got away before, but this time Conor makes sure she begs for more.

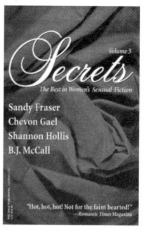

Insatiable by Chevon Gael
Marcus Remington photographs beautiful models for a living, but it's Ashlyn Fraser, a young exec having some glamour shots done, who has stolen his heart. It's up to Marcus to help her discover her inner sexual self.

Strictly Business by Shannon Hollis
Elizabeth Forrester knows it's tough enough for a woman to make it to the top in the corporate world. Garrett Hill, the most beautiful man in Silicon Valley, has to come along to stir up her wildest fantasies. Dare she give in to both their desires?

Alias Smith and Jones by B.J. McCall
Meredith Collins finds herself stranded at the airport. A handsome stranger by the name of Smith offers her sanctuary for the evening and she finds those mesmerizing, green-flecked eyes hard to resist. Are they to be just two ships passing in the night?

Secrets, Volume 6

Flint's Fuse by Sandy Fraser
Dana Madison's father has her "kidnapped" for her own safety. Flint, the tall, dark and dangerous mercenary, is hired for the job. But just which one is the prisoner—Dana will try *anything* to get away.

Love's Prisoner by MaryJanice Davidson
Trapped in an elevator, Jeannie Lawrence experienced unwilling rapture at Michael Windham's hands. She never expected the devilishly handsome man to show back up in her life—or turn out to be a werewolf!

The Education of Miss Felicity Wells by Alice Gaines
Felicity Wells wants to be sure she'll satisfy her soon-to-be husband but she needs a teacher. Dr. Marcus Slade, an experienced lover, agrees to take her on as a student, but can he stop short of taking her completely?

A Candidate for the Kiss by Angela Knight
Working on a story, reporter Dana Ivory stumbles onto a more amazing one—a sexy, secret agent who happens to be a vampire. She wants her story but Gabriel Archer wants more from her than just sex and blood.

Secrets, Volume 7

Amelia's Innocence by Julia Welles
Amelia didn't know her father bet her in a card game
with Captain Quentin Hawke, so honor demands a
compromise—three days of erotic foreplay, leaving
her virginity and future intact.

The Woman of His Dreams by Jade Lawless
From the day artist Gray Avonaco moves in next door,
Joanna Morgan is plagued by provocative dreams.
But what she believes is unrequited lust, Gray sees
as another chance to be with the woman he loves. He
must persuade her that even death can't stop true love.

Surrender by Kathryn Anne Dubois
Free-spirited Lady Johanna wants no part of the bind-
ing strictures society imposes with her marriage to the powerful Duke. She doesn't
know the dark Duke wants sensual adventure, and sexual satisfaction.

Kissing the Hunter by Angela Knight
Navy Seal Logan McLean hunts the vampires who murdered his wife. Virginia Hart
is a sexy vampire searching for her lost soul-mate only to find him in a man determined to kill her. She must convince him all vampires aren't created equally.

Winner of the Venus Book Club Best Book of the Year

Secrets, Volume 8

Taming Kate by Jeanie Cesarini
Kathryn Roman inherits a legal brothel. Little does
this city girl know the town wants her to be their new
madam so they've charged Trey Holliday, one very
dominant cowboy, with taming her.

Jared's Wolf by MaryJanice Davidson
Jared Rocke will do anything to avenge his sister's
death, but ends up attracted to Moira Wolfbauer, the
she-wolf sworn to protect her pack. Joining forces to
stop a killer, they learn love defies all boundaries.

My Champion, My Lover by Alice Gaines
Celeste Broder is a woman committed for having a sexy
appetite. Mayor Robert Albright may be her champion—
if she can convince him her freedom will mean they can indulge their appetites together.

Kiss or Kill by Liz Maverick
In this post-apocalyptic world, Camille Kazinsky's military career rides on her ability to make a choice—whether the robo called Meat should live or die. Can he prove
he's human enough to live, man enough… to make her feel like a woman.

Winner of the Venus Book Club Best Book of the Year

Secrets, Volume 9

Wild For You by Kathryn Anne Dubois
When college intern, Georgie, gets captured by a
Congo wildman, she discovers this specimen of male
virility has never seen a woman. The research possibilities are endless!

Wanted by Kimberly Dean
FBI Special Agent Jeff Reno wants Danielle Carver.
There's her body, brains—and that charge of treason
on her head. Dani goes on the run, but the sexy Fed is
hot on her trail.

Secluded by Lisa Marie Rice
Nicholas Lee's wealth and power came with a price—
his enemies will kill anyone he loves. When Isabelle
steals his heart, Nicholas secludes her in his palace for a lifetime of desire in only a
few days.

Flights of Fantasy by Bonnie Hamre
Chloe taught others to see the realities of life but she's never shared the intimate
world of her sensual yearnings. Given the chance, will she be woman enough to
fulfill her most secret erotic fantasy?

Secrets, Volume 10

Private Eyes by Dominique Sinclair
When a mystery man captivates P.I. Nicolla Black
during a stakeout, she discovers her no-seduction rule
bending under the pressure of long denied passion.
She agrees to the seduction, but he demands her total
surrender.

The Ruination of Lady Jane by Bonnie Hamre
To avoid her upcoming marriage, Lady Jane Ponson-
by-Maitland flees into the arms of Havyn Attercliffe.
She begs him to ruin her rather than turn her over to
her odious fiancé.

Code Name: Kiss by Jeanie Cesarini
Agent Lily Justiss is on a mission to defend her country
against terrorists that requires giving up her virginity as a sex slave. As her master
takes her body, desire for her commanding officer Seth Blackthorn fuels her mind.

The Sacrifice by Kathryn Anne Dubois
Lady Anastasia Bedovier is days from taking her vows as a Nun. Before she denies
her sensuality forever, she wants to experience pleasure. Count Maxwell is the perfect man to initiate her into erotic delight.

Secrets, Volume 11

Masquerade by Jennifer Probst
Hailey Ashton is determined to free herself from her
sexual restrictions. Four nights of erotic pleasures
without revealing her identity. A chance to explore her
secret desires without the fear of unmasking.

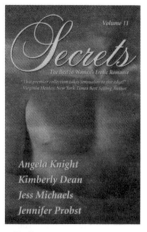

Ancient Pleasures by Jess Michaels
Isabella Winslow is obsessed with finding out what
caused her husband's death, but trapped in an Egyp-
tian concubine's tomb with a sexy American raider,
succumbing to the mummy's sensual curse takes over.

Manhunt by Kimberly Dean
Framed for murder, Michael Tucker takes Taryn
Swanson hostage—the one woman who can clear him.
Despite the evidence against him, the attraction is strong. Tucker resorts to uncon-
ventional, yet effective methods of persuasion to change the sexy ADA's mind.

Wake Me by Angela Knight
Chloe Hart received a sexy painting of a sleeping knight. Radolf of Varik has been
trapped there for centuries, cursed by a witch. His only hope is to visit the dreams of
women and make one of them fall in love with him so she can free him with a kiss.

Secrets, Volume 12

Good Girl Gone Bad by Dominique Sinclair
Setting out to do research for an article, nothing could
have prepared Reagan for Luke, or his offer to teach
her everything she needs to know about sex. Licen-
tious pleasures, forbidden desires... inspiring the best
writing she's ever done.

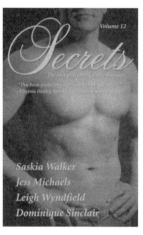

Aphrodite's Passion by Jess Michaels
When Selena flees Victorian London before her evil
stepchildren can institutionalize her for hysteria,
Gavin is asked to bring her back home. But when he
finds her living on the island of Cyprus, his need to
have her begins to block out every other impulse.

White Heat by Leigh Wyndfield
Raine is hiding in an icehouse in the middle of nowhere from one of the scariest men
in the universes. Walker escaped from a burning prison. Imagine their surprise when
they find out they have the same man to blame for their miseries. Passion, revenge
and love are in their future.

Summer Lightning by Saskia Walker
Sculptress Sally is enjoying an idyllic getaway on a secluded cove when she spots a
gorgeous man walking naked on the beach. When Julian finds an attractive woman
shacked up in his cove, he has to check her out. But what will he do when he finds
she's secretly been using him as a model?

Secrets, Volume 13

Out of Control by Rachelle Chase
Astrid's world revolves around her business and she's hoping to pick up wealthy Erik Santos as a client. He's hoping to pick up something entirely different. Will she give in to the seductive pull of his proposition?

Hawkmoor by Amber Green
Shape-shifters answer to Darien as he acts in the name of long-missing Lady Hawkmoor, their ruler. When she unexpectedly surfaces, Darien must deal with a scrappy individual whose wary eyes hold the other half of his soul, but who has the power to destroy his world.

Lessons in Pleasure by Charlotte Featherstone
A wicked bargain has Lily vowing never to yield to the demands of the rake she once loved and lost. Unfortunately, Damian, the Earl of St. Croix, or Saint as he is infamously known, will not take 'no' for an answer.

In the Heat of the Night by Calista Fox
Haunted by a curse, Molina fears she won't live to see her 30th birthday. Nick, her former bodyguard, is re-hired to protect her from the fatal accidents that plague her family. Will his passion and love be enough to convince Molina they have a future together?

Secrets, Volume 14

Soul Kisses by Angela Knight
Beth's been kidnapped by Joaquin Ramirez, a sadistic vampire. Handsome vampire cousins, Morgan and Garret Axton, come to her rescue. Can she find happiness with two vampires?

Temptation in Time by Alexa Aames
Ariana escaped the Middle Ages after stealing a kiss of magic from sexy sorcerer, Marcus de Grey. When he brings her back, they begin a battle of wills and a sexual odyssey that could spell disaster for them both.

Ailis and the Beast by Jennifer Barlowe
When Ailis agreed to be her village's sacrifice to the mysterious Beast she was prepared to sacrifice her virtue, and possibly her life. But some things aren't what they seem. Ailis and the Beast are about to discover the greatest sacrifice may be the human heart.

Night Heat by Leigh Wynfield
When Rip Bowhite leads a revolt on the prison planet, he ends up struggling to survive against monsters that rule the night. Jemma, the prison's Healer, won't allow herself to be distracted by the instant attraction she feels for Rip. As the stakes are raised and death draws near, love seems doomed in the heat of the night.

Secrets, Volume 15

Simon Says by Jane Thompson
Simon Campbell is a newspaper columnist who panders to male fantasies. Georgina Kennedy is a respectable librarian. On the surface, these two have nothing in common... but don't judge a book by its cover.

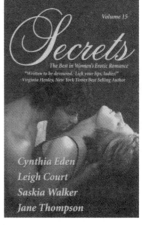

Bite of the Wolf by Cynthia Eden
Gareth Morlet, alpha werewolf, has finally found his mate. All he has to do is convince Trinity to join with him, to give in to the pleasure of a werewolf's mating, and then she will be his... forever.

Falling for Trouble by Saskia Walker
With 48 hours to clear her brother's name, Sonia Harmond finds help from irresistible bad boy, Oliver Eaglestone. When the erotic tension between them hits fever pitch, securing evidence to thwart an international arms dealer isn't the only danger they face.

The Disciplinarian by Leigh Court
Headstrong Clarissa Babcock is sent for instruction in proper wifely obedience. Disciplinarian Jared Ashworth uses the tools of seduction to show her how to control a demanding husband, but her beauty, spirit, and uninhibited passion make Jared hunger to keep her—and their darkly erotic nights—all for himself!

Secrets, Volume 16

Never Enough by Cynthia Eden
Abby McGill has been playing with fire. Bad-boy Jake taught her the true meaning of desire, but she knows she has to end her relationship with him. But Jake isn't about to let the woman he wants walk away from him.

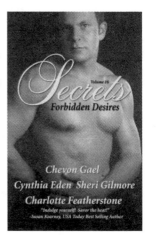

Bunko by Sheri Gilmoore
Tu Tran must decide between Jack, who promises to share every aspect of his life with her, or Dev, who hides behind a mask and only offers nights of erotic sex. Will she gamble on the man who can see behind her own mask and expose her true desires?

Hide and Seek by Chevon Gael
Kyle DeLaurier ditches his trophy-fiance in favor of a tropical paradise full of tall, tanned, topless females. Private eye, Darcy McLeod, is on the trail of this runaway groom. Together they sizzle while playing Hide and Seek with their true identities.

Seduction of the Muse by Charlotte Featherstone
He's the Dark Lord, the mysterious author who pens the erotic tales of an innocent woman's seduction. She is his muse, the woman he watches from the dark shadows, the woman whose dreams he invades at night.

Secrets, Volume 17

Rock Hard Candy by Kathy Kaye
Jessica Hennessy, descendent of a Voodoo priestess, decides it's time for the man of her dreams. A dose of her ancestor's aphrodisiac slipped into the gooey center of her homemade bon bons ought to do the trick.

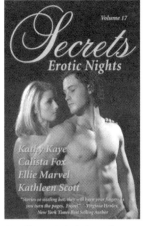

Fatal Error by Kathleen Scott
Jesse Storm must make amends to humanity by destroying the software he helped design that's taken the government hostage. But he must also protect the woman he's loved in secret for nearly a decade.

Birthday by Ellie Marvel
Jasmine Templeton's been celibate long enough. Will a wild night at a hot new club with her two best friends ease the ache or just make it worse? Considering one is Charlie and she's been having strange notions about their relationship of late… It's definitely a birthday neither she nor Charlie will ever forget.

Intimate Rendezvous by Calista Fox
A thief causes trouble at Cassandra Kensington's nightclub and sexy P.I. Dean Hewitt arrives to help. One look at her sends his blood boiling, despite the fact that his keen instincts have him questioning the legitimacy of her business.

Secrets, Volume 18

Lone Wolf Three by Rae Monet
Planetary politics and squabbling drain former rebel leader Taban Zias. But his anger quickly turns to desire when he meets, Lakota Blackson. She's Taban's perfect mate—now if he can just convince her.

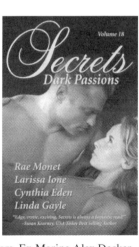

Flesh to Fantasy by Larissa Ione
Kelsa Bradshaw is a loner happily immersed in a world of virtual reality. Trent Jordan is a paramedic who experiences the harsh realities of life. When their worlds collide in an erotic eruption can Trent convince Kelsa to turn the fantasy into something real?

Heart Full of Stars by Linda Gayle
Singer Fanta Rae finds herself stranded on a lonely Mars outpost with the first human male she's seen in years. Ex-Marine Alex Decker lost his family and guilt drove him into isolation, but when alien assassins come to enslave Fanta, she and Decker come together to fight for their lives.

The Wolf's Mate by Cynthia Eden
When Michael Morlet finds "Kat" Hardy fighting for her life, he instantly recognizes her as the mate he's been seeking all of his life, but someone's trying to kill her. With danger stalking them, will Kat trust him enough to become his mate?

Secrets, Volume 19

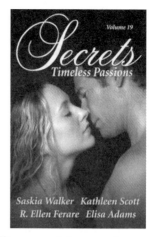

Affliction by Elisa Adams
Holly Aronson finally believes she's safe with sweet Andrew. But when his life long friend, Shane, arrives, events begin to spiral out of control. She's inexplicably drawn to Shane. As she runs for her life, which one will protect her?

Falling Stars by Kathleen Scott
Daria is both a Primon fighter pilot and a Primon princess. As a deadly new enemy faces appears, she must choose between her duty to the fleet and the desperate need to forge an alliance through her marriage to the enemy's General Raven.

Saskia Walker Kathleen Scott
R. Ellen Ferare Elisa Adams

Toy in the Attic by R. Ellen Ferare
Gabrielle discovers a life-sized statue of a nude man. Her unexpected roommate reveals himself to be a talented lover caught by a witch's curse. Can she help him break free of the spell that holds him, without losing her heart along the way?

What You Wish For by Saskia Walker
Lucy Chambers is renovating her historic house. As her dreams about a stranger become more intense, she wishes he were with her. Two hundred years in the past, the man wishes for companionship. Suddenly they find themselves together—in his time.

Secrets, Volume 20

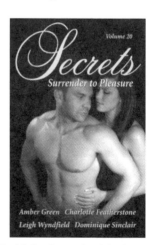

The Subject by Amber Green
One week Tyler is a game designer, signing the deal of her life. The next, she's running for her life. Who can she trust? Certainly not sexy, mysterious Esau, who keeps showing up after the hoo-hah hits the fan!

Surrender by Dominique Sinclair
Agent Madeline Carter is in too deep. She's slipped into Sebastian Maiocco's life to investigate his Sicilian mafia family. He unearths desires Madeline's unable to deny, conflicting the duty that honors her. Madeline must surrender to Sebastian or risk being exposed, leaving her target for a ruthless clan.

Amber Green Charlotte Featherstone
Leigh Wyndfield Dominique Sinclair

Stasis by Leigh Wyndfield
Morgann Right's Commanding Officer's been drugged with Stasis, turning him into a living statue she's forced to take care of for ten long days. As her hands tend to him, she sees her CO in a totally different light. She wants him and, while she can tell he wants her, touching him intimately might come back to haunt them both.

A Woman's Pleasure by Charlotte Featherstone
Widowed Isabella, Lady Langdon is yearning to discover all the pleasures denied her in her marriage, she finds herself falling hard for the magnetic charms of the mysterious and exotic Julian Gresham—a man skilled in pleasures of the flesh.

Secrets, Volume 21

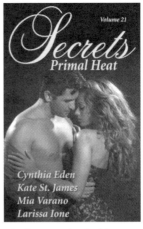

Caged Wolf by Cynthia Eden
Alerac La Morte has been drugged and kidnapped.
He realizes his captor, Madison Langley, is actually
his destined mate, but she hates his kind. Will Alerac
convince her he's not the monster she thinks?

Wet Dreams by Larissa Ione
Injured and on the run, agent Brent Logan needs a
miracle. What he gets is a boat owned by Marina
Summers. Pursued by killers, ravaged by a storm,
and plagued by engine troubles, they can do little but
spend their final hours immersed in sensual pleasure.

Good Vibrations by Kate St. James
Lexi O'Brien vows to swear off sex while she attends
grad school, so when her favorite out-of-town customer asks her out, she decides to
indulge in an erotic fling. Little does she realize Gage Templeton is moving home, to
her city, and has no intention of settling for a short-term affair..

Virgin of the Amazon by Mia Varano
Librarian Anna Winter gets lost on the Amazon and stumbles upon a tribe whose
shaman wants a pale-skinned virgin to deflower. British adventurer Coop Daventry,
the tribe's self-styled chief, wants to save her, but which man poses a greater threat?

Secrets, Volume 22

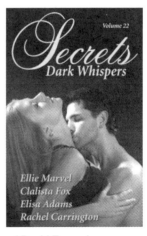

Heat by Ellie Marvel
Mild-mannered alien Tarkin is in heat and the only
compatible female is a Terran. He courts her the old
fashioned Terran way. Because if he can't seduce her
before his cycle ends, he won't get a second chance.

Breathless by Rachel Carrington
Lark Hogan is a martial arts expert seeking vengeance for the death of her sister. She seeks help
from Zac, a mercenary wizard. Confronting a common enemy, they battle their own demons as well as
their powerful attraction, and will fight to the death
to protect what they've found.

Midnight Rendezvous by Calista Fox
From New York to Cabo to Paris to Tokyo, Cat Hewitt and David Essex share
decadent midnight rendezvous. But when the real world presses in on their erotic
fantasies, and Cat's life is in danger, will their whirlwind romance stand a chance?

Birthday Wish by Elisa Adams
Anna Kelly had many goals before turning 30 and only one is left—to spend one
night with sexy Dean Harrison. When Dean asks her what she wants for her birthday, she grabs at the opportunity to ask him for an experience she'll never forget.

Secrets, Volume 23

The Sex Slave by Roxi Romano
Jaci Coe needs a hero and the hard bodied man in black meets all the criteria. Opportunistic Jaci takes advantage of Lazarus Stone's commandingly protective nature, but together, they learn how to live free... and love freely.

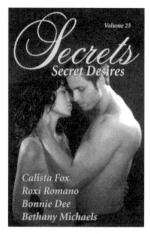

Forever My Love by Calista Fox
Professor Aja Woods is a 16th century witch... only she doesn't know it. Christian St. James, her vampire lover, has watched over her spirit for 500 years. When her powers are recovered, so too are her memories of Christian—and the love they once shared.

Reflection of Beauty by Bonnie Dee
Artist Christine Dawson is commissioned to paint a portrait of wealthy recluse, Eric Leroux. It's up to her to reach the heart of this physically and emotionally scarred man. Can love rescue Eric from isolation and restore his life?

Educating Eva by Bethany Lynn
Eva Blakely attends the infamous Ivy Hill houseparty to gather research for her book *Mating Rituals of the Human Male*. But when she enlists the help of research "specimen" and notorious rake, Aidan Worthington, she gets some unexpected results.

Secrets, Volume 24

Hot on Her Heels by Mia Varano
Private investigator Jack Slater dons a g-string to investigate the Lollipop Lounge, a male strip club. He's not sure if the club's sexy owner, Vivica Steele, is involved in the scam, but Jack figures he's just the Lollipop to sweeten her life.

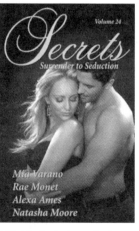

Shadow Wolf by Rae Monet
A half-breed Lupine challenges a high-ranking Solarian Wolf Warrior. When Dia Nahiutras tries to steal Roark D'Reincolt's wolf, does she get an enemy forever or a mate for life?

Bad to the Bone by Natasha Moore
At her class reunion, Annie Shane sheds her good girl reputation through one wild weekend with Luke Kendall. But Luke is done playing the field and wants to settle down. What would a bad girl do?

War God by Alexa Ames
Estella Eaton, a lovely graduate student, is the unwitting carrier of the essence of Aphrodite. But Ares, god of war, the ultimate alpha male, knows the truth and becomes obsessed with Estelle, pursuing her relentlessly. Can her modern sensibilities and his ancient power coexist, or will their battle of wills destroy what matters most?

Secrets, Volume 25

Blood Hunt by Cynthia Eden
Vampiress Nema Alexander has a taste for bad boys.
Slade Brion has just been charged with tracking her
down. He won't stop until he catches her, and Nema
won't stop until she claims him, forever.

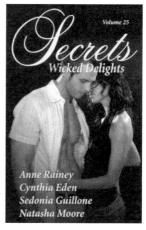

Scandalous Behavior by Anne Rainey
Tess Marley wants to take a walk on the wild side.
Who better to teach her about carnal pleasures than
her intriguing boss, Kevin Haines? But Tess makes
a major miscalculation when she crosses the line
between lust and love.

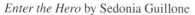

Enter the Hero by Sedonia Guillone
Kass and Lian are sentenced to sex slavery in the
Confederation's pleasure district. Forced to make love for an audience, their hearts
are with each other while their bodies are on display. Now, in the midst of sexual
slavery, they have one more chance to escape to Paradise.

Up to No Good by Natasha Moore
Former syndicated columnist Simon "Mac" MacKenzie hides a tragic secret. When
freelance writer Alison Chandler tracks him down, he knows she's up to no good. Is
their attraction merely a distraction or the key to surviving their war of wills?

Secrets, Volume 26

Secret Rendezvous by Calista Fox
McCarthy Portman has seen enough happily-
ever-afters to long for one of her own, but when her
renowned matchmaking software pairs her with the
wild and wicked Josh Kensington, everything she's
always believed about love is turned upside down.

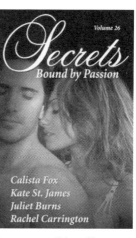

Enchanted Spell by Rachel Carrington
Witches and wizards don't mix. Every magical being
knows that. Yet, when a little mischievous magic
thrusts Ella and Kevlin together, they do so much
more than mix—they combust.

Exes and Ahhhs by Kate St. James
Former lovers Risa Haber and Eric Lange are partners
in a catering business, but Eric can't seem to remain a silent partner. Risa offers one
night of carnal delights if he'll sell her his share then disappear forever.

The Spy's Surrender by Juliet Burns
The famous courtesan Eva Werner is England's secret weapon against Napoleon. Her
orders are to attend a sadistic marquis' depraved house party and rescue a British spy
being held prisoner. As the weekend orgy begins, she's forced to make the spy her
love slave for the marquis' pleasure. But who is slave and who is master?

Secrets, Volume 27

Heart Storm by Liane Gentry Skye
Sirenia must mate with the only merman who can save
her kind, but when she rescues Navy SEAL Byron
Burke, she seals herself into his life debt. Will her
heart stand in the way of the last hope for her kind?

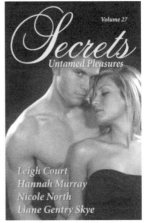

The Boy Next Door by Hannah Murray
Isabella Carelli isn't just looking for Mr. Right, she's
looking for Mr. Tie Me Up And Do Me Right. In all
the wrong places. Fortunately, the boy next door is just
about ready to make his move...

Devil in a Kilt by Nicole North
A trip to the Highland Games turns into a trip to the
past when modern day Shauna MacRae touches Gavin
MacTavish's 400-year-old claymore. Can she break the curse imprisoning this *Devil
in a Kilt* before an evil witch sends her back and takes Gavin as her sex slave?

The Bet by Leigh Court
A very drunk Damian Hunt claims he can make a woman come with just words. He
bets his prized racehorse that he can do it while George Beringer gambles his London townhouse that he can't. George chooses his virginal sister, Claire, for the bet.
Once Damian lays eyes on her, the stakes escalate in the most unpredictable way...

Secrets, Volume 28

Kiss Me at Midnight by Kate St. James
Callie Hutchins and Marc Shaw fake an on-air
romance to top the sweeps. Callie thinks Marc is a
womanizer, but as the month progresses, she realizes
he's funny, kind, and too sexy for words, damn it.

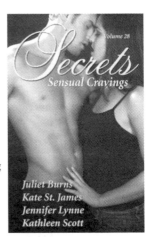

Mind Games by Kathleen Scott
Damien Storm is a Varti—a psychic who can communicate telepathically to one special person. Fear
has kept his Vartek partner, Jade, from acknowledging
their link. He must save her from the forces who wish
to see all Varti destroyed.

Seducing Serena by Jennifer Lynne
Serena Hewitt has given up on love, but when she
interviews for a potential partner she's not prepared for her overpowering sexual
attraction to Nicholas Wade, a fun-loving bachelor with bad-boy good looks and a
determination to prove her wrong.

Pirate's Possession by Juliet Burns
When Lady Gertrude Fitzpatrick bargains with a fierce pirate for escape, but unwittingly becomes the possession of a fierce privateer. Ewan MacGowan has been
betrayed and mistakenly exacts revenge on this proud noblewoman. He may have
stolen the lady's innocence, but he also finds the true woman of his heart.

The Forever Kiss
by Angela Knight

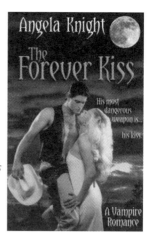

Listen to what reviewers say:

"*The Forever Kiss* flows well with good characters and an interesting plot. ... If you enjoy vampires and a lot of hot sex, you are sure to enjoy *The Forever Kiss*."

—*The Best Reviews*

"Battling vampires, a protective ghost and the ever present battle of good and evil keep excellent pace with the erotic delights in Angela Knight's *The Forever Kiss*—a book that absolutely bites with refreshing paranormal humor." **4½ Stars, Top Pick**

—*Romantic Times BOOKclub*

"I found *The Forever Kiss* to be an exceptionally written, refreshing book. ... I really enjoyed this book by Angela Knight. ... 5 angels!"

—*Fallen Angel Reviews*

"*The Forever Kiss* is the first single title released from Red Sage and if this is any indication of what we can expect, it won't be the last. ... The love scenes are hot enough to give a vampire a sunburn and the fight scenes will have you cheering for the good guys."

—*Really Bad Barb Reviews*

In *The Forever Kiss*:

For years, Valerie Chase has been haunted by dreams of a Texas Ranger she knows only as "Cowboy." As a child, he rescued her from the nightmare vampires who murdered her parents. As an adult, she still dreams of him—but now he's her seductive lover in nights of erotic pleasure.

Yet "Cowboy" is more than a dream—he's the real Cade McKinnon—and a vampire! For years, he's protected Valerie from Edward Ridgemont, the sadistic vampire who turned him. Now, Ridgmont wants Valerie for his own and Cade is the only one who can protect her.

When Val finds herself abducted by her handsome dream man, she's appalled to discover he's one of the vampires she fears. Now, caught in a web of fear and passion, she and Cade must learn to trust each other, even as an immortal monster stalks their every move.

Their only hope of survival is... *The Forever Kiss*.

Romantic Times Best Erotic Novel of the Year

Object of Desire
by Calista Fox

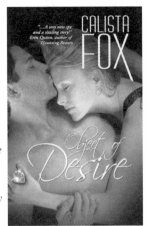

Listen to what reviewers say:
"Bombings, kidnappings and hot, hot sex fill the pages of this engaging story. Not only are the alpha hero and heroine strong, they have intriguing flaws too."
> —*Romantic Times Magazine*

"…a sexy new spy and a sizzling hot story."
> —*Erin Quinn, author of Haunting Beauty*

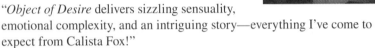

"*Object of Desire* delivers sizzling sensuality, emotional complexity, and an intriguing story—everything I've come to expect from Calista Fox!"
> —*Rachelle Chase, author of The Sin Club and The Sex Lounge*

"*Object of Desire* was a very good book! The plot was fast paced, the adventure was thrilling, and the espionage angle added a whole new edge to the book. The developing relationship between Devon and Laurel was fun to watch, and the romance between them was intense! … I loved it!"
> —*Romance Junkies*

In *Object of Desire*:
When treasure hunter and spy Laurel Blackwood raids Victoria Peak in Belize to recover a rare Mexican fire opal rumored to evoke dark desires and passions, she unwittingly sets off a sequence of dangerous events—and finds herself in the midst of a battle between good and evil… and lust and love. Being chased through the Yucatan jungle is perilous enough, but Laurel must also keep the opal from falling into the hands of a deadly terrorist cell, a greedy Belizean dignitary, and one particularly hot and scandalous treasure hunter named Devon Mallory.

For ten years, Devon has had his eye on the thirty-million-dollar prized opal and his heart set on winning Laurel for keeps. But her web of secrecy and now her betrayal over recovering the legendary stone without him has Devon hell-bent on stealing the opal from her and collecting on the massive pay-out. Unfortunately for Devon, there is much more to Laurel Blackwood than she lets on. And soon, he's caught in the eye of the storm—falling under her sensuous spell, willing to put his own life on the line to help her protect the mystical jewel.

But Devon will eventually have to decide which gem is his true object of desire…

Check out our hot eBook titles available online at eRedSage.com!

Visit the site regularly as we're always adding new eBook titles.

Here's just some of what you'll find:

A Christmas Cara by Bethany Michaels

A Damsel in Distress by Brenda Williamson

Blood Game by Rae Monet

Fires Within by Roxana Blaze

Forbidden Fruit by Anne Rainey

High Voltage by Calista Fox

Master of the Elements by Alice Gaines

One Wish by Calista Fox

Quinn's Curse by Natasha Moore

Rock My World by Caitlyn Willows

The Doctor Next Door by Catherine Berlin

Unclaimed by Nathalie Gray

Red Sage Publishing Order Form:

(Orders shipped in two to three days of receipt.)

Each volume of *Secrets* retails for $12.99, but you can get it direct via mail order for only $10.99 each. Novels retail for $14.00, but by direct mail order, you only pay $12.00. Use the order form below to place your direct mail order. Fill in the quantity you want for each book on the blanks beside the title.

_____ *Secrets* Volume 1	_____ *Secrets* Volume 12	_____ *Secrets* Volume 23
_____ *Secrets* Volume 2	_____ *Secrets* Volume 13	_____ *Secrets* Volume 24
_____ *Secrets* Volume 3	_____ *Secrets* Volume 14	_____ *Secrets* Volume 25
_____ *Secrets* Volume 4	_____ *Secrets* Volume 15	_____ *Secrets* Volume 26
_____ *Secrets* Volume 5	_____ *Secrets* Volume 16	_____ *Secrets* Volume 27
_____ *Secrets* Volume 6	_____ *Secrets* Volume 17	_____ *Secrets* Volume 28
_____ *Secrets* Volume 7	_____ *Secrets* Volume 18	Novels:
_____ *Secrets* Volume 8	_____ *Secrets* Volume 19	_____ *The Forever Kiss*
_____ *Secrets* Volume 9	_____ *Secrets* Volume 20	_____ *Object of Desire*
_____ *Secrets* Volume 10	_____ *Secrets* Volume 21	
_____ *Secrets* Volume 11	_____ *Secrets* Volume 22	

Total _____ *Secrets* Volumes @ $10.99 each = $_____

Total _____ Novels @ $12.00 each = $_____

Shipping & handling (in the U.S.) $_____

US Priority Mail:

1–2 books .... $ 5.50
3–5 books $11.50
6–9 books $14.50
10–24 books $19.00

UPS insured:

1–4 books $16.00
5–9 books $25.00
10–24 books $29.00

SUBTOTAL $_____

Florida 6% sales tax (if delivered in FL) $_____

TOTAL AMOUNT ENCLOSED $_____

Your personal information is kept private and not shared with anyone.

Name: (please print) _____

Address: (no P.O. Boxes) _____

City/State/Zip: _____

Phone or email: (only regarding order if necessary) _____

You can order direct from **eRedSage.com** and use a credit card or you can use this form to send in your mail order with a check. Please make check payable to **Red Sage Publishing**. Check must be drawn on a U.S. bank in U.S. dollars. Mail your check and order form to:

Red Sage Publishing, Inc. Department S28 P.O. Box 4844 Seminole, FL 33775

It's not just reviewers raving about *Secrets*. See what readers have to say:

"When are you coming out with a new Volume? I want a new one next month!" via email from a reader.

"I loved the hot, wet sex without vulgar words being used to make it exciting." after *Volume 1*

"I loved the blend of sensuality and sexual intensity—HOT!" after *Volume 2*

"The best thing about *Secrets* is they're hot and brief! The least thing is you do not have enough of them!" after *Volume 3*

"I have been extremely satisfied with *Secrets*, keep up the good writing." after *Volume 4*

"Stories have plot and characters to support the erotica. They would be good strong stories without the heat." after *Volume 5*

"*Secrets* really knows how to push the envelop better than anyone else." after *Volume 6*

"These are the best sensual stories I have ever read!" after *Volume 7*

"I love, love, love the *Secrets* stories. I now have all of them, please have more books come out each year." after *Volume 8*

"These are the perfect sensual romance stories!" after *Volume 9*

"What I love about *Secrets Volume 10* is how I couldn't put it down!" after *Volume 10*

"All of the *Secrets* volumes are terrific! I have read all of them up to *Secrets Volume 11*. Please keep them coming! I will read every one you make!" after *Volume 11*